THE
END
OF
LOVE

RICHARD JOHN GAWLER

Published in Australia by Richard John Gawler

First published in Australia 2025
This edition published 2025
Copyright © Richard John Gawler 2025
Cover design, typesetting: WorkingType (www.workingtype.com.au)

The right of Richard John Gawler to be identified as the
Author of the Work has been asserted in accordance with the
Copyright, Designs and Patents Act 1988.

ISBN: 978-1-7641905-2-7

Author's Foreword

This novel is an attempt to explore two of the central concepts in western love. These are the concepts of immutability and immolation.

Those of us who have been in love, almost all of us I suspect at some time in our lives, have become painfully aware that, exquisite though the sensation is, it is caught in time and, like everything subject to time, grows old and dies. For most of us the course of love is brief, two years, three years, sometimes four. But love also longs for continuity. So intense is its happiness that we want it to endure forever and we want a "lasting relationship" that endures over the years. It is this desire that makes us embark on marriage or a long-term partnership. Sadly, many relationships entered into with optimism do not survive the cessation of romantic love and, as a consequence, many marriages end in divorce. Indeed, I am tempted to say that the more intense our belief in the redemptive and enduring power of love the more likely we are to end in marital failure.

However, love contains a yet darker strand. It is a reaching out for another self, an attempt to escape our essential isolation and loneliness. We wish to penetrate the being of another, to merge with them, to become one, a complete and perfect being when the "we" becomes " I".

Such a reaching out is really, a desire for the extinction of the self and the ultimate form of self-extinction is death. Hence love becomes, while seeming to be life affirming, the ultimate weapon of death. Love is what draws us to the great abyss which eventually will claim us all. Love becomes a form of destruction, of self-immolation.

It is this understanding, albeit very imperfect, that leads to Milton Harper's erratic experimentation with art, exercise and relationships. It is his hope of finding a path through mutability and immolation that leads Jim Wilson to his intense relationship with Melissa Gibson, a relationship which he did not seek but was thrust upon him.

A former teacher of mine, the only great teacher I have ever known, once said: "Plato was the greatest philosopher who ever lived. He asked all the right questions and came up with all of the wrong answers." I have no idea whether this novel asks all the right questions and I make no attempt to come up with the right answers, if there are any answers at all. What I hope the novel does is explore the landscape of the problem.

RJG

To Rosemary, my wife of 50 years.

Each and every heart throws up its barricade
Each piles up his own mountain of karma
How could they guess that what they clasp so close is sorrow?
Unwilling to ponder, as day and night
They do embrace the falsehood of the flesh

Shih-te

Chapter 1

Milton Harper was an ascetic, he neither smoked nor drank. His condition had not been a planned choice; he had arrived there by degrees. Several years earlier he had looked at his young boy's body and had realised that, while he had the mind and passions of an adult, he was really still a child. Consequently, he had cut down his smoking and taken up weightlifting. Next, to complement his weightlifting, he had taken up running and that had caused him to give up smoking altogether. Then the clean empty ache of his body mirrored the clean empty ache of his days. He no longer wanted to relax with a drink in his hand, so he had taken the obvious step of stopping drinking as well. His body and his life became like a taut fence wire and he used ritual, not pleasure, to get himself through his days. Sometimes in the dusk he would lie on his bed and cry, wishing there was a way that the graft of his life might ease, at least for a few hours a night; but he couldn't go back to smoking and drinking because it would destroy his feeling of purity.

That particular Monday, after lunch, Milton Harper was asleep on the front veranda of his white weatherboard cottage. He was sheltered from the sun by the veranda's red corrugated iron roof. His head had fallen to one side in the deckchair, his mouth was wide open and a small trickle of spittle glistened on the green and red striped deckchair. It was his after-lunch siesta before he did his weightlifting and went on his run.

A small, white Datsun car rolled to a stop underneath the Pohutukawa trees outside the Harper's house. Father Jim Wilson got out of the car which seemed to leap to attention as his seventeen and half stones were removed from the springs. The priest slammed the door and the car rocked. He took a crush pack of unfiltered cigarettes from his shirt pocket and pulled one out with his lips. He lit the cigarette with a silver cigarette lighter. Then he inhaled and looked at the cloudless blue sky. He wished he was just in his swimming togs and jandals and could rub his hand through the sweaty hairs on his fat, pink stomach. He reached up and plucked one of the red Pohutukawa blooms from the tree and sniffed it. He could smell nothing. *Bloody cigarettes* he thought and threw away the flower in disgust.

Father Wilson strode round the front of his car, leapt the gutter and the pavement and strode across the closely cropped grass of the Harper's lawn. Not one flower grew around the house. Father Wilson was vaguely aware of the nasal whine of a lawn mower and the faint hiss of the surf, which gave the impression there was a wind, though it was completely still at that moment. He mounted the wooden steps and stood over the sleeping writer. He scratched his nose with the thumb of the hand that held the smouldering cigarette.

"Fire," he whispered, rather like the sea itself. Milton Harper shifted his weight in the chair and went on sleeping. "Hey, Milt! Wake up!" said the priest sternly. Milton Harper's head jerked to the front and, for a couple of seconds he stared in front of himself as a dead man might stare. Then he blinked.

"Hi Jim," he said. He sat up slowly. Father Jim Wilson sat at the top of the veranda steps with his back to Milton Harper and went on smoking. Milton Harper looked out across the bright lawn to the black road on which the tar was melting. He could smell the sweet acrid smell of the priest's cigarette. He didn't want to see the priest. Conversation irritated him. He had nothing he wanted to talk to his fellow human beings about. Writing was his form of self-expression. He didn't need to talk as well. A blow fly droned around in the still air of the veranda and then flew away into the blue sky as though it had been snatched back by an enormous elastic band. The porch was silent again.

"Well, how's God?" asked Milton Harper pulling his singlet away from his wet armpits.

"How would I know? I only talk to him. He doesn't talk back."

"Sounds like an ideal marriage," said Milton Harper standing up.

"Like yours you mean?"

"Not at all like mine. You want a beer?"

"I thought you'd never ask. I was seriously thinking about jogging your memory."

"No need to do that. I know you religious lot are all hedonists at heart."

"Mine is a taxing profession. No reason why I shouldn't have a few humble pleasures."

The aluminium fly door banged shut behind Milton Harper as he disappeared into the darkness of the house.

When Milton Harper came back carrying an open bottle of beer and a glass, Father Wilson was sitting with his elbows on his knees and his chin in his hands. He was watching his cigarette butt smoulder on the dry lawn. Milton Harper tipped the beer glass on one side and let the beer slide down the inside of the glass and pool in the bottom. As the pool of beer increased in volume Milton slowly straightened up the glass.

"It's easy to see that you're a reformed sinner. Still, I suppose that reformed sinners are the most fanatical. Thanks," said the priest taking the beer. "Cheers." He took a sip of the beer and then wiped his mouth on his wrist. "That's good. Cool as a mountain breeze, as the saying goes."

"You do that too?" asked Milton Harper.

"What's that?

"Look at the idiot box?

"When you work with the people you've got to be able to talk to the people."

"I thought only the Protestants did that? I thought that all you bods had to do was make the right magic passes.

"Ah Milton, conversation may be largely meaningless and full of the common place, but you can't tell the people that." Father Wilson poured the rest of the glass of beer straight down his throat and reached behind him for the remainder of the bottle. He groped the bare wood for a couple of seconds before he found the bottle.

""What do you want anyway?" asked Milton Harper.

"Why do you assume I have an ulterior motive for coming?

"You can get a beer at any bar."

"I don't like to, given the colour of my cloth. Besides, you're not available at any bar." Milton Harper looked piercingly at the priest and then shrugged. Father Wilson's comment made little sense to him. He never courted anyone. People always betrayed you in the end so it was better not to like them in the first place and avoid the subsequent pain.

The priest swung his feet onto the porch and leaned his back on one of the wooden columns that supported the veranda roof. He looked speculatively at Milton Harper. He's a poor man he thought.

He only trusts his own cleverness and his ability to create beauty. All other things he seems to despise. Milton's voice interrupted his reverie.

"Uncovered any good stories of corruption and perversion in the confessional lately?" asked Milton Harper.

"I can't recall any," said the priest. "Besides, I wouldn't be at liberty to divulge them if I did."

"The letter of the law, eh?"

""Gossiping has never been much a temptation to me. If I was to succumb to that I would never be forgiven for surrendering to more virile temptations."

"Well, you might like to look at it this way. You come here to amuse yourself and bring nothing in return. A little scandal from the confessional might compensate me for satisfying whatever it is that I satisfy in your visits here."

"You're such a merchant Milton."

"Everyone's a merchant, including our wives, our parents and our children."

"You don't have any children Milton."

"Yeah, well someone's got to support this set up. I can't, so Liz has to do it. Children would interfere with my vocation Father, just as they would interfere with yours. It's not that I don't want them, or that I do."

Milton Harper looked at the line of Norfolk Pines that rose immaculate, like living lino cuts, behind the houses and motels which hid the beach. A walnut brown girl, her honey blond hair bleached by the sun and wearing a blue, faded dress waved to Milton Harper as she swung along the footpath on the opposite side of the road. Milton made a movement that was more like a salute than a wave.

"Who's the girl?" Father Wilson asked.

Oh, I don't know," shrugged Milton Harper. "I wave to her and she waves to me. You fancy her, do you?"

"She's attractive," the priest said defensively. He rather liked women, so he didn't really want to discuss them. In fact, he had a terrible suspicion that there was something ungodly about women. He feared that they may be able to take the place of God.

"When are we going fishing next?" asked Milton. He saw that he had touched the priest at a weak spot and wanted to steer the conversation into calmer waters, at least for the time being.

""Don't know," said the priest fumblingly trying to light a cigarette. Milton Harper put his head back and laughed spontaneously.

"What's funny?" asked Jim Wilson looking up and spitting a speck of tobacco off the tip of his tongue.

"How about Saturday week?" asked Milton with smiling eyes.

"That'll be alright," said Father Wilson looking down at the palm of his hand.

Milton Harper also looked down, down at the dial of his watch. Now it was after one o'clock and he should have been going to the YMCA gym before returning home to run. Jim Wilson put down his now empty beer glass. Froth clung to the sides of the beer glass like soap suds.

"I know this is a breach of the rules of friendship," said Father Wilson looking at Milton Harper, "but why not come to church?"

""I don't have a religious disposition," said Milton, shoving his hands in his pockets and hunching his shoulders. Father Wilson looked at Milton Harper.

"Liar," he said with a trace of a smile on his lips.

Chapter 2

The blond girl that Milton Harper had waved to was Lillie Foster. She sold material, buttons and dress patterns in a dress shop, but that Monday she hadn't felt like going to work so she had stayed at home. Home was a large, run-down, old house where she lived with one other girl and four boys. The boys all admired Lillie because she would go anywhere and do anything. The girl, however, was suspicious fearing the Lillie might entice away her boyfriend, one of the boys in the flat.

Lillie ran across the road feeling the tar seal accept the imprint of her toes. The synthetic material of her dress slithered across her legs as she ran. Her nylon panties stuck to her stomach and her pubic hair felt cool and damp. Then there was the soft, cool feeling of grass against her feet and she seemed to enter a new, dark world as she passed behind the tall, flowering hedge which shimmered with droning bees. Lillie kicked a wet, decaying pile of grass which, like many others, lay on top of ground after the last mowing.

Lillie mounted the veranda of the old house. Grey paint flaked off the doorstep and grey dust sat silently on the unpainted boards of the veranda. The green straps of the cabbage tree moved almost imperceptibly in the faint gusts of air. She paused a moment in the doorway looking into the cool musty smelling darkness. She lifted up the front of her dress and pressed the edge of her hand into her stomach. She took her hand away from her stomach, flattened out her dress and walked down the long, high-roofed hall of the old villa. The wallpaper was yellow with age and in some places had been ripped off the wall exposing the rotten orange scrim. All the doors in the hall were shut. Lillie walked around a pot, half full of water that had been catching water from a leak in the roof.

When she entered the sunny kitchen she realised, to her annoyance, that she was not alone. Matt, a dark-headed Australian boy, was sitting at the kitchen table smoking a cigarette and eating a piece of bread. Lillie was irritated. If he had been one of the others, she might have propositioned him. Lillie had slept with all the other male occupants of the flat at various times but had sworn them all to secrecy.

"Hi, Matt," she said smiling sweetly, "how come you're not at work?"

"Got fired," said Matt through a mouthful of bread.

"Three jobs in six weeks, Matt." Lillie whistled.

"All you kiwi cunts hate Aussies."

"You want to go back to Aussie then Matt?" said Lillie walking across to the stove.

"Can't keep a job long enough to earn the dough to get back." It fleetingly crossed Lillie's mind that if Matt stayed too much longer, she might find herself giving him the money to go back.

"Never mind, Matt. Things 'll get better."

"They bloody well need to. It makes you depressed not being able to hold down a job."

Lillie filled the blackened kettle with water and walked to the gas stove. She put the kettle on the element and glanced distastefully at the large puddle of congealed fat under the griller. She had already decided that she wouldn't clean up that mess under any circumstances. The boys needed to learn, if they were capable of learning.

"Throw me the matches will you, Matt? You can throw me your cigarettes too, if you like. I'll give you one of mine tonight. I don't feel like walking through and getting them.

"Forget it. I'll give you a smoke." He threw her the matches and then a packet of cigarettes. Lille found herself wishing Matt would stop turning all his "i" sounds into "ee" sounds. Lillie put a cigarette in her mouth, struck a match and lit the gas and then her cigarette. She took the cigarette out of her mouth, inhaled the smoke and popped the dead match into the open top of the old wood range. She walked across to Matt, put the packet of cigarettes and the matches on the table in front of him and said:

"Thanks."

"You want to come to the pub and help a man drown his sorrows, Lillie?" said Matt looking up.

"No thanks Matt."

"You're a really stuck-up chick, aren't you?" said Matt.

"I'm tired Matt," said Lillie turning her back on him and walking back towards the stove.

"Aw, just a few drinks Lillie," Matt whined.

"Go to hell, Matt!

"You're a bloody mean bitch!" said Matt getting up and kicking over his chair. He slouched off into the corridor. "A stingy, kiwi bitch." His footsteps retreated down the corridor. The front door slammed noisily.

"Fuck you too," said Lillie looking down the hall.

There was hiss as the heaving water lifted the lid of the kettle and flopped onto the gas flame.

"Fuck!" said Lillie and pulled the kettle away from the flame. Lillie stood watching the dead part of the gas flame hiss, spark and finally catch light again. She put her half-smoked cigarette on the stove and reached under her dress to pull off her panties. Then she stopped, ran down the corridor, across the lawn and poked her head out of a gap in the hedge which served as an extra gate. Matt was about a hundred yards along the road wandering listlessly from one side of the footpath to the other.

"Poor bastard doesn't mean to be a creep," said Lillie quietly to herself.

Back in the kitchen she draped her panties over the arm of the old sofa. She flopped her dress up and down to cool her stomach. I'm twenty-four year's old she thought and the rest of these kids are only about twenty. She rocked from the balls of her feet onto her heels and back again several times. Sometimes Lillie regretted ignoring her aptitude for mathematics but, after a moment's reflection, she always decided that her life of sensual and mindless hedonism suited her better.

She walked to the table, lifted up the brown china teapot, tilted it and watched the tea bubble out of the spout into the plain white cup. She leaned one hip against the table and elegantly sipped her tea. She felt the thin, hot liquid run down her throat.

Lillie finished her tea and wandered through to her bedroom. She shut the door and pulled off her dress over her head. She sat down on the bed and took a silver framed picture of a dark young man off the chest of drawers next to the bed. On top of the chest of drawers was a white lace edged cloth. He was beautiful, she thought. Her stomach seemed to tingle as she thought of his hard, ivory-smooth muscles covered with thick black hair. He had gripped her painlessly, but with such power she could not have wriggled free.

By then Lillie had her fingers deep inside herself. She threw the heavy framed picture onto her pillow and rolled her hips. It's just a little way she thought, just a little way around the corner, in the next white-sanded bay. She tightened and relaxed the muscles in her thighs until it seemed her body would crack with the tension. Then, suddenly, she was over the top and her mind and body rushed down like a wave. Down, away from hardness towards softness and perfect relaxation towards a heat-laced desert shrouded with sleep.

Lillie arched her back again, pulled back the blanket and crawled between the cool sheets. She lay on her side in a foetal position. There was no need to worry now, only a need to be still. A breeze moved the yellowing lace curtains and the plain brown blind that covered the tall window. Underneath the bottom of the blind Lilli could see the warm sun on the grey window sill. She shut her eyes. She could hear a circular saw whine in the distance. A horse suddenly neighed. The sparrows that frequently roosted under the eaves chirped incessantly. A blowfly got in and flew around and around up near the high roof. Then the sounds changed. They were just as loud but somehow gentler. The breeze is so cool and the sheet is so smooth thought Lillie. Just as well I didn't go to work today.

Chapter 3

On the ridge Dave Gibson sat under a slender, yellow barked willow having smoko. Periodically he would break off a piece of fruit cake and eat it. Gunn, a long haired black and white huntaway dog, sat with his head tilted on one side watching his master eat.

Gibbo looked through the hot air, which sparkled like a silver stream in the gully. The grass on the other side was long and thick and silky. Clumps of brown rushes mottled the wetter areas of the gully floor. A dark green ribbon of thistles, covered in purple blooms wound their way down into the gully. They had grown on a road that Dave had bull dozed two years before. Springy heaps of bone-grey manuka showed in places above the long grass that had grown so high because of the wet summer. In the distance, further up the ridge, an old horse was scratching itself against a fence. Both the fence and the horse looked like sinister illusions against the blue sky and through the trembling air. Dave Gibson pushed his hat back then slapped at a green and black grass fly which had landed on his bare leg.

Dave Gibson was not a happy man. His daughter had gone astray. It was all the teachers' fault. They were always saying how intelligent she was and how she should make something of herself; as though being a famer or a farmer's wife was somehow only a low occupation filled by stupid people. So, first of all, she had started calling him names, saying he was an ignorant old boor. He had complained to the teachers, but he could see they probably only agreed with her, so he didn't persevere. Eventually she wanted to go to university to study philosophy and he had refused to let her go. She ran away. He took the matter to court but, even though she was under eighteen, the judge seemed to think she ought to go to university. Those townies had control over everything. They didn't have any respect for a parent's wishes and they wondered why there were bikies and hooligans all over the show.

Anyway, he hadn't seen her now for eighteen months and he didn't really want to see her much either. If she could stay away for two Christmases, he didn't see why she should come home now. But there was something fishy going on. Myra had got a letter, but when he had asked to read it she said she had burnt it. Perhaps the girl had married some university pansy. If she had he wouldn't be having her home. At least the law still allowed him to have whoever he liked in his own home.

Gibbo poured out some tea from his thermos. Then he bit out the cherry from the remaining piece of fruit cake and threw the rest of the bit of cake contemptuously in the direction of Gunn. The dog slunk towards the cake, picked it up delicately and chewed it back into its throat. Then Gunn backed back to where he had been sitting. Gibbo took a sip of his tea and started to roll himself a cigarette. A lark came fluttering out of the sky like a lolly paper and sat on a grassy clod, no more than fifty feet away, looking at the man. When Gibbo lit his cigarette the bird flew away, startled by the pop of the igniting match. Gibbo blew some smoke through his nose and undid the leather cover of his wrist watch. It was only a quarter to three. He wasn't going to leave until four-thirty. He stood up, picked up his slasher and walked up to the ridgelet where he had finished cutting fifteen minutes ago.

There was no reason why Dave Gibson should cut manuka. He could afford to hire contractors to do it. Nor did he get any pleasure out of the physical labour involved. Working hard was his main source of pride and it was that that made him do it. It was not even so much a matter of doing it well, but doing it hard. In fact things that were delicate or complex seemed to be the product of idleness rather than hard work. Instruments should be ruthlessly utilitarian. Gibbo even preferred workers who groaned and toiled rather than workers who did things quickly and easily. That particular prejudice had probably cost him a lot of money.

Dave Gibson went on chopping scrub, slicing the manuka bushes at ground level and almost running from one manuka bush to the next. The dog lay in the shade of the uncut manuka with its chin on its paws, looking at its master with what seemed like pity. The leaves of the manuka clung to Gibbo's wet flesh and got down his black singlet and the fury of his working became intensified by the discomfort. He was continually brushing his hair off his forehead with the back of his hand. Once he stopped in his runaway course and, still breathing heavily, rolled himself a cigarette. But he had no sooner lit it in the darkness of his cupped hands and thrown away the match than he started working again.

At almost exactly four-thirty Gibbo stood up as though an alarm had gone off in his head. He put his slasher on his shoulder and walked back to where he had left his flax basket and his thermos. He dropped the thermos into the flax basket and, leaning on his slasher, looked at his watch. By then it was two minutes after four-thirty. Gibbo rolled himself a smoke and walked back up the ridge to where he had left his motor bike. Gibbo hung his flax basket on the mud encrusted bike and got on, holding the slasher across the handlebars. He kicked the starter and the bike roared into life. Gibbo drove off down the hard clay track pitted with miniature gullies where the water had coursed down the track during heavy rain. He rode so slowly he was in constant danger of falling off from mere lack of momentum. Gibbo may have had abundant energy, but he saw no point in taking risks of any sort. He was probably one of the few men in New Zealand who owned a Jaguar that had never been over sixty miles per hour except when driven by his tearaway daughter.

The bike strained up and down the bumps and dips of the ridge, occasionally passing through patches of rushes and thistles. At one stage Gibbo stopped the bike and got off with his butcher's knife drawn and cut a variegated thistle. He got back on his bike and briefly cursed his neighbour for running a stud for variegated thistles as well as cattle. The next door neighbour, of course, had his stud fifteen miles away on flat land.

Finally Gibbo's bike mounted the last knoll and there, at the bottom of the ridge, on a wide, green flat backed by a creek, was Gibbo's red, painted woolshed; its windows dark, mysterious holes, the sheep-yards looking like some puzzle board with their grey fences and their hoof-trampled black dirt. A shadow fell on the roof of the woolshed from the big walnut that grew behind it. All along the creek bank were weeping willows, golden and still. Further up the flat was the house, low and brown walled with a grey roof. From the knoll you could see the large, unpainted patio. The whole house was surrounded by a high mesh fence of the sort you see around tennis courts.

Gibbo rode down this last steep piece of ridge on to the flat. He had to dismount to open a gate. Gunn was pleased to stop. His unreasonably long, pink tongue flopped out of the side of his mouth and his chest pumped like a bellows. Then they were off across the flat, their shadows behind them; the dog starting to draw ahead of the man and the bike as they followed the two wheel tracks of crumbling, white stone across the hot green flat to the house. A weka, which had been pacing peacefully, squeaked and fled with ruffled feathers towards shelter underneath the woolshed. The other sheepdogs began to bark. Gibbo skirted the house and stopped his bike by the garage. Gibbo looked over at his concrete floored dog cages. The dogs were leaping against the netting barking hysterically.

"Si' down!" bawled Gibbo. The dogs took no notice. Gibbo walked into the car shed and came back out again with a stick. The dogs went on barking, but not so loudly. Gibbo clicked his fingers at Gunn and the dog fell in behind. As Gibbo walked towards the cages the dogs fell silent one by one and disappeared inside their kennels. When Gibbo reached the cages he opened the door of Gunn's cage and let him in. Then he walked along the other cages, chose one at random and walked in. Stooping slightly because of the low roof, he reached into the kennel and grabbed the dog by the collar and dragged it out of its kennel. Then, holding the stick in the middle, he hit the dog's bony back. The dog yelped and tried to pull back into the kennel, but Gibbo twisted the collar tighter and dragged the dog back towards him.

"Si' down you bastard! Si' down!" shouted Gibbo, hitting the dog with short, sharp blows. The dog went on yelping and whimpering. Its claws scraped on the floor of the cage. All the other dogs hid in their kennels completely silent. Finally, Dave Gibson let the dog go and it ran back into its kennel, bumping against the side of the doorway in its haste. Gibbo backed out of the cage and shut the mesh gate. He turned his back on the kennels and walked back to the shed using his stick as a staff. First one dog and then another peered out of the door of his kennel. Finally a big yellow dog bounded out and stood with his

16

ears half pricked and his tail in the air. In another minute all the dogs were back out, milling around looking for something else to bark at.

Gibbo wheeled his bike back into the shed and came back out carrying his flax basket. He walked through the gate in the high fence and pulled it shut. There were hydrangeas growing inside the fence and roses running on either side of the path to the back door. Gibbo was always threatening to cut out the roses because he often caught his flesh or clothing on their sharp thorns.

Gibbo sat on the porch steps and began to unlace his hobnail boots. The porch was covered in gumboots and other old boots and shoes. Gibbo noticed his wife's blue, rubber, gardening gloves and an old butcher's knife, whose blade had been worn down to a sliver of metal, lying by the back door. Some fresh, damp earth was clinging to the knife where the blade joined the handle. He realised that his wife must have gone inside when she heard his bike on the hill. Gibbo bent one knee almost up to his chin, pushed the boot off his heel and kicked the loose boot onto the path.

"Hello dear," said his wife from the back door.

"Where is she?" asked Dave Gibson, unlacing the other boot.

"She's in the lounge."

Well, shouldn't she be out here?"

"No," said his wife quietly.

"Get her out here or get her out of the house!" Dave Gibson shouted suddenly.

"I'm here Dad," said his daughter stepping into the doorway beside and slightly behind her mother.

"Hello," said Dave Gibson without turning, as he pulled off the other boot.

"Hello Dad," said Melissa.

Dave Gibson stood up, turned around and looked at his daughter for the first time. His eyes narrowed for an instant. Then he said:

17

"Is that what you went to university for, was it? That was a waste of time and money, wasn't it? Any one of my shearers could have done that for you." He moved to brush past his daughter. She put her hand out and stopped him.

"I wouldn't have let any of your shearers do it Dad. They wouldn't understand me."

"I bet my rams don't understand the ewes much but they still manage to get them pregnant."

"Not all life is lived on that sort of basic level," said the girl.

"That's what you think," said Dave Gibson. "Now get out of my way. I want to have a beer. Anyway, if he understood you that well, how come he's not around understanding you now?" Melissa looked away.

"We no longer love one another. It wouldn't have been fair to me, him or the baby to stay together."

"Oh, very nice! That justifies everything. At least one of my shearers would have married you. Now get out of my way," he said menacingly. This time the girl got out of his way.

Chapter 4

ather Wilson lived just a little up the side of the valley. Poverty Bay was only about seven miles wide here and he could see across the endless paddocks of brown headed maize and white headed sweet corn. Beyond the monotony of the maize and corn, broken only occasionally by a tree, a house or an old stump, was the muddy Waipaoa River, at this point on the other side of the valley. You couldn't see the river itself, only the sloping land and the silver poplars which formed a solid wall on the other side of the river. Behind the poplars were the rough hills, which always reminded him of serge. This year though, the grass almost entirely concealed their scars; but they were too steep to pretend they were smooth and fertile. They were stubbly and rough and steep right into the blue distance.

Jim Wilson turned back to the stove and switched off the element. Then he took the pot off the element and removed the eggs, one by one, with a tablespoon before running them under the cold tap. After that he put them on a large, white plate. Normally he had a housekeeper to cook his meals, but today she had taken the day off. He didn't mind. The chores took his mind off the evening. The evening was mellow, soothing and beautiful. Faced with this beauty, man felt he was alone.

When he was young Jim Wilson had craved for women, but he had chosen to serve God. If the terrible, infuriating emptiness that the evening's beauty exposed, perhaps even created, was to be denied only God could deny it. Without God life would be awful, ecstatic and perhaps even pagan and man could do what he wished in celebration of this empty beauty. This was a horror you could reach out and touch.

It seemed not to be so for many of his parishioners, however. They seemed to possess a purely practical notion of God. They seemed to want to ensure that they had a good time in the next world just as they paid money into insurance schemes to make sure they had a good time in their retirement in this world.

Then there were the parishioners like his housekeeper, Mrs Carmichael. She spent almost all of her spare time rushing over to the church and, when she wasn't at church, he had little doubt that she spent her time thinking about it. Why? Simply to fulfil the pious self image she had of herself. Her religiosity was a form of vanity, just like dressing well or being careful with your make-up was for other, different women.

Then there were the elderly woman who frowned upon the vigorous passions of the young and whose frowns were tinged with envy.

The male parishioners were a little different. Men were, after all, allowed to sin, they couldn't help it; whereas their wives, being naturally virtuous, felt little inclination. Not many of his male parishioners wanted to be virtuous. A few on the various parish committees were frustrated city and county councillors, but there weren't many of those. No, most men came to church because it lent a certain decorum and dignity to their lives. Perhaps they came looking for something that was uncorrupted, something that could be taken seriously. There was something tender and unsentimental about mass. It was quiet and unhurried, just as Sunday mornings were quiet and unhurried. Perhaps the feeling was more important than all the ideas in the mass.

Father Wilson stopped thinking and knocked the top off his egg. The yolk was slightly soft, just the way he liked it and he put some salt, some pepper and knob of butter on top of the orange yolk. While he waited for the butter to melt, he stood up, put his tray on the arm of the couch and walked over and pulled aside the curtains so that he could look across the flats as he ate his evening meal.

Father Wilson sat on the couch and ate his eggs. When he had finished, he set his tray down on the plain, green carpet and lit a cigarette. He looked at the enormous bookcase that ran along the wall to the edge of the large, full-length window. The full bookcase made him feel secure.

Father Wilson took a lung full of smoke and eyed the television which obscured the last two feet or so of his bookcase. There was instant oblivion if he wanted it, oblivion more complete than any alcohol, nicotine or art could offer. Work offered a similar oblivion to TV but at least it gave you, in the end, the pride of achievement, the pride of creation. But work too was painful; it was difficult to drag through the hours of labour. Work, even work you admired, was barren and harsh; but at least when you worked you didn't have to worry about the pain of beauty, which came knife-sharp through the relaxed warmth of pleasure.

Jim Wilson reached behind his head and slid open the door of the cupboard. He turned in his chair and took a crystal decanter and a crystal whisky glass from the cupboard and, holding both the decanter and the glass in one hand, slid the door shut again. He sat back, removed the stopper from the decanter and filled the glass three quarters full of whisky. Then he stubbed out his cigarette on the heavy glass ashtray which sat on the arm of the leather sofa and, picking up the glass, quickly took a large slug of whisky. He grimaced, put the whisky glass by his feet and lit another cigarette.

A flock of starlings flew across the sky looking like a black pennant carried by the wind; but there was no wind and it was still unnaturally sunny and hot. No point in looking at the scenery too hard, thought Jim Wilson. He knew that looking too hard made everything more elusive than ever. Father Wilson looked down the front of his blue cotton shirt at his shiny, pink stomach. He took another swig of whisky. It burned all the way down. New bubbles of sweat seemed to burst from his flesh.

He stood up and walked over to the windows again, hoping it would be nearer to dusk by now. It was evening alright, still and golden with the hot sun scorching across the valley and even the shadows looking hot and uninviting. I'm going to get drunk and go to bed thought Father Wilson. I can only absorb so much through my senses and, when they cry out for more, I can't supply them with the extra they require. Solitary pleasure only winds you up like a spring.

The priest walked back to his whisky, the landscape shining like a halo behind him. He bent over, picked up the glass and tossed the remaining whisky down his throat. The priest looked at his empty glass and wondered what Milton was doing. Probably standing on his head doing press ups with his ears. Father Wilson gave a tipsy laugh. He could understand Milton in a way. The physical pleasures of eating, drinking and smoking were not really animal pleasures, but human ones. Besides, Jim Wilson could dimly remember that there was a certain pleasure in physical exertion. He couldn't remember what sort of pleasure though. Tonight it was all getting a bit beyond him.

He poured himself another whisky. It wouldn't be much fun being married to Milton though. Jim Wilson tried to imaging Milton's relationship with his wife. He must have been different once, thought the priest. Perhaps she lives on that.

Father Wilson sat down and listened to the creak of the leather sofa. He kicked off his slippers and drew his feet beneath him. I must weed my garden tomorrow, he thought. His melancholy still lingered, but now it was being replaced by a sense of physical well being. A couple more big whiskies and Father Wilson wouldn't be in the least concerned about what was outside his window. I really must get Milton here and get him drinking and get him to have a cigar or two, thought the priest. Already he was pouring himself another whisky. Come to think of it, I'll have a cigar. It'll remind me of some of the pleasant unsanctified moments of Christmas. Jim Wilson rolled onto his feet and walked over to his bookcase. On the top was a paua shell box. Jim Wilson opened the box, took out a long cigar and lit it with his lighter. He took a couple of puffs and then held it between his thumb and forefinger, at head level. He savoured the smoke and a delighted smile passed across the face of this huge, pink-faced man with pale blond, almost white hair. He took another puff and walked back to his whisky.

It's funny, he thought sitting down, that a chemical can achieve what no amount of prayer can achieve. The chemical might be powerless to cheer without God, but allied with him it's insurmountable. There are other, more dignified pleasures, but it is a major pleasure and sometimes it's pretty miserable being sober. I'm a priest, but it's only my function, my job, my sphere of expertise. When I'm not doing my priestly duties I'm just a layman like any other man, except in relation to woman of course. I'm obliged to observe God's edicts, but no more than a lawyer or a carpenter is expected to follow their codes of conduct and the expectations of their profession. A man must work, but he must also relax.

Slowly the priest drank himself into a stupor. He laid full length on the couch and tried to blow smoke rings with his cigar. He tried to drink his whisky lying down, but eventually ended up pouring it out of the glass and letting it run in a stream into his open mouth. Unfortunately, some went down the wrong way and he sat up coughing and spluttering.

The crickets began to chirr and the hot air cooled a little. The sun disappeared behind the ridge and the air around the house became like a dark pool of water. Further away the air was molten and flowed orange over the emerald, brown-tipped corn. The far hills became cut-outs under the fiery light.

Father Wilson staggered out his back door and stood on his dappled lawn watching the sand flies dance beneath his red leafed plum. A tractor carrying some discs went bouncing up the road at breakneck speed. "Fool," muttered Father Wilson as he staggered barefooted, down his shingle drive to the front gate.

When he reached the front gate he had forgotten why he had come down. A car sped by and tooted. Father Wilson looked vaguely at the fleeing vehicle, lifted his hand and then dropped his hand again. His sinuses felt sore. He thought he had better get the paper and then remembered that it was the paper that he had been trying to remember. He pulled the paper out of the top of his letter box, pulling much too hard, so that he staggered back a couple of paces when it came free. He opened up the paper and went slowly back up the drive following an erratic path and looking down into the open paper. When he reached his back door, he suddenly crumpled up the paper and threw it under the plum tree. "I must castigate my lungs with one more cigarette," he said loudly. "That's a malapropism, isn't it?" he asked the unresponsive plum.

Inside he lit another cigarette and wandered around gently jolting the walls and door frames, checking that everything would be tidy when Mrs Carmichael turned up in the morning. He put the almost empty decanter back in the cupboard and took the glass out to the kitchen. Then he went back to put the decanter away, saw that it was done and brought through the tray instead and put it on the kitchen table. He stood in the kitchen smoking his cigarette trying to think of anything else he had to do. It occurred to him to put the light on, but he figured it wasn't worth it. He ran the butt of his cigarette under the kitchen tap and left the sodden butt on the kitchen bench.

Through in his bedroom he knelt down and, taking his rosary beads off the bedside table, he slowly worked his way through the rosary. He finally finished, but before he crossed himself, he looked up at the picture of Christ that hung on the wall and thought to himself: You made the world beautiful Lord, but you also made it too painful to bear. I don't see it as wrong to try to forget the pain with alcohol from time to time, providing that we do not allow the alcohol to let us forget you. I am your creature and in everything I try to do your will. Try to help Milton Harper who will bow to nobody and lives in a state of torment. The priest crossed himself and dragged himself to his feet. He looked at the feminine Christ with the soft, brown eyes. Then he sunk onto the bed fully clothed.

Father Wilson slept.

Chapter 5

"You're not romantic to me anymore," said Liz Harper throwing a large pot she had been drying under the sink.

"Yeah," said Milton Harper, placing the soapy electric fry pan on the fawn terrazzo on the bench in front of his wife. He pulled the plug out of the sink and the water ran out with a hoarse, sucking sound. "Who is romantic to you Liz? Elvis Presley?"

"Stop being scornful Milt. You may find romanticism a fit subject for humour, but it's the essence of female sexuality."

"What makes you think you have any accurate notion of female sexuality?"

"Damn it all, I'm a woman, aren't I?"

"Maybe you're an atypical woman. Perhaps your sexuality is entirely perverted. Has that never occurred to you?" asked Milton Harper, sending waves of water rolling down the bench top in front of his blue sponge.

"So, you think my sexuality is perverted?" said Liz, throwing the wet tea towel over the back of one wooden chair and sitting down in another chair and lighting a smoke.

"I didn't say that," said Milton Harper, squeezing the sponge into the sink. "I was only helping you to be objective."

"Bloody smart fart!"

Milton Harper threw the sponge into the corner of the empty sink next to the pot mitt and leant against the sink wishing he could smoke. He resisted the urge. He considered it weak to give into your urges, they should be crushed. A man could have no self-respect unless he could control his desires. Life could have no continuity and safety unless you controlled your desires.

"Perhaps we should take lovers," said Liz blowing out a cloud of smoke in a thin stream.

"You take a lover and I'll leave you."

"Don't be so corny Milt."

"If I take a lover I'll leave you too."

"You don't have to."

"You really believe in your own freedom, don't you?"

"Why not?"

"A person manacled in a dungeon always looks a bit pathetic if they believe they're skipping around ankle deep in clover."

"Where are my manacles, Milt?" asked Liz, shaking her wrists at him.

"Oh, get fucked!" said Milton Harper, walking out of the kitchen and into the lounge.

He flopped down on the pale grey divan, which was covered in orange flowers and green leaves. He looked through the dull, gauze fireguard at the ash-grey bricks in the hearth. I try to be kind, he thought and just when things are starting to go well dissatisfaction breaks out again, like a boil. His body felt warm and relaxed as he sat there; as though each cell was flushed and breathing. There's nothing I can do though, he thought.

Liz appeared in the gloomy doorway.

"Shit it's hot!"

"Why don't you have another beer?" said Milton, turning around and smiling at his wife.

"I will, if you have one with me."

"No, I don't want one."

"I get tired of your puritanical abstention. Life's no fun with a teetotal husband. Here," she said thrusting a packet of cigarettes at him, "have a cigarette."

"No thanks."

"Fuck you! Have a bloody cigarette."

"No," shouted Milton Harper, standing up. His wife, who had been kneeling by the divan, stood up, burst into tears and ran out of the room. Milton paced around the room swinging his arms, his red singlet showing through the gloom of the curtained lounge. Suddenly, he left the room, walked through the kitchen and into the bedroom. His wife was lying on the double bed, a pillow over her head, still sobbing. He sat down on the bed beside her. She pushed at him, but he just sat there. Then he reached out and touched her hand, but she drew it away.

"Come on," he said. Let's go for a walk."

"Don't want to go for a walk."

"I'm sorry," he said, sounding kindly. Liz took the pillow off her head and looked at him.

"You only care about your body. Once you were hungry for the world. Now you just drift. You're completely barren, as barren as a brick."

"My life's got to have some order to get everything I want done."

"You do too much. Why can't you just live?

"There isn't anything in life except boredom and art."

"You make art sound more boring than working on an assembly line.

"It is for those who practise it."

"I don't believe you."

"I never asked you to." Milton Harper stood up. He wanted to get out of the house. "I'm going for a walk anyway. Come on, Liz." Liz took hold of his hand and he pulled her off the bed.

Milton Harper locked the front door and let the fly door slam shut. "Come on!" he shouted, leaping off the veranda and running across the lawn to the footpath. Liz ran too in her slightly ungainly, girlish way, her black hair streaming out behind her. When she came up to him Milton Harper slipped his arm around her shoulder. They walked along the pavement in the glaringly, dark light of the evening sun, the shadows falling long and distorted on the fiery road. They could hear the hush, hush of the surf behind the houses. A faint off-shore breeze gently moved the olive green Pohutukawa's, most of which had already bloomed. In between the gaps in the houses and the motels you could see the white sand of the beach. They passed some palm trees, with clusters of orange fruit growing in among the leaves. Hibiscus flowers were blooming in many of the gardens. The quiet cars of the well to do, out for a drive, went slowly past them. A teenager rode by on his bicycle, a surfboard under his arm.

Finally, the houses on the seaward side stopped and Milton and Liz crossed on to a lawn which seemed to lead only to distant cliffs and an empty sky.

"Jim Wilson dropped around today," said Milton as they walked across the tough, close-cropped grass to the sea.

"Oh! How was he?"

"Okay, I suppose."

"He's quite an attractive man really."

"You're only fascinated to see if his cock's as big as the rest of him." Liz laughed.

29

"I don't deny I'm curious, but only in a speculative sort of a way."

"Why's he attractive then?"

"I just think that he could genuinely care for a woman."

"I told you God was a woman."

"Don't be ridiculous!" Liz laughed.

Liz and Milton stepped off the grass, over a little bank and looked out to sea. There, on the dark surface, surfers in wet suits were bobbing like seals. To the west, above the hills that minute by minute merged into one pink, satin mass, the sky burned hot orange. Against this furnace mouth flew the gulls, whirling like bits of soot from a fire. Beneath the gulls, three children on ponies looked out at the low waves that slid, curling towards them. Liz and Milton reached the smooth, shiny, wet sand at the water's edge and watched the dark water, laced with foam, fleeing the land, only to be caught by the next wave and thrown back on the wet sand that shone like coal in the dusk. Up the beach people moved mysteriously like figures in the apocalypse.

"I'm going to have a paddle," said Liz, slipping her feet out of her leather jandals and picking the jandals up by the thongs. Milton Harper watched the water close round his wife's calves as she stood there like a statue, holding her dress around her thighs. He started to wander up the beach towards the sunset. A young girl of about eleven came running across the beach towards the sea. As she passed close in front of him Milton saw that her togs were emerald green. The girl ran straight into the sea, lifting her knees high in the water and squealing with delight. Her cries became lost in the cries of the seagulls.

What, thought Milton, is art compared to all this?

Milton looked back at his wife, wandering without purpose in the swishing water, lost in the fresh, almost painful feeling of the sandy, salty water scraping and slapping her legs and feet. She was happy now. But soon she would make a bigger demand, desire more and then she would be unhappy.

And what of me? thought Milton. He found it easy to lose himself in the purely physical, the almost being in the moment. Yet he feared a life without art. Art would provide the knowledge, the understanding. He didn't care to be completely naked before the stones and thorns of reality.

Liz came plopping out of the water and stood on the sand. The sand had been roughed by many feet and was all small hills and small hollows. She lit a cigarette. The sand clung to her feet like socks, the pure white grains standing out against the darkness of the rest of the beech. The smoke from the cigarette stung her eyes and she shut them tightly. She opened them to see a clump of pampas grass paralysed against the now pale evening sky. A car, parked face on at the top of the beach and looking like an overgrown insect, turned on its headlights. In the dim light of the dusk, they burned like half blind eyes.

Milton turned and looked past his wife to the river mouth where the breakwater lay like a sodden dog oblivious of the waves. Behind it Kaiti hill seemed like a dull egg in the sky.

"I'm glad we live near the beach," said Liz, giving her husband a quick hug. "It makes me feel real."

They set off back along the beach. Liz was rising on her toes taking unnaturally long strides to keep up with her taller husband. Milton Harper suddenly stopped dead and turned around and stared at his wife. He wondered why he kept the marriage going. He had never thought so pernicious a thought before. It had always seemed obvious to him that his relationship with Liz came first and that other things had to be sacrificed to it. Had the sacrifice been to a barren God? Once he had expressed his living self to Liz, but the mechanism had taken over and now, it seemed, he only lived beside her.

"What is it Milt?" asked Liz.

"Nothing," he said and looked again out to sea, while she wandered further along the beach on her own.

When Milton looked back up the beach Liz was drawing in the sand with a stick, her back towards him. Suddenly Milton ran up behind Liz, lifted her off her feet and ran up the beach carrying her like a baby. Liz screamed and shouted.

"Put me down. You're hurting me you fool, put me down." Milton lowered her feet first to the ground.

"It's easier lifting weights," he panted.

"You've bruised my bloody ribs. You don't know your own strength, Milton."

"Come on. Let's go home."

They walked back up towards the edge of the road, their feet sinking in the sand and sliding backwards. They reached the grass verge and looked through the dim light at the warm yellow glow of the surf club which was partly hidden by the squares of sacking that surrounded the recently planted trees. On the other side of the road the pine trees in the motor camp loomed over them. Underneath the trees a little man with an enormous Alsatian dog was walking about flashing his torch. The sky in the east was still quite light, though the air was darkening quickly.

Liz and Milton walked arm in arm along the road past the old weatherboard houses with their corrugated iron roofs. The gardens were dry and warm, the perfect combination of the desert and the tropical. They walked slowly beneath the telephone wires that ran sagging from pole to pole.

It was dark now, but you could still see everything distinctly, except for a little blurring at the edges. Liz and Milton passed the Pohutukawa's, at that point almost growing into the telephone lines. The street lights suddenly came on creating snowy pools, a sort of visual ether that turned men into shadows. The pavement was still warm under Liz's bare feet. The thick air flowed smoothly over their faces and arms. They passed a house with large French windows facing the road. Loud music poured from the doorway and inside a room full of people twisted and writhed to the music, silhouettes lighted by a table lamp somewhere behind them.

"Do you think I've ruined your life, Milton?" Liz said out of the soft darkness. Milton looked at her shadowy face.

"Na."

"We're really like all those people though, aren't we?"

"Yeah, I'm afraid so. We've got two arms, two legs, all the same number of things they've got."

"We've even got two mortgages."

"That's a lot better than one landlord."

"Our life's appalling."

"Utterly depraved."

"Don't be flippant."

"I've just got to keep writing. Maybe that will save us."

"Why should it. We're rotten anyway."

"Okay, so what?"

"Nothing. It's just that our life stinks."

They turned in and walked across their lawn to their house. The pale white moon above the eastern hills was almost half full. They reached their front door and Milton felt around in his pocket for the key.

"We'd better think about putting in some shrubs, Milton," said Liz looking across the lawn to the road.

"Yeah, well, I don't mind doing some gardening." Milton found the key and unlocked the door, holding the fly door open with his outthrust backside. He turned the handle and pushed the door open.

"Perhaps we ought to have a hedge?"

""No, I don't like being closed in," said Milton walking back out onto the veranda, the fly door scraping across his back and banging shut. "A lot of low shrubs and a few taller ones; but no hedge."

"Well, you'd better get on with it then," said Liz.

"I wonder if you've got to plant certain shrubs at certain times of the year. I'd better go to the library and get a book," said Milton absently.

"Your family lived on the land. How come you know nothing about shrubs and gardening?" asked Liz.

"I was too busy reading books," said Milton Harper walking through the door of their lounge and turning their light on. He stood there, just inside the doorway, holding the fly door open for Liz.

Chapter 6

Melissa Gibson sat on the edge of her bed. She was afraid sitting there in the country darkness. Darkness in the country seemed to her so hollow, so unending. She didn't believe that the light would ever return that she would wake in the morning and find the warm sun on her face. Her parents had talked for a long while after she had gone to bed, but now the grumble of their conversation had stopped and the world was empty. So Melissa sat there in the dark not wanting to put on the light because the white of the light was even worse than the darkness.

She looked down at her stomach. She even felt afraid of that. It had seemed such a triumph to her once. That was before her long-haired, moustachioed boyfriend had gone pale and looked away out the window at the sprinkling of lights below them in the city. He was so young and tender, yet strong. She had felt protected by him, yet not controlled. Then he started to cry and, as the tears ran down his cheeks and dripped off the end of his moustache, they washed away her trust. He was only a boy after all. After that she had no longer been able to love him as she had before. They had started to live together as husband and wife and he had even been happy, very happy really: but finally she had had to tell him that it was all over. He had cried again, more loudly and much longer this time. He had told her that he loved her as he had never loved anyone and that he wanted their child which was the monument they had created to their love. She had comforted the young man, made weak by his loss, but she only comforted him as she might a stranger. She could not confuse love with humanity.

She had shifted after that, but she was unable to get rid of him. He had rung so often that eventually she had stopped answering the phone. He used to lean against one of the lampposts outside her flat and wait for her to come out. So, she had to come home to Poverty Bay, because he couldn't follow her there without deserting his studies and she didn't think he would do that.

Melissa drew her feet up and covered herself with the blanket again. She wished she could have a smoke, but she had given that up for the baby. Still, it was only about another month now and she would be able to smoke a whole packet of cigarettes one after the other. It was a treat she had promised herself.

She lay back, wishing she had a man with her. A man for her wasn't exactly a specific person, but a sort of an abstraction and she was drawn to men who came nearest to this abstraction. She didn't have a carefully calculated specimen of manhood: so many feet high, with a certain occupation and a certain accent. She just looked at a man and she knew, even though an outsider might have seen no similarity between two men that she loved.

That was the worst thing about coming back home. Here, where love was concerned, men were vulgar, unrefined little creeps like her father. Love was a quick grunt and a hitching up of strides or an interlude between drunkenness and sleep.

There was a soft thud against her stomach. The damned thing kicked so much she sometimes mused that she must have been fucked by a horse. She was sweating again now. Her nightdress stuck to her legs and she felt a large, cold drop of water slide down her rib cage from her armpit. The scratchy sheet seemed to be coiling around her body and her limbs, closing on her like a boa constrictor. She threw off the sheets again and laid her legs in the moonlight, staring at the ceiling.

She wished now that she didn't have to have a child. She would always be cool to it, now that she no longer loved its father. She would be as indifferent to it as she was to the rest of the world that she didn't love. It would know kindness and gentleness and it would be well clothed and fed. She might even marry and it would have a father. But there, at the bottom of everything, would be the corrupting seed of lovelessness. Not, of course, that that would make it very unique. Many children had abundant affection lavished upon them without being touched by the hand of love. Melissa chuckled softly. The chuckle coiled and floated around the room.

She was twenty years old, well nearly twenty anyway, and the all encompassing sin of the world was as clear to her as a germ under a microscope is to a biologist. By some fluke she had been born a vessel of truth. All the wiles of education had been unable to wean her from the nipple of the world. She knew the world without needing to open her eyes, while others who scuttled with notebooks and magnifying glasses and the objective method would never see it for all their looking.

Melissa stood up and walked soundlessly across the room. She turned the door handle and drew open the door. She walked down the corridor, though the darkness of the lounge and out into the moonlight. Her feet sunk deeply into the white carpet. She reached the sliding glass doors which led to the patio and pressed them apart.

There was a faint rumble as they rolled easily open. The new air forced its way in the door and Melissa was surprised at the cold. She stepped out onto the patio. The chill of the concrete rushed up her legs and pooled in the womb with her baby. It reminded her of going to school barefooted when there was almost a frost. She snorted in the cold air. It burned the top of her sinuses and all the way down to the bottom of her lungs. She heard the" hoosh, hoosh" sound of a hedgehog feeding on the lawn. The sweet smell of grass and the pungent smell of sheep dung hung in the still air. The air here was thin though, not thick with scent as it was in some other parts of the country. It was, above all, healthy.

She looked out into the grey jumble of shapes. Nothing was discernible in the landscape except for the perfect flatness of the cloudless sky. It looked as though, if you reached high enough, you could caress its smooth, flawless surface. Somewhere, within or behind the sky, were the stars like fiery, frozen moths. A morepork sounded in the night. Out there was such space that if you walked out you would never return to the daylight. No human would ever see you.

Melissa returned inside, shut the door and went through to the kitchen. She filled a glass of water by sound as she looked out the window at the shadowy dog kennels through the spidery boughs of the silver birches. She turned around and stopped with a jolt. Water slipped over the rim of her glass and splashed on the floor.

"Mum, you frightened me."

"Can't you sleep?"

"It's hot in here."

"I thought it was quite cool, myself."

"That's the trouble. With the blanket on it's too hot and with it off it's too cold."

"Don't worry dear."

Who's worried?" Melissa's mother looked at her for several seconds and then turned back towards her bedroom. Melissa filled her glass again and followed her mother out of the kitchen. Her mother was waiting for her just outside her bedroom door, a shadow in the dark hall.

""Don't take too much notice of your father," said Mrs Gibson in a stage whisper. "He's a little bit uncouth and he thinks he's the only person in the world who's entitled to hold an opinion, but he means well."

"Okay Mum." Melissa despised these muttered confidences which were really more like betrayals.

"Once you've had the baby, don't be afraid to leave it with me and go out whenever you want to."

"You mean I'd better leave the baby with you and get out there and round up a husband."

"Of course not; but you don't want the child to ruin your chances, do you?"

"Okay Mum. I'll see you in the morning."

"Do you want one of my sleeping pills?"

"No thanks Mum. I'll go to sleep eventually. I'm probably just a bit excited about being home." Melissa opened the door of her room, slipped in and closed it again before her mother had a chance to say any more. Her mother stood there looking at the closed door for a little while. Then she shrugged and walked back to her bedroom.

Melissa sat on the edge of her bed and bounced up and down. She was wondering how the hell she had ever emerged from a liaison between her father and her mother. Some God must have watched over her or she would have ended up a strange and perverted girl. It wasn't so much that her mother thought that there was anything wrong with sex, but that she thought it was unmentionable. Sex was fine as long as it was hushed up in marriage. Once you were married no one ever thought of you making love, whereas if you were single all you ever did was make love. You fucked under hedges and in the backs of cars and it wasn't healthy. Once you were married and you slept together every night sex was relegated to its rightfully minor place.

Melissa walked over to the sliding cupboard door opposite her bed and pushed it aside. It was too dark to see into the cupboard so she reluctantly walked back to her bedroom door and turned on the light. Everything went a searing yellow and her eyes smarted through their half-closed lids. She rubbed her eyes and watched the colours change from black to red. When she reopened her eyes everything was less bright, though unnaturally clear edged. Melissa walked back to her wardrobe and looked into it. It was full of old clothes, clothes she had worn as a child: a little coat with a furry collar, school uniforms all hanging on their coat hangers, a costume museum of her past. On the floor beneath the coats were old shoes, the leather dulled and misshapen by long disuse. Spider webs stretched across the mouth of some of the shoes. Her tennis racket, a very expensive one, lay in its cover in the back corner.

But Melissa had come for none of these things. She looked up at the shelf above the coats. That was where her dolls were. She could see her squat Koala bear with his flat black nose and his button eyes. She remembered that he had a zip in the back. Even now she couldn't work out why the zip was there. There too was her cloth Gollywog with his flaring hair, bright red coat and green trousers. He had a maniacal grin on his dull black face. That Gollywog had been a failure though; she had neither loved nor feared it. Then she saw the red velvet leg of her favourite doll sticking out from underneath a blue teddy bear. She lifted up the teddy and dragged out the slender doll. The doll was dressed like Father Christmas, her hood trimmed with white, woolly material. The doll's legs and arms flopped down towards the ground, hanging straight from the shoulders and hips. Melissa cradled the doll in her arms and went and turned off the light again. She stood perfectly still at the door for some time, her hand against the light switch until, little by little, the objects in the room began to disentangle themselves from the darkness. Once the room had reformed itself Melissa walked through the square puddle of moonlight and got back into bed.

She lay on her back with the doll against her cheek and the sheet under her chin. She felt again the warmth and security that a child feels encased in sheets. She felt again the tender, uncomplicated love that a child feels, not just for a doll, but for all things living and dead. She knew that this love could not last. It was too sweet, too non-carnal and she instinctively began to rebel against it. It was carrying her away from herself, from the tongues of fire produced by the savage muscular frailty of men, away from the tongues of fire that melted her to her essential being. The child's love is based on a feeling of safety, but an adults is based on beauty and both loves cannot survive simultaneously in the same person.

Sleep was coming now and as each wave of sleep rolled across her mind, she could almost feel the waves inside her skull as she sank down into the world of the child. When the wave subsided, she struggled frantically to escape back to herself, bobbing to the surface only to relax and surrender to the next wave. The detached part of her was afraid, but the wave came and she responded against her better judgement.

Then, suddenly, she was very lucid. The child kicked and stopped her descent into whatever place she was going to. She felt tired now. She didn't have to go away anywhere to sleep. She could simply lie there and sleep in perfect safety. She dropped the doll on the floor. She no longer needed it.

Chapter 7

The next day in the afternoon it began to rain. The rain came in from the south and it rained intermittently for a week. All week the sky remained dark and the cold wind came swooping in over the backs of the muddied waves. On the Saturday it rained without let up. The rain made a permanent link between the drab earth and the dark sky, swallowing the hills and imprisoning everyone in a wet, windy cage a mile square. Never had there been such a wet summer in Gisborne!

Milton Harper sat through the rain in misery. It hadn't curtailed his activity for he still ran, even though the sudden squalls of rain sprang out of what seemed an impassive sky and the raindrops pierced his singlet like icy quills. He just resented the fact that there was no sun to shine on his muscles, muscles that were hard and well defined. The cold froze up his body and his body became a drab, inanimate thing like the winter soil.

Jim Wilson, however, enjoyed the rain. Sitting in his warm house, wearing two jerseys, a heater scorching his legs and turning his face a darker red, he would read and smoke and look across the valley. He felt like an eagle in his warm nest, up above lowland humanity. He even enjoyed being out in the rain, the cold penetrating his warmth without destroying it. When he went out he wore a white silk scarf beneath his black overcoat and a black, felt hat on his head. He even enjoyed running across the street from one lot of shop awnings to another. So many people stared at the large priest leaping lightly over the puddles in the road, one hand on the top of his head to hold his hat on. Sometimes he would even hide in a shop doorway and light a cigarette in his cupped hands, pretending to himself that his white scarf had turned him into a gangster.

On the last day of the rain Milton Harper was visiting the greengrocers. He stood there, his head thrust slightly out in front of him as though he wanted to see what was going to happen to him before it even occurred. His eyes, hard and expressionless, were buried beneath his brows. He was wearing a tan duffel coat. Duffel coats were seldom worn anymore, though several years before they had been quite common. He stood there looking at the vegetables. A neat Chinese woman with dirty fingernails hovered within striking distance of him. She was waiting until Milton straightened up, showing that he had made a decision.

Melissa Gibson, her stomach preceding her, entered the shop. She looked around vaguely. She had not been in this shop for a couple of years and was trying to get her bearings. Her gaze came to a halt on Milton Harper. He looked interesting, though not her type of course. Too much frigid indifference and bitterness, she thought vaguely. She wondered what he was like when he had sex. It was so hard to imagine a man like him abandoning himself to anything, even pain.

Milton Harper plucked the lobe of his ear a couple of times. He

43

couldn't decide what to buy. He had just decided to buy a cabbage when Melissa, who was standing beside him, said:

"Not much choice is there?"

"No," he said. Milton looked sideways at the very pregnant swollen faced girl. The water had run off the bottom of her parka and left wet patches on the front of her long dress. Her white feet in water logged roman sandals poked out from under the hem of her dress. Milton wondered what this cheeky hippy wanted. Perhaps she was going to try to sell him one of Moses David's pamphlets.

"You're just visiting Gisborne?" asked Melissa.

"No, I live here." The girl didn't have the frail air of a hippette. She had the air of an attractive, successful professional woman. She seemed too young though and the impression made no sense.

"You look like a student to me."

"Too old," said Milton Harper bending over and picking up a cabbage. He looked around for the Chinese woman, but she was serving another customer. He was caught. He turned back towards Melissa.

"You used to be a student though, huh?" she said.

"Yeah," Milton agreed. They stood there looking at one another without saying anything.

"Why don't you come out and have tea with me?"

"I'm married," said Milton wanting to see how she would respond.

"Bring your wife too, then."

Milton's wet trousers were beginning to cling uncomfortably to his legs and he tried to shake them loose. He clutched the cabbage tightly under his left arm and said."

"Why me?" Melissa, who was squeezing a lettuce, looked over her shoulder and said:

"I just think you'd make an interesting friend."

"Aw, I'm very boring really."

"You might as well come out. I'm a good cook," said Melissa turning back to the other vegetables after having failed all the lettuces. "You'll have to put up with my parents though and I hope you've got a car. We live a fair way out." The Chinese woman came up expectantly and Milton thrust the cabbage at her.

"Good, Liz likes the country?

"Fine, what day suits you?"

"Any day but Thursday, Liz has yoga on Thursday."

"That'll be thirty-five please," broke in the Chinese woman, holding the cabbage firmly under her arm and thrusting out her palm. Milton pulled up his duffel coat and took a handful of change out of the pocket of his jeans. He looked at the change in his palm, picked out thirty five cents and gave them to the Chinese woman while he put the rest of the change back in his pocket.

"How about tomorrow?" asked Melissa.

""Better make it Wednesday. I'll have to check with Liz."

They went through all the formalities of exchanging addresses and phone numbers and Melissa drew Milton a map on a brown paper bag showing him how to get to the farm. Melissa asked the Chinese woman if she had any garlic. There was no garlic, so they both turned and walked back along the shiny black rubber mat past the vegetables in their wooden bins. Just in the entrance of the shop a violent gust of wind checked their progress. They stepped further out onto the street and turned into the wind. Sinking their heads into their shoulders they walked slowly along the street, their clothing curling and flapping in the wind.

When they reached the end of the block they dawdled to a halt and Melissa pulled the hood of her blue parka over her head. She tightened the cord around the opening of the hood.

"What do you do anyway, Milton?" she asked.

"Oh, I write."

"What do you write?"

"Novels."

"I've never heard of you."

"I had one published in America three months ago. That's all I've ever had published." A loose strand of Melissa's wet, brown hair flapped in the wind.

A car came to a halt beside them, water dripping from the insides of its mudguards. The old black car's side windows were foggy, and drops of rain broke loose and ran down the outsides of the windows. The windscreen wipers swished backwards and forwards, backwards and forwards. There was a graunch as the driver put the car in gear and drove away across the main road. The little pennants, hanging from wires strung across the main street, flapped in the wind sounding like a flock of angry birds. Their colours were dull in the rain.

Do you make a habit of picking up men who intrigue you?" asked Milton.

"What was that?"

"You usually pick up men in the street?

"All the time," laughed Melissa. Their relationship was in suspension now until they met again.

It had suddenly stopped raining and she looked acrss the road through the water clean air at the muscular, slightly round-shouldered Māori kid who was leaning against the display window of a department store. He was wearing a yellow sleeveless singlet and had his arms wrapped tightly around his body. Periodically he would lower his head and take a puff out of a cigarette he had smouldering in his hand. In front of him on the pavement, people moved as erratically as moths. Melissa noticed the ribbon of dry pavement which ran along the street hard in against the shops and laughed. The air under the awnings was solid and sombre. It was no medium for hurrying people.

Milton looked at the preoccupied girl standing there staring into the distance.

"Well, see you Wednesday," he said. Melissa slowly turned around and looked at him. Then she said, quite suddenly:

"That's right. Ring me if you can't make it."

"I will. Make sure you don't slip on the wet road or you'll be in hospital on Wednesday instead of at the dinner table."

"Don't worry. It won't be leaving early. It likes kicking me too much."

"It must be a dangerous puritan."

"You could be right."

"Well, I'd better get home and cook a meal."

"Alright, see you Wednesday."

"Right, see you Wednesday."

Chapter 8

iz Harper stood on the front veranda of her house and shook the water off a heavy, shiny, red raincoat. A plump, cheerful, young man was standing looking at her, his hands in the pocket of his three-quarter length tweed coat. Liz draped her raincoat over her arm and took a key out of her glossy, brown, leather shoulder bag. The young man pulled back the fly door for her.

"Thank you," she said smiling at him.

Liz had decided that it was time to take action. She wasn't quite sure whether this was revenge, an attempt to arouse in her husband renewed sexual interest or simply a wish to be fucked by a man who actually desired her. Liz glanced at Hugh as she turned the key in the lock.

She had been encouraging Hugh ever since the term began at the start of the previous week. On Friday night he had taken one of the young, first-year teachers out, plied her with drink and tried to fuck her. There was no doubt about old Hugh. He was definitely keen. They would have a quick roll on the sofa in the front room and she would send him off with the promise of another time soon.

They went into the lounge. Hugh stood there in the middle of the floor, not quite knowing what to do.

"Let me take your coat," said Liz. She was amused by Hugh. The poor guy didn't know whether he was going to get it or not. Hugh unbuttoned his coat, put his arms behind his back and Liz pulled the coat off.

"This is a nice, homely room," said Hugh walking around the room trying to find something to look at on the wall.

"Milton hasn't made much from his writing yet so we can't afford anything much," shouted Liz from the kitchen.

"Where is Milton?" asked Hugh idly, staring at the reproduction of a Picasso nude on the wall.

"He usually wanders around town until about 5 o'clock. He probably thinks of it as part of his research." Being a new staff member Hugh had never met Milton Harper, but he was beginning to form a picture of him as an ineffectual asthmatic with glasses.

Hugh walked over and sat down on the divan. The old fashioned, wooden Venetian blinds excluded much of the light. Rain suddenly rattled again on the iron roof. The dark varnish on the edge of the floor seemed to glint in the gloom. The light coming through the kitchen door looked like a solid block of glass.

Liz broke through the glass and moved into the weightless darkness. She had taken off her boots and was walking in her stockinged feet. Hugh suddenly stood up and moved towards Liz, like a fat worm fired from a catapult. He put out his hands, grabbed her by the hips and dragged her roughly towards him. This was his version of masculine assertiveness. He ruffled her lips with his lips and then he glued his lips to hers, feeling her breath on the back of his palate. He rammed his pelvis against hers and held her tighter. Liz was in pain by now and struggling to free herself from the grip of this lecherous Billy Bunter.

"Come over to the couch," she croaked. He released her. She walked backwards towards the couch. He stood there, face flushed, eyes glinting.

"Get 'em off!" he panted. Liz pulled her pants and panty hose down round her ankles. stepped out of them and kicked them away across the room. The underwear rested against the concrete hearth. Hugh struggled with his belt. He got it undone, ripped open his trousers and pushed them and his underpants to his knees. He tried to draw one leg out, but couldn't get his shoe through the cuff. Hugh knelt on one knee, his pants hanging around his thighs. He almost fell over as he did so. He began to undo his shoe. Liz sat neatly on the edge of the sofa and watched Hugh's fevered struggle with his clothing. She could see his pink penis bobbing up and down between the front flaps of his shirt. Hugh got the shoe off and fell over backwards. He got up, a smile of triumph on his face, and began to undo the other shoe. It crossed Liz's mind that Hugh should never have given her the opportunity to reflect upon his indignity. He was hardly the most attractive of men. Hugh got the other shoe off and stepped out of his pants. He walked up to Liz, thrust his penis in the direction of her face and ended pulling her forehead against his testicles. If he doesn't let me go I'll bite one of the pearls he's got inside those wrinkled red purses, thought Liz.

Hugh pushed Liz suddenly backwards on the divan and fell on top of her. He wriggled about, probing with his penis, trying to find the channel to slide inside of her, "sheath his sword" as he thought of it. He felt the softness of her flesh and the electric brittleness of her pubic hair as he probed with his soft ended hammer. He struggled frantically to enclose his penis in her flesh.

The rain stopped and everything was still and silent. He could smell Liz's scent and the material of the settee. The divan creaked slightly. He found the right place and pushed slowly forward, his penis sliding into the hugging wetness. He heard a scratching noise and then a click.

He felt Liz try to sit up. Suddenly the room was light and he could hear water running from a spouting overflow. A gust of wind ruffled the hairs on his backside and some beautifully cool fingers played with his testicles. Hugh straightened his arms and looked over his shoulder. There, standing in the doorway, his shape blurred by grey light, was a slim, powerful man, with heavy arms and shoulders almost too large for his slim torso. His hair seemed to be sticking out of his head like bristles on a broom.

Hugh withdrew his penis from Liz. He stood up and turned around. The shadow had grown to terrible proportions as it swept towards him on a river of light. Then, suddenly, it was no longer a shadow, but a man his jaw set and his eyes like cold, grey seas between his eyelids. *This can't be her husband,* thought Hugh. He felt his face flush with embarrassment at being caught without his pants in public, especially with his penis pointing half to the front and half to the sky.

Then the man was upon him. Hugh felt his hot breath on his face, breath that was unusually sweet. He felt his feet lift off the ground and then a terrible pain shot from his testicles along the top of his legs and around his abdomen. The pain got worse, like a landslide gathering momentum. It got so intense that it almost destroyed itself, so intense that it didn't seem to belong to him anymore. Hugh saw the fly speckled light and light shade going away from him. He heard a long guttural scream of agony coming from somewhere quite close. He felt a jolt as his back and head hit against someone's soft flesh. He slipped down that slide of flesh on to a hard surface like sacking. It smelled of dust and it made him want to cough. Then his right eye felt hot and wet and his nose felt as though it was packed with cotton wool covered with ether. He really was coughing now, as though some tea had gone down the wrong way. There were two screams now instead of one, the second one high pitched, made up of words, but words that seemed like a foreign language.

Then nothing was happening. He seemed to be floating, surrounded by a strange muttering sound. Suddenly there was a blank space filled with nothing, absolutely nothing. Then Hugh realised he was lying on the floor a ridiculously large shoe specked with blood next to his eye. There was a terrible pain in his abdomen and he tried to scream, but only ended up emitting a sound like a cistern filling. He couldn't see out of his right eye and he could feel blood coursing out of his nose. He sniffed and the blood gurgled in his nose and pain rushed to either side of his temples and exploded like a bell ringing. He realised that Liz was screaming.

"You've killed him you idiot! You've killed him, you've killed him!"

"Yeah," said the man with an assumed drawl. "You'll be able to go and put violets on his grave then?"

"I'd better ring a doctor, Milt," said the woman.

"I wouldn't bother unless you want to end up like him." The man moved slowly and rhythmically to the door, looked up and down the road and fixed his eyes on an elderly gentleman who was sitting on his bike staring at Milton Harper. Hilton stared at him until the elderly man looked away and began cycling back up the road. Milton pushed the door shut with his foot. A sudden gust of rain rattled against the window sounding like fine stones.

Hugh Black sat up against the couch still clutching his abdomen and whimpering in long, rasping gasps. He watched Milton Harper pick up his trousers from the floor and walk to the fireplace with them. Milton took the fireguard off the empty fireplace and threw the pants and the underpants in. Hugh lifted up his hand in a feeble gesture of protest, but then dropped his hand to his side.

"Don't be a bloody idiot, Milt!" said Liz angrily. Milton Harper looked at her and his features lost all their mobility. Instead of being a living face it became as hard and sharp edged as slate. He took two ridiculously long strides towards Liz. Her eyes became round and her mouth became a cave and, for a second, it seemed to Hugh that Milton would disappear down it. Liz screamed and put her hands over her face. Milton hit her sharply in the stomach as he flashed past and Hugh saw Liz sliding down the wall, her eyes still round, but completely blank.

Liz sat there on the floor. She couldn't believe she would ever breathe again. She felt she was vomiting in one long stream and completely unable to get her breath. She doubled over, trying to expel the last drop of liquid so she could inhale, but it didn't seem to make any difference. At the back of her throat, in her nostrils and behind her eyes was the terrible ache of grief. Even if she lived, even if she breathed again, the world was changed forever. She had never really recognised the legitimacy of any passions but her own. She had never understood that there were times when men were the mere puppets of their own machinery. She knew now that she could be hurt, that she was frail and weak and that what she did really did affect other people.

A shadow seemed to pass over her. She looked at the brown leaf pattern on the old carpet. That was life and she must hold on to it. Just as she felt her eyes were about to roll onto her cheeks she became aware of a pain in her stomach. She snatched a little breath. The kerosene fumes burned her lungs and nostrils. There was a "whoosh" and her face was suddenly hot and orange shadows seemed to be writhing on the floor. But this was all unimportant. She grabbed a little more air. Something was moving in front of her. Whatever it was it was white and sticky, but it was a piece of matter without significance. She got a bigger breath this time. She looked again and saw a pair of naked calves and feet sidling towards the door. She heard Milton saying:

"Go on fats. Get out."

"Be reasonable Mr Harper. I live on the other side of town."

"That's your problem." Liz sucked in an even bigger breath. She looked up at Hugh standing there, his hands over his genitals, the structure of his face somehow distorted and strings of blood and mucous hanging from his nose. Hugh was looking from the door to Milton and then back to the door again.

"Liz," said Milton from just behind her, "show your Adonis out." Liz's gaze travelled up Milton's body. His chest and head looked oddly small and his eyes seemed to be aiming down either side of his aquiline nose. "Go on, get up," he said nudging her knee with the toe of his boot. Liz turned around, kneeled on all fours and then pulled herself up on the back of the divan. She stood there swaying, holding her stomach with one hand. "Come on. Don't keep our guest waiting," said Milton sinking down on the divan. Liz crossed the room with a staggering rush and held the door open, looking like a cripple parodying a courtier. Hugh looked at Milton appealingly, but Milton simply sat on the divan picking his weight-lifting calluses. Hugh's eyes began to glitter with tears, like tinsel on a Christmas tree. He turned and looked out under the low roof of the veranda at the sodden grass on the lawn. The steely, grey air was streaked with silver. The sun was about to break through. The road was a ribbon of coal in the almost sunlight backed by the sodden hutches of houses and the eerie silhouettes of the Norfolk pines.

Suddenly Hugh just ran. He ran in a crouch, his shirt flapping up and down exposing his pink buttocks. Halfway across the lawn he swerved to the right and was no longer in the door frame.

Milton sat there looking at the still life, sans Hugh. Liz started to shut the door.

"You'd better get my duffel coat and cabbage off the veranda. Otherwise, you won't have enough vegetables to cook for tea.

"Aren't you cooking tea?" asked Liz. Milton shook his head and went on picking his calluses. "Oh, well. I don't mind cooking tea just for tonight." said Liz pulling open the door again.

"It's not just for tonight. You're doing all the cooking from now on."

"But that's not fair, Milt."

"It's not supposed to be, but you'll do it."

"I'll leave you, Milt."

"No, you won't, because when I catch you, I'll kill you." Liz looked at Milton, trying to gauge if he was genuine. He looked at her with a sad, soft smile. He wasn't joking. He would kill her.

Liz walked quickly out the door, picked up the cabbage and the duffel coat and walked back inside and through to the kitchen. Milton sat on the couch flexing the muscles in his arms. He looked like a child, deserted by his friends and trying to put a good face on it.

In the kitchen Liz inspected the fridge and all the cupboards. Having memorised their contents, she lit a cigarette and tried to submerge herself in the nicotine and the laborious ritual of cooking. Life had seemed boring before, but at least it was safe. Now there was to be the misery of living with a man who would show her not the least kindness, not the least warmth. Worse still, there was the fear of physical injury, which hung over her for the first time in her life. Worse again was the knowledge that she would have to subjugate herself to Milton to have him ever accept her again. She would have to become his lackey, his valet if they were ever to have anything together again. The only other alternative was escape. Either she must live in obedience and pain, like a sort of secular nun, or try to escape in the knowledge that if she was caught, she would be destroyed. She could not believe that such a situation could arise in the twentieth century. She took the heavy bladed French chef's knife from the drawer and looked at the dull gleam of the blade. This of course was another alternative. Liz sawed vigorously through the cabbage.

In the lounge Milton Harper stuck out his chin and scratched his bearded throat. People had always dominated him and now, at last, he had someone in his power. Not that she was completely in his power, not yet; but eventually she would be. Eventually she would love him with tenderness and fear, or one of them would die. Milton didn't greatly care if it was him. This would be his great experiment with reality. Other men raised crops, built homes for their families, carved out positions of eminence in their professions. But he was a writer and did not live in reality. He toiled in the void, like some demon blacksmith who never saw the light. He lived in neither reality nor imagination, but in a reality where anything was possible, a reality where understanding was more important than the gratification of appetite. Well, now he would have his little piece of reality. He would make his wife love him or he would destroy one or both of them.

Chapter 9

ugh Black was bobbling in a world of grey and green and he knew from the jarring on the soles of his feet that it was he who was moving, not the world. The sound of a bicycle bell fractured the air. He fled it, but encountered the grey boards of a garden wall. He dragged and clawed his way to the top of the wall and teetered there on the top like a seesaw, his stomach the fulcrum. It looked a long way down to the flower bed on the other side. The bicycle bell rang again. Hugh let himself fall forward. The dahlias in the garden rushed towards him in a jumble of colours and Hugh felt the rough wood on the top of the fence tear at his legs.

There was a sharp thump as Hugh landed on his elbows, but the bicycle bell was gone. Hugh had got a piece of dahlia stem in his mouth and he tried to spit it out. He told himself several times that he was upside down. Then, slowly, he let himself fall over backwards. He found himself lying, his buttocks refreshingly wet, in the crushed dahlias.

He sat up. He seemed to have fallen into a new world. There was the bliss of a low concrete walled house with a smooth lawn and the lawn was dotted with neat round circles of black earth powdered with lawn clippings. Through the lawn clippings roses grew with knotty elegance. Drops of water glistened like pearls on the rose petals that had fallen on the lawn. Against the wall of the house was an area of red scoria through which cacti and small conifers were growing. Above this garden there was a grey concrete patio and some white wrought iron furniture. Civilisation was so soothing.

Then Hugh noticed the woman, who was sitting in one of the wrought iron chairs looking at him over the rim of a magazine. Her face seemed to flicker with one emotion after another. No specific emotion was able to gain control of her face. Hugh grinned sheepishly and cupped his hands over his genitals. He licked some blood from his upper lip. The silence folded around Hugh and the unknown woman and froze their attitude of confrontation. The water-logged ground beneath Hugh hissed. A plane flew over head, like a crucified Christ shot through the sky. All action hung suspended; for one second, two seconds, three. Hugh fell through the bottom of the silence and began to co-ordinate his apparently frozen and uncoordinated limbs.

He ran across the front of the house like an arthritic seagull taxiing for take-off. Two muddy, white heels whirled in the air and a white shirt tail flapped in the air as Hugh leapt a spiky cactus and disappeared around the corner of the house. The garden returned with a jolt to green normalcy.

Hugh ran along a dark corridor smelling of pine. The fronds of the trees scratched at his face. He emerged into the sliver prairie of the back garden. Hugh ran on through the fading gloom past a revolving clothesline. He grabbed hold of the centre pole and came to an abrupt halt. There was the grass, a couple of silver leafed feijoas, a white walled garage, a back fence of red, corrugated iron and there, where a hedge joined the fence, was the hole to freedom. Hugh trotted across the backyard, his senses numbed by the overwhelming presence of reality. Awareness and rationality were somewhere on the edge of his consciousness, rendered useless by the danger of his situation. Like a cork on a stormy sea he was at the mercy of whatever information his brain chose to admit to his consciousness.

Hugh's brain admitted pain and he hopped around like a spastic stork trying to extract thistles from his left foot. Finally he managed to also hop on the thistle with his right foot and he fell to the ground, his body jerking with sobs as he rocked backwards and forwards and pulled the thistles out of his feet.

A fresh chill crept out of the once milder air. The light dimmed and a couple of large, cold spots of rain fell on his bare legs. Surely, he thought, even I can't be that unlucky. He stood up, trotted the rest of the way across the lawn and stepped carefully through the gap between the fence and the hedge.

Hugh emerged from the gap with the cautious alertness of a Weka emerging from a woodheap. He had come out onto a large, empty field of grey stones and long, brown grass. The grass though, was so wet it had a greyish tint. Two hundred yards across the paddock a chestnut horse lifted its tail, shifted on its feet and shook its mane. Houses backed onto the field on both sides, older houses on Hugh's side and new ones on the other.

Hugh shrunk back into the hedge. He knew he couldn't stay there very long in case the woman he had just seen called the police. But he couldn't get home either without the same incident repeating itself ten or twenty times, perhaps more. He would have to steal some trousers. He looked across at the new houses, brightly painted on their barren sections, looking like beach balls in a rubbish dump. Behind one of them was a clothesline of sodden sheets. All the other lines were empty. Hugh realised that after a week's rain there wouldn't be much washing on any of the lines. He poked his head further out of the hedge and looked at the houses on his side of the field. About

50 yards away, behind a fawn-coloured house with a brown roof were three long lines held up by manuka props and full of clothes. He scanned the back yards of the two houses between himself and his goal. The nearer one had a long, sombre lawn edged with ferns and black trunked pongas sticking out of the thin grass like wigged skittles. It was deserted except for birds eating worms brought to the surface by the rain. The back yard of the other house, further away, was dominated by a swimming pool with a grey concrete edge and a shattering blue underwater surface. Hugh peered into the dark porch which ran along most of the back of the old white house with its green roof. He could see no flicker of movement there.

He stepped out from the covering of the hedge and ran gingerly across the stony surface of the grassy paddock. He skirted a tangle of rusty barbed wire and, bending his knees, approached the old fence making sure he kept the washing between himself and the house. He gripped the top of a fence post encrusted with fungus and began to put his weight on the wire. He was about to lift his back foot off the ground when the wire gave out a long, metallic groan. A shock passed through Hugh's body. He felt as if his back was going to collapse. His heart began to jump in his chest and he was gripped by nausea. He also became aware of his chilled and naked backside and he tried to pull his shirt tail down to cover it. All the beautiful clothes hung on the line a few strides away. Beyond the first row of towels, he could see socks and trousers. He imagined the warm clamminess of the socks and the wet slap of the baggy, khaki trousers. Donning that drab, shapeless pair of trousers would be akin to the most potent pleasure of paradise.

This time Hugh drew two of the lower wires apart and climbed through the fence. The muscles in his legs felt weak as he cautiously approached the pants through the ankle-deep grass. All he could see of the house was the roof above the hedge of clothes. He parted the sheets and passed through. He reached out to unpeg the pants.

"Hey, boy! Whose garden you think you're in?" said a gruff, but not unfriendly voice. Hugh turned and looked along the corridor of clothes. There at the other end of the corridor, his black, singletted stomach hanging groundwards like a fig, was a large Maori, a stained, extinguished cigarette sticking to his lower lip. He looked at Hugh expressionlessly, his hands on his hips. Then he turned his head towards the house and yelled out: "Hey, Agnes! Come and look at this." Then he turned back and looked at Hugh, checking to see that Hugh had no thought of running off. Hugh stood still. For some odd reason he felt at peace, as though he could stand there forever. The Māori looked away and said in a low voice, apparently to no one: "We got a streaker. He was trying to streak off with a pair of my pants." A large Māori woman waddled into view and looked down the corridor of washing.

"I wonder why he's got no pants."

"He probably came to rape you, Agnes."

"He can come and rape me any time he wants, providing he comes decently dressed." The Māori man fixed Hugh with a serious gaze. Then he said:

"Hey! How come you're dressed like my ancestors? I thought you white men were supposed to be more civilised than us?" The Māori woman lit a cigarette and the cloud of smoke floated straight above her head. Hugh stared, almost hypnotised by the cigarette smoke.

"If you want some pants Lady Godiva, you better come in and get some dry ones. You better come up now before my daughter gets home, otherwise she'll see what she's been missing and I'll never be able to hold her back then." The Māori woman took a few more puffs of her cigarette.

Hugh stood there looking at them both. He couldn't take charity from someone in his humiliating state. It was better to steal than accept charity. He ducked underneath the sheets and ran back towards the fence. He climbed over the fence in a squawk of wire.

The Māori woman came running out from behind the washing, her bulk being tossed from one side to the other like water in a bucket as she ran over the uneven ground.

"Hey, boy! Come back here and get some pants. You can't run around like that. They'll put you in jail. Come back here! We won't hurt you."

Hugh took no notice. He was only aware of the jumble of the distant houses across the paddock and the crunch of shingle under his feet. The houses flashing by on his left, he hardly noticed. The long, sticky paspalum pulled at the hairs on his legs. Ahead, a large hedge came bumping towards him. Above the hedge Hugh could see orange boards the colour of faded brick and the rusting, unpainted roof of an old house. He figured that with any luck the old house would be deserted and he could hide there until dark.

He approached the hedge which stuck much further out into the paddock than any of the other hedges. The hedge seemed unbroken and Hugh turned around the corner created by the hedge and the back fence of the neighbouring property. A large pine tree stood there and the ground was covered with rust-coloured needles and mounds of horse manure. The stinging, sweet smell of wet pine hung in the still air. Hugh picked his way between the pine cones, the fallen pine branches and cairns of fresh horse dung and went round to the back of the tree. There was a hole in the hedge there alright, but it would only take a small dog. In fact, there was an old grey bone lying in the small corridor. Hugh got on all fours, reached in and scraped out the bone. Then he slithered into the hole trying to flatten and elongate his body. He got his hair caught in a branch and had to jerk it painfully free. Finally, his legs jerking like a frog, he managed to push his head through the hedge and into the long, sodden grass, which grew between the wall of the old house and the hedge. There were no skirting boards on the house just there and Hugh could see the old bottles, decaying sacks and bits of rusty roofing iron which lay in the dust under the house. Hugh tried to get the rest of his body through the hole in the hedge, but his shoulders wouldn't move. He lunged violently forward and the hedge above him shuddered. There was a noise of snapping branches, a tearing pain in the back of his right shoulder, but he was through. He stretched out his arms and then stood up and walked towards the other side of the house.

He walked carefully. It didn't look too good for him. The other side of the section was in deep grass, but there was a flattened, muddy track leading to the incinerator, a rusty forty-four-gallon drum with a lid on it, and the long wire with a single prop that was obviously the clothesline. Absurdly too, in the middle of the yard, was a peach tree of huge proportions, completely bare of fruit and dripping wet beneath the dark sky. The green hedge all around the house was a solid as a prison wall.

Hugh hesitated before he rounded the corner. With his luck there would be some aging, dirt encrusted old woman waiting round the corner with a pitch fork. He peeped around the corner and saw Lillie Foster standing in the kitchen door smoking a cigarette. She was humming some unintelligible tune and swinging her right leg back and forth across her body. Her hair hung in damp rat's tails and her dark brown legs glistened with moisture. She looked up and saw Hugh's white face and tousled red hair, from which a large sprig of foliage dangled.

"Hello," she said and smiled. "Are you looking for someone?" Hugh's head disappeared from sight. Lillie flicked the ash off the end of her cigarette, put the cigarette back in her mouth and walked towards the corner of the house, lifting her feet high so that the grass didn't drag off her jandals. She had almost reached the edge of the house when Hugh's head appeared again around the corner.

"Don't come any further," he panted.

"Why on earth not?"

"I don't have any pants on."

"Is that a threat or a promise?" asked Lillie laughing.

"I'm perfectly serious." Lillie frowned.

"Well, if you're a flasher, flash."

"You don't understand. Someone took them off me."

"Took what off you? Are you alright?" asked Lillie as she noticed Hugh's face for the first time.

"Yes. I'm alright. You couldn't get me some pants though, could you?"

"I doubt that any of mine would fit you."

"Please get me some."

"Oh, okay. Come with me." She turned and started to walk back towards the kitchen. Half way back she stopped and looked around. Hugh had disappeared. "Well, come on! I won't rape you." She stood there watching the corner, cigarette leaning downwards from her lips. A couple of seconds later, Hugh came marching round the corner like a headmaster walking across the quadrangle to cane a miscreant. His head was erect and his chest was pushed out. "For God's sake relax," said Lillie turning around and walking towards the kitchen.

Hugh sat down behind the kitchen table, his legs tight together. He looked around the room and thought what a hovel it was. Lillie materialised out of the gloom of a doorway and threw him a pair of jeans. Hugh put them on, crouching behind the table.

"How are they?" asked Lillie.

"Very nice thank you," said Hugh, struggling to do up the dome at the top. Lillie suddenly seemed to be looking at him very hard. Hugh looked at her and started to back away out the door.

"You've got a broken nose and that eye's a real mess as well." Hugh stopped and stood up. She was right. He had been badly injured. All his pains now seemed to register at once. His right eye felt as though someone had sewn the brow and the cheek almost together. He realised he couldn't see very much out of that eye. His nose felt as though the top of it was clogged with plastoscene. He snorted. That seemed to clear it. Then he saw the blood making fresh, scarlet dots on his shirt, which already had a large dark red stain on it. He staggered back to the chair, weakened by the sight of his own blood. He collapsed on the table crying uncontrollably.

"Oh, Jesus and bloody hell! I'll kill that bastard, I'll kill him!" He felt someone pull him up from the table and force his head back. He shook his head free and lowered it into his hands again.

"Put your head back, or the haemorrhaging won't stop," said Lillie.

"I don't care. I just want to get him," groaned Hugh, his courage growing stronger in the presence of his pain and the absence of Milton.

"Oh, stop talking tripe!" said Lillie, shoving a large handkerchief against his nose and grabbing a handful of hair and forcing his head back. "How did this happen?" asked Lillie, looking out the window.

"I was making love to a woman and her husband came home," sniffled Hugh through the handkerchief. "I didn't know he was a muscle man." Hugh squirmed in his chair.

"Sit still!" said Lillie shortly.

"I think she wanted him to catch us."

"That's the guy in the funny little house with the big lawn, isn't it? Just up the road."

"Probably. His name's Milton Harper."

"I see him out running quite a lot. Not a bad looking guy."

"He's square."

"Look who's talking."

"What's square about me?"

"Nothing."

Life drained into the darkness of the high-ceilinged room. The tap dripped and the crisp linen pressed into Hugh's face cutting off the flow of air. Lillie was moving slightly back and forth, her pink satiny blouse approaching his left eye and then retreating exposing the smoke-stained cream wall to his eyes again. Hugh relaxed. Way, way above him he could see the fly speckled ceiling. He knew that if Lillie took the handkerchief away, he would smell the smell of dirt, clean and musty. Being there was like living in a flower pot under a walnut tree on an early summer morning. *Perhaps this place does have its virtues,* thought Hugh. Something clunked on the roof. The noise seemed to linger and become a part of the stillness rather than disappear. Hugh's pain buzzed like an insistent mosquito. All around him was the cool caress that only a big, old, empty house possesses, a caress arousing like the hands of a strange woman but not so disturbing, a caress like the first sublimely slow descent into cool, thick water on a warm summer's day. It was a house where each inside sound became like a tinkle of crystal. What was needed was a fresh Christmas tree with its sweet smell and clinging, syrupy gum.

"I'll make you a cup of tea. One of the boys can take you to outpatients when they come back from work. Want a cigarette?"

"Oh, great!" Lillie lit Hugh's cigarette and took the flaming match to the gas jet. She turned on the gas tap and applied the match to the jet. There was a pop as the gas ignited. Hugh looked at the blue flames. They seemed like demon dancers in a faery glade. He tried to blot them out with a cloud of cigarette smoke. But the dancers kept frenetically on until Lillie turned them into slothful, yellow leaves by half smothering them with the blackened bottom of the old kettle.

Lillie leaned against the stove. She could feel the tingle of the cold metal through her dress. She only needed to be touched by something, whether animate or inanimate, to feel aroused. She looked at Hugh sitting there, his face rendered inhuman by bruising, completely engrossed in his cigarette. She shook her head gently. He was too flabby. That guy up the road, Milton whatever his name was, would be alright though. He was a little too hard perhaps to be a real animal, but he was close.

"You don't know what Milton does do you? With a name like that he ought to be a poet, or a Maori."

"He writes. He can't be much good though, or Liz wouldn't teach."

"No one makes any money out of writing, not in this country anyway."

They shouldn't do it then."

"Why not?"

"Writing doesn't feed anyone. It's immoral."

"Who wants to feed people all the time?"

"It should be our aim to feed people adequately."

"I've got better things to do with my time. Anyway, I'm not the one who eats too much. You are."

Hugh looked at Lillie and wondered why so many people were bereft of idealism. He talked and thought about feeding people in the third, fourth and fifth worlds all the time. He thought about them as he guzzled his way through his twice daily three course meal, he thought about them as he swilled through his large, daily intake of beer. He even thought about them as he took his yearly holiday in Fiji. So many people, so little compassion!

Hugh looked at Lillie appraisingly.

"You've been nice to me," he said.

"Yeah."

"Would you like to come out for dinner on Saturday night?"

"I don't intend to be that nice."

"What's the matter?"

"Nothing. Why?"

"Well then. How about it?"

"I've seen your prick once. I'm not hankering for another look."

Hugh went red. He felt angry and embarrassed.

"You've got no more manners than a rhinoceros!" he squeaked.

"At least I don't look like one." This catapulted Hugh right onto his highest horse. He forgot his pain and his recent humiliation in one red flush of superiority.

"You are so uncouth!" he spluttered rising to his full height. Lillie shrugged.

"So what?"

"Well, apologise!"

"Don't be a pain!"

"You may live in the gutter but I'm a humanitarian and a schoolteacher."

"Who's just been screwing another man's wife?" Hugh winced and looked away.

"Really!" he muttered.

"You just can't face the facts. That's your trouble."

The kettle of water on the stove boiled. Hugh stood at the window trying to smoke, his hand shaking, the cigarette burnt down to the filter. A gust of wind came and rattled the window pane. Drops of water fell from the peach tree in the garden like a settling flock of birds. The hedge shimmered. Lillie's words cut sharply through the cocoon of his misery.

"I'm sorry," she said.

That's all right," said Hugh, turning away from the window. Lillie turned back to the tea.

What an obscene little man, she thought. Men like that make sex ugly.

Chapter 10

About five minutes before six o'clock Dave Gibson was wandering around the lounge in a green tweed suit, tan shoes that shone like a car in a second hand car sales yard and wet, neatly parted hair. He looked a bit like a ten day old bone coated with Béarnaise sauce. The change of clothing had reduced him to a state of neurotic nervousness.

"What the hell's happened to my tobacco?" he shouted to his wife.

"I've hidden it."

"What in the name of God for?"

"It's too messy. There's a packet of filtered cigarettes on the bookcase." His wife's voice, a near miss at refinement, descended to the floor in a series of swoops like an autumn leaf. Gibbo reached the bookcase and lit a cigarette, bending over it, protecting it with his body. He turned, walked to the fireplace, threw the match in and leaned back against the chimney. Through in the dining room he could see his wife waving a table cloth over the table like a magician making magic passes over a box from which he intended to produce a gross of rabbits. The table cloth settled on the table and she smoothed it with the palms of her hands. Outside was the desert blue of the sky, the fiery yellow light of the cooling evening and the motley jungle of shadows on the lawn. Gibbo could see pulsating swarms of sand flies hovering in the shade of the silver birches. A starling landed on one of the birch branches, tottered momentarily and then settled securely on the thin whippy branch bobbing up and down. Just on the other side of the tall fence a sheep was grazing, its frantically moving lips and teeth seeming to pull its relaxed and idle body after it. The dogs began to bark, their voices sounding weak in the thin evening air.

"It looks like the shithouses are arriving," said Gibbo to his wife.

"Don't be so childish. Go out and meet them, Dave."

"What for? Surely they've got enough brains to find the door?"

"I'm going Mum!" shouted Melissa walking through the lounge past her father and on into the kitchen.

Milton Harper turned off the ignition of his Morris Mini. He looked at Jim Wilson. Jim was sitting with his head drawn into his shoulders to keep it out of permanent contact with the roof. Jim's elbows were together on his lap. The priest looked like Finn McCool in his son's cradle.

"You look happy," said Milton undoing his seat belt.

"I should never have agreed to come in this sardine tin Milton."

"I wouldn't grouch yet. This might have been the good part."

"I reckon I'd rather have tea with Satan, Lucifer and Beelzebub than ride in this thing."

"Well, I'll see if I can borrow some roller skates from our hosts and I'll tow you back home."

"Don't be silly. This thing couldn't tow a mouse, let alone an elephant." Father Wilson opened his door, drew up his legs, swivelled in his seat and put his feet on the ground. Milton Harper jumped dexterously out of the small car and slammed his door.

"You'll have to take up exercising Jim. All your idleness is seizing up your joints." Jim Wilson stood up and staggered around bent kneed beside the car. Finally, he stood up shaking one leg and then the other.

"Exercising? Hell! I think I'd better have a cigarette." The smoke from his cigarette blew away like a blue chiffon scarf against the blue hills. The chill vapours in the breeze slid over their bodies.

"It's a bit cold."

"Yes. Nice garden."

"Yes. Liz'd really like this place."

"How come you didn't bring her?

"She was busy," said Milton looking away.

Milton looked up and saw Melissa coming down the path towards them on the tips of her toes despite the pregnancy. She pushed open the gate in the tall wire fence. The gate squealed.

"Hi!" said Milton smiling warmly.

"Hi Milton!"

"Melissa, this is Jim Wilson."

"Hello Mr Wilson."

"You'd better call me Father or Jim. I'm no Mr." Melissa laughed gaily.

"Come on in then, Jim."

"What about me?" said Milton.

"We don't care about him, do we?" said Melissa nudging the priest.

"Certainly not," said the priest. "Would you care for my arm?"

"Oh you are gallant!"

They walked along between the waist high roses. Jim and Melissa moved ahead with laboured solemnity, like a couple approaching the altar through the glaring light of the day of judgement. Milton looked sideways at his shadow, bent by the roses but straight and elongated to caricature, on the lawn beyond. The house looked as though it was wearing sunglasses over all its windows. The crickets battered the air with their trills. A magpie flew like a black stone through the light laden air. The shadows had all turned solid. Milton waited for someone to shout and have the sound magnified a thousand times until he was crushed to death by noise. Instead, Jim and Melissa mounted the steps of house and Jim opened the door for Melissa. She disappeared and then he disappeared. Milton was left gaping at the mundane and empty porch.

Milton hurried to the back door and walked into the kitchen. Jim was just telling Mrs Gibson what lovely roses she had and she was blushing like a flower girl at a wedding. *Silken tongued heathen* thought Milton as he pulled the door shut.

"Mum, this is Milton," said Melissa dragging her mother's doting eyes away from the priest.

"Hello Milton," said Mrs Gibson putting out her hand. Milton squeezed her hand, which was smooth and almost feverish, though quite dry.

"How are you Mrs Gibson?"

"I'm so sorry your wife couldn't make it tonight."

"Yes. You seem delighted with the replacement anyway."

"Is he allowed to drink?" Mrs Gibson hissed at Milton under her breath.

""I don't know whether he's allowed to, but he does."

""That's good. It wouldn't be much fun sitting there while we were all drinking."

"No, I suppose not."

"Well, you'd better come through with me and Jim to meet the trog," said Melissa.

"You shouldn't call your father names, Melissa."

"But it's so descriptive, Mother. He likes to skulk up here in this black hole away from the light of civilisation."

"She's a terrible girl," said Mrs Gibson confidingly to Milton.

"I can quite believe it."

Milton followed Melissa and Jim through to the big lounge. He saw a small, apparently frail, little man hovering nervously above a chair which obviously, at that moment, held an almost irresistible attraction for him. Finally the little man managed to drag himself out of the chair's magnetic field and advance across the room, his hand preceding him.

"How are you your highness?" said Dave Gibson shaking hands vigorously with Jim Wilson.

"I'm fine thanks mate," said Jim Wilson, clapping Gibbo on the shoulder with his left hand.

"The Catholic church must have pretty rough congregations if they've got to get big jokers like you in the priesthood."

"Ah well, we've got to make sure that the husbands keep their wives off the pill somehow."

"Too right!"

"Dad!" Gibbo shot a quick glance at Melissa and then moved towards Milton.

"Who's this runt over here?" he asked as he went.

"Milton Harper, Dad."

"How do you do, Mr Harper?"

"I'm not doing too badly," said Milton grinning and shaking Gibbo's hand.

"Take a seat, boys," said Gibbo waving his hand around in the general direction of the chairs.

"Don't go in the brown leather rocker. That's Dads," said Melissa.

"Might I have an ashtray?" said Jim as they moved towards the couch.

"Sure thing."

"Gibbo went wandering off in a distracted way in search of another ashtray and Melissa went back to the kitchen to check the dinner. Jim

Wilson decided he didn't like the couch and shifted to an armchair. When they were alone Milton said:

"Jesus! You've got enough social savvy to charm a meal out of a Northern Irish Protestant."

"Jesus hasn't got anything to do with it."

"You're probably a descendant of Sir Walter Raleigh."

"It's better than being a descendant of Dangerous Dan McGrew, like you."

"All of us genuine colonials are of convict stock," said Milton as Gibbo wandered back with a crystal ashtray for Jim.

"I was looking for a bigger one, but my wife made me take this one."

"That's perfectly all right," said the priest.

"Well, what can I get you?" asked Gibbo looking from one to the other.

"Do you have whisky?" asked Father Wilson.

"And water?"

"Yes, water please."

"And you, Mr Harper?"

"Nothing, thank you."

"Don't you feel well? Do you want an aspirin or something?

"No thanks, Mr Gibson. I don't drink."

"Milton is an ascetic. He believes that mortifying the flesh and the soul is the true course to earthly delight." Father Wilson smiled gently.

"And what do you think, Father?"

"We don't believe in earthly delight, so I can afford to have a bit of pleasure."

"All right, whisky then." Gibbo stomped away over to the liquor cabinet thinking what a rum evening this was going to be when words like "ascetic" and "earthly delight" were already flying around.

Gibbo and the priest drank and smoked their way through the spasmodic conversation and deep silences, while outside the garden and the hills slipped towards the throat of evening. Milton sat in his chair in a state of profound discomfort. This was what he hated about dinner parties, the relaxing. His path to pleasure was through mortification. As far as he was concerned you were either doing something or going to sleep. Pain, work and sleep were the only themes in his life. Once he had believed in pleasure, but then he had started to work at writing and what was required was discipline and habit. So eventually he put pleasure aside and it was at these moments, when it was unavoidable, that it took its revenge. Milton glared out at the evening. What right did it have to be beautiful? He never had time to see the morning, because he was in his study working, so why should he have to look at the evening? How ironic that someone, who almost made his living describing the natural world, should not be able to look at it. Milton longed to escape from that room and enter the world of dizziness and sweat, when the world could slip unnoticed into his heart.

Maybe, he thought, if he could make his wife love him pleasure would come back. Really though, that was just another one of his inhumane, little experiments. His life had no place for his wife's love. There was no place on his schedule for him to fit it in. He kept her because he feared to live alone. Divorce would be the slipping of the final bolt into place and he would be locked into hideous isolation forever. He would be locked in the black, rich, man-hating loneliness which was at the centre of his being. Human beings had always been a nuisance as far as he was concerned. Yet he knew too that surrender to this final depravity, this ultimate self-realization, would destroy him forever. It was as though the whole of his bitter life had been a struggle against this intrinsic misanthropy which he found rationally absurd. But if he were to jump into this sea of hatred and fury, whose waves continually called to him in soft whispers, he didn't believe that his flesh could stand the retaliation of humanity. Besides, he couldn't bear to be entirely separated from humanity and surrender to the tossing of the waves. Perhaps he only loved rationality because it kept him away from the horrible dangers of his misanthropy. Something would have to be decided soon though. He couldn't go on working harder and harder and running further and further and lifting weights for longer and longer. Something would have to tear in the end.

Milton blinked and looked across at Gibbo and Jim, who suddenly seemed to be talking without making any sound, like two demons from the dance of death. In the shadows at the back of the room a huge pendulum seemed to be swinging monotonously. Gibbo's chin and nose seemed to have become elongated and his body withered, while Jim seemed to have swelled up like some inflatable toy. The whisky in their glasses glowed eerily. An electric beater was buzzing in the kitchen, though their voices still seemed mute. Something is wrong with me thought Milton. Jim and Gibbo laughed and nodded on in the silence. Milton relaxed back in his chair to enjoy the show. What was the use? Might as well surrender. The carpet became the grey, stained, back of a sheep and Milton sat there gripping the arms of his chair expecting at any moment to be thrown in the air. Briars had sprouted out of the backs of the chairs and hung, curving towards the floor around the heads of the conversationalists. Gibbo and Jim talked on behind their thorny cages, the red rosehips jostling from their conversation. The coffee table next to Gibbo tilted to forty five degrees and the glass ashtray rushed up and down its inclined face as though it was searching for something. A stream of water fountained out of a bowl of apples and bananas and splashed back on to their partially moss covered surface. Milton threw his feet in the air expecting to bang his knees on his forehead. His chair went over backwards and, as he struggled to get off his back, Gibbo and Jim came rushing around the back of the chair.

"What the hell happened?" asked Gibbo.

"I must have leaned too far back in the chair," said Milton.

"Anyone would think it was you that had been drinking," said Jim Wilson. "Stay where you are." Jim Wilson bent over and effortlessly righted both Milton and the chair. Gibbo looked at the priest, struggling to conceal his admiration.

"You wouldn't want a job pulling ploughs I suppose?"

"Only if you have a horse that can save souls."

"You think too much," said Gibbo to Milton. "That's why you're always falling off chairs." Milton looked shocked. The man made sense.

Gibbo and Father Wilson sat down again and their spasmodic conversation continued, this time with Milton's head stuck towards them listening intently. It wasn't much of a conversation and Milton didn't contribute much, but it was better than the other thing.

After a short time Melissa joined them for a drink. Jim Wilson took out another cigarette and lipped it to moisten the end.

"Don't light up again," said Melissa. Tea'll be ready in a moment." Jim returned the cigarette to its packet and Melissa drained the whisky from her glass in one, slow, steady draught.

"You're well versed in sin I see," said Father Wilson.

"Not all my boyfriends were poor," said Melissa leading the way through to the dining room.

* * *

They ate their meal in a certain contemplative melancholy, except for Mrs Gibson who got a little tipsy on the wine and conversed and squeaked with laughter with all the vigour of a hamming actress. Even Milton could appreciate the food. In fact with his animal vigour and sobriety he appreciated it more than anyone. That still didn't stop him gazing darkly out at the miraculous close

77

of day. He watched the land slowly merge into one dark mass while the sky remained blue, though shadowed by a darkness which seemed to emanate from the earth. All around the horizon the sky became a faint brick colour.

Melissa lit the candles as it darkened and the diner's arms gyrated in the white light above the white table cloth before disappearing towards the silhouettes that manipulated them. Melissa sat in her place toying with her food and staring across at Jim Wilson. He seemed so charming, but perhaps he was too soft and affable. He seemed to lack that savage, secret, single mindedness of a man who could love. It seemed improbable to her that he suffered either. He got on so well with her father that she was tempted to believe he must be wholly insensitive. She watched his wine glass disappear and then reappear, glinting faintly, as the candle penetrated the darkness around Jim Wilson's face. He delicately sipped the wine. He was physically very delicate. She wanted to love. The question was would it be him that she loved?

Jim Wilson put down a pork bone, wiped his fingers on a paper napkin and dropped the crumpled napkin on the table. He withdrew further into the gloom away from the table. As he sat there in the rich misery of his happiness he fumbled for his cigarettes. He was hot, he had eaten too much and his stomach was vaguely sore. His vision was a little blurred because of the alcohol. She was a nice girl and had a nice mother. The old man was a good sort too, the salt of the earth, a sort of peasant democrat. That tricky bastard Harper was ballsing the whole evening up though. Teetotallers shouldn't be allowed to mix with the rest of humanity. Jim Wilson breathed in a lung full of cigarette smoke and felt cured of his physical and spiritual discomfort, for the moment at least. Drugs, drugs, long live drugs! His eyes were half closed, though he felt wide awake. Just as well I've got Harper to chauffer me though, he thought. It's a pity Harper couldn't eat in the servant's quarters though, assuming the Gibsons had servants.

The trouble with Harper was that he had too much dignity and pride. It galled him to make a fool of himself. Everyone ought to walk around with his trousers around his ankles now and again. He'll never make heaven because he's always trying to be perfect. Satan tried to be perfect and look what happened to him; hell. Harper is trying to be perfect and look what is happening to him; hell too. Oh well, everyone to his just desserts. I may well end up in hell with Harper because of sloth, drunkenness and gluttony. Still, at least sloth, drunkenness and gluttony don't give people a pain in the arse.

Father Jim Wilson rose to his feet.

"Excuse me a moment please," he said, looking down at the table which reminded him of the time he had flown in a light plane over a fairground at night.

"Certainly Father, certainly," said Mrs Gibson who was in the middle of a sentence about how young Melissa was when she had learned to swim. Mrs Gibson's conversation continued at breakneck speed towards infinity. Possibly there would be an ending, but there would be no conclusion. Milton Harper continued to make sporadic remarks as Mrs Gibson raced solo for outer space. Gibbo, isolated from the rest of the table because he sat at its head, looked as though he had collapsed in his chair. Only the smoke from his cigarette which dribbled upwards, gave any indication that he was lucid, or at least conscious. Jim Wilson began to wade through the darkness. As he passed Gibbo the latter said:

"Bloody women turn off the lights when you're eating just to make eating an obstacle course."

"Yes," said Jim without stopping.

Through in the lounge Jim wound his way between the furniture. He quite enjoyed his weaving path and he also enjoyed watching his glowing cigarette bobbing just beyond his nose. The cigarette smoke drifted back into his eyes and made them water. Jim looked at the weird, square pool of moonlight over by the French windows. It's the impersonal milk of hell, he thought. I must wind some more among these rocks and find some running water.

Jim Wilson located the room with the running water. He put his hand on the light switch. The light came on. It was like suddenly being enmeshed in a fine spider web. The white walls of the bathroom shone like the surfaces of lakes. Jim Wilson walked over to the mirror and thumbed his nose at himself. Then he pretended he was broken hearted and rolled his eyes and put his head on one side. The fat, red faced oaf in the mirror did exactly the same.

"You watch it, you protestant skut," muttered Jim Wilson, shaking his finger at his reflection. He walked to the toilet bowl. His cigarette spat as he threw it in the water. He adopted the Colossus at Rhodes position in front of the toilet and unzipped his fly. There was a hiss of urine and the occasional gurgle as the stream was accidentally projected into the water. The sharp smell of urine purged Jim Wilson's nostrils of food, wine and cigarettes. The painful deflation of the bladder was better than the relief of tears.

Jim Wilson zipped up his fly and turned on the cold tap. The tap wailed as the water raced around the basin and disappeared down the plughole. There was shock of cold water on his hands and the soap, faintly caustic and sticky between his fingers. He turned off the tap and shook his hands over the basin to shake off the loose drops of water. Then he carried his hands, like a chalice, to a towel and rubbed them vigorously on the fresh, coarse, soft towel. He felt a new man. He took a black comb out of his pocket and, bobbing down, combed his hair in the mirror. Even my housekeeper would find no fault with me now, he thought.

Melissa came swaying down the dark corridor towards the toilet. She could see the light around the edge of the sliding door. There was a soundless explosion and the priest's silhouette appeared in the brilliant light, like God appearing to an Old Testament prophet. He came on through the light with a smooth, sinister momentum and then pressed his back against the corridor wall.

"You ought to be preceded by someone carrying a sign saying 'Caution! Wide Load Following,'" said the priest from his position against the wall.

"It won't be for much longer now," said Melissa, feeling a slight touch of distaste at the priest's comment.

"You'll be free again then?"

"Sort of," said Melissa, lingering in the bathroom doorway.

"Oh well. I hope you will find some man that will make you happy, permanently."

"So do I."

"I thought that people of your age didn't believe in permanency?"

"I do. Everyone wants to be happy all the time." Melissa slid the bathroom door shut.

The priest came out of the dark corridor into the lounge. He paused and lit another cigarette. He felt very clear headed, but his body hurt as though all his watercourses had had the barnacles scraped off them. It was as though his pain was the echoing of water in the empty pipes.

A funny girl! I think I must be drunker than I thought. He smacked his lungs with another wall of nicotine. There's definitely something funny about her though. Some sort of unique quality that she possesses that no other girl has. It's not that she's cleverer, or wittier or anything. She's just in some way remarkable. I wonder if I could talk to her with the same frankness that I talk to God. It would be a much greater achievement to be totally honest with someone you could get away with lying to. I'm more nearly honest with Harper than I am with any other human being. But even with him, there's an element of concealment in my conversation. Why is it that I suddenly have the need to tell the truth, to make a confession? I don't really know if I've got any truth to tell in the first place. Everything seems to have become amazingly simplified though, all of a sudden. It is almost an ungodly simplicity. I want to tell, but I don't know what it is that I want to tell.

Back in the dining room the light was on. Gibbo was rolling a cigarette having now managed to get his quite abandoned wife to tell him where she had hidden his tobacco. Mrs Gibson came steaming through the dining room with a large pavalova thrust out in front of her. This was to be the coronation of this culinary orgy. She put it down in the middle of the table, seized Milton's water glass and filled it up with white wine.

"I don't want to see you get dehydrated Milton," she said sitting down. "What on earth has happened to those other two? I hope they haven't got trapped in the toilet together. What an earth would Father Wilson do?"

"Play with his Rosary beads I suppose," said Milton.

"Well he wouldn't want to play with Melissa in her state," said Mrs Gibson and she put her hand over her mouth and enlarged her eyes to indicate how naughty she thought she was.

"What's the matter with you Myra?" asked Gibbo. "You look like a chook that's just laid twenty eggs."

"I was just wondering where Jim and Melissa were."

"They're probably out in the kitchen eating carrots so that they can see the food when the lights go out again."

Jim Wilson strolled into the dining room and casually sat down.

"Where's Melissa?" asked Mrs Gibson.

"What's that?"

"Where's my daughter?"

"She was last seen south of the lounge and about to turn east."

"Ah, you've bought in the pav mum," said Melissa entering the room.

They ate the pavalova under the white lights, bending over their plates, crunching the meringue and licking the cream off their lips. The table seemed to have become relaxed and proper. Mrs Gibson's vivacity seemed to have dissipated without being replaced by depression. Gibbo even whipped out his top set of false teeth; dredged something out of them and slipped them back in like a Komodo dragon swallowing a chicken. Jim Wilson seemed to have become quite different. He suddenly seemed to have become possessed of the smooth, self-absorbed, disinterest of youth as though what he was thinking about was infinitely more interesting and important than the mere trivia of external events. Even his skin seemed younger. Milton Harper looked across the table at the priest and wondered what had happened to him when he was out of the room.

Melissa looked across at the priest and wondered what she could have said to make him change so suddenly. I must say it again, she thought. I like him even better this way. He seems to have lost that comfortable, faintly used look like a favourite coat or an overused pipe. He's also lost his look of faint dissipation. I don't love him though. It's so hard wanting to be possessed. You never know until the very moment whether or not it's going to work. A man's got to know beforehand and that's his safety and danger. His self knowledge must be a burden. But a woman doesn't know until it's happening and her uncertainty makes her so vulnerable. Oh well, it's in his hands now. I can do nothing, only wait and hope. It's a pity desire is so much more than simply a physical urge.

* * *

Later, much later, Milton was hurling the little car through the landscape made barren by the darkness. A wind had come up and, whenever they drove past a line of poplars, leaves swirled and rolled on the smooth, dew-damped dust of the road's surface. The white, disdainful eye of the moon shone over the hump-backed hills. The trees moiled in a nightmare rhythm. Jim Wilson looked at Milton's face, lit up by the lights of the dashboard to a line below his eyes.

"What do you think of that girl?" asked Jim Wilson.

"Melissa?" Milton shrugged. The car slid around a corner and small stones pattered on the grass beside the road. Then the headlights steadied on the white road and a grey mound of shingle disappeared behind into the animal landscape.

"She seems a special, almost unique person to me."

"You're in love!" said Milton with jocular contempt.

"I don't think so."

"What do you mean you don't think so?"

"I don't want her, physically."

"Give it time." Milton swung the wheel, sending the car's headlights sideways across the face of a bank as though they were seeking something out.

"Don't drive so fast."

"What's the matter? Aren't you in a state of grace?"

"I'm trying to think."

"There's no point in writing a thesis on whether or not you've got a hard on."

"Shut up, Milton or I'll give you a thick ear."

Milton looked at the hulking silhouette of Jim Wilson, stolid and immovable against the almost geometric precision of the passing trees, fence posts and hillsides. The ash grey landscape fell steadily behind. They were whirling like a compass needle in the basin of the hills; the skyline and the clouds moving in slow gyrations as the car compass swung backwards and forwards. Sometimes they climbed a hill and seemed about to leap into the sky, only to descend again into the bowl of the hills.

"It seems an awfully long way home," said Jim Wilson.

"You must be frightened of being alone."

"It's not that."

"Oh for a long embrace with a piece of warm comfort amidst these flecks of whirling flesh."

"Is that really what I want Milton? How come you know anyway?"

"I'm a poet, remember. I know everything because I am nothing."

"You seem even bitterer than usual tonight."

"Liz was unfaithful the other day."

"Oh, I'm sorry."

"Not half as sorry as she is."

"That's why she didn't come tonight then?"

"Yes."

"Aren't you afraid of her doing it again when you leave her alone?"

"Not half as frightened as she is of being caught."

"You hit her, then?"

"Yeah."

"I never thought I would see the day when you hit anyone."

"Neither did I."

"It's probably a step in the right direction."

Finally, they came over a ridge and looked down on a lake of level darkness pierced by lights, some of them strung in long rows and others moving like the eyes of predatory fish. Down they came through a cacophony of hisses, the moon sitting just on the jagged edge of a pine plantation. The pink eyes of an opossum swirled on the moist, needle-littered tar seal and the creature galloped off like a shadow. There was a moment of empty stomached excitement as the car shot through a hollow and on down a gentle slope of sky topped manuka towards the flat ground. Milton looked out his side window and wondered what place God could have in all of this.

Father Jim Wilson shook another cigarette clear of his packet and clicked his lighter. Even by his standards he had smoked a lot that evening. There was something empty about his body. It was like an estuary when the tide had run out; leaving only pitted mud and mangroves.

At the same time he felt a sort of gnawing peace. Perhaps this woman could quell his pain. He longed for a life on earth beyond his current life when every little event would be of joyful significance; in which sorrow would have its part in the tapestry of life and sorrow would be tolerable because of that. Instead of achieving things in spite of yourself you could achieve them because of yourself, because of your happiness. Instead of life being dreary, tense, hectic and purposeless life would be peaceful, happy and purposeful.

But would there be a place for God in such a world? Religion seemed so bound up with misery. Was it possible to need God out of joy?

Jim Wilson subsided into his cigarette. They were driving now beside fields of towering maize. Occasionally they passed a house that the maize had generously allowed to remain in a barren bight of the field. Sometimes they passed between walls of fennel and sometimes they looked out over white waves of sweet corn that had engulfed the flat. The smell of fennel was vaguely reminiscent of cow's breath. Once they passed through a choking band of grass smoke, though they saw neither the smoke nor the fire.

The intoxicating chill of the country night made Milton's blood race. Milton wound down his window and wished he was out there somewhere, running through the maize, in a race that knew no other end but dawn. To move and kill, that was his real destiny. To splash, dripping wet, out of the seeming solid river in the dawn and dry in the sun in a meadow. To be part of the forest: indistinguishable from faun and dog. To have no individuality and know only magic, the magic of the cave and the forest shadows.

The little car hummed through a collection of state houses, built in the middle of nowhere, crushed together with tanks on tall stands.

There were no streetlights and the car was through the settlement so quickly and the countryside was so much the same as before that you could doubt the settlement ever existed.

Milton heard the noise of another car travelling very fast, but still a long way away. He wondered how far away it was. The noise kept getting louder. Milton began to tense. He couldn't see any lights. The car should have been and gone. Then, a big American car leapt out from behind a bank and came fishtailing up the wrong side of the road towards them. Milton pulled over and stopped. The other car came on like a sardine can with two blazing headlights. The sound of its engine seemed to shatter the night air into slivers.

"Bloody idiot!" stormed Father Wilson, scrambling out of the car. The other car weaved frantically backwards and forwards and then slithered to a halt. It sat there, its engine chugging slowly with an insinuation of brutal speed.

"You guys all right?" said the driver, poking his head out the side window.

"Yes, thank you," said Jim Wilson. "How about you?"

"Why should there be anything wrong with me reverend? I don't believe in God."

"He probably doesn't believe in you either."

"He must be thinking there's something wrong with us," said the driver into the back of the car. Muffled laughter drifted lazily through the car window.

"You want a fuck, reverend?" shouted a female voice from the back of the car.

"Don't mind her," said the driver. "How about a drink, reverend?"

"I'm afraid I'll have to decline both your kind offers. It's past my bed time."

"Aw, come on. Have a drink reverend," said a skinny youth in a denim jacket with no sleeves, getting out of the car door. He walked towards Jim Wilson, a bottle thrust aggressively out in front of him. As he got closer, though, his pace slowed and his hand moved slowly towards ground level until he was standing in front of Jim Wilson, his hands by his sides looking up at the priest. "Hey, Pogo!" he shouted.

"What's the matter Pee Wee?"

"I think I might need your help."

"You don't need my help. You need a machine gun."

The youth stood there looking up at Jim Wilson. There was only the rustling of the breeze in the swaying fennel, the sound of the crickets and the chugging of the engine of the big American car.

"Well, I'm going to get cold if I stand out here any longer," said the youth.

"That's right," agreed Jim Wilson. The youth turned and swaggered back to the car, taking a swig out of the bottle as he went. Cheers and shouts erupted from the car as he approached it.

"Shut up!" he shouted. "Shut up!" He kicked the back door with his boot.

"Lay off him you guys," whined the girl. The car became silent again and Pee Wee climbed into the driver's seat. A match flared, making his face look for a second like an orange pumpkin. He flicked the match on to the road, stuck his elbow out the window and revved the engine. The wheels of the car started to spin, the tyres squealed on the tar seal and the car, after resisting movement, suddenly jerked forward and slid away into the darkness. The car became a shadow among the other shadows, except for its noise, its red tail lights and its white headlights, which shimmered and flickered on the fennel. It went round a corner and then there was only the sound, fading.

Jim Wilson made himself small and got back into the car.

"You missed your vocation," said Milton.

"Weak kids who act tough make me mad."

"He was alright."

Milton drove on to the priest's home and sat at the top of the drive with his headlights shining on the priest's back door while the priest unlocked it. He saw Jim Wilson's body apparently seep into the wall and Milton tooted the horn and began to back down the drive. Jim Wilson stood at his back door waving at the retreating headlights. Then he walked through the darkness of his momentarily alien house and turned on the kitchen light. But the light was a part of the darkness rather than something that repelled it.

All this paint and stainless steel and what does it add up to? thought Jim Wilson. Hell! In the night a man alone becomes a shadow, a ghost, a premonition of his future self in torment after death. I am lonely, thought Jim Wilson. Yes, I am lonely.

Chapter 11

The next morning Father Jim Wilson went to see several parishioners, friendly visits to see that these people had no personal reasons for failing to attend mass. Too many people in country parishes neglected God because of some personal grudge against the priest.

Father Wilson enjoyed the reverence shown to him by the women, a reverence they didn't display towards their husbands. It was, he supposed, a tribute to purity. At every home he visited he was offered and accepted a cup of tea, so the visits had a practical aspect as well.

In the afternoon he went to visit one of his parishioners, who was in hospital. The woman had cancer. She was going to die, but nobody admitted it because there was a one in a million chance that she might live. Father Wilson hated participating in what he saw as a deceit.

Mrs Murphy lay in her bed in a frilly pink night dress. She looked straight ahead with a sort of tormented indifference. Father Wilson sat down on a wooden stool beside her and waited for her to say something. Nurses moved like flies from bed to bed. The woman in the next bed along smiled at the priest and he smiled back. Then he glanced quickly back at Mrs Murphy. She was still lying there, tense and immobile. Father Wilson's eyes wandered out the window to the hot, sunlit lawn.

"You're too late," said Mrs Murphy. Father Wilson looked back to her, surprised. She was in exactly the same position as she was before. It was as though she had never spoken.

"What do you mean Mrs Murphy?"

"The church isn't going to feed on this carrion."

"Why would the church want to do that, Mrs Murphy?"

"Muck!" It was silent apart from Mrs Murphy's breathing, the squeak of a passing trolley and the sound of a couple of nurses laughing as they walked outside in the land of the living.

"What can we expect out of you, Mrs Murphy?"

"Money."

"Oh that. That doesn't interest me, or the church."

"Don't lie."

"You don't have much money."

"So, you know then?"

"Know what?"

"How much money I have."

"I was only guessing."

Mrs Murphy seemed paranoid. She had lost her equilibrium at the thought of losing her life. Not that her life was much: a drunken husband on a small income with whom she lived alone now that her children had gone. The two sons didn't come home because their father picked on them in a desperate attempt to assert physical control in a house where he had lost all moral control. One of the daughters had married a local truck driver and no one knew anything about the other daughter, except perhaps her mother.

Father Wilson fumbled for his cigarettes. He usually didn't smoke when he was actually working but this was very difficult. He drew on his cigarette and felt his body return to normal.

"I thought the church was wonderful once. But a painful death on top of a painful life straightened me out."

"Bitterness against man or God won't help you, Mrs Murphy," said Father Wilson while quietly reflecting that it was probably a great help.

"Those who are happy and those who suffer all go to heaven alike, providing they are in a state of grace. My stinking life will be of no advantage to me at heaven's gate."

"The important thing is to gain admittance to heaven, irrespective of how fortunate or unfortunate you are."

"No, the important thing is revenge on the happy."

"But why?"

"Don't enquire father. Only we, the dying, know."

Father Wilson looked down at the emaciated woman who seemed to go on living in defiance of nature. He knew he had all the pat answers, but he knew they were of more interest to a student in a philosophy class than to a human faced with the enormity of death. In the end all answers are overwhelmed by the brute fact of death.

"Is there anything at all I can do for you Mrs Murphy? Anything you want?"

"I want to see my husband."

"Doesn't he come of his own accord?"

"I wouldn't be asking for him if he did."

"Do your children visit?"

"Oh yes, but Jimmy was alive before they were."

The swinging glass doors at the entrance to the ward flashed as a nurse pushed them apart. The glass doors rocked back to stillness as the nurse advanced down the ward, wading in the silver river between the beds. The nurse passed Father Wilson and Mrs Murphy, paying them no heed. In this hall of tragedy, she did not contemplate tragedy; she only executed one task after another in the hope of postponing tragedy another day, or occasionally overcoming tragedy completely, at least for the time being.

"I'll go and see your husband, then."

"Yes. And be nice to him."

"Why shouldn't I?"

"You think he's worthless."

I never think of anyone as being worthless."

"Don't be smart sonny."

The priest went red with anger. He hated being patronised because of his age.

"You're human too are you, Father?"

"Of course," said Father Wilson sharply. Mrs Murphy's face contorted and her chest heaved with wheezing laughter. Finally, when the laughter had let go of her body, Mrs Murphy said:

"You can go now, Father. Make sure you send Jimmy."

"All right, Mrs Murphy. Goodbye." Father Wilson stood and made a little bow from his hips. He picked up his hat from the bedside table and holding it at his side, gripped between his thumb and forefinger, walked down the ward. He passed the high, white covered beds. In some beds patients lay, as though their necks had been broken, their mouths open, gummy chasms. On silver stands the saline bottles slowly bubbled. As he approached the doors of the ward two young girls were sitting up in their beds talking to each other. Their flesh was white and thick and soft. They were very much alive.

Once in the hospital corridor Father Wilson walked, shoes squeaking, towards the light at the end of the dark corridor. The air in the corridor was metallic and vibrant and the voices of the nurses sharp and clear. He passed an elderly man in a green dressing gown being wheeled down the corridor. The man smiled warmly and Father Wilson lifted his hat in recognition of the smile.

As he neared the doors, he felt the strong desire to run. He strode past the office at the end of the corridor and leapt off the front steps, stumbling slightly as he hit the ground. He straightened up and took an enormous lung full of air. His whole body relaxed. His relief was even greater than he had anticipated in the corridor. He stepped off the tar-seal and on to an island of grass and stood there lighting a cigarette next to the white "Please Keep Off the Grass" sign. He threw the match on the grass and watched the wisp of white smoke trail mysteriously off into the blue air. The sun burnt his shoulders through his black shirt.

Turning he strolled off towards the car park beneath some karaka trees. The karaka berries, shrivelled by the sun, smelled richer and sweeter than raisins.

He reached the large area of tar seal where a couple of hundred cars glinted in the sun. The trembling heat made the cars look as though they were set in aspic. The tar seal itself was as black as smoke. Down in the gully, between the car park and the main hospital, there was a tangle of convolvulus and orange flowered nasturtium. Tall bamboos grew above this tangle of tendrils. On the other side of the gully, below the hospital grounds grew tall, slender, grey-trunked gums. Father Wilson leaned on the white railing of the car park wishing he could rush into the gully and play cops and robbers. Children, he reflected, had the richest of all lives.

He turned and looked back at the hot, unfriendly metal of the cars. He wondered why men should create things that were so profoundly unlike themselves. Mrs Murphy had wanted her husband. She had wanted her husband more than she had wanted God. He doubted that she had thought much good of her husband through the entire course of their marriage. He wondered what strange compulsion made her call for him now.

He wandered in among the cars, thinking of Melissa. He felt dizzied by the grief of his desire. This terrible possession of his body must be what possession by the devil felt like. He had, like any normal person, felt lust before. However, that was just a phenomenon in a certain part of his body. This desire swept his self away like a swollen river sweeps away a bridge. It destroyed his self and his morality.

Jim Wilson pulled open his car door and collapsed onto the car seat. He rolled a little sideways and tried to pull the keys out of his pocket. His skin was prickling with heat. A young woman came walking along in front of the cars, led by a child that could hardly walk. The child was leading the mother by the finger. The young woman talked and laughed with the child who was gurgling with jollity and trying to make its bandy pink legs turn faster so that its mother would have to run with it.

Father Wilson wrenched the keys out of his pocket and jammed them in the ignition switch. He started the car, backed out of his parking space and drove towards the car park entrance, which was between a toilet and a collection of tool sheds. Across the main drive, opposite the car park entrance, was a round mirror to show if any vehicles were coming along the drive. The mirror was empty. Jim Wilson swung out of the cap park and raced away past three tennis courts.

Over the hill he glimpsed the flat tedium of Gisborne and then the sea, a romantic blue and the sun burnt, houseless coast to the south of the city.

He swung down the hill and passed beneath the gums and some oaks and came out amongst the houses, less tedious now that he was among them. There was sanity in there, concealed behind the fences and hedges. They were the product of sanity and sense, of the certainty of childhood, when no one could harm themselves.

Everything seemed clear and definite to Jim Wilson at that moment. Yesterday he had no future, only a gap which would be inevitably filled with something. Now he could paint his future in a picture and not a very large picture at that.

Chapter 12

After Milton had run about a mile, he began to feel less breathless and the weakness and aches in his legs seemed to disappear. It was as though, initially, Milton's body refused to accept the fact that it was running at all, but then he felt he was moving without effort, carried by his own momentum. He felt his heels bang on the ground and the muscles in his rump thrust his legs out and drive him forward.

He began to increase his speed, making sure he didn't break up his rhythm. It was very hot, though Milton did not feel the heat itself, only the ache and nausea that the heat was beginning to cause. The sweat began to dam up in his eyes and Milton wiped his right eye with his right shoulder. He regretted it immediately because his eye began to sting as the salt from his perspiring shoulder entered his eye.

Milton began to enter the void created by his own effort. He was unaware of his own pace. He didn't turn to his right to watch the fence posts flashing past. He was aware of the landscape changing but, because he was a man running, its sameness was more noticeable than its difference. He could see things coming towards him, but even though he knew he was running quickly, the trees or houses that he was approaching seemed to linger in the air until he was alongside or past them.

Milton took in the white sand hills on his left, which were covered in onion green grass, almost silvery, and the occasional car among them like a dollop of heat. He could see the far- out part of the sea, but not the waves which were obscured because there was so much sand between the waves and the water's edge. Single pine trees were planted at intervals in the sand dunes, looking rather like fountains of green water.

Milton ran on, bathed in his own perspiration. His body had become an independently functioning thing now and it had left his mind entirely free, not just from directing the pace and speed of his movement, but from thinking anything at all. His mind could swoop in the grey stillness of the cloud now. It floated light and cool and unfettered by the banal. This concentration on the physical led directly to heaven.

Milton looked on up the road which ran through brown, beach tussock and white salt spray to the lake-blue mountains. Away to his left, across the sea, were the grey-white cliffs of Young Nick's Head looking like a face peering over the sand dunes from out of a bath. Ahead was the painted silver drum, which was his turn around point. But there were several of these drums at intervals along the road and, for a moment, Milton could not remember which of the drums he ran to. Then, about fifty yards up the road on the other side of the road from a bin, he recognised the gateway that was his turning point.

Now there was the trip back and his systematic betrayal by his body. Not that the running ever quite lost its automatic quality, but the side effects of those remorselessly rotating limbs became more and more pronounced and, instead of being freed by his effort, he became slowly dragged into the pain by the body machine which drove him down the heat black road.

It was now that the real battle began. No one ever ran against another man. You always ran in isolation because you did not have the energy to invest your opponent with humanity. Your opponent was only a spur to the real contest, the contest with your own machine. Whenever the machine slowed Milton willed it back to its proper rhythm and pace. There was him and there was it and the two things could never become a unity.

Milton looked at the houses back around the coast and the low, frothy waves rushing at the white sand. He thought of being finished, but that had no reality. It was like the thought of a distant holiday. A cattle truck rushed past, knocking him sideways with its blast and leaving him breathless, his lungs full of diesel fumes. He stumbled, but then drew himself together and ran on. He knew he could not cope with too many disruptions like this or he would stop. The body relied on its own momentum to keep it going.

His skin was on fire now, a burning sensation that seemed to generate no warmth, but chilled him. His nose and throat were sore and he felt that if he increased his pace he would not be able to get enough air to sustain his body. He noticed his shadow on the road in front of him and he was surprised at how fast he was running. He took joy in his speed and the inert, normally unutilised part of his brain began to help him. He turned inland towards the golf course. Somehow he seemed to speed up. Somewhere in some part of his mind he wondered if he would get round his course faster than he had ever done; but he didn't know because he never wore a watch. The reality of time could be too demoralising.

Then he was beside the pine shaded golf course, three hundred yards inland and below the top of the dunes.

The road widened. He left the golf course and passed several small factories, unpainted corrugated iron and their sections overgrown with weeds. Ahead the blackened tar seal took a turn to the right and the road would rejoin the beach, but for the moment on his right there was waste ground, grey stones and long brown grass stems growing out of rust coloured moss. A pool of black, stagnant water, in a pit of grey stones, flashed past him.

Now was the time when he should increase his pace, but the corner to the beach seemed impossibly far away. He increased his speed anyway. He had no idea whether this was the sensible thing to do. Considered judgement was no longer possible. It was time to magnify his pain to the point where it no longer mattered.

He crossed a median of shrubs and he was back beside the beach. He went past a two storied, concrete surf club, past the fawn, corrugated iron fence of the motor camp and into the houses. A girl came out from behind an enormous, unkempt hedge covered in pink and white flowers. She seemed vaguely familiar but there was the final two hundred yards to his gate. Milton put his head down and tried to make his legs move faster.

Lillie heard his heavy breathing behind her and spun around. She saw a red face, flopping blond hair and a sculpted body slick with sweat rushing towards her. She stepped aside. Milton Harper stormed past, his eyes glazed, his breathing a rapid, rhythmic wheeze. The back of his red singlet was black with perspiration.

Lillie Foster smiled as she strode after him up the road. They had been "up the wall" at lunch time and she had taken a late lunch.

Milton only had a hundred yards to go and he had found his extra speed. His style broke up a little as he sprinted.

Five yards from his gate Milton eased back and stopped at the entrance to his drive. He bent over and put his hands on his knees. He could feel a little pain start above his Achilles tendons. He stood up and put his knuckles on the small of his back and arched his back.

His breathing began to slow.

Lillie Foster came up to him, stopped, pulled a packet of cigarettes out of her string bag, flipped open the top of the packet and extracted a cigarette with her lips. She snapped the top of the cigarette packet shut and threw it back in the bag. She rummaged in the bag, brought out a lighter and lit her cigarette with rather a grand flourish. She inhaled and then blew out a cloud of smoke. Milton was bent forward again, his hands on his knees.

"Don't you ever worry that you might expire?" she said with a smile. Milton glanced back at her with a look of irritation.

"No," he said. Lillie's eyes narrowed as she looked at him. There was a long pause. Milton was looking away from her again.

"Why do you do it?"

"In my own way I like it. It makes my muscles happy."

"I wouldn't be happy if somebody treated me in that way." Milton stood up, turned around and looked Lillie in the eye.

"Well, the body thrives on punishment, unless you have a physical defect of course." This time Lillie looked away.

"You believe in living through your body, do you?"

"What else is there?" Milton said simply. Lillie looked back at him.

"Your mind?"

"The mind is a gateway to hell. Running stops it's functioning. It stops you thinking about crap."

Lillie took another long drag on her cigarette and blew smoke out of her nostrils.

"What about food, cigarettes and alcohol? They're physical pleasures."

"I've got nothing against those things, except that they make running more difficult."

"You can't have it both ways you mean?"

"Yeah."

Milton stood there looking at Lillie Foster, the sweat flowing from his body. She was staring vacantly past him, smoke dribbling from her mouth and nose. Milton wondered why she was talking to him. Why would a hippy be talking to him, Milton Harper? Still, she was nice enough. In fact, she was very charming. But Milton didn't trust charming women. They were charming to the fool and the wise man alike. It didn't matter, just so long as the man liked them. He knew what the score was with attractive women. He gave them a rough time and they hated and feared him for that.

"Look, I don't mean to seem rude, but I've got to get inside before my muscles cool down."

"Oh, yes. Sorry."

"Well, I'll see you then."

"I had a visitor of yours the other night."

"What would a visitor of mine be doing at your place?"

"This one had no pants on."

"Well, I hope you called the police and had him arrested for indecent exposure. I don't like to think of my guests roaming round the country half naked and giving me a bad reputation."

"No, I didn't turn him in. I gave him some pants instead."

"That must have excited him - walking around in a pair of your pants."

"It's not healthy to be violent you know."

"Who's violent?"

"You are. All the time. Even when you're holding a normal conversation like this."

"Yeah, that may be so, but if you think I'm going to stand round and listen to some hippy give me a lecture on how I should love everybody, you' better think again."

"I wasn't going to lecture you, just express my opinion."

"Same thing," said Milton turning away and walking across the lawn to his front door. Lillie strode after him and grabbed a handful of his hair when she reached him.

"Who in the hell do you think you are?" she hissed as Milton swung around, unbalancing her.

"I'm me. Now if you don't let go my hair, you'll be cold." said Milton lifting his clenched fists. Lillie let go his hair and stepped back.

"I don't hate you. The amazing thing is, I don't hate you."

"Why should you? You've only just met me." They stood there looking at each other on the yellow, sunlit lawn. Milton coughed as he inhaled some of Lillie's cigarette smoke. The afternoon was strangely quiet. Somewhere above was the nasal wheeze of a jet. Milton looked up, trying to locate the silver fleck in the depthless blue. He could see nothing. He looked back at Lillie again. Then he shrugged and turned away.

"You can't bear me to be comfortable in a situation, can you?" she said.

"What's that?"

"You can't bear me to be in command of myself." Milton stopped and stood looking at her over his right shoulder and tugging his left ear lobe.

"I don't care."

"Don't lie."

"You don't mean anything to me; but as a matter of interest I don't like self-possessed people, especially women."

"You like everyone to mirror your own insecurity."

"Look, fuck it! I don't want to get involved in a heavy conversation. Understand?"

"All right then. I'll see you round." Lillie turned and moved rhythmically away across the lawn, her rubber jandals snapping at the bottoms of her heels, her long skirt moving as though it was alive. As she reached the footpath, she tossed her sun-bleached blond hair and threw her cigarette nonchalantly into the road.

Must be nice to be certain of yourself like that, thought Milton. Must be nice to believe you owe no one anything and that you can come to no harm. Women like that usually have daddies who own half of New Zealand. I wonder how she turned out to be a hippy. She could have married a doctor or a lawyer and had a sports car to drive. Bloody upper-class bitches who own the entire world.

Chapter 13

Milton walked naked through to the bedroom and stood there behind the closed green curtains, looking through the coarse green material at the sunlight, the lawn and the wooden fence. He had dried himself thoroughly in the bathroom, but his skin already glistened with moisture. He pulled a fresh singlet over his head and felt it immediately stick to his back. He put on some corduroy trousers. They were heavy on such a hot day, but he liked the feeling of corduroy on his limbs. He put on some clean socks and picked up his boots. He frowned as he noticed a faint brown smear on the toe of the right boot. He looked at the faint bloodstain from various angles. Then he put on his boots and laced them up.

He stood up, put his hands in his pockets and pushed the trousers comfortably onto his hips. He brushed his hair with the woman's hairbrush he always used, looking in his wife's hand mirror. His hair was caked close to his skull. It was just too hot. He threw the brush and the hand mirror on to the bed and went back to tidy up the bathroom.

After that he sat in the cool, dusty lounge and waited for his wife to come home. This pause in his life between work and his wife's return was always the worst part of the day. He sat there transfixed by nothing, vaguely wishing that there was some sort of hectic activity to take his mind off the slow drip of time. He needed his wife's return to release him from the cage of his inactivity.

Milton knew he had allowed their relationship to wither behind the facade of their marriage. But once you married a certain waning of sexual enthusiasm was permissible, even normal; whereas when you first went out with a woman you were expected to be sexually obsessed.

Milton had loved Liz in the beginning, but she had demanded her rights, equality and, rightly or wrongly, that had killed their love, or rather his. She had stayed with him out of ignorance and because he titillated her mind. But now that Milton had drifted into the inarticulate physical world and no longer wished to destroy everything with words he was no longer so satisfying to her.

Milton lay full length on the divan facing the front door. He could see the light and the heat through the slats in the wooden venetian blinds. But that world seemed far away. Only sound and the faint oyster smell of the sea penetrated the room.

Milton sat up and pulled the wet front of his singlet away from his chest. His relaxed muscles seemed to glow in the dim room. He lay down again. Then he sat up again.

Time passed slowly in a flurry of different poses, each uncomfortable and unnecessary, except to occupy the space of time. Finally he heard the crunch of the car on the shingle drive, then silence and then the bang of Liz's heels on the veranda. He watched the door handle turn and the door open a little. Then Liz pushed the door open with her shoulder and looked at her husband sitting on the divan, his body looking boyish and frail, despite his obvious strength. She straightened up and walked across the room without looking at him again. He followed her to the kitchen, rather like a poodle. He stood in the doorway of the kitchen, one hand on the door frame, looking at her as she spilled an arm full of groceries on the bench.

"Well?" he said.

"Well, what?"

"What sort of day did you have?" She shrugged. She was resisting him in the only way that she knew how, passive resistance. "You still in a shitty mood?" She leaned back against the bench, lit a cigarette and said nothing. "I meant what I said that night."

Liz blew out a stream of smoke and looked at Milton as though he wasn't there. She was resisting him and Milton desired her. She was stirring up that little weak fire of sexual will that Milton Harper had been pleased to let languish until he came home and found her with Hugh. He walked towards her and stood right against her. She looked to the side and wouldn't face him. He snatched the cigarette out of her hand and threw it in the sink. She still didn't face him. He took her in his arms and felt the tense resistance of her body. Once her resistance would have overcome him and sent him off for a melancholy walk alone. Now he looked upon it as something to be overcome. He kissed her on the jaw, since she wouldn't look towards him. He began to kiss her hair line as she leaned backwards over the sink to try to escape him. He jerked her head back up and went on kissing her.

"Don't Milton," she said. This time he resisted with silence and went on kissing her. He reached up underneath her skirt and pulled off her panties. She didn't physically resist. She just said "Stop it, Milton!" He ran his hand over the smooth, hot heavy flesh of her rump and he started to kiss the soft skin which covered her thin neck. He tried to get his hips between her thighs but she held her knees tightly together.

"Let me," he said quietly.

"No."

He tried again, but she kept her knees together. He crushed her to him and they fell on the floor together. He lay upon her panting and trying to kiss her lips. She rolled her head backwards and forwards to stop him kissing her. She began to cry, hot tears of grief, not of terror. Something had burst and she cried with relief, crying towards relaxation. Her legs fell apart and Milton undid his belt and pushed his pants off his hips. He slowly lifted himself inside her. She had never seemed more beautiful and he undid her blouse and pushed it off her shoulders. He moved inside her trying to get deeper and deeper to sample more completely her softness. He felt himself start to come in one, slow, quiet, warm rush and he lay there as his sperm flowed into her. Then he collapsed guiltily on to her breast and waited to be comforted.

She lay there, relaxed and indifferent, as though grief had been her orgasm. She did not comfort him and he stood up and turned away from her so that she could not see his penis and did up his pants.

He was overcome with remorse and guilt. He had destroyed his home, his comfort, his security. This non-violent violation, which had made her seem so beautiful before his orgasm, now only filled him with bitterness and shame. He understood now why men sometimes killed the women they raped. They could not bear to look at them and remember their guilt. All he could do now was flee, put distance between himself and his wife, himself and the kitchen. Perhaps distance would destroy this feeling of self-loathing.

He burst out of the house, much as Hugh had burst out of the house and, like Hugh, he fled. He fled across the lawn with explosive power and then, as he got further from the house he dropped into his usual running gait.

When Milton arrived at the beach he sat down, dug himself a hole in the hot white sand and looked across the brown pieces of driftwood to where the sea, now grey, curled and flashed. He watched the sun, which barely seemed able to stay in the sky, glimmer like a globule of molten glass.

Milton played with the sand and tried not to think of anything at all, like a child who has broken his mother's favourite vase and can't bear the responsibility.

The sun got lower and turned a copper colour. Milton started to get cold. The air seemed to be covering the landscape now, like an almost transparent black scarf which wound round and round the houses and trees until they disappeared. As the sky darkened Milton looked at the arriving and departing people on the beach as figures in a pantomime.

Finally even the sand became hostile. It renounced the acquired warmth of the sun and began to exude a moist chill. On the horizon there was a smudge of red, left by the setting sun, though the sky was still an intense, though darkening blue. The beams of the cars headlights began to congeal in the darkening air.

As Milton sat, with his back to the road a woman wearing slacks and a white jersey came silently across the thinly grassed lawn towards the beach. The tip of her cigarette glowed intermittently.

"Your tea's cold," said Liz. Milton stood up, wiping the sand off his trousers, but not turning round. He slowly rubbed his hands together to remove the clinging sand. "What the hell's the matter Milton?"

"Use your imagination."

""Why throw a big sulk just because I didn't want to screw you? You got what you wanted, so why the fuss?" Milton turned around and looked at Liz standing on the bank above him. His nose was sore and his eyes were smarting and watering.

Milton climbed the bank to where Liz stood, his feet slipping on the sandy bank. He paused for a minute in front of her and then walked on.

"I almost rang the hospital, Milt." said Liz, running after her fast striding husband.

"Yeah."

Milton stepped off the grass on to the road in front of an oncoming car. Car tyres squealed and the car stopped. Milton stood on the road, his hands on his hips, looking at the darkened car. A head poked out the driver's window and said:

"Get out of the way." Milton took a step forward and kicked the number plate of the car. Liz jumped onto the brightly lit stage. A second car drove up behind the original vehicle, stopped and then sounded its horn. When this had no effect the second car pulled out and drove around the stationary car and began to move off up the road.

"Why don't you two dopey bastards take it out the back and stop blocking the road?" said the driver of the second car shouting through the open passenger window as he accelerated away. Milton picked up a stone and hurled it at the shadowy vehicle that was receding up the road. There was a clunk as the stone hit the tin fence of the motor camp.

"Don't be a child, Milton!" said Liz putting her arms around him in a bear hug and trying to drag him off the road. Milton kept his eyes fixed on the receding car as Liz jerked and yanked to try to get him off the road. The driver of the first car took advantage of Milton's inattention to back his car off a little. Then he tried to drive past Milton, but Milton tore free of Liz and jumped in front of the car again. The driver put the car in reverse and backed away up the road at top speed, Milton in pursuit. Another car swept by, its horn making a sustained blast in the darkening evening. Milton caught up with the fleeing vehicle, jumped on the front bumper and hit the bonnet with his fist, using it like a hammer. Unexpectedly the driver turned at ninety degrees into a driveway, throwing Milton off his precarious perch and on to the jagged edge of the tar seal. Milton looked up and saw another car, coming the opposite way, bearing down upon him. He crawled off the road on all fours and onto someone's wet front lawn.

Milton vaguely wondered why the lawn was wet.

His elbow was sore. He lifted up his arm close to his eyes and saw a slash in the muscle of the arm below the elbow, from which blood was flowing freely. The blood barely had colour, but it was warm and sticky. Milton felt dizzy. The car, that he had so recently been terrorising, drove madly back out of the drive, spraying Milton with stones as he lay on the wet grass.

Milton stood up and looked at the deep blue sky. He looked at the tops of the even darker pines over by the motor camp and then quickly looked down at his feet. The streetlights suddenly came on and the objects in the landscape seemed to leap at him all at once. He took a step out of the light. Milton looked at his feet again. He was afraid that if he looked up, he would vomit. He felt as though his nose was going to bleed.

Liz came up, looking sallow beneath the bright light and then disappearing into semi darkness as she approached him.

"Are you okay?"

"I'm bleeding."

"Badly?"

"I don't know. I can't see."

"Come over underneath the street light then."

No, I'd rather go home.

"Come on then."

Liz reached out and took him by the injured elbow. Milton tore it out of Liz's hand shouting indignantly.

"Watch out!"

"All right! We'd better hurry Milt. I think it's bleeding quite badly."

The light in their lounge shocked Milton into a reality he would have liked to avoid. His side was wet and sticky and he could see the dark stain of blood on his red singlet. Though everything was sharp and clear under the electric light it seemed faintly ethereal. Milton's throat felt as though it had a piece of string tied around it. He moved his arm and it slowly peeled away from the singlet. The cut was long and fairly smooth, but the skin was wide open and blood began to seep immediately into the fissure.

"You'll have to get it stitched," said Liz. "You're white as a sheet Milt. Your eyes have almost lost their colour. You know how they go when you're sick."

"Stop talking shit and let's go to the hospital."

"I'll bandage it first."

"Well, hurry up then."

* * *

Later, Milton was at home sitting on the divan while Liz made some coffee. Everything had returned to normal. The electric bulb glowed feebly in the roof and the venetian blinds clacked from time to time in response to the intermittent breeze. Milton looked vacantly at his stitched arm, now covered in a bandage.

"When he finished the arm looked like a stuffed chicken's arse at Christmas time," he called out to Liz.

"Yeah," said Liz coming to stand in the doorway.

"I'm going to have to control myself a bit better, or I'll come to a sticky end," said Milton looking enquiringly at Liz.

"I'm not going to disagree with that," said Liz looking him straight in the eye.

"Maybe I've got a brain tumour?"

"I doubt it."

"So do I. But everything seems to have gone haywire since the other night. It was like undoing the lid of Pandora's Box and now I can't keep it on anymore."

"That's your problem," said Liz, turning back to the kitchen.

Chapter 14

Dave Gibson was shearing for a week. It was a time of ceaseless activity. Every day Dave and his shepherd Les would muster the sheep, starting at dawn. Every day they would deliver them to the woolshed by breakfast time and every day, all day long, the shearers would lay the white-yellow fleeces on the dark yellow wood of the woolshed floor and the fleecos would sweep them away and put them in bales to be pressed.

It was about this time that Dave Gibson began to think of his daughter's child as an heir. He wanted to leave his kingdom on earth to someone. He couldn't see the point of having worked hard for so long just to sell what he had created. To sell would just be to admit defeat. If he sold he might as well have never been there at all. His daughter couldn't be relied upon to marry someone who would take over the farm, so if her child was a son, maybe he, Dave Gibson, could hold out long enough for the boy to succeed him. I wonder what sort of blood the boy will have in him? Probably he'll just want to stand around and sniffle and play the piano. Still, we'll have to wait and see. If we can get Melissa to leave him here maybe he'll grow up wanting the right things.

Now and again, Melissa would wander up to the shed to watch the shearing. One day one of the female Māori fleecos asked Melissa where her old man was. Melissa just laughed and said:

"I'm not married."

"But you've got to have an old man or you wouldn't be fat."

"I didn't like him. I got rid of him."

"Oh, someone better come along, eh?"

"No. I just got rid of him."

"Well, who's going to look after you?"

"I'll look after myself."

"You must like to work hard," said the Māori girl and went on with her work.

Melissa liked the shearing shed. She liked its darkness and the way the light, which was so bright it was almost blue, pierced the darkness in shafts when it entered the doors and the windows. Small explosions of white light could be seen above the rafters where there were nail holes in the corrugated iron. There would be the continuous rumble of sheep's hooves on the wood floor and occasionally the cough of a sheep, deep and raspy. The smell of wool hung in the air as well as the smell of oil, burning on the hot cutters. She liked to drag a bare foot over the layer of faintly sticky black dirt which covered most of the floor of the shed. She liked to read the names scrawled in raddle on the walls along with dates left by members of the previous gangs. She looked at the Maori workers and felt isolated from them as the boss' daughter.

She would stand there as though she was in between breaths, only half present, a person who could not live again until she had rid herself of her burden. She half thought of ringing Jim Wilson, but she knew she couldn't until the child was born. At this late stage carrying the child de-personalised her more than anything ever had before. She could not feel for anything except herself and the child and, since human beings only know themselves by responding to what surrounds them, she really knew nothing of either herself or the child.

Each day seemed to wither into a black nut of darkness, shrinking painfully slowly, while Melissa stood there and watched it shrink, wishing time would move faster. She wished she already had a home and children and was required to do some sort of labour. Anything was preferable to living in this void bereft of appetite except to eat, sleep and evacuate her bowels and bladder. I bet I look like a normal, alert human being too from the outside, she thought with bitterness.

When she wasn't at the shearing shed, she spent a lot of her time sitting on the hot, grey silt beside a shallower part of the creek. Often when sitting there she fell asleep and, when she woke up, she felt as though she had the flu, the sweat running down her body like worms. She would stand up feeling dizzy, her dress would stick to her moist body and she would feel suddenly cold. She would look at her watch and realise only half an hour had gone and she would sit down again and stare at the water, bumping over the stony bottom of the creek, its deep gurgle backed by the hush, hush of the wind in the trees. Now and again a fantail would come to visit her, flitting around in a neighbouring willow, chattering incessantly as though he could barely contain the excitement of his own story. Eventually Melissa would stand and wander off at her customary laborious pace. Every time she did so she wished her journey would take a long time but, however long it took, it was always too short.

Then, eventually, the day was dead, although it was never quite clear to Melissa quite how it had died and why it was not still there; keeping her moving, keeping her awake like a secret service interrogator.

She and her parents would sit in the lounge, her father watching television when he wasn't asleep in front of it, her mother knitting with almost sinister speed and her, sitting there waiting for a reasonable excuse to go to bed. She was on her second time through her mother's collection of women's magazines. Her mother got both sorts of women's magazines: the ones that said only sex counted and ones that said only sponge cake counted, but which threw in a bit of sex to reinforce the value of sponge cakes. Melissa read recipes for cakes that she couldn't eat and dress patterns for dresses that she couldn't wear. She read about the royal family who, unintentionally support several thousand journalists simply by continuing to breed. She read about menopause and mastectomy, goulash and gonorrhoea. Best of all she read about pregnancy and babies; or rather she didn't because she could see no point in reading about anything that remotely concerned herself. All the time as she sat and wasted time, she had this terrible suspicion that she was small, that they were all small and at the mercy of giants.

So, Melissa sat in the dim light of the lounge turning the pages of woman's magazines until about nine o'clock when she would stand up uncertainly and say:

"Well, I suppose I'd better go to bed Mum."

"Yes, you go and get a good night's rest.

"Goodnight Dad."

"Be quiet. I just want to hear this bit." So Melissa waited looking at the TV screen until that particular news item was over.

"Good night, Dad."

"Christ, was that all you wanted? Good night then, dear."

"Make sure you wake us up if something starts to happen."

"I've seen Dad deliver too many lambs to want to entrust myself to his tender, loving care."

Chapter 15

Shearing was finished and Dave Gibson duly got tipped drunk on the back porch by the shepherd. On Saturday morning, the morning after the night before, he not only had a hangover but he got an ear bashing from his wife for going out with the car and getting drunk when Melissa might have chosen Friday night to go into labour.

Dave Gibson got on his bike with his ears stuffed full of cotton wool to keep out the noise of the engine and rode to the back of the farm to keep out the noise of his wife. By the time he returned on Saturday night he felt physically and morally purified by a day of remorseless physical labour. In fact, by his standards, he was in a remarkably fine mood.

On Sunday they all drove into town to the beach. When they arrived Dave Gibson rolled up his trousers and walked across the sand to the water, his white feet flapping like sea gulls. He stood in the water staring out to sea dropping cigarette ash in the clear, foam flecked water. The water swirled and flopped about the feet of the pre-occupied man. Mrs Gibson walked into the waves and stood beside Dave, grasping his elbow with one hand while she held up her dress with the other. Then they promenaded along the silver-surfaced, dark sand which had been made wet by the slithering waves.

Melissa walked where the sand was dry, her hands behind her back, sinking her feet in the sand and kicking the sand that covered her instep into the air. The coarse grains of sand fell heavily back to earth while the fine particles were caught up in the onshore breeze and whipped away. After awhile Melissa sat on a sand-softened piece of driftwood and watched a gull dropping a shell on the sand and diving to retrieve it, only to fly up and drop it again. Finally, the gull landed, waddled up to the shell and plucked out a tongue of white flesh. Then it ran off along the wet, stone studded, near sea sand, wings flapping and heaved itself into the air. A small plane, the sunlight bursting occasionally on its wings suddenly went silent in the cold blue sky. It hung there, apparently still for a long time. Then its engine burst into life again and it continued its journey.

Melissa saw a boy come walking along the beach towards her, emerging out of a silhouette on the flat sand. He had been in the same class as her at school. She turned her back on him and walked away up the beach towards the sand dunes, meandering, snapping a twig of driftwood in her hands into smaller and smaller pieces. The sand clung to her damp feet. Bugger this for a joke, she thought. Bugger this for a joke!

She hauled herself up the dunes pulling on the stems of the pale grass. She reached the car and leaned against its hot metal. She pulled her eyebrows down and formed a black haze over her eyes. She could smell the charred paper in the rubbish bin, just across the hard white sand. If I had the energy thought Melissa I'd grab the crank-handle out of the boot and wrap it around the head of the first person to cross my path. Melissa stared out at the intense blue sea which seemed to be sitting right on top of the dunes. Thousands of leaves of light fell off the waves each second and drowned on the ocean floor.

Suddenly there was her mother in front of her, looking as though she was pasted on the blue surface of the sea.

"You ought to go in for a paddle. Salt water's good for your skin," said Mrs Gibson beaming and waving her shoes around.

"Fuck!" said Melissa.

"Don't get despondent dear. It'll be over soon enough." Melissa shrugged and a tear wriggled down her cheek. "Oh darling, baby!" said Mrs Gibson rushing towards Melissa and trying to encircle her in her arms.

"Don't squeeze me. I don't want to expel it on the beach."

Dave Gibson came over the top of the dune looking vaguely like a zebra with his white feet, his brown legs and his grey pants.

"What the hell's going on here? A soccer match?"

"Be quiet Dave, you wouldn't understand."

"Bullshit! I've had thirteen kids and four miscarriages didn't you know." Melissa began to laugh. "I told you I knew what I was doing," said Dave beginning to unlock the car.

Chapter 16

The next day Melissa sat on a high stool in the kitchen watching the leaves of the silver birches flutter like the eyelids of an amorous woman. Her father poked his head in the door and dropped a letter on the floor for her. Melissa walked warily across the kitchen and knelt to pick up the letter. As she was kneeling on the floor, reaching out, she felt her first contraction. She thought it was nothing and struggled to her feet. Then another contraction came.

"Fuck!" she muttered as she shuffled across the floor and leaned her elbow on the bench. She got her thumb inside the flap of the letter and tore it open. She didn't recognise the writing and turned to the end to see who had written it. It was from Jim Wilson. He had written:

Dear Melissa,

It is getting on for a fortnight now since I met you and, in spite of my best efforts, I think of you every day. It is a disaster and a sin for me to do so, but I cannot help it. I realise that I am not a very handsome man and that any dash that I might possess is rather negated by my occupation. Consequently you must realise my fear at admitting my affection for you. It must be easy for a man to make advances to a woman if he does not fear rejection or if he is generally considered handsome and is normally successful when he makes advances to women. I, however, do care if you reject me and, as I have already said, I am not handsome or experienced in the ways of love.

So please, even if you feel nothing for me, have sufficient respect for me to reject me without reviling me and making my earnest affection seem ridiculous.

Personally, of course, I do not care for earnestness in any shape or form, but in this instance I find it infuriatingly unavoidable. I have always been a rather detached and worldly man; a reflection perhaps on the religion I follow, which has always looked upon enthusiasm with a jaundiced eye and prefers the predictability of dry intellectual resolve and the odd descent into sin. So the purity and the intensity of the emotion I feel for you comes as something of a revelation to me, albeit a revelation that I would rather not have received.

I do not know what you will be able to say in reply to this, even if your emotion towards me is as overwhelming as mine towards you. I cannot imagine you sending me a panegyric on the incomparable beauty of my left shoulder. However, perhaps you could give me some indication of your feelings for me no matter how indefinite they are.

You must tell me the complete truth though. I would rather have my love, and that is what it is, rejected than falsely accepted. Freedom is a difficult, if not impossible, matter to define; but once you love, it becomes relatively simple. You must be free. Free to choose me or reject me. I wish to be loved by, you but probably, if you reject me, I will survive. But if you accept my love falsely then I will give you everything and once you inevitably spurn me I will be lost both to myself and to my friends.

I have never known such excitement or risk as this. I imagine this risk-all love is very similar to battle and I understand much better those men who become soldiers even if I believe their killing to be a mortal sin. My life has never been beyond my control before. Please take from me all chance of controlling it.

I hope that you are well physically and that the child, born or unborn, is also well. Not that I care for the child personally, in personal terms it does not exist for me, but one would be a brute indeed to wish harm on a creature who had influenced your life either for good or ill. I hope your parents are well and that your father's eyes have recovered from the candle lit meal.

Everything is in your hands now. I can only wait until I am ordered over the top or ordered to return to my parishioners. Please forgive the impersonality of my ending, but you have not really given me permission to be more familiar.

Yours faithfully,

Jim Wilson.

Melissa, holding her stomach walked to one of the kitchen drawers and pulled out a small, thin-leafed pad, the sort on which letters are written. She took an envelope and a pencil from the drawer as well. She headed her letter with her parents address and then wrote:

Dear Jim,

I probably love you. I will know the next time I see you. Right now I have an urgent appointment at the maternity ward.

Your good friend,

Melissa.

She put her letter in the envelope, addressed and sealed it. Then she tore up Jim Wilson's letter and buried it in the rubbish tin, under the previous night's potato peelings and vegetable scraps. She walked unsteadily but quickly through to her room, put the letter in her packed case, she had packed it the day before, fell into a sitting position and called her mother.

Mrs Gibson rapped on the window pane. Melissa looked at her mother who was gesturing to Melissa to open the window. Melissa pointed to her stomach. Her mother pointed to Melissa's stomach, her mouth fell open and her eyes dilated.

"Now?" Melissa could just hear her through the closed window. Mrs Gibson had on her blue gardening gloves. Melissa realised that her mother was standing on the lawn and leaning against the house to avoid standing on a newly planted flower bed. Melissa nodded her head in response to her mother's question. Mrs Gibson's throat and then her shoulders rose into view before she disappeared altogether, leaving the sun glinting dully on the mesh fence that separated the hill from the front lawn. Melissa could see that some of the distant valleys were still in shadow. The shadows looked thick and cold. The sky was blue, but it had a slightly pallid tinge and the sunlight had a slight trace of white in it. Melissa realised that it was getting towards autumn.

Eight hours later Melissa had an eight pound one ounce son. Gibbo started drinking at eleven o'clock that night. He finally went to bed at dawn the next morning.

Chapter 17

illie Foster sat clicking the cigarette lighter that belonged to a young doctor who was her latest acquisition. Eventually she adjusted the flame until it was nearly a yard long. At that point it didn't look like a flame because it was so long and thin.

"Cut it out Lillie, you might start a fire."

"Great, I could do with some excitement."

"Don't you like it here?

"Give me another cigarette, will you?" The doctor offered Lillie one of his Black Russian cigarettes, adjusted the jet on his lighter and clicked the lighter underneath her cigarette. Lillie lowered her head and pushed the tip of the cigarette into the flame. She sat up straight, taking a couple of puffs as she did so.

"We can go somewhere else if you like. We can go back to my place."

"What'd be exciting about that? Balls are balls are balls."

"Well, if that's what you feel, I might as well be off."

"You'd do a lot better if you were impervious, or even aggressive."

"Well, I'm not."

"Yes, that's tough for both of us. Perhaps I'll go to Australia.

"What would you want to do that for?

"I'm getting restless."

"You can't go on flitting from country to country like you've been doing; especially without qualifications."

"I've got qualifications. You've been seeing some of them the last few nights.

"You mean you'll work as a prostitute."

"Don't be ridiculous! A fuck in the right place works wonders though.

"What about when you get old?"

"Then I'll have to pay."

There was a burst of laughter and a whoop from one of the billiard tables on the other side of the bar. One of the Māori at the next table stood up on his chair to see what was going on.

"Can you see what's going on Sonny?" said the white guy in the woollen hat.

"Not a show man," said Sonny, climbing down from the chair.

"Well, we'll let them lose their money playing pool. We'll drink ours."

"Sure thing," said Sonny, picking up the half empty jug and filling the glass of his pakeha companion.

Lillie stood up and walked to the window. She took out her red handkerchief with the white spots and wiped a square on the steamed-up window. Water was running in streams down the outside of the window pane. Lillie looked between the rivulets at the curtain of rain illuminated by the orange lights in the car park. The rain was leaping off the roofs of the hump backed cars in the car park. A drunk was tottering and lurching amongst the cars and the rain like a cork in the ocean.

Beyond the road there were trees looking like wet lumps of papier-mâché in the darkness. Further away was the velvet black river, which in the darkness looked neither wet nor liquid. Silver plates of light floated motionlessly on the river. Beyond the river were more houses; domed shells of wood in the wet night. Above them, like a row of orange teeth, were more street lights.

Lillie looked back at Dr Hathaway who sat at the table in a crouch. He looked emotionally dishevelled.

"I'm sorry Alan," said Lillie standing, walking towards him, stopping by his chair and touching his head.

"That's okay," said Alan managing to be pleased through his suffering.

"Shall we have some more beer?" said Lillie picking up their empty beer jug.

"Yes, but it's my round."

"Is it?"

Yes."

You'd better go then."

Lillie sat down and watched Alan sidling between the chairs on his way up to the bar. It had really been her round of drinks. It was nice of him to pick it up. If he had been on the same wage as her, Lillie never would have allowed it, but since he was a doctor, it was only fair that he should pay a bit more. Lillie reached down into the string bag that was hanging from her chair, took out her own cigarettes, counted them and put them back in her bag.

Alan was standing by himself at one end of the bar trying to attract the barman's attention by staring at him. The barman went calmly on serving the customers who were in front of him. A large, muscular man rose momentarily into the air as he threw down the winning card, then flopped back into his seat and leaned forward to sweep up the winnings. A young guy in a T shirt at a neighbouring table gave

Lillie a cheeky grin and winked. Lillie looked away. Cigarette smoke was funnelling up from the tables and accumulating under the ceiling. The tables were so stacked with foam flecked glasses they looked like three dimensional models of American cities. Here and there amber ribbons of beer would break from a tilted jug and glut the tilted glass below. Lillie could see Alan twisting towards her, lifting a full jug high to stop it being bumped.

Lillie was definitely getting bored, but it wasn't Australia she wanted. She wanted the right man. She wanted the indifferent dominance of masculine flesh. She had thought it was going to be a long, hot autumn but now, after a fortnight of almost unbroken heat, there was wind and rain and there had almost been a frost the previous night when it had been still and clear. It was time to take her body inside and inside there was nothing to do without a man.

Alan was no good. Even if he had had the body, he didn't have the indifference. He could not coolly exploit her for his personal satisfaction, a satisfaction that removed the man from her and even from himself as though he had fled, at the moment of ejaculation, to some high mountain and lived through his pleasure there before coming back to his body. It was this exploitation of her body that was her highest excitement. Once the man's face became an impersonal mask of desire she was safe inside her pleasure. After that they could loll around in her room smoking and looking out the window and having more sex until they were exhausted. But she didn't know any man with the right body or the required level of indifference, except perhaps that guy Harper and she hadn't had much luck with him.

Alan sat down and poured Lillie a beer. He drank what was left in his own glass and poured himself another. Lillie dropped the smouldering butt of her cigarette into the circular ashtray and blew out her last lungful of smoke.

"You like being a doctor, Alan?" she asked and took a sip of her beer.

"I suppose so."

"It fulfils you then?"

"I don't know. It's what I was always going to do."

"Surely you like serving humanity?"

"I don't serve humanity. I just diagnose, prescribe and cut things out, or off."

"You don't like anything about it?"

"I like the power and respect."

"Oh yes."

"Everyone thinks you're an expert; that you know exactly what you're doing. All the obvious things are fairly certain, but a lot of the time you're making judgements on scattered bits of evidence."

"Doesn't that worry you?"

"Not really. If you walked around with an atom bomb in your pocket long enough, you'd grow indifferent to the danger after a while. I'd rather go to bed with you than save a patient's life. Not that I'd let anyone die or anything."

"You sound like a motor mechanic that works with people rather than cars."

"Yes, except that if you do a bum job with someone's car, they'll moan like hell. If you do a bum job with someone's wife, they're inclined to look on the outcome as an act of God."

Lillie looked at Alan and realised that this was a fruitless line of conversation. He had the unfortunate knack of making everything sound indescribably dull. Lillie suspected that that was because Alan himself found everything indescribably dull and afflicted the world with his own dullness. Lillie turned in her seat. She could still see the streetlights through the hole she had created in the foggy window. She turned back and looked at Alan, who was fumbling in his coat pocket for his cigarettes.

"Let's go after we finish the jug?" suggested Lillie.

"If you like," said Alan, looking up without taking his hand out of his pocket. He found his cigarettes and pulled them out of his pocket saying: "What are we going to do?" He moved the open cigarette packet to his mouth and pulled it away again leaving a cigarette dangling from his lips."

"I don't know," said Lillie. "It must be going to be a surprise."

They drank their way through their third jug of beer. Alan, who didn't really want to leave, dragged his beer out and smoked more cigarettes to use up time. Lillie had lost the desire to drink, so the jug lasted for a long time. She always drank beer because it took a long time to get through a jug of beer, but she didn't really like beer that much, except when she was hot and thirsty.

It was after nine o'clock when they finally got up from their table and wound their way between the full tables towards the stairs. Lillie felt as though she was being crushed by the expanse of people that surrounded her. For a moment they all seemed to lose their humanity and become inert and she felt as though she was standing in a silent expanse of flax. Then there was the noise and the smoke and the raucous, open-mouthed laughter again. Lillie felt as though she had been hit hard on the head. As she skirted a card game she would catch a whiff of male perspiration coming from the jocular collection of labourers at the table.

Then Lillie and Alan were through the multitudes who were consuming beer and cigarettes instead of loaves and fishes. The pool tables near the door looked very green in the dim light. Men leaned over the tables, flexing their arms. Then, with a quick strike, they would send the white ball into one of the coloured balls. The colours would rattle and roll around the table, or disappear down one of the pockets at the side of the table. The men at the tables moved with a clipped purpose. They were the heroic players on centre stage and needed to make a dramatic impression, even if they weren't winning the game.

Lillie and Alan passed through the frosted glass doors which swung shut behind them with shocking finality. They stood at the top of some stairs which ran downwards between pale, varnished walls. A thick turquoise carpet flowed down the stairs, softening the edge of each step. At the bottom of the stairs was another frosted glass door. On it were the words "Lounge Bar", but back to front.

"I'd better go water my horse," said Alan. He disappeared into a darkened corridor which ran to the left off the landing. To the right, down another corridor two Māori girls emerged from the women's toilets. They walked towards Lillie, rearranging things in their handbags, not paying much attention to where they were going.

"She needs a bloody good belting, that one," said the girl in the red satin blouse.

"Yeah, she thinks she owns him, eh?"

"Well, she does. He's so soft."

"You wait till he finds out about her and Willy. She'll be for it then."

"Nothing happened. They were just fooling around."

"Is that right? I heard that someone found them in the cupboard without anything on."

"That's all bullshit. That's one of Mike's bullshit stories."

They reached the top of the stairs, still preoccupied with their handbags.

"Look out!" shouted Lillie. The two Māori women stopped and looked up.

"What's the matter?" asked the one in the red satin blouse.

"I thought you were going to walk over the edge without looking," said Lillie, grinning with embarrassment.

"Don't worry about us, girlie," said the other Māori girl. "We know our way around here by memory." They both shuffled off down the stairs.

"Lillie lit herself a cigarette, thinking as she did so, that she had already smoked far too much that day. I'll have to make sure that I don't smoke before lunch tomorrow, she thought. Alan emerged from the dark corridor with an almost jaunty swing.

"You look as though seeing it just reminded you of how big it was," said Lillie taking his elbow.

Out the door they stopped in the entrance way of the hotel, while Lillie did up her heavy cardigan. Now that she was outside Lillie could hear the rain drumming on the iron roof. Over by the river the branches of the palm trees pawed at the darkness in the wind and the rain. A solitary car swished past. Lillie stuck her head out of the doorway and looked along the pavement of the long main street at two figures on the pale grey pavement that looked like vultures in a desert landscape. Most of the shop windows were unlit, but a few sickly-looking neon signs clicked on and off above street level. The telephone and power wires swayed and bumped in the wind. Lillie wished she had worn her raincoat and a pair of heavy socks.

"What a hell of a night," said Lillie drawing back into the doorway.

"The car's not far away."

Alan put his arm around Lillie and they walked along the street, Lillie slightly ahead using Alan's body as a shelter from the wind. They came to a part of the street where there was no awning and no eaves. Alan let go of Lillie and they both ran across the slippery pavement. Lillie ran with her shoulders hunched and he feet curled, trying to stop the ripple soles of her jandals slipping in the rain. When she reached the other side she shook her hair like a dog shakes its ears and rubbed her palms over her wet face, which the cold had made warm a little way below the surface.

They went on, Lillie sheltering behind Alan's body again. They crossed a side street through a jungle of rain drops. Then Lillie stood with her back against the window of an empty cake shop, her hands tucked under her armpits, while Alan stood manfully in his three-quarter length coat, in the pouring rain, trying to insert a key in the car door. It was one of those moments when, for some inexplicable and never reoccurring reason, he couldn't get the key in. Finally, the key went in, he yanked the door open, hurled himself into the car and the light in the car went off as the door slammed closed.

In the car Lillie turned on the inside light and inspected her cigarette, which somehow smouldered on. She looked at Alan who was struggling to take off his overcoat, twisting from one side to the other in a desperate effort to free an arm from the sleeve. The front window of the car was already starting to fog up. Alan finally got both of his arms out of his coat, hauled it out from underneath his backside and threw it into the back seat of the car.

"Bloody thing!" he muttered. He sat there wiping his face with his handkerchief and thinking gloomily about his next day's work in the hospital. Lillie's wet, bare legs were beginning to feel cold now that she wasn't moving. She suddenly shivered, as though someone of enormous strength had grabbed her and shaken her violently.

"Take me to the beach!" said Lillie suddenly, undoing the little passenger side window and dropping her cigarette butt out of the car.

"Which beach?"

"Wainui."

As they drove through the dark, the rain drops flattening and spreading as they struck the windscreen, only to be wiped away by the tireless wipers, Lillie pulled the car rug that she had wrapped around her body up above her nose and peered out at the world from her tent of warmth. She was ready for sex. She wondered though at her own strange impersonality, at her own untouchability.

As far back as she could remember she could not recall needing anybody, not once calling for her mother or her father. She could never remember being afraid of a teacher, only perhaps feeling a certain irritated pique with them for denying her something. Nor could she remember being afraid of another girl. Once an older girl had picked on her and they had fought. Lillie had got a bloody nose and the other girl a black eye but nothing conclusive had resulted from it. Physical pain had no psychological significance for Lillie.

While she had never been afraid of anything Lillie had never really loved anything either. She had never gone into sleeping with dolls. She played with dolls of course, but they had never comforted her. All she had ever liked were trees, beaches, mountains, the things of nature, and boys' bodies. She had spent a lot of her time spying through the holes in the boys' dressing sheds at the swimming baths. Now and again, she would take a boy somewhere secret and pull down her pants so that the boy could have a look. This always seemed to her unsatisfactory, although at the time she couldn't understand why. She really much preferred swimming and rolling down hills of long grass and making herself dizzy or jumping off haystacks until her legs were sore and red from the spiky, brittle straw. Also, of course there were the undulating rhythms of a horse with its waves of damp heat like the inside of a pile of grass clippings, the heavy thump of its hooves and its purring snorts.

Her girlfriends were all talking about kissing by now, but Lillie could see no point in that.

Lillie's mother had given her a talk about lambs and things and about how Lillie would be able to have lambs once she started to "bleed" and once she started letting boys put their "thingies" inside her. Lillie had looked at her mother without surprise or speculation and wandered off to play in the far paddock. She understood what had been said, but it had no significance for her.

A short time later she had begun menstruating and she adapted to the physical inconvenience of that with the same imperturbability as she adapted to everything else.

During the Christmas break between primary school and

secondary school Lillie and her father were out rabbit shooting on horseback one day. Lillie was an exceptional shot, just as she was exceptional at all sports, without being in the least bit interested in them. She liked shooting, though, because it was connected to the things that attracted her. Her father: ruddy, cheerful, vigorous, a trifle uncouth and built like a bull looked at her and said:

"Your mother's been talking to you about sex?" Lillie had nodded. "I see that you're your normal, talkative self this morning." Lillie shrugged. There was a rumble as they rode over a culvert. "I've no doubt your mother got all the facts right," her father continued, "but she probably didn't say often enough that there was nothing wrong with sex. I wouldn't have much money if these sheep didn't have sex every year. Everything wants to have sex and anyway, it's fun. The only thing is, if you start having children, you'll have to get married. Understand?"

"Yes Dad."

"Remember though, it's normal to want sex."

"Yes Dad."

"This discussion bores you does it, Lillie?"

"Yes Dad."

"Maybe you're a bit young for it then. Remember it though." He leaned over and tousled Lillie's hair.

Because her father's farm was rather large, he kept two shepherds, one married and one single. He would have kept two married shepherds, except that the cottage that the single shepherd lived in was too small for a married couple. Anyway, his current single shepherd was no trouble. He was big, raw-boned boy who was very shy. It was almost as though he was embarrassed by his own size and strength. He had never been up late from a hangover on a working day. Lillie would see him around from time to time but never took much notice of him.

One night, just before dark, Lillie walked out to the paddock by the tractor shed to see her horse one last time that day. The sky was a deep, sinister, pre-night blue and pressed down on the brown hills which rolled monotonously away to the dark mountains. The few clouds that floated thin and flat on the horizon were orange, marbled with flecks of black. All the chickens were sitting like feather dusters on their perches in the coup. The Foster's one milking cow was cropping grass at the very end of her rope lead. Lillie wandered along the tangled line of Lawsonianas behind the shepherd's cottage. She used to play in there because there were so many pine-smelling, secret places. The Lawsonianas cast long shadows up the hill. It was damp there, between the line of trees and the slope of the hill, even in summer. Lillie lifted up a solid green frond and crept into a hollow place in the hedge. She lay there on her back on the brittle, brown carpet of fallen leaves and looked up through the lattice of dark, brown branches to the unbroken roof of green fronds. It was such an exciting place.

It would be a good place to bring Herby Green for a look. Lillie rubbed her stomach and thought of Herby's hard knees and fists. She began to caress her short, dark pubic hairs. She thought of Herby Green's twisted nose and flat-topped hair-cut. She began to stroke her cunt, which was wet, and she began to understand why girls let men put their "thingies" inside them. She wriggled out of her panties and pushed two of her fingers inside of her. The air was still and silent and the secrecy of the place freed her from the sordid limits of her existence. She wished that Herby Green was really there on top of her so that she could lick him and bite him. Then she was muttering Herby's name and there was a sudden shock and she was free, free of her stupid games and her mother's stupid worries about how she was doing at school. Her whole body seemed to laugh as she lay there with her eyes shut and her face screwed up, liberated from time, space and circumstance.

After that she opened her eyes and looked again to see if she was really under the Lawsonianas. She laid there, the warm air firmly gripping her buttocks. This was what she had been aiming for all this time without ever knowing. She squeezed her legs together and wished Herby Green was there. Lillie put her panties on and crawled through to the other side of the Lawsonianas. The light was on in the back window of the shepherd's cottage. It was almost dark now and the grass felt cool around Lillie's bare feet. She realised that her mother would be wondering where she was. Then she saw the shepherd's head and naked shoulders appear at the lighted cottage window. She felt excited again. She ran to the corner of the cottage and crept along the back wall until she reached the window. She had to stand on tip toes to see in. The shepherd was lying on his stomach on the bed in his underpants. Lillie felt herself lose her breath, her face go hot and her thighs weak. She wished he would take off his pants. He was reading a magazine full of pictures of naked woman. Then, he casually looked towards the window. His body stiffened and he shoved the magazine under the pillow with extraordinary swiftness. Lillie ran. When she reached the house her mother asked why she had been running so fast and Lillie replied that she was just seeing how fast she could run back from the other side of the Lawsonianas.

Lillie was very preoccupied with Herby Green in bed for the next week or so, but Herby Green's non presence made her lose interest in him. She decided that if it was that nice with your fingers it must be fifty times as nice with a man's prick. Now, when she began to pass the shepherd she would smile at him. He would take no notice or go red and work even harder at what he was doing. After a week or so of being nice to him it was perfectly obvious to Lillie that he wasn't even going to ask her for a look, let alone anything else. She would be at school in another couple of weeks and even if it was a girls' boarding school at least it was in town and she would have more chance of seeing some boys. She might even get to see Herby Green.

Then, one evening her parents went off to a party about six o'clock. Lillie seemed so independent that neither of them worried. Besides, she could easily ring up the married shepherd down the road or go and get John out the back if he was at home.

Lillie watched her parent's car speed away down the drive leaving a tunnel of dust slowly dissolving in the air behind it. The car jolted as it went over the cattle stop at the end of the drive and accelerated away up the road, the horn tooting. Lillie stood on the front veranda waving vigorously to her parents. Then she went inside and sat in the lounge. TV had recently come to the area, so she turned on the set and watched the grey picture. But she couldn't concentrate on the Donna Reed show, so she walked resolutely out the back door to the shepherd's cottage. She climbed up the two wooden steps and knocked at the door. No one came to the door and she paused and listened carefully to see if anyone was moving around inside. She turned the door handle, pushed the door open and went in closing the door behind her. The air in the dark lounge was thick and smelled of beer and stale cigarettes. She went through to the kitchen which smelled of mutton fat. The bench was covered in breadcrumbs and there was an open can of golden syrup on the bench with a dead fly stuck on the surface. Lillie walked back into the lounge and went into the shepherd's bedroom. This room smelled of cigarettes as well and sweaty socks. There was a pile of dirty washing in the corner of the room over by the windows. The bed was neatly made and Lillie sat down on the prickly grey blankets, like the sort you get in the army. Lillie pulled off her panties, lifted her dress up around her waist and lay on the bed. The flecks of dust swam in the sloping box of sunlight like tadpoles in a pond. Lillie looked up at the fly spotted light shade, which hung completely still in the hot air. The shadowy tallboy on the other wall seemed almost human in the dark, hot, room.

Lillie heard the door open and someone in creaking boots walk

137

across the floor. Lillie opened her knees and shut her eyes and watched the beautiful red mist swirl slowly before her eyes. There was no noise of boots now, only the rustling of paper. Then the clump and creak of boots started again. The clumping stopped as the shepherd walked over the mats in the lounge. Then there were two more bangs and Lillie could feel him standing in the doorway. All she could hear was her own breathing and the mist in front of her eyes changed to dawn purple as she shut her eyes harder. Nothing happened. Lillie opened her eyes and lifted up her head and looked at the shepherd who was standing in the doorway on the verge of flight.

"Come on," said Lillie impatiently. The shepherd slowly shook his head and looked as though his limbs were all going to give way at the joints. "What's the matter?" The shepherd opened his mouth and then shut it again, like a beached fish.

Lillie stood up, marched grumpily across the floor, undid the fly on the shepherd's khaki pants and put her hand in. She was amazed. It was so hard and straight and big and heavy. She rubbed her hand up and down it. The shepherd gave a little groan and fell back against the door frame. She grabbed the shepherd's work swollen hand and put it between her legs. He didn't seem to know what to do though. Lillie pulled out the shepherd's beautiful, shining penis and began to kiss it. Then, suddenly, she was lifted in the air and bourn across the room and she could feel the prickly blankets under her buttocks and she almost coughed because of the cigarette-soaked breath of the shepherd. His face was so sunburnt it was like being close to a brick wall. She felt a little pain and then she felt filled up. and she started to throw herself against him and then he started to disappear as she was free again and trembles like waves, but stronger, flowed up and down her body and her buttocks clamped in and out like breathing ribs and saliva flooded into her mouth. She floated in her silver world, vaguely aware of the cries of the man on top of her.

Then there was a moment of frightening calm, like the moment when the wind stops and the rain begins. Then the shepherd was no longer on her and he was retreating away across the room, bent over, doing up his pants.

"Come back," shouted Lillie. The shepherd got his fly done up and felt his manliness return. He stood up to his full height and looked at the smooth skinned blond girl lying in a wanton position of the bed.

"You little slut! You've buggered everything up for me now."

""What's the matter? Didn't you like it?"

"What's that got to do with it?"

"Please come back. I don't want to stop yet."

"No. Go away Miss Foster. Please?" Lillie got off the bed and put her panties back on. "I'm sorry for doing what I did."

"What are you sorry for?"

"You know. For rooting you. Don't tell anybody. Please?" Lillie shrugged and walked out.

The next day the shepherd quit. Lillie spent most of the next week wondering if she was going to have a baby. When she didn't, she decided that she would never take a chance like that again.

Lillie was very successful at school but her indifference to her success made her disliked by her teachers who couldn't believe that anyone could take what they had to say lightly. It wasn't that Lillie had the antipathy to intellectual pursuits that some very talented people have. All she wanted to do was go home for her holidays and be with men who, in her own impersonal way, she adored. The trouble was though that so many men were not just flesh and blood, but glue as well; you couldn't shake them off. So many of them were adoring and affectionate and nice. Their bodies were like the bodies of kittens, sinewy and malleable. Even the boys with radical minds were somehow a bit domesticated.

Occasionally Lillie would pick up labourers. She liked their bodies, but so often their worlds were bestial and harsh. Lillie longed for a man of intelligence with a hard strong body and a heart as distant and blue as the steel that composed his body. In the town where she went to school Lillie had a reputation as a school girl harlot.

When she went to university that reputation meant nothing. At university women were supposed to be free, so she drifted through university passing exams as nonchalantly as she lit her cigarettes. She didn't like the lecturers. They seemed weak, conceited and physically very unappealing. They were able to conceal their defects beneath a cloak of not entirely unattractive erudition and at least they were intellectual all their waking life. And most of the male students Lillie met were full of intellectual vanity. The only entertainment Lillie got out of that group was pricking their vanity. They, of course, dismissed her as a reactionary farmer's daughter.

Then she left university and went overseas on her father's money. She had spent her time in North America and Europe, especially Greece. On the way back she had spent two months in Australia. She had been back only eighteen months and had wandered around most of New Zealand before settling for the summer in Gisborne. She loved her life, she loved all of it, but sometimes she felt as though she was floating through it, leaving it all behind without being able to hold onto anything.

Lillie looked over at Alan who was squinting, trying to see through the water which lay on the windscreen in one, opaque, ruffled sheet. Splinters of light from an oncoming car flew around Lillie's head. Alan slowed down. There was a rumble of water under the floor of the car as Alan went through a deep puddle. The car slowed momentarily, retarded by the spray of water.

Lillie shivered suddenly. It was not a shiver of cold, but a shiver of fear. It had been happening to her occasionally in the past year. The world had suddenly become empty of significance and Lillie would feel a fear that she had never known from any human agency. She felt, at those moments, that she wanted to leave some monument to herself in the world, some sign that she had been there, something that she could turn to and say, without being foolish, "this is mine".

Somehow her education had not geared her to create anything. It had been all about acquiring certificates and appearing to be intelligent. "Creativity" had been a word, repeated over and over again like certain religious groups repeat ad nauseam the expression "The Lord will provide." Lillie suddenly realised that she had been cheated. She could do a job which was something more than a sponge to soak up time and a way of making a meagre income. Perhaps, she thought, sculpting was the answer. I ought to sculpt. Not something small that I can manipulate with deft movements of the fingers, but something that will involve my entire body. Something I have to wrestle into beauty.

Alan drove the car off the road underneath some asymmetrical and wind-flailed Norfolk pines. The car bumped softly over the sandy track and then stopped. In the absence of the engine noise Lillie heard the pinging thud of the rain on the roof and the crackle of the drops on the windscreen. The wind boomed in the pines and, behind it all were the waves in their rising, breaking, falling, whispering shout, the embodiment of nothing.

Alan turned off the headlights. Now Lillie could see the black, rolling sea underneath the lighter sky. The sky looked weak and thin above the inscrutable, swirling power of the ocean. The white lines of the waves' crests were like disconnected impositions on the seas muscular back. The waves came in; white line on white line. To the south the lights of a handful of bachs shone weakly above the beach, while sheets of spray, like pages of wet newspaper raced across the sand to clamp themselves on the houses. Where the water was finally halted by the land the white foam shone as though it was a source of its own light. The dark sea, across which lines of waves scooted to become part of the iridescent white confusion of the shore, roared. All this was seen through the dimming curtain of rain on the windscreen and was exposed by the lights of the bachs and the eerie, grey light of the night sky.

"I'm going out," said Lillie.

"Out where?" said Alan, his back humped and his face and hands glowing like a lampshade as he lit a cigarette.

"On to the beach."

"Don't be mad. You'll get your clothes all wet," said Alan settling back in his seat because of his apparently irrefutable argument.

"I'm not going to wear any clothes," said Lillie, pulling one arm out of her cardigan.

"Don't be mad! You'll get exposure."

"The only exposure I'll get," said Lillie leaning forward and unzipping the back of her dress, "will be if there's a reporter from the local rag here somewhere." She pulled her dress over her head and Alan lurched out of his corner and began to kiss the thick, deeply tanned flesh of her right shoulder. Lillie took no notice and kicked off her jandals.

"I want you," said Alan weakly, as though in pain.

"You'll have to come down the beach then," said Lillie, slipping off her panties and diving out the door just as Alan made another lunge for her.

Lillie fell on the wet, needle-strewn sand and slammed the car door shut. There seemed to be a permanent layer of water on the surface of the ground. The hard pellets of rain stung as they bounced off her skin. She stood up and was shocked by the wind, but she leaned into it and steadied herself. She could smell the wind-bruised pine needles and the sea salt driven up her nostrils by the wind. Lillie moved deeper into the pines treading carefully in case she stood on a stone. Ten yards away from the car she stopped, bent forward and waggled the white triangle of her bikini mark at Alan. Then she laughed, waved at him and ran to the edge of the near vertical bank of sand at the edge of the beach.

She stood on the top of the bank and the salt-roughed wind was swirled up to her by the bank and ran its salt-roughed hands over her body. Lillie looked out to the edge of the sea where the waves were falling among the rocks like belly-flopping children. One of the pines in the plantation creaked. Lillie charged down the steep bank of sand feeling her feet dig deep down into the sand where it was almost dry. Gravity carried her down the bank at an exhilarating speed. Her legs were only there to stop her falling over. She ran out free on the beach. She was cold, but she knew if she kept moving the cold would not affect her.

Then she thought of the sea. The sea would be warm. She ran into the shallow, coursing, foamy water, little wavelets flopping at her calves as she ran. The sea was like a warm bath. She was down on the seas level now and she could see the tumbling rise of the waves, well above her head and the horizon, which was higher still and the sky which seemed to have descended ever lower. She ran deeper into the water and flopped on her stomach. Then, she turned on her back and closed her eyes. She felt the water move gently around her. Then she felt the savage, stinging pull of the swash as the water rushed back out to sea, like a train behind schedule. Then there was the gentle, running rise of the warm water again. It seemed wonderful that such gentleness could exist so close to the vicious, blustery air. She lay there wishing Alan had come down. It would be better still if the sea would take me she thought. Her body was suddenly heavy and weighed down with a great, impersonal desire, a desire directed to no man, to no sexual object, a desire which seemed to exist without reason. *I mustn't let the salt water get inside me* thought Lillie as she wriggled on her back towards the land.

"Oh, fuck," she groaned as she crab walked on her elbows towards dry land, one hand pressed against her groin. Finally, there was only a little sea lapping around her feet and she lay on the altar of the beach, on the edge of the ocean, her flesh flailed by the rain, her fingers inside herself until the dam burst and she started to flow towards something very far away which she knew would take a long time to reach. "Oh hell, oh Jesus, oh fuck," and on into unintelligible mutterings until she became aware of the rain and Alan in the car and was even faintly suspicious that she might have fainted. She clambered back up the sliding dune occasionally putting her hands on the steep slope for support.

She felt quite a different person.

Chapter 18

The hot autumn that had promised seemed suddenly dead and the world turned over to mildew and decay. But then the cold clapped its preserving hand on the moisture and the trees began to turn, so the autumn became clear, precise and beautiful, preserved in the aspic of the cold. The grass became green and the soil black. Only the maize, which turned from green to yellow, remained as a testimony to the heat dimmed air of summer. Men had been around slashing the fennel from the roadsides and Jim Wilson used to drive over the roads, littered with vegetation, half ill from the reek of fennel, which did not agree with him. So green did the grass become that the smell of grass occasionally penetrated Jim Wilson's sensory world. The cold seemed to insinuate its way into his body and move in little tunnels along his bones. He contracted his first cold of the year and, though he never coughed much, he walked around with a red nose and a slightly silvery upper lip for nearly a week. His back and neck ached all the time.

But that meant nothing to him. Jim Wilson had always feared the year destroying autumn, but even this was trivial beside the fire of desire and remorse which made his eyes sparkle and his face glow with wellbeing. He received a note from Melissa and then a longer letter saying she would come to see him after she had recovered from having the baby. Father Wilson spent hours speculating on how she would have her hair done, how she would look now that she was thinner, what sort of dress she would wear, even what underclothes she would wear, assuming she wanted him to take them off.

He still performed his parish duties, but his heart was no longer in them. He had to drive himself to pray, whereas once he had done it as a matter of course.

Late one night, as he was making himself coffee, he told himself that it wouldn't matter if God died tomorrow because Melissa would still be alive. He tried to pretend he hadn't thought such a thing but it came back to him time and time again. It was like a marker of his corruption. He wanted to do nothing except to be with her and experience her love. Each night he lay in bed and imagined the feel of Melissa's skin on his lips.

His love increased his fear of being dead. He would look out of his car at the passing trees and think that if God's will did not hide behind them there would be nothing to order the universe, no reason to live or die. If God wasn't there behind them there was only the pitiless chasm and that thought drove him more feverishly back to his thoughts of Melissa. His love reduced the world, nature itself, to something merely horrible and, in so doing, threw Father Wilson completely into its power. His life was like some game, organised by the devil, in which every step brought him closer to hell.

Father Wilson drove past fields of sheep and thought that they would die to feed man and past trees and thought that even if they were not chopped down they would die and fall and be beautiful no more. The more beautiful a thing was the more you were aware of its mutability and the more you wanted to flee into the arms of the creature who made it like this and who yet was the only person who offered any consolation for it.

Father Wilson gave up drinking too. He had been drinking one night and found himself masturbating. This seemed to him a terrible sacrilege, though not against God, but against Melissa. It was like worshiping a false idol, a synthetic substitute for the only source of pleasure and truth. So he had given up alcohol at least until Melissa could be with him. He was waiting for her to visit him so that his life could begin.

One night, when the moisture dripped from the trees with a noise like fate's dice falling into the shaking cup, a car with insect-eye headlights stopped at the top of Jim Wilson's drive. Jim Wilson walked to the door, opened it and stood in the doorway. He heard the car engine stop and saw the beams which leapt out of the eyes disappear and the eyes themselves turn orange and fade away. Milton Harper, looking short and squat because of the parka he was wearing, came crunching across the gravel towards the priest. He was looking up at the pure orb of the white moon hanging dangerously large over Jim Wilson's dew-glistened roof. Then Milton looked away from the moon and walked with blind determination towards the mysterious bulk of the house.

"Hello, Milton," said Jim out of the darkness of the doorway. Milton's arms started to move up towards a boxing guard and then suddenly dropped back to his sides.

"You shouldn't do that. I'm very suspicious of anything I can't see."

"That's the story of your life really," said Father Wilson turning on the light and standing in the doorway like an elephantine vulture. Milton walked up to the priest, stood against his chest and said:

"Out of the way you papist dog. My hands are cold."

Jim Wilson made coffee and they sat in the lounge with the curtains drawn. The room looked as small as a cupboard once the French windows had disappeared behind the curtains. Jim Wilson sat back on the couch drawing on a cigarette stretched out in a position of invulnerability. Milton sat on the chair hunched over his cup, watching the steam mysteriously disengage itself from the surface of the liquid. Periodically he would look up at the priest, his eyes coldly speculative, waiting for the priest to say something. Finally, tired of waiting, he said:

"How come I haven't heard from you lately?"

"Things haven't been going too well."

"Why not? What's the matter?"

"I'm in love with Melissa."

"Melissa?" asked Milton struggling for a second to place the face. "Oh yeah, Melissa. I predicted it that night we went to tea, remember? I never believed my own prediction though, really."

"It's the best and worst thing that's ever happened to me Milton," said the priest, leaning forward and stubbing out his cigarette in a glass ashtray on the floor.

They sat there, staring at one another across the lighted room, each cemented in their loneliness. Finally Milton said:

"What's bad about it?"

"It's destroyed my faith."

"God's not much of a guy anyway."

"How's that?"

"Anyone who could condemn even one man to eternal damnation must be a monster. If God was a man, we'd try him for war crimes and we'd convict him more easily than we convicted Goering."

"I don't care for that sort of reasoning."

"Have you ever met anyone you thought rated eternal torment?"

"No, I suppose not."

Jim Wilson's mind had often been down this path, of course, but he always thought to himself that there must be some mitigating factor in God's favour. Perhaps no one went to hell and we all only went to purgatory, but even that wasn't a very nice thought. If men did go to hell the world was best pictured by the works of Bosch and Brueghel and their pictures were so earthy, violent and horrific that it was impossible to reconcile them with the bucolic peace in which Jim Wilson lived. Jim Wilson's God existed to stop the world becoming a jumbled confusion, not to harry sinners with implacable mediaeval viciousness.

"How's Liz, anyway?" he asked, trying to take his mind off Milton's obnoxious comparison.

"Alive," said Milton draining the last of the coffee from his cup and falling back in his seat so that he looked as though he had been recently deposited there by a violent explosion.

Outwardly Milton's relations with his wife had neither improved nor deteriorated since the night he had received his stitches. Usually, he sat in his chair waiting for some sign of weakness in his wife, some sign of surrender. But she did not show it. It was as though she had withdrawn inside her body and gone into hibernation while the rest of the body went on functioning according to a pre-determined programme. She would talk to him, but the talk was only an insult because it was only to fill in the empty time. Milton watched her go through her day without showing any need of him and each day he hated her more. At night as he sat there watching her smoke and read, he thought of killing her. If she did not bow to him, he would kill her. He had superior strength. It was only fitting that she should bow to him. This resistance, this refusal to acknowledge his superior force slowly filled him with a cold fury.

In addition, the absence of the little love he needed made him depressed.

Finally, Milton had gone on a different tack. He had taken to going out and leaving Liz at home. He never told her where he went or even that he was going. He would simply get up and walk out. Sometimes he would go to the pictures, sometimes he would just walk around the streets alone for three or more hours. Tonight, he had come to see Jim.

All this, however, had no effect on Liz. For one thing she sincerely believed herself to be in the right. As far as she was concerned her behaviour with Hugh had been justified by her husband's intellectual and sexual neglect. It was a fair and permissible act of revenge and Milton had over reacted. If he had said nothing, that would have been alright; if he had protested that would have been alright, but she would never accept intimidation even though she was intimidated. She was ready to forgive everything, even apologise as long as Milton apologised first. She did not desire their current wordless union and, in a sense, she was even gratified by Milton's possessiveness. But she was not going to apologise. He had a debt he needed to pay.

Milton lay back on his chair watching the smoke from Jim Wilson's newly lighted cigarette gyrating upwards. Milton's eyes moved around the room as he momentarily envied the priest his bachelor life.

"Why don't you let her go, Milton?" Jim Wilson suddenly said out of the bleary silence.

"She doesn't want to go."

"Do you want her to go?"

"Maybe."

"Well, send her away."

"Not until she surrenders.

Jim Wilson blinked. On one level he felt disconnected from Milton's problem; but he was also puzzled. Here he was sitting and waiting for a woman to come through the door to make his life whole for the first time and here was Milton, who had a woman in his life, who no longer knew whether it was love or hate which held him to her most strongly.

Have you ever thought of going to a psychiatrist, Milton?"

"No. Why?"

"I think your sanity is in grave danger."

"Aw, shit. I'm already mad."

Milton gazed at the curtains across the windows and felt as though he was sitting in a theatre waiting for the show to start. The smell of cauliflower lingered amid the smell of cigarettes. Milton flexed his shoulders and wriggled his hips. He looked across at the priest. At this moment Milton hated Jim with a vigour that shocked even him. I'll tell him thought Milton; I've got to tell him.

"Don't ever bargain with her Jim."

"What do you mean, Milton?" asked Jim Wilson looking up."

"Make her give you everything you want. When you love it's tempting to give in, but don't or you won't love."

"I believe she will give me everything Milton."

"She won't. She isn't you."

"What do you mean?"

"People love in spite of their personalities, not because of them. You'll disagree over politics or God and from that tiny wound you will rot until your relationship is a festering mess. She will force you to be her so that you can be united and that will destroy you."

"I can't say Milton that I'm entirely optimistic about love, but I believe that it is predominantly tender."

"Yes, until she is smitten by another man or decides, quite unexpectedly, to become a Buddhist or a Hindu. I warn you, women have no heart. You have sacrificed your God for her. She is incapable of doing the same for you, because she is a woman."

"Don't be ridiculous Milton. Women are no more selfish than men."

"That's what you think, but she will wade through the flood of your love and emerge dry on the other side."

"But Melissa has told me that she loves me," lied the priest. He was beginning to feel angry at this attack on his new God. He had always known that Milton was not a Christian but both of them had refrained from discussing it. They would have to come to a similar tacit agreement over love.

"Her love is not the same as yours. Men's love always has a touch of the eternal while women's is something they do for today, like blackberry picking. They accept time, they live in time. They do not care about eternity."

"I could never believe any human being to be that dishonest."

"Women find lust and affection as satisfactory as love."

"I'm getting tired of this discussion Milton."

"You should go back to your God and leave the world to garbage like me."

Milton had passed too near to his woman hating centre to be comfortable any longer. His intellectual and moral contempt for the treachery of women, which normally he kept so well hidden that he even forgot it, had come out after a long, long incarceration. If there had been a handy woman he would have manoeuvred her into a corner and shouted in her face about the iniquity of her sex until she had been reduced to tears, as he had done on several occasions many years before.

But in the end the women had won. He couldn't live alone and he still wanted women's bodies. He was driven back, time and again to these creatures, which he hated. He had to find a sane and secure basis on which to build a relationship with women. Desire and his search for some sort of moral guidance had provided this basis. Sometimes, in the seconds after his desire had been satisfied, he felt a genuine bond of physical tenderness which he could almost convince himself was real love. Indeed, this physical tenderness brought him closer to these women that he did not love than he had ever been to the women he had actually loved, one of whom he had had no sexual relationship with at all.

Liz had been by far the most successful of these relationships until

Milton had undermined their equilibrium by trying to pass back into the "normal" world which he had left so many years ago. Milton had relaxed and ceased inventing myths to explain his unhappiness and confirm his intelligence. Providing he could be intelligent and perceptive for the few hours he sat in front of the typewriter each day he didn't mind being inarticulate, a body, for the rest of the day. But Liz had minded and that had been the end of that. Liz had not been able to cope with Milton's absorption with the physical at the expense of the intellectual. That is what had led to Hugh and the whole nasty mess. Milton grinned as a man might grin who had a nasty taste in his mouth.

"You're silent Milton," said Jim Wilson standing up and stretching.

"It's a decorous way to be at a funeral," said Milton standing up and also stretching.

"She might never come and visit me."

"She'll come. You're a virgin. That will intrigue her, one way or another."

"I hope she'll come because she loves me. I need her."

"I'm sorry Jim. Everything in my life is pretty fucked up at the moment. What I said is true for me. Maybe you'll be lucky. How about a game of chess?"

They put the big, cardboard chess board on the floor and set up the varnished, yellow and black pieces on the green and white squares of the board. Jim Wilson picked up two pawns, held them behind his back and Milton pointed to his left hand. Milton chose white and made the first move. Both of them hunched over the board like a pair of peasants trying to look into the same hole in the ground. The board shone as though the cardboard had been waxed. Milton loved the big board. It gave a tremendous sense of panorama; of the beauty of the pieces and the sweep of the territory they controlled. Periodically Milton would have to escape from his hawk's eye view of the board to escape the fumes generated by Jim's cigarettes. Jim was a jovial and

153

good-humoured chess player who was continually withdrawing his disastrous moves and often substituting moves of brilliance. Jim's brilliant substitutions for his stupidities were particularly galling to Milton who was inclined to mutter about people not observing the rules. Milton played miserly, safety-first chess; at least he did against Jim Wilson. Against players with an inclination to be defensive he was prone to take an attacking role. In the first game Jim Wilson's queen sacrifice was unsuccessful, and he resigned. In the second game, despite "unlosing" his queen twice, he made a knight and rook sacrifice which led to most of Milton's pieces being eliminated from the board as Milton tried frantically to protect his king. Milton refused to play a third game. He didn't want to end up losing more games than he had won.

Jim Wilson and Milton strolled slowly out across the gravel to Milton's car. Emerging from behind the house they saw the fog, a white streaky plain of moisture lying over the valley, pieced by trees and oddly illuminated. Above was the black, hollow emptiness of the sky, dimpled by pin points of golden light. The moon, which had looked so large and impressive earlier in the evening, was now an insignificant bauble which looked as though it had bits of its shiny, white surface picked off by a bored child or gnawed by mice. The hills, though, stood out sharply against the horizon making the edges of the sky seem white. Trees of steam appeared and disappeared from the mouths of the two men. Milton stopped beside the front door of his car and drew an outline of a man with big ears in the condensation of his windscreen.

"You need to keep in touch," said Milton putting his hand in his pocket and pulling out the car keys.

"I always have in the past."

"Oh, you'll get preoccupied. You'd better call often though. In your situation a lot can happen in a week."

"Anyone would think that I was going to the Eastern Front." Milton laughed his wolf laugh and got into the car. He leant forward in the seat and Jim Wilson heard the labouring cough of the starter-motor. There was silence. The cough started again. The motor sprang into life, roaring fast and loudly until Milton took his foot off the accelerator and left the car running at a level putter. Milton turned on the headlights, tooted and backed down the drive; the car inside a whirling ball of smoke and steam. Jim Wilson stood at the top of the drive, feet apart; waving until Milton disappeared around a bend in the drive. Then he turned, put his hands in his pockets and walked slowly inside.

Chapter 19

Milton drove home through the fog, or rather in and out of it. Sometimes he would pass into a huge mass of whiteness when the headlights no longer seemed to penetrate and the light would be thrown all around his own car like a halo. At other times it was like gliding down a plane of clarity between two plates of fog, the headlights seeming to penetrate for an enormous distance between the unconnected layers of fog. Then, suddenly, he would charge through a few floating wisps of moisture into the clear light, tensing as though he was expecting an impact. His little car bumped aside the freewheeling wisps of moisture and ploughed through the ankle-deep drifts of mist scattering it as though it was snow. From a long way off Milton could see the horizontal columns of the headlights of approaching cars bouncing in the smoky fog.

When Milton finally got nearer the coast there was no more fog. He passed through the wide fields in which intruder houses sat like poor boxes, while the fields were their own masters until dawn, when men would descend upon them as flies sometimes descend upon a bull. Milton could see the pale light of the sea spray above the black line of the land's end. The star pierced sky was flat and as hard as ebony.

Then Milton was on the coast. Here in the new sea light the houses seemed like skeletons in the sea dry air and the power wires sagged silver between the shanty poles. At sea, under the guard of a hummock of rock, Milton could see the four tiers of lights of a big ship. The blazing beacons were like an invitation to a party. It seemed to him odd that Kaiti Hill should look like a mere rock behind the lighted ship.

Milton's headlights brushed over the neighbours drive as he turned into his own drive. Milton stopped and watched a hedgehog caught in the beam of his headlights. Then the hedgehog scuttled away looking like a sausage on four legs.

Milton walked around the back of his car. The dew had barely dampened the dust on his drive. Milton walked out onto the moisture lightened lawn and threw his car keys into the air. The keys seemed to hang, for a moment, at the top of their flight before falling safely into Milton's hands. The keys were reassuringly cold and heavy.

In the street, a white streetlight hung above his drive like an eye that must be worshipped. He walked out onto the street and stood under its beam. The sea hissed and fell silent, hissed and fell silent, the night's constant heart beat disturbed by the occasional burst of sound from a neighbours television set.

Milton walked along the footpath watching his shadow stretch out as he walked away from one streetlight and then disappear as he came within range of the next one. Milton's parka made a scratching sound as he walked and began to think about the clammy moisture that would shortly gather inside the plastic.

About three lampposts up the road, Milton noticed a shadow with a red spark in front of what was presumably a face. Periodically the point of light would whirl away, only to return there after a pause. Milton wondered whether he should keep going. He didn't want to frighten the woman, whoever she was.

Milton shuffled, hands in pockets, under the last light before the woman. She gave a start and turned towards him quickly. Milton heard a long exhalation of breath.

"How come you're not running?" asked Lillie Foster.

"A bit dark, maybe."

"I would have thought someone like you would have used every available minute to improve your physical condition."

"Probably not." Milton stood in the gap in the hedge beside and slightly in front of Lillie. She went on smoking. He kicked the edge of the pavement with the heel of his boot, just as you would dig a hole in the turf for a rugby ball. Lillie watched out of the corner of her eye. He seemed in a strangely gentle mood, as though he had been made uncertain by her reluctance to talk to him. Anyway, as far as she was concerned, he had chosen a bad night. For some reason her body felt as dead as a sack of wet sand. She flicked her cigarette with her thumb and some sparks flew free from the tip. She breathed in deep and hard and the cold scraped the inside of her sinuses so that they felt raw. She also felt sore just at the top of her eyes.

"I must be getting a cold," she said quite impersonally.

"You ought to give up smoking. It deprives you of energy. You never bound out of bed thinking it's a wonderful morning if you smoke."

"And you do?"

"Not really."

"Anyway, I don't smoke much."

I've hardly had a cold since I stopped."

An old, high, box shaped car came squealing around the corner, slipping across to the wrong side of the road, swaying as it straightened up. It came straight towards Lillie and Milton. As it seemed to be about to leap on top of them it swerved again in pursuit of the tar sealed strip of road. It went off the road on the other side and joggled on the grass verge, before it leapt back onto the road and, grass flying out behind its back wheels, disappeared around the next corner.

"Someone's having a good time," said Lillie.

"Yeah." Lillie flicked her cigarette butt in an illuminated arc out onto the road.

"You want a drink?"

"I don't drink."

"You don't drink?" Oh, I see what you mean. I meant a cup of coffee."

"All right."

Milton sat at the table in the dim, high ceilinged kitchen which smelt of dirt and sawdust. He looked at himself leaning on the table in the black mirror of the window. They had decided on tea and Lillie, in jeans, a white polo necked jersey, a short woolly coat and wearing a scarf over her head, moved with quick power between the stove and the table making it. Finally, she was just waiting for the kettle to boil, leaning on the table with one hand.

"Why do you think you write?"

"I don't know. It's the only thing I ever wanted to do really."

"You don't think it's the noblest of occupations?"

"No. It's morally unhealthy to think like that. You're trying to say that what you do is better than what others do. Some people dig ditches. I write."

"You never had any reason for writing?"

"Oh, when I was young, I thought that life was a stupid and painful mess and that the only way of coping with that was to write about the mess. Life makes more sense now, but it's still not very nice."

"I've never been unhappy."

"Yeah, well you're nice looking."

"What difference does that make?"

"Are you going to tell me that your personality's been stunted because men found you attractive?"

"Of course not."

"You could always treat men as you wanted, because there was always another one coming around."

"And you're just another one in the line." They locked eyes momentarily. Then Milton laughed.

"It's funny. There are some very attractive women you don't mind falling for. Tonight, you're one of those. Other women I wouldn't admit to finding attractive." Lillie walked over to the stove where the water in the kettle was gurgling and steam spurting into the air. She poured water into the teapot and carried it across to the table.

"Enough tea for me, Lill?" asked an olive skinned tousled haired boy, poking his head in the kitchen door.

"You'll have to wash yourself a cup."

"Aw hell!" The head disappeared.

"One of the leeches," said Lillie, leaning her head towards the door and picking a crumb out of one of the tea cups.

"You mummy around here?"

"Sort of. They appreciate it and I can drop the role when I like." Lillie picked up the teapot and poured the tea.

"You ought to use that thing," said Milton pointing at the coal range.

"The boys won't go and get any wood. I've even found a farmer who will supply it, but they're too lazy." She pushed a cup at Milton and some tea flopped over the edge. "Sorry," she said reaching across with a damp dish cloth and soaking up the tea.

Lillie lit another cigarette and threw the dead match vaguely in the direction of the coal range.

"I've decided I ought to sculpt," said Lillie, wrapping her hands around the mug of tea.

"Oh, yeah?" Milton was wary. He hadn't realised that Lillie was an arty, though probably he should have guessed. "What for?"

"I just thought that one day I ought to do something important with my life."

"Yeah. What's important about sculpting?"

"I don't know. I suppose I feel the need to point to some concrete thing that I have created."

"You must be going nuts. All nuts like to freeze a moment of their life and say: 'Look, I've got this.'"

"You think so?"

"Yeah. It's the first step towards nutterhood." Milton was looking at Lillie who was staring at the far wall without looking at it. "I thought you said you were never unhappy?"

"My turn must be starting to come round."

"I hope not. It'd make me feel better to believe that money and social position protected you against unexpected misery."

"What makes you think my family are rich?"

"It's written all over you."

"Am I really that transparent?"

"Does it matter?"

"Tonight, it matters."

Lillie stood up, walked over to the sink and flung half a mug of tea into the sink.

"You attract me you know," she said without looking at him.

"Why's that?"

"You possess the detachment of all truly physical people." Milton dropped his hand and laughed silently into his cup. "I know it probably isn't as pretty as it looks."

"You do?"

"You're married, aren't you?"

"Yeah."

"What's your wife doing?"

"I don't know."

"Will you stay with me tonight?"

"I ought to go home."

"Please? I'm asking. I don't often ask." Milton said nothing but stared hard into his tea cup. "For fuck's sake! Even if your wife loves you, I need you more than she does tonight."

Milton wanted to refuse her. He wanted to reject her honesty and her vulnerability. At the same time he wished all women were like this instead of hiding their needs and weaknesses so that you finally came to believe that they were creatures of stone. Women were so safe behind the mask of feminine passivity. Even when they desired you, they concealed this by praising your character or your talent. They would have sex to cement a meaningful relationship. Or else they would take you casually, in hope of taking you permanently.

Milton stood up.

"Which way's your room?"

"Straight through. I'll just wash my teeth." Milton laughed at Lillie's unromantic response.

Milton sat on Lillie's bed, in a white pool cast by her bedside light. His shadow, long and angular, fell on the orange sacking wall. He sat with his elbows on his knees, picking his weight lifting calluses. Milton saw the door open and Lillie's shadow fall on the bedroom floor. Lillie appeared herself, stepped into the room and pushed the door shut with the heel of her right shoe.

"How come you're not in bed?" said Lillie as she walked across to her dressing table next to the window.

"I don't know."

You're shy?"

Yeah. A bit."

"Well, disrobe and dominate me," said Lillie, looking in a hand mirror for a piece of dirt she imagined she had in her eye. Milton laughed.

162

"You really are very charming." Lillie put down the mirror and turned to look at him.

"Do I have to undress you?"

"No."

"Well, don't just sit there. Do something." Milton laughed and fell back onto the bed. Lillie walked out of the shadow and kicked his leg.

"Hey! Don't do that," he said rising up on his elbows. Lillie kicked him again, coldly and deliberately. "Cut it out." She kicked him yet again. Milton jumped up, his eyes flaring with anger. His swollen hands, whose very knots and hardness radiated threat, closed on Lillie's arms just above her elbow. Lillie reached under Milton's jersey to feel the thick slabs of muscle that covered Milton's abdomen. At the same time, she kicked him in the shin once again. "Don't!" said Milton crushing her to him in a bear hug. He seemed to know just how hard to hold her without hurting her. Lillie pressed her body against his solidity, against his dominating masculine substantiality.

"Use me," she whispered in Milton's ear, "use me."

Then her flesh was in confusion as she felt her clothing being roughly pulled off and the cold air flowing around her flesh and rough feeling of Milton's jeans as she pressed her stomach against them. Her ears went hot and sore as Milton pulled her jersey over her head. She grabbed Milton's belt and jerked it undone, unzipped his fly and dragged his pants to his knees. She stepped back and knelt holding his penis in her hands. He closed his eyes and pulled his jersey over his head. Then there was the jolt of his body against hers, his limbs like steel snakes binding her body, the heartless strength of his penis parting her flesh and then moving against her attempts to capture it and her body like a village in the shadow of a mountain. Then her pores opened like flowers and she flowed out of them, though not to him, but into the world, so that as well as being in a room entangled with another body, hot and panting like her own, she was disappearing into the air, flowing smoothly over the night-wet grass and around black trees that seemed themselves made of flesh.

Then, once again, there was only the man and she felt tears inside her cheeks and in her spine. She crushed her burning, tired flesh to him in gratitude.

"Come properly onto the bed," she whispered, stroking his blond hair which, in strange contrast to his body, was light and soft. He crawled across her and collapsed beside her. She sat up and pulled herself down to the end of the bed, still in a sitting position. She sat on the end of the bed, her feet dangling over the end, undoing Milton's boots. She pulled off his boots and socks and pushed his jeans all the way off. She crawled back up the bed and began to lick his body. It felt like being brushed with autumn leaves falling from a tree. His body began to tingle, but he lay there completely immobile, his veins feeling as though they were filled by a dark, heavy river, which pressed him to the earth and deprived his body of that spark which provided the strength to heave the loaded barbell above his head. His stomach muscles flickered as he felt his faintly aching penis absorbed into her mouth. He reached over and pulled her legs towards him and nibbled with his lips at the thick, soft woman flesh, which lay richer than solid cream beneath her salty, soft, brown skin. Something in his stomach seemed to be knotting and twisting like a rubber band being wound tighter and tighter by a matchstick. Then her thighs blotted out all sound. He sorted through the stiff hair, pulled open the lips of her cunt and began to kiss and suck the rubbery inner surface. Then there were more floundering limbs and her face appeared beside his and she kissed him quickly and said:

"From behind this time."

She knelt on the bed and Milton slipped behind what had become an hour-glass of flesh and lifted himself inside her. Lillie pushed back towards him and they bumped together. Milton's body felt almost lifeless except for the sexual compassion he felt for Lillie. He closed his eyes, hugged her rump against him and moved. He entered a world of solitary blackness. Somewhere, at the end of it all, he would become free. He heard Lillie coming and wished he could lift her up and hold her against his chest.

"Don't stop," she said weakly. He closed his eyes again. Each time he pushed he imagined he was trying to penetrate deeper into the chasm of her being, as though somehow, if he could get deep enough, he would touch some mystic trigger and shatter her being and bind her to him forever. He felt her moist, warm, loose flesh around him and he felt mournful. He wanted to ejaculate, but it seemed like an impossibility. Then Lillie was coming again, her back twisting stiffly in quick jerks as she tried to drive her head into the bedclothes. Then her body sagged and seemed to lose all tension. Milton held her by the hips and tried to push harder and deeper. He felt as though someone had tied a piece of string around the top of his head and put dollops of hot olive oil on either side of his head just where it joined his neck. The eternity of his unsatisfaction seemed to stretch out like an empty cellar before his eyes. Then, suddenly and unexpectedly, he realised that he loved her and that he had to go on. The muscles in his thighs were as tight as violin strings. Something in his abdomen seemed to be contracting into a small, tight fist. I've got to explode it, thought Milton.

His head seemed to be drawn magnetically towards his abdomen. His whole body seemed to want to fold and disappear into his abdomen.

"Oh, darling, hold me up!" said Lillie coming again, this time with more pants than groans. Milton let out a long, high powerful groan of agony and, when he came back from the groan, he realised that all he had to do was fall off the top of the wall and into release. He banged his pelvis into Lillie's body, jolting her whole body and then he screamed with relief and went on screaming as though the happiness would never end.

Then, suddenly, it was ended and he was there looking around the room and then down at Lillie who was spread-eagled on her stomach on the bed. He did not feel like himself and he stared savagely around the room. He was angry and he didn't know why. He looked back at Lillie. She looked beautiful and he bent over and kissed her rump. For some reason he wanted to lie there with his head up her vagina, she was so beautiful.

He stood up and looked suspiciously around the room again. Lillie rolled over onto her back and smiled at him weakly and warmly. Milton pulled the blanket out from beneath her, covered her up and put a pillow under her head.

"Come and lie with me." Milton shook his head. Part of him actually loved her. Part of him thought that she was the most beautiful thing he had ever seen. But another part of him, that cold, distant, detached, blue soul said that it didn't matter. Milton thought: If I walked out the door now and never saw her again, I wouldn't care.

He walked slowly across the room then struck a savage hammer blow to the wall with the bottom of his fist. Fuck freedom! He didn't want to be free, but there was nothing he could do to escape his freedom. He couldn't sell it, or frighten it away. I am only free, because there, in the centre of myself, I hate women. That is all my freedom consists of; hatred. I wonder if, at the bottom of all things who live only for their bodies, lies hatred. Perhaps animals are basically evil because, like me, at their centre lurks hatred. If hatred is the only thing that can cancel love among human beings, perhaps it also cancels love among the animals. Maybe that is the most basic way that God made us different from the animals.

Lillie sat up.

"Let's get into bed Milton. You'll catch a cold if you stand over there."

Milton got into the single bed and he and Lillie sat there, side by side. Lillie slipped her arm behind Milton's back and laid her head on his shoulder. He was a man she could live with if they could find a broader basis for their relationship. What they needed was a work in common, something they could both do together towards the same end. But it would never work out. He was a writer and art was a monument to narcissism. Perhaps that was unfair, but it was certainly solitary and lonely, somewhere where she had no place. I would do anything with him if we could both do it together.

Milton looked down at Lillie who seemed to be looking at the two joggling lumps at the end of the bed made by her feet.

"I'd better ring Liz."

"You can go home if you like," said Lillie. Milton smiled. "No, I'm serious. I'm not being shitty or anything."

"Going home would only be pretending that everything was still the same."

"Isn't it?"

"Not between me and Liz anyway."

"She might think it is."

"Yeah, but it only takes one to make it different."

Milton got out of bed, disentangled his jeans from his underpants and put the underpants on.

"You got a dressing gown?"

"Yeah. Over there, in the wardrobe. What did you put your underpants on for if you're going to wear a dressing gown?"

"If it had fallen open while I was on the phone, I might have been raped by some lust crazed cockroach." Milton pulled a large, heavy, blue and grey dressing gown from out of the wardrobe. It was as coarse as an army blanket. "How come you wear such an unfeminine dressing gown?"

"It's warm. Anyway, the flesh inside the dressing gown is wanton.

There's no reason why the dressing gown should be too." Milton Laughed.

"See you in a minute."

Milton stood in the hall looking up towards the almost unlit ceiling, feeling as though he was looking up towards the surface of some water. He turned and faced the old, black phone which was attached to the wall at the same level as his throat. The dull, aging lino was cold and gritty beneath his oddly sticky feet. All the doors off that long corridor with its yellowing wallpaper seemed to wrench everything out of proportion. Milton pressed the hand piece closer to his ear as he listened to the rhythmic buzz of the ringing phone. He followed with his eye the pipe which ran under the wallpaper from the light switch to the base of the light chord.

"Hello," said a tentative voice on the other end of the phone.

"Oh, hi Liz."

"Milton?"

"Yeah."

"Is anything the matter?

"No. I'm just ringing to say that I won't be home this evening."

"Why not?"

"I'm with another woman."

"All right." There was a long pause. "Will I see you tomorrow?"

"Yeah, I'll be home by breakfast."

"I'll make breakfast as usual then."

"No. Forget about that horseshit. I'll make it when I arrive."

"You'd better be on time then. I don't want to be late for school."

"No. I'll be on time. You think you'll be alright?"

"What the hell's the matter with you?"

"I must feel guilty." Milton listened to Liz laughing. She seemed a long way away down the phone.

""We're equal now. I'm glad really."

"Yeah, well let's talk about it in the morning."

"All right Milton. Sleep well."

"Yeah, same to you."

There was a click and the hum of an empty line. Milton stood there, the phone still against his ear, listening to the hum of an empty line. He looked at his shadow stretching along the floor and bending up the wall. Something seemed wrong. He had expected Liz to be angry, scornful and vindictive, but she had been calm, almost happy. This was not the world he knew. Perhaps he was not quite as perceptive as he thought.

He put the receiver back in its cradle on the black box. As he walked along the corridor, he kicked a nail which went pinging across the linoleum and cracked on the skirting board. He pushed on the door and passed into the dark kitchen. He looked into the darkness at the mysterious bulk of the table and the dark cave of blackness above the coal range. He heard the scratching rattle of a mouse running somewhere through the kitchen. The window was a shining square in which you could see the dark plane of the hedge and the sky, brightened by the city's lights.

Milton went through to Lillie's room. She was lying on her back blowing smoke at the roof. She turned her head and looked at him.

"Ready to go to sleep?" she asked.

"Yeah. What time do you get up in the morning?"

"About a quarter past seven."

"I'll go home then."

"Sure thing," said Lillie, leaning out of bed and stubbing out her cigarette in a saucer on the floor. Milton got into bed and Lillie reached up and turned out the light. "I very seldom, go to sleep with men," she said rubbing her hand over Milton's body.

"That's probably why you like them so much."

"You're right. I don't find men much of a comfort, usually."

169

Chapter 20

Milton Harper woke up a little before Lillie's alarm went off. He turned towards her as softly as he could. It was just light enough for him to see her breathing softly through her pale, parted lips. Her blond hair had turned into a series of dark ropes and her face was slightly swollen by sleep.

Milton could smell Lillie's ashtray under the bed. His clothes were lying in a heap on the floor. Lilies were stuck on the chair. Then the alarm went off. Milton's body lashed like a startled eel. He grabbed the alarm clock and pressed the knob to turn it off. He looked back at Lillie.

"Shit!" she said looking blankly at the ceiling. She sat up, yawned and turned towards Milton. Her breath was a bit like the smell of an outside toilet on a warm day. It was oddly arousing. "Don't you have to go home or something?"

"Yeah."

"Well, don't just sit there strumming yourself. I want to get up."

"Where's the place you want to go to?"

"The toilet, stupid."

"Yes. Where's the toilet?"

""Opposite the kitchen."

"Good, I want to use it," said Milton jumping out of bed, grabbing Lillie's dressing gown and running out the door.

"Damn you," said Lillie standing up, yawning and scratching her pubic hair.

They had a cup of tea together in the kitchen. There was a pale blue sky out the window above the hedge. There had been no frost and the outside air had a peculiar dry sweetness to it.

"I'm no great beauty in the mornings," said Lillie, looking over the rim of her cup. "Takes me a while to get wound up." Milton shrugged. "You having regrets in the cold light of dawn or something?" Milton smiled and shook his head. "For fuck's sake, SAY SOMETHING."

Milton fiddled with his teaspoon for a few seconds. Then he looked at Lillie and said:

"Can I come and see you if I want to?" Lillie looked momentarily shocked. Then she laughed.

"Don't worry. I'll tell you when I'm tired of you."

"When will that be?" Lillie looked across the top of her cup at Milton for a long time. Then she looked away quickly and said:

"Maybe never." Milton looked down at the table and pushed some crumbs around with his fingers. Lillie was still looking away. Suddenly she made a croaking sound as she drew in her breath. She stood up, rushed across the room, grabbed her packet of cigarettes, took one out and lit it. She took several puffs and then turned around to Milton beaming. "Sorry about that."

"You sure you're, okay?"

"Perfectly." Instinctively Milton wanted to take her in his arms, but he knew he couldn't. Sometimes the complications of life just get in the way.

"I'd better be off. I might drop in tonight though."

"Sure thing."

"See you."

"Yeah."

Milton jogged along the moisture blackened street. The dew on the walls and roofs of the houses made them seem as though they were perspiring. A cyclist in a heavy coat came bobbing through the grey morning air. The sun, promising a hot day, was hiding behind the hills. Lights were shining weakly in some of the houses.

Milton ran across his lawn leaving a trail of dark, green footprints behind him. The sea was hissing and the air over the sea was slightly whitened by the spray. He jumped the steps and landed lightly on the veranda. He unlocked the front door, entered the house, walked through the cold, creaking lounge and into the kitchen. He got out a frying pan from the cupboard under the sink, took some eggs from the fridge and began to fry four eggs. The bedroom door clicked, then opened and Liz poked her head out. She was trying to look through the slits between her eye lids. "That is you Milton?"

"Of course."

"What time is it?"

"Twenty to eight."

"Bloody hell! Give me a cigarette." Milton threw her cigarette packet at her. She dropped it and then bent over and picked it up. She stuck a cigarette in her mouth and put her hands on her hips. "I think I need a match, Milton."

"You don't say?" he said grinning.

"I do say." Milton threw her some matches too. Liz leant back against the doorway restoring her body to equilibrium, completely absorbed in the cigarette that was effecting the change. "I don't feel like going to work today," said Liz suddenly.

"So?" queried Milton, as he leapt away from the frying pan as it spat hot fat at him.

"So, you ring and tell them I'm sick."

"Do I have to?"

"Yes, goody-goody, you do."

"Aw, fuck Liz."

"Come on poetic anarchist. Strike a blow for your wife's freedom."

"All right, all right. Let's have some breakfast first though."

Liz and Milton ate their eggs looking at one another across the oil cloth covered table. Liz was still finishing her cigarette, but she was eating as well. "What's she like, your mistress?"

"Don't use such an archaic word, Liz."

"Well, if you tell me her name then I'll use her name."

"Lillie."

"Oh. Is she a flower, Milt?"

"She's a hippette."

"I thought you didn't care for that sort of woman."

"She's not defensive like most of them."

"You mean she's not aggressive?"

"Same difference."

They finished their eggs, Milton scraping his plate to get as much as possible of the runny, yellow yolk off the white plate. Liz lit another cigarette and shook her hair back off her face. The little back window over the stove had turned a dazzling silver, though the rest of the room was dark and chill. Milton plugged in their bar heater and aimed it at Liz's dirty scuffed pink slippers. He plugged in the electric jug and put some tea in the teapot. The two orange bars of the heater shone brightly. "Are you going to move out?" asked Liz, looking up from her toes which she was wriggling in front of the heater.

"I don't know. I suppose I ought to think about it."

"You mean you're going to stay here?'

"I don't know. It just never occurred to me that one of us would have to leave."

"I never said you had to leave. You can stay here if you fuck me." Milton grinned and shook his head. "Well?"

"Well, what?"

"Are you going to stay?"

"It seems a bit ridiculous, having two women. Not evil or immoral, but conceited in a harmless sort of way."

"I'll have other men of course; if I want them."

"Why not?"

"I might leave you for someone who wanted me alone."

"There's a surprise."

"You'd better ring up the school then and tell them I'm sick. Then I'll claim some conjugal rights."

Chapter 21

Melissa Gibson looked at her collection of clothes. She had decided upon a dress or skirt rather than a pair of slacks. She wanted something simple, but attractive. She wanted to look ordinary as well as appealing. She finally picked a bright green skirt made of a heavy material and matched it with a fawn polo necked jersey. She laid them out on the bed and examined her body in the mirror, hands on hips. She had just had a bath and her body, warmed by the water looked an almost unhealthy pink.

Melissa shrugged. It wasn't her fault she hadn't been able to do much sunbathing in the latter part of the summer.

"Melissa!" Her mother's voice seemed to hang in the still afternoon air. Behind her mother's call Melissa could hear the howls of her son. He sounded like a chainsaw.

"What is it mum?"

"Mark's crying."

"There's a surprise," muttered Melissa quietly to herself.

"Well, change his nappies, or bung up his mouth with a bottle or SOMETHING!" Melissa shouted back.

"He's not dirty or wet and he doesn't want the bottle."

"Well, we're not mind readers. He'll just have to cry."

"He probably wants his mummy."

"Maybe he wants his daddy. Did you ever think of that?"

"Don't be like that Melissa."

"Oh, shut up and let me get dressed, mum. I'll be out in a minute."

Melissa got dressed and brushed her hair yet again. She was excited. She felt weak round the hips and her solar plexus was tight. Pleasure was about to return to her life for the first time in quite a while. As a child there were many things that had been exciting, but as you grew up pleasure fled as imperceptibly as autumn leaves from trees. Each time you looked at the trees they were a little barer until, finally, there was nothing. Men though, could bring back those pleasures; they could bring them back through love. Uniting with them made you whole again and the earth breathe again. But once you stopped loving you returned to the arid wilderness, a place of stones and sand, and you had to leave that man and find a new guide to lead you back to the nearest thing to Eden that there was. Melissa had never been promiscuous because sex with a man she didn't love left the world unchanged, so there was no point.

Melissa walked through into the lounge. The baby had stopped crying and was being nursed by her mother.

"I quietened him," said Mrs Gibson, looking pleased.

"Good for you, mum," said Melissa buckling up her watch.

"You look nice dear," said Mrs Gibson looking uncertainly at her daughter.

"Thanks mum."

"Why don't you tell me who you're going to see?"

"I can't. I'm sorry."

"I hope he has good intentions."

"Don't make me puke, mum."

"Well, we don't want another little Mark."

"Look, unless I've made a big mistake about what the world's like I won't ever be married, so get used to it."

"You'll find someone dear." Melissa opened her mouth, widened her eyes and looked towards the heavens. Then, without saying anything more she left the room.

She paused on the back step and lit a cigarette. She had thought she would smoke like a chimney once the child was born, but it was so long since she had smoked, she was unable to find much enthusiasm for it. She was only smoking five to ten cigarettes a day. She blew out her match and cast it beneath a rose bush. She looked at the smoke wiggling upwards from the end of her cigarette and wondered if the smoke made her milk taste funny to the baby.

A few fragments of leaf still hung on the silver birches. On the hills you could see the odd basket willow, looking like an orange fountain now it had lost its leaves. The weeping willows though, were still stubbornly resisting the change of season, even though some of their leaves were beginning to turn brown or yellow. Melissa followed the line of weeping willows up the creek with her eye. They looked limp and out of place amid bright green grass and black mud.

Melissa entered the garage and edged along the side of the car, stepping over old paint tins, half full cans of oil and boxes of nuts and bolts. She almost cut her ear on an old, rusty scythe that was hanging on the garage wall. She opened the car door and fell sideways onto the seat. She drew her legs up and shut the door.

She drove to Jim Wilsons along roads that were dry but no longer dusty. Alongside the roads the leaf clogged ditches occasionally flashed silver. The bare poplar trees pointed into the winter blue sky like the up-thrust hands of the dying. She drove through cuttings whose moss-grown faces glittered with water. The low sun battered the cold landscape with waves of light. The deep shadows of one range of hills fell darkly on the next. In the many little nooks of the valleys, where the sun had not penetrated, the grass was still pale and sparkling from the morning dew. The muddy waters of the dams reflected the trees and the sky. Bulls in muddy gateways gazed glumly across the landscape. Sheep, flung by an unseen hand, were scattered in small groups between the khaki slips on the hillsides. The dark brown of the manuka muted, a little, the heavy green of the early winter feed.

Driving through the pine plantation the water had formed strange globular patterns on the road, where it mixed with the oil that seeped from below the ground. It was very cold in there and, at the side of the road; the water lay in indentations left by the last mob of cattle that had walked along side it.

Once out of the plantation Melissa drove past two shooters wearing thick, tartan shirts. One was already across the fence in Max Tippet's property and the other one was handing two shotguns across the fence. Melissa passed their muddy car around the next bend. She stopped and wrote down the number of the car on a notebook that was in the glove box. She decided to ring Max Tippet later on and give him the number. Max was a fanatical opponent of hunting as well as being a collector of antiques and a demon actor in the local drama society. Those shooters didn't know what they had let themselves in for.

When Melissa was finally on the flats it struck her how dry everything was there. Decay there was brittle. Many of the maize fields had been harvested leaving only serried ranks of yellow stubble sticking out of the grey dirt. The slightly tatty houses seemed to merge into the landscape, even though smoke was seeping and curling from their chimneys. The kids were all wearing gumboots, sometimes their fathers. They stared at you with sullen curiosity as you passed by their houses.

The tar sealed road rocked backwards and forwards between the knolls. Melissa came up behind a tractor, a large, flat tray attached to the hydraulic system on the back. The man who was driving wore a battered and shapeless felt hat and pulled over without even turning around. Melissa tooted thanks as she drove past. The Jaguar moved effortlessly over the road, as though it floated on air rather than ran on wheels. Melissa flashed in and out of shadows on the dappled land.

She swerved across the road with no diminution of speed and the car seemed to move in one leap from the bottom of the drive to the top of it. It screeched to a halt, wheels locked, at the top of the drive. Melissa twisted the rear vision mirror of the car and checked her makeup. She looked uncertainly towards the back door. She hoped she had got the right house.

To her relief Jim Wilson opened the back door as she walked towards it. He was wearing tight, black corduroy pants and a navy-blue polo necked jersey. The sleeves of the jersey were pulled up to his elbows. She felt herself smiling as she walked towards him and she resisted the instructions of her legs, which told her to run. He opened the door wider. All his usual ruddiness had gone from his cheeks.

"Come inside quickly," he croaked. He stepped back from the door and some strange force swept her past him, along the short corridor and into the lounge.

Melissa stood in the lounge, blinking with confusion. Jim Wilson entered the door and stood just inside, his hands, one inside the other, held low in front of him. He just looked at her. She didn't seem real; she didn't make sense. He had thought about her flesh so often and now she had no flesh.

She looked at him and smiled awkwardly. She didn't know what to do either. She ached to be loved but the desire did not transmit itself to her flesh.

Jim Wilson began to open his mouth and stopped. He realised that talk, at this moment, would destroy everything. He didn't want to touch Melissa either, but it seemed less dangerous than talking. He walked towards her and stood in front of her waiting. She returned his look blankly. They stood there hoping that their feeling, the feeling they believed they had, would find a way out.

Nothing happened except that the pain that both felt grew stronger. Finally, the pain was too much for Jim Wilson and he pulled Melissa to him and bent over and nuzzled her hair in the hope that its scent would possess him. The scent was a disappointment.

He wanted to kiss more of her, but she was far too short to do that easily. He could feel her small arms hugging him tightly to her. He gently pushed her away and then took her by the hand. They walked through to his bedroom and they stood there beside his bed, both hands joined, smiling at each other. Then Melissa sat down on the bed, withdrew her hands, bent over and knocked off her shoes and lay, full length, on the bed. Jim Wilson knelt beside the bed and squeezed then kissed her feet. Then, out of the corner of his eye, he saw the picture of Christ on the wall. Christ looked so pure and saintly. Jim Wilson scrambled to his feet. He walked around the end of the bed and turned the painting to the wall.

"Why did you do that?" asked Melissa.

"The look on that face makes it impossible to love you. I'm sorry. Can I have a cigarette? That might drive it out of my mind."

"Of course. You can give me one too if you like." Jim Wilson stuck two cigarettes in his mouth and lit them.

They sat there without talking, without even looking at each other. Jim Wilson's head sunk towards the floor, and, for a time, he closed his eyes hoping to drive the memory of the picture away. Finally he stubbed out the butt of his cigarette and Melissa said:

"Pass me the ashtray please." Jim Wilson stood up, picked up the ashtray and held it over his bed while she ground out her cigarette. He put the ashtray back on the bedside table and looked at Melissa. She looked up at him and patted the bed beside her. He shook his head.

"Can we get undressed and get into bed?" Melissa looked at him blankly and then grinned.

"All right." Jim Wilson sat down on the bed; bent over, untied his shoelaces took off his shoes and then his socks. When he stood up and turned around Melissa was already getting into bed.

"Don't. Let me see you?" Melissa paused and, with a slightly embarrassed smile, stood up her hands dangling self-consciously by her sides. Father Wilson looked at her. She was very beautiful and her nakedness made her look so frail, even though she was far from thin. Her full hips and her swollen breasts were made to be worshipped. But it was her softness that was best. Her softness would protect him and calm him and heal him.

"You'd better get into bed before you get cold," he said. Father Wilson pulled his jersey and singlet off over his head and turned away from Melissa and took off his pants. Then he sat down on the edge of the bed drew his feet under the blanket and turned on his side to face Melissa. He only had to move an inch to touch her. Then he felt her flesh brush his and she was kissing him and her brown hair was falling across his face and becoming tangled in their lips and he pressed Melissa to him so that they might no longer be separate and he kissed the flesh that he revered and he drew the small, soft body beneath him and felt her slowly slip around his penis and he felt weak and he loved her, he knew he loved her and they strained together so that with and through their labour they might love one another. Their bodies were the paltry tools with which they loved. Jim Wilson shut his eyes and there was no room and no world, only Melissa and her small soft, moist body, her lips muttering somewhere down by his chin. He felt Melissa lift herself against him, making the sound of a wild beast, though quietly and there was a flicker like a mild shock at the base of his spine and his body became cat warm as the semen flowed out of him.

He opened his eyes and looked down at Melissa who smiled and kissed his chest.

"I love you," he said.

"I love you too," she said and kissed his chest again.

"My love doesn't feel any less than before, but the pain has gone."

"Yes," she said, kissing his chin. He rolled over pulling her with him so that she lay almost on top of him.

"There's peace," he said, "like I always imagined the peace of God. But God never brought peace like this."

"He's brought it now."

Jim Wilson was shocked into silence. She was right. This warm-faced happiness, in the purity of the early winter afternoon's light, was God's gift, just as everything was God's gift. He pulled Melissa tighter to him. She was beautiful and yet her beauty was not material. To describe it was impossible except to say that it was a warm celestial light.

"I think I'll pull back the curtain so that we can lie here and watch the world."

Jim Wilson walked heavily across the room and pushed the partly open curtains wide apart. He stood there, a shadow in a blaze of light, and then turned and walked back across the darkly varnished wood of the floor. Melissa looked at the fantail hovering under the eaves of the house where it was probably catching spiders. She felt the bed lurch as Jim got in. She reached out and rolled over on top of him and lay there, feeling safe under the sheets, this warm, hairy mountain of flesh beneath her. There was no need to act, just the need to lie there naked, touching him, watching the afternoon fade. There was no need to do anything exciting or thrilling, just the need to walk around the same secluded house as him. Even to sit opposite him, at the meal table, would be more significant than the most startling philosophical revelation. It seemed, lying there, that they had time, endless amounts of time even though Melissa knew that she would have to leave just as dusk was falling. Jim Wilson had confessions to hear and Melissa had a child to feed.

"I wish we could stay here forever," said Melissa, rubbing her head on Jim Wilson's chest.

"Yes, so do I."

"The world conspires to keep us apart just as it conspires to keep all lovers apart."

"Us more than most. You have a child and I am a priest. We can only expect to be hounded."

"I think I'll tell my parents. That'll make it a bit easier."

"Marriage is the only real way out though. That's the only way they will leave us alone."

"That's talking about the distant future Jim. Let's not let the future destroy what we have at this moment."

"I love you and I'll love you ......" He tried to say forever, but Melissa put her hand over his mouth.

"Don't tempt fate. Today is full of sweetness, but tomorrow we may hate one another."

"All right. I'll try not to think about the future."

"As long as we love one another there is today. Once we stop, there is neither today, nor tomorrow, nor yesterday." The priest turned away from her and buried his face in the pillow in anguish.

"Why do we have so little?" he asked. "Why are we so mean and impoverished?"

"How should I know? I'm not God."

Father Wilson turned on his back and sat up in bed. He didn't feel nice. Love had so many pitfalls. He wanted to cry out and hit his head against the wall. He looked down at Melissa, who looked back up at him and smiled.

"It's not that bad," she said.

"Kiss me and rescue me. Show me the face of love again." Melissa crawled up his chest and kissed him. and they slid down under the sheets into their world where it was warm and secret and he felt the sweetness of her sugar sticky body and the healing softness of her kisses and the need to plunge into the waiting void, the gap she had prepared for him within herself, so that his self would disappear and he wouldn't be separate from her any longer. He was floating in the sunny, thin aired heights of sexual exertion. He laboured, not for the end, but for the pleasure of the labour itself, which was a tender blessing from Melissa to him and from him to Melissa. Finally all else was excluded from their thoughts. They did not think of the tinkling of the lark or the thud of the spade striking the earth and when Jim Wilson had his orgasm both felt a joyful grief as they lay there still loving without having been successfully united.

They slipped off into a short sleep, merely half a step from their waking state. Jim Wilson woke first and leaned over and kissed Melissa's forehead and then lay very still as she rolled against him, almost awoke and then slipped back into sleep once again. A short time later her eyes suddenly opened. She smiled and said:

"What's the time?" Jim Wilson picked up his watch off the bedside table and looked at it.

"Quarter to four."

"Fuck! It's getting late."

"We don't have to get up yet, do we?"

"I wouldn't mind a bath."

"All right, but only if I can bathe you."

"I'd like that."

"We can't both bathe unfortunately. I can hardly fit in there on my own."

"You ought to get a shower."

"Yes, but it's a bit late now. I've got confession next week."

"I thought you had it tonight?"

"I mean I've got to confess next week."

"Why not lie. I'm sure a lot of people do. After all you're not really lying to God; only to another priest. You can repent to God and ask his forgiveness privately."

"God can only absolve me through an intermediary."

"I see."

"I'll have to resign. My life may not be completely devoted to God anymore, but he still deserves respect."

"Come on and bathe me."

"I'll just get another cigarette. It must be years since I went this long without a cigarette."

The priest bathed Melissa and, after she was dressed, brushed her hair. She, of course, had to re-brush it since he knew little about the finer points of doing a woman's hair. Then they sat in the kitchen and Father Wilson began making a cup of tea. Melissa sat at the table smoking one of her filtered cigarettes while Jim Wilson sat opposite smoking one of his "lung busters." They held hands across the table as they waited for the electric jug to boil.

"I'd offer you a whisky if you were going to stay the evening," said Jim Wilson. Melissa looked up from the table. Her eyes seemed hard and expressionless. "Don't look like that."

"Look like what?" she asked and laughed.

"As though you don't love me."

"I love you even when I don't look like I do," said Melissa looking out the window at the blue sky, which was losing its white glare and returning to its natural colour. Jim Wilson sighed and pushed his head forward to his cigarette and drew in a mouthful of smoke.

"What will you do when you stop being a priest?"

"Become an alcoholic." Melissa laughed.

"Seriously?"

"What can I do? I've always been a priest."

"Can you teach?"

No. Anyway, I only believe in two things, you and God. I could never come to believe in anything else."

"There must be something you could do."

"I wouldn't mind being a gardener, but I don't know anything about flowers."

"I'm sorry Jim. Would you like me to leave Gisborne and go back to Wellington? I can do that."

"There's no need to do that. It's funny though that we can sacrifice our love for the benefit of the person we love."

"That's a paradox, isn't it?"

"Yes, I suppose it is."

Jim Wilson heaved himself out of his chair and walked over to the now boiling kettle. The water slopped and pinged into the shiny teapot. He pushed the lid on the teapot and bore it to the table.

"We'll have silence, shall we?" said Melissa.

"Yes, silence. And cigarettes of course." Jim Wilson leaned over the cups and poured the tea.

""I've smoked so much today. I'm getting a sore throat."

"All trainee nicotine addicts do."

"I think I might give up."

"What for?"

"I don't enjoy it anymore. I smoke because I feel as though it ought to be a source of pleasure, but it isn't."

Then it was nearly dark and they stood out by the car in the clammy cold where sand flies whirled in a bobbing cloud. Their grief was as heavy as the cold air. Their sorrow at parting was suffused with rage towards the circumstances that caused them to part.

"When will you stay the night with me?" asked Jim Wilson.

"Tomorrow?"

"Yes, that's all right. My housekeeper comes on Thursday morning though. I'll have to put her off."

"Does that matter?"

"No. I'd better come and pick you up though. It's better not to have a strange car in the drive all night."

Jim Wilson lit another cigarette and looked at the ground. There was nothing more to say, absolutely nothing to say. Profound feelings did not give rise to eloquence but to a distrust of eloquence. He looked at the sky above the squat hill on which they stood. The sky was crimson, but lined with horizontal bars of black cloud. Across the flats the lights shone feebly in the semi darkness.

"It's a red sky," said Melissa. "Must be going to be fine tomorrow."

"Does it matter?"

"No."

Melissa got into the car and wound down the window.

"I'd better not kiss you goodbye, someone might see us," she said.

Yes, I suppose you're right. I love you."

"I love you too," said Melissa, reaching out and squeezing his hand.

"Go now!" said Jim Wilson, his voice suddenly harsh. "I'll go inside. I'll pick you up at five o'clock tomorrow."

Jim Wilson walked towards the house, his head back, drawing in gulps of cold air to keep back his tears. The sky was light but the land had disappeared. He heard the car start as he reached his doorstep. He quickly stepped in and shut the door leaning back against the door so that the noise of the departing car could not be heard. His shadow appeared on the glass door as Melissa turned on the headlights. He froze where he was until the headlights no longer surrounded him. Then he turned quickly and saw the ray of the headlights curving away and downwards. Then the car and Melissa were gone. There was only darkness.

One hour later Jim Wilson walked out the back door. He was on his way to hear the confessions of others.

Chapter 22

The first suspicion that Father Wilson had that he had become one of the flock rather than the shepherd came on the next evening when he picked Melissa up from her home. It had been a persistently windy day. The long trailers of the weeping willows had swum in the wind and the loose, light debris from the harvested maize fields was hurled up against the blue sky. The unharvested maize made a scratching noise in the wind and the soot black maize flowers bobbed. The last leaves of the oaks, the brown ones (the red leaves had already gone) were pushed at a sunbeam slant to earth. The smoke from the chimneys lay down flat.

Driving to Melissa's the dams were all ruffled and the surging manukas made the hills look alive. The sun sat on the edge of the hills firing his blinding rays with the impudence of a muddy faced boy with a slug gun. Jim Wilson had almost hit a harrier hawk that he had come on just around a bend in the road. The priest had braked and run his front wheel into the papa shiny water table while the hawk rose with mechanical clumsiness into the air, wheeling away to hang, buffeted, over the rush bottomed, willow strewn valley. Jim Wilson got out of the car and bounced it away from the bank. There was a long scratch on the side of the car between the headlight and the front wheel. Jim had the dusty, musty taste of fern stalks in his mouth and had to pause to pick a piece of fern stalk out of his eye. He backed the car onto the road and drove on.

Going across Gibson's wooden swing bridge he looked down at the fat bellied, brown pool and the grey facetted water of the rapids below. The grassy banks of the stream were covered with grey silt, the grass barely peeping through. The lower branches of the streamside willows wore garlands of debris where the water during the last flood had reached its highest point.

The car bounced on across the flats, the magpies carolling and the sheep nibbling the grass with unabated haste. The barks of the dogs were jumbled with the hiss and roar of the big trees.

Jim Wilson stopped in front of Dave Gibson's empty garage. The blinds in the house were all down. Father Wilson felt nervous. He hoped that Melissa had told her parents about their relationship. The gate shrieked above the wind as he opened it. The wind slithered between the brittle, black spikes of the silver birches. The stiff backs of the roses were bent in the unrelenting wind, their bushy tops acting like sails. Many rose petals lay on the black earth and the dry, grey, concrete path. The coats at Gibson's back door looked sinister moving above the empty boots and shoes.

Father Wilson stood on the back step and knocked on the door. There was no sound, except for the hoot of the wind from around the house. Jim Wilson nervously scraped his feet on the rubber doormat, slowly one foot, then slowly the other. He knocked again. There was a faint click and the door opened with sinister readiness.

"Come in Mr Wilson," said Mrs Gibson from half behind the fully opened door. Jim Wilson walked blithely into the kitchen and Mrs Gibson shut the door behind him and leaned on it. Jim Wilson lifted the lid of a big pot and a cloud of steam billowed out.

"It smells good!" said Father Wilson putting the lid back on.

"Oh yes," said Mrs Gibson wiping her hands on her apron and stepping way from the door.

"Where's Melissa?"

"Primping I suppose."

""You sound as though you don't approve."

"Does it matter? I'm only her mother."

""Poor thing," said Father Wilson before he knew what he was saying. Mrs Gibson went back to rolling her pastry, silently, purposefully and a little viciously. "I'm sorry, Mrs Gibson."

"Oh, that's all right."

"But it's not, is it?" said Father Wilson slapping his pockets and finding he had no cigarettes on him.

"Why Melissa?"

"I don't know. It was an accident."

"She's already had one baby." Mrs Gibson faintly smiled as she thought of the child. "She can't go on having them."

"A lot of women do. Anyway, I'll marry her."

"She mightn't want to get married."

"She loves me."

"She doesn't believe that love lasts forever."

"I think ours will. I wouldn't be throwing away the priesthood for a petty infatuation."

"Unfortunately, that doesn't mean it will last forever."

"Don't be ridiculous!"

"As you like." Mrs Gibson trimmed off the overlap on the top of the apple pie and turned the trimmings into a crimped edge. She put a slit in the top of the pie and put it in the oven.

Mrs Gibson straightened up and began to wipe down the bench.

"Why did you let the little bit seduce you?" she asked with sudden venom.

"What? What did you say?"

"Men ought to know better."

"Know better? Why should we know better?"

"Women are emotional, they can't help themselves. Men can."

"Why can they?"

"Because they only feel lust and aren't emotional like women."

"You mean your husband has no emotions?"

"Of course not! But he has no emotions in that way."

Father Wilson lifted his hands in the air and let them fall back, helplessly, by his sides. What a terrible, Spartan world the woman must live in he thought, walking around and around the room. He could smell the rich smell of the pastry beginning to cook and the thick, peppery smell of the bubbling steak and kidney. It made him feel safe and warm.

Melissa poked her head through the kitchen door.

"Hi Jim. Want to come and see Mark?" Jim was taken aback. He had no feeling for the child. In fact, thinking of the child diminished his feeling for Melissa.

"Go on Jim." He felt Mrs Gibson pushing him lightly in the back. "Go and see the wee fellow."

"All right," he shrugged. Melissa took his hand. They walked through to the lounge, turned and looked to see if Mrs Gibson was following them and then kissed passionately, Jim lifting Melissa off her feet. Finally, Jim lowered Melissa back to the floor. She took one of his hands and squeezed it.

"I do love you, Jim," she said and squeezed his hand again.

They walked down the dark corridor and into Melissa's room. The bedroom looked very cluttered with the cot in it. The child was lying asleep with its mouth open. It looked small, vulnerable and pink, though pinkness was its primary quality. It seemed the embodiment of cleanliness. It was cute, huggable and apparently happy. Yet there was something odd about the creature. It seemed almost like a little machine designed to take in matter at one end and expel it, transmuted, at the other.

"Do you like him?"

"He seems not to matter. I'm sorry. I love you."

"He matters and he seems very serious to me. In a sense he's my life's work."

"Doesn't he detract from your love for me?"

"Not as long as I keep the two of you separate."

"Don't you want to be with me all the time?"

"I do. But once you have a child, at least a very young one, you can't be a one hundred percent lover, unless of course your lover is the father of the child."

"He will always be between us, won't he?" He looked at Melissa. She nodded.

"Yes - always - a little."

Father Wilson looked down at the child, its fine, warm little lips wide apart, its nostrils absurdly small. He felt a sudden wave of hatred towards the child. He wanted all Melissa's love and was not willing to share it with anyone. If the child had been his it would have been different. He would have been their creation, a monument and testimony to their love. But, at that moment, he wanted the baby dead. For the first time in his life his mouth went into a crooked smile, the sort of smile that could be seen, from time to time, on the face of Milton Harper.

Father Wilson sat down on Melissa's bed and took her packet of cigarettes off her bedside table and lit one.

"Given up yet?" he asked.

"No." She sat down on the bed beside him.

"I'd like to make love to you in your room. Being in your room makes me feel that I know you better. In a sense I love your room as I love you." Melissa put her arms around Jim Wilson and hugged him tightly.

"Come on. It's time to take me away to your dark castle."

"You make it sound as though it's a den of iniquity."

"Every woman likes to think there is something a little evil about her love."

"Really?"

"Yes. Don't you think like that?"

"Of course not. I think of love as only innocent."

"Come on. Let's go."

As Jim Wilson drove Melissa back to his house under the blue sky with the orange afterglow of the sun behind the black plasticene textured hills and the paspalum beside the road bending before the wind he asked her about where her father had disappeared to.

"He went out," said Melissa looking in her bag for her matches.

"Why?"

"I don't know." Jim Wilson looked at Melissa. She was searching too deliberately for her matches. Even in the dim, dusk light Jim could see she was lying.

"He was trying to avoid me," said the priest.

"He's very violent." She lit her cigarette.

"Why's he hostile to me?"

"He doesn't hold anything against you personally, but you've got to get married and perpetuate your line."

"Perhaps I ought to ask him for a job when I resign from my parish?"

"Don't Jim. I'd lose all my respect for you if you became one of father's creatures."

"And he'll hate me if I don't?"

""That's right," said Melissa, blowing out a cloud of smoke.

That night Melissa and Jim Wilson forgot about the world. They ate tea surrounded by air thickened by their love. They drank whisky, smoked cigarettes, made love and finally fell asleep in a stupefied heap. Periodically during the night one or the other would wake, seek out and kiss the other and fall back asleep, their bodies pressed together.

Chapter 23

The day came around when Father Wilson had to go into town to confession. He normally went to confession and had afternoon tea with his confessor. It was a civilised and enjoyable afternoon. This time though the fat would be in the fire and he would have to put himself in a public position.

Father Wilson stood in the cold shadow on the front steps of the church watching cars drive along the road, sunlight flashing on their windows and roofs. The bare, dappled trunked plane trees looked like trolls sitting in the wide road with their stubby branches. An elderly man in a grey suit and a grey felt hat stood in the line of plane trees supporting his wife by the elbow. The wife wore a long black coat, a little grey hat and had her grey hair in a plaited bun. Finally they made their move across the other half of the road, the woman tilting on one leg and swinging the other leg in a stiff arc. Two short haired young men wearing jerseys and ties strolled airily past the priest exploring and embellishing some incident they had both observed.

Father Wilson turned and went into the even deeper shade of the church itself. He walked past the collection of pamphlets in the vestibule and stopped in the entrance proper and crossed himself with holy water. The church was silent and clean smelling. Father Wilson walked up the aisle past the stained-glass windows, brilliantly illuminated by the white winter sunlight.

There was a cough and Father Wilson noticed a man on the far side of the church praying. He was kneeling, head bowed, holding his forehead with thumb and forefinger while holding a grimy looking white handkerchief to his mouth with the other hand.

Father Wilson dipped his knee in the direction of the altar, entered the pew and, taking out his rosary beads, crossed himself and started the rosary. The light that poured in the three stained glass windows above the altar lay on the carpet at the foot of the altar like sunlight on a forest floor. In here there was a thick, booming, high roofed stillness. The cars outside sounded very far away. Father Wilson self-consciously shifted his knees and went on praying. Here, in the silence, you really felt that someone was watching you.

There was a faint clatter on the other side of the church and Father Wilson saw his companion tip toeing back up the aisle toward the door. He was all alone now in this reverential emptiness. This was the void, but the void was filled by God, frightening yet reassuring, dark yet pierced by light, still but with a stillness that was musical.

Father Wilson began to say his rosary again rolling the beads in his fingers as he said the prayers. He felt filled by God's love, able to repent without feeling humiliation. That was one thing no one could take away from religion, its beauty. He was even free from Melissa, just for a moment. Here, in fact, was a completeness he had never achieved with Melissa.

Perhaps, he thought, I ought to renounce her and devote more time to prayer. Perhaps I have taken too intellectual an approach to

God. Perhaps, instead of experiencing God, I have simply used him to explain experience.

Still, I can be committed to both Melissa and God, though not as a priest. Perhaps this experience of love has opened my mind to the experience of God. Yet they are so different. God is peace, honour and clarity of vision. Melissa is tumult, anguish and confusion, mingled with tenderness and joy. Melissa offers fulfilment through the world; God only fulfilment in it.

I think that perhaps I mistook my vocation. After all, who at school told us we ought to do what we wanted to do. If we were bright, we were obviously going to be priests or scholars. It never occurred to anyone that an intelligent man might find fulfilment as a street sweeper. Even now I don't know what I want. Do I want the tranquillity of God, the sort of quiet peace that surrounds me now; or do I want to be expanded into the state of glimmering significance that can be brought about by a loved woman? She promises me peace through life; God promises peace away from life. Melissa promises satisfaction through turmoil and violence. Prayer promises satisfaction without turmoil.

Father Wilson looked up. The light above the entrance to the confessional was on. God's business, it appeared, could not wait until God was understood. Jim Wilson got up slowly. His knees clicked as he stood up. He bobbed rather than walked towards the confessional. Then he was in a little cupboard, like a child playing hide and seek; small, confined and trembling. Silver light was seeping through the grill and he could make out a vague silhouette. "Bless me father for I have sinned."

The confession took its normal course. Father Wilson recited his normal sins, swearing, drunkenness and a few other errors, mostly of the venial variety. Then there was a pause. He could not bring himself to say what he had to say next. It didn't seem like a sin. The act itself was insignificant. It was the implication of the act that was important, not the act itself. Even though all their life was summoned into the act it still didn't seem important. It certainly seemed anything but sinful.

Finally he said it. There was a little shuffling on the other side of the confessional. The confessor told him that it was a serious sin and that he must repent and try not to repeat the act. Father Wilson said simply:

"I sincerely regret offending God." He was given a large penance, he and the confessor prayed together and Jim Wilson left the confessional, crossing himself with holy water as he went.

When Father Wilson finished his penance he stood in the sun, blinking at the brightness of God's world. It was as though the world itself had been renewed while he had been in the church. He felt sad without feeling depressed. It was the end of part of his life and anything was hard to give up, especially this about which he had no regrets. He put his hand on the breast pocket of his coat and heard the envelope crackle. He lit a cigarette. The blue air above the two storied buildings was blurred with light. Away to his right, the cars on the main road flashed past the street entrance. There was always something slightly festive about this town because so many of the shoppers were country people in town for a day's shopping and relaxation.

Jim Wilson stepped out of the shadow of the church and walked around to the large building where the town priests lived. The garden behind the big hedge was wet and shady and full of foraging thrushes and blackbirds. The black earth in the flower beds was sprinkled with dead leaves. The sunlight was a sickly yellow on the green lawn. Father Mulligan was reclining in a bright, yellow deck chair against the funny little ramshackle garden shed. He was smoking his pipe. He was young and slim, though well built. He appeared rather homely in spite of this. He simply sat there absorbed in his smoking as Jim cut across the lawn towards him. When Jim reached him, Father Mulligan shaded his eyes and looked up smiling.

"Good day, Jim. How are things?"

"Not too bad."

"Zip over and grab a chair from by the door. I've got Mrs Jarvis to bring tea out here today."

It was quiet sitting beside Tim Mulligan. Father Mulligan emerged from his reverie to take a quick glance at Jim Wilson's chair. The chair seemed under strain, but it would probably survive. Father Mulligan leaned forward and knocked out the contents of his pipe on the concrete path. Mrs Jarvis came waddling across the lawn with the tea on a tray with legs. She put it down, then lost her balance and almost fell on top of the tray. She stood there resting one hand on the tray-table puffing slightly.

"This is the last time I'm doing this, Father Mulligan."

"It's good for you, Mrs Jarvis. Keeps you fit."

"I'm too old to be fit."

"Nonsense, you're just due for your second wind. In a couple of years, you'll be running five miles before breakfast."

"The only way I'll be running five miles before breakfast in a couple of years' time is inside the stomach of a worm, Father Mulligan."

"What makes you think the worms would be interested in a tetchy old lady like you, Mrs Jarvis?"

"Oof! You are rude!" exclaimed Mrs Jarvis and she waddled back across the lawn, pleased to be insulted by someone she admired.

"Black, two sugars?" asked Father Mulligan pouring the tea.

"Yes." Father Mulligan sugared and stirred Jim Wilson's tea and handed it to him. Jim Wilson flicked his cigarette butt onto the lawn and watched it smoulder.

"Why don't you give up those dirty things? They'll kill you."

"A pipe doesn't hit you like a cigarette." Jim Wilson took a sip of his tea. Father Mulligan settled back in his chair with his cup of tea.

"What are you going to do with this girlfriend of yours?" he asked

Jim Wilson, looking over the rim of his tea cup. Jim Wilson tapped his pocket with his forefinger.

"My resignation."

"That's a bit rash. Why not hang on a bit? You might get tired of her."

"I'll chance it. Besides, I can't carry out my duties in a state of sin."

"Why not? No one can be blamed for your sin, other than you." Father Wilson shrugged and watched a blackbird fly off with a beak full of wet straw. A crowd of sparrows was rolling a piece of bread around on the far side of the lawn. Cars hummed by out on the road.

"You don't understand, Tim. I love her."

"Huh, huh."

"That doesn't mean anything to you?"

"Not really. It's why most people get married, isn't it?" said Father Mulligan grinning. Jim Wilson laughed. He was a talented young man, Tim Mulligan. "Tell me about love. Enlighten a stranger to paradise."

"There's no point in telling you. It wouldn't make sense unless you've experienced it."

"Mmm," said Father Mulligan caressing the tip of his nose. He put his cup down on the smooth, grey concrete and relit his pipe. "You're just the same as the schoolgirls who confess to having sex. They all say, 'But I love him' ". He said the last piece of direct speech in a high pitched, breathless voice.

"I'm not a complete stranger to the confessional myself Tim."

"It can't be a very exulted emotion if so many people experience it." He blew out his match

"Perhaps all men are exulted, remarkable?"

"Rubbish! Men are vulgar, petty, stupid and ordinary."

"You're a snob and an elitist Tim. I know a lot of people with half your brains that live a richer life than you do."

"How come they can't tell me about it?"

"They can't. They lack the linguistic subtlety. That doesn't mean it isn't there."

"I've got to give them the benefit of the doubt, do I?"

"You're full of hatred, Tim. You're a very unhappy man. You know that other people live more fully than you and that is why you are scornful of them."

"Nonsense, Jim. I don't envy you your love."

"I know. You hate me for it." They sat there, in silence now, each trying to hide in their own world to escape the animosity between them. Finally, Father Mulligan looked across at Jim Wilson.

"I accept your criticism."

"Perhaps I was too harsh."

"No. I'll never be a good priest. I just do the best I can."

"You've got a good brain."

"But my personality prevents it from functioning properly, at least in this context. I'm doomed to be a second-rate priest."

"You could resign."

"Why? I believe in God and I'm not in any danger of loving anyone."

"Do you still coach rugby?"

"Naturally. I've got some good kids this year. They'll win the competition."

"I hope they do."

"Would you like a game of chess before you go?" asked Father Mulligan, reaching under his chair and taking out a portable chess set in a cardboard box. Each square on the board had a hole in it and each chess piece had a peg on the bottom so that it could be fitted into a hole.

Jim Wilson lit another cigarette and they played. He was thoroughly beaten. With each move his position got worse without him being able to determine exactly why and each of his moves he knew was only a postponement of his eventual defeat. Finally, he resigned, with an inevitable checkmate two moves away.

"I don't know why you don't join a club. I ought to have more sense than to play you," said Jim Wilson shaking his head.

"Oh, I'm good all right," said Father Mulligan, "but not quite brilliant. That's one of the reasons I'm so resentful of life. I've been almost brilliant at almost everything, but I've never quite been the best at anything."

"Being the best doesn't matter."

"It does to me. My parents always told me I had to be the best. I see now it's silly, but it's too late. The need to be the best is part of me and there's nothing I can do to change it. So, I don't enjoy any of my talents, because I'm not the best."

"Oh well. I suppose we'd all like to change things about ourselves."

"Tough, isn't it?" said Father Mulligan grinning.

"You might as well send this off for me," said Father Wilson handing him the letter of resignation.

"Are you sure this is the right thing to do?"

"Positive."

Chapter 24

Father Wilson entered the airport building and went into the cafeteria. The air was thick, hot and dry as a result of the winter heating and the sun shining through the glass windows. Father Wilson took off his overcoat and hung it on the back of a chair. He sat down and looked at the wooden counter. The counter was covered with plates. Also on top of it was a display case half full of cakes and a warming cabinet with a glass door, which contained a solitary meat pie. Behind the counter were shelves containing cigarettes, chocolates and packets of sweets. Above the shelves was a menu offering items such as "Pie and Veg" and "Lamb Stew with Mashed Potatoes." Jim Wilson could hear noisy chatter and the clash of crockery coming through the door from the back room.

A woman approached the counter and stood waiting for someone to come and serve her. She had a child in a canvas stroller and she pushed and pulled him backwards and forwards as she waited to be served. Finally, a scruffy looking, middle-aged woman in a dark green smock, came out of the back. The woman stood there with her left hand on her hip, as though she was daring the woman with the stroller to complain about the service. Instead, the woman with the stroller purchased a Milky Bar and wheeled the child away to the far corner of the lounge.

As the woman in the green smock began to exit a suited and waist-coated businessman approached the counter. The woman in the smock spun around and walked, beaming, back to the counter. "Another cup of coffee please, May," said the businessman.

"Certainly, Mr Harris," said the woman in the smock. She smiled broadly and dribbled some coffee out of an urn into the businessman's cup.

"I see the plane's late again," said the businessman, taking his cup back off the woman.

"Bloody National government! They take the trains off us and now they want to take the planes off us as well. They must want us to swim to and from Wellington. One thing's for sure, if I've got to swim to the polling booth to vote them out next time I certainly will."

"Give them time, May."

"If I give them too much time, I'll be so weak from starvation I won't have the strength to get out and vote."

"We've all got to tighten our belts."

"I reckon you ought to shed your waistcoat before I tighten my belt."

"I only wear these clothes because businessmen need a certain amount of decorum, not because I like wearing them."

"I don't know about that. If you conducted business in the nick the cold'd probably make you work faster."

"You're incorrigible, May."

"Yeah, and your words are too long. You use them because you think that makes you a cut above the rest of us."

"Balderdash!"

"Why not say bullshit? I've heard the word before, you know." She turned her back on him and walked away back out to the kitchen. The businessman shook his head, smiled and walked away from the counter.

Jim Wilson sat there rubbing his thumb and forefinger on a twenty-cent coin, wondering if he had enough stamina to stand long enough at the counter to get served. There was a neigh of laughter out in the kitchen and Father Wilson returned the coin to his pocket and lit a cigarette. He looked out the window towards the runway again. Immediately outside the glass were three small children and a farmer. The farmer had the rim of his green, felt hat turned down at the front. His trouser cuffs were wrinkled where they were caught on the top of his slip-on boots. The farmer, noticing that one of the children had wandered off, turned and shouted at the little child to come back. The little boy, who had very white hair and was wearing long, loose, pants and gumboots came stumbling back to his father. Father Wilson picked up his own short-brimmed, black, felt hat and began fiddling with the brim, thinking of emulating the farmer.

A couple more families entered the lounge through the door from the car park. Jim Wilson realised that they must have anticipated the plane being late. A little girl, in one of those little-girl short dresses, was pulling at the hand of her tartan-skirted, twin-setted mother, who had not a hair out of place and a flawless layer of makeup.

"Can I have a sweetie, Mummy?" Her mother did her best to ignore her. The little girl rose on her tip toes. "Can I have a sweetie mummy?"

"Shh," said her mother putting her finger to her lips and scowling with just her eyebrows.

"Can I have a sweetie mummy," whispered the little girl.

"No, they're bad for your teeth," said the mother a little too loudly. She looked quickly around to see if anyone had noticed her embarrassing loss of temper. She caught Jim Wilson's eye, smiled guiltily and looked quickly away.

"I'll wash my teeth as soon as I get home," the little girl offered in a tone of tragic resignation. Her mother bent over her and said in a half whisper:

"If you're a good girl until nanny arrives, I'll buy you an ice-cream on the way home. Is that all right?"

"Oh, yes," said the little girl, giving a restrained jump of joy. The mother pulled the little girl's head against her hip and smiled affectionately to herself. Then she looked suddenly at Jim Wilson.

"She's terribly spoilt I'm afraid." Jim Wilson went red with embarrassment.

"I'm sure it doesn't matter," he managed to mutter.

"I hope not. Are you waiting for someone?"

"Yes."

"Jenny's waiting for her nanny, aren't you Jenny?"

"Yes," said the little girl dropping her chin on her chest and letting her head roll around.

"Don't be shy darling. The reverend won't hurt you."

"I'm a priest, not a reverend," said Jim Wilson grimacing.

"Oh, I'm sorry. I'm not religious you see. My husband doesn't go, so I don't go." Jim Wilson smiled broadly because he couldn't say it didn't matter and he certainly wasn't going to give her a lecture on the benefits of religion. He left that sort of thing to laymen.

Jim Wilson looked desperately out the window and then sighed with relief. There, on the seaward side of the runway, wafting gently to earth was a shiny plane. It jolted gently as its wheels touched the ground and then ran smoothly along the runway, its tail clear of the brown hillocks in the background, but moving against the blue of the sky.

There was an announcement over the loudspeaker, even though the man at the desk just across the foyer from the cafeteria could have communicated the obvious simply by raising his voice.

Everyone was drawn into the doorway which led to the tarmac like water into an empty plug hole. As the crowd drew in around him Jim Wilson shivered. He hated to be in physical proximity to so many people.

Once through the door the crowd spread out as everyone waited to pounce on their friends, family or business associates. The service crew all had their ear muffs on now. There were two tractors on the tarmac, one with a trailer to carry baggage and one with a thing that Father Wilson assumed was a battery charger. The plane reached the end of the runway and turned around. It taxied back along the runway and then swung in a slow arc on to the path that led to the airport building. It got slowly larger as it approached the terminal. The whistle of the turbo-prop engines became louder and more piercing. Jim Wilson could see two pilots sitting in the cabin of the aircraft. The plane swung side on to the terminal. Jim Wilson felt like shouting, to drown out the noise of the plane. An overalled man with ear muffs and waving coloured disks was walking backward in front of the plane, guiding it into position. He dropped his hands. The plane's engines stopped. Two men in overalls put blocks around the plane's wheels. The two tractors lurched forward towards the plane. Two more ground crew wheeled the steps into position and the door of the plane opened. A pink uniformed air hostess stepped smilingly out and stood to one side, grinning and nodding her head as the passengers disembarked.

Jim Wilson watched them come out of the door one by one. Then a diminutive little man with a black beard and dressed exactly the same as Jim Wilson, save that he wore a bowler hat, bounced out of the plane, made a joke to the hostess, or seemed to, came down the steps in a series of jumps and came across the tarmac at breakneck speed. Jim Wilson tilted his hat back and scratched his head. The little man saw him and waved cheerily, altering slightly the direction of his wild charge. Jim Wilson rearranged his hat on his head and stuck out his hand, thinking that the little man would need to arrest his headlong rush somehow. The little man's eyes suddenly turned into two pools of water, then back to eyes again. He was wearing rimless glasses. He grabbed Jim Wilson by the hand.

"Father Wilson, I presume?"

"Not Doctor Livingstone anyway."

"I'm Father Swift."

"I'm not surprised."

"What's that? Oh, yes. Rather prophetic, wasn't it?"

"I take it you've got some baggage to collect?"

"Yes, where should I go?" All these jerky, rather abbreviated sentences were uttered in the deepest of base voices. Jim Wilson couldn't help grinning with amusement. It seemed to him that this man ought to be a scientist in a castle that he was slowly reducing to rubble with his ill-conceived experiments.

As they walked out the door of the terminal building Father Swift drew a churchwarden pipe from his pocket in much the same way as you might pull a fly rod from its cover. They paused facing the parked cars and the city while Father Swift, arms at full length, lit his pipe. Jim Wilson stood there waiting to see if any smoke came out of his ears, or perhaps his socks.

"Don't you find a pipe that long a bit inconvenient?" Jim Wilson finally asked.

"Yes, but it's cool, a connoisseur's pipe."

"Really?"

"You know, it's a scandal. You're not allowed to smoke a pipe on those planes. You'd think that they could produce a plane that you could smoke a pipe on wouldn't you? The aircraft designers probably all have shares in the cigarette companies."

"So does the church probably."

"My dear Father Wilson the church probably has shares in hospitals performing abortions. The pope is father to so much money he doesn't know what it's all doing."

An airport assistant wheeled the white NAC trailer out of the goods' shed and people started pulling their bags free from the confusion of baggage.

"Which one's yours?" asked Father Wilson.

"Oh, I'll get it," said Father Swift, swinging round towards the baggage trailer and almost decapitating a passing woman with his churchwarden. "Hold my pipe, will you?" he said thrusting the pipe at Jim Wilson. He rushed at the trailer, grabbed a large, leather suitcase with both hands, rather like a pre-adolescent Davey Crocket wrestling with a bear and, lifting it aloft, staggered back towards Jim Wilson.

"Are you sure you wouldn't like me to carry it?"

"No, no. I'm alright."

Father Wilson walked just ahead of the panting Father Swift along the row of cars between the terminal building and the control tower. Some of the cars were backing out and driving away smoothly and quickly out the airport gate, their exhaust fumes trailing behind them. Periodically Father Wilson would look back to check if the little man was still there.

They reached the car, Jim Wilson opened the boot and Father Swift hurled the suitcase into the boot rather like a wrestler might throw an opponent out of the ring. He stood there panting, hands on hips, looking pityingly at the suitcase.

"I'm a silly man. Every time I go somewhere for a day I take enough clothes for a month. Just as well I've never been away for a month." Father Swift put his left ankle on his right knee and knocked out his pipe on the sole of his boot. Then he joined Jim Wilson in the car.

Jim Wilson began to drive home while Father Swift re-filled his pipe. Then he lit it and held out the match while Jim Wilson lit his cigarette.

"Well, Jim, what's it like living in this idyllic rural setting?"

"I like it," said Jim Wilson overtaking a car as they left the thirty miles per hour limit and passed the smooth, green undulations of the city golf course. "That's our school over there," said Jim Wilson, indicating with his head the Catholic secondary school on the other side of the road. Father Swift half turned in his seat and sniffed.

"Looks like a lot of toilets built to resemble spaceships," he said looking back to the front. "That's a nice old cemetery in there though," he said, pointing with the stem of his pipe. "Grassy, overgrown, but dignified."

"You like old things?"

"People were more certain of their tastes then for some reason. Now people don't know what they're doing anymore and most of what we make is a mess."

"Perhaps you ought to come and take my place. The past has managed to survive here, living rather than preserved."

"Please, please," said Father Swift, "let's not start just yet. What are you; a barbarian or a masochist?"

"I'm sorry, but I see no point in avoiding the issue."

"No one's avoiding the issue, just postponing it. You're like all modern men, no sense of time or place. You've got to take your time, make things pleasant and be comfortable. That's why I smoke a pipe. A pipe is comfortable."

"What would you like to discuss then, rugby?"

"Rugby? A heathen game. Only fit for Angles and Saxons and Jutes."

"Name a topic."

"Don't be so vulgar Father Wilson. Don't you have some refined interests like hunting, or walking or riding?"

"No, I don't do any of those things."

"Yes, it's such a pity they're so expensive, unless you actually live on the land. I do hope you have a fireplace?"

"I'm afraid not."

"When was your house built?"

"About 1960 I think."

"Yes, that boor, Father Günter. Fortunately, the Lord put him out of harm's way before he could build too many houses."

Father Swift was put in the spare bedroom. The house was close and cool and smelled of cigarette smoke, the sweetness of decaying apple cores, cauliflower leaves and cooking oil. Father Swift walked into the lounge rubbing his hands.

"Would you like a cup of tea?" asked Jim Wilson who was standing at the window in the sunlight watching hordes of sparrows feasting in the newly harvested maize fields. Autumn and early winter were certainly the best seasons for the birds.

"Tea? Never touch the stuff. I think I'll bathe and then you can pour me a whisky and water. You do have whisky I presume."

""Yes I, do."

"Very good."

Father Wilson sat in a wicker armchair with steel legs, right up against his French windows so he could catch the last of the sun before it got too far to the west to enter his lounge. He could hear the crackle of the running bathwater and clouds of steam were swirling threateningly around the doorway to the lounge. Then he heard Father Swift break into a rendition of "Singing in the Rain."

Father Wilson looked at the remains of last summer's growth in his garden. It was brittle and black. The shadows of the hills and trees were already long and cold. Shadows at this time of year took on the solidity of rock. A solid carpet of winter grass choked the soil. The leafless trees somehow reminded him of coughs made matter. Everything was collapsing towards the earth, until that moment of ultimate lowness, out of which spring would come and everything would leap away from the cold, entombing earth towards the sun, only to be betrayed again and pulled back into the black soil.

Nature goes nowhere in the end and my love, which is the child of nature, will probably go nowhere too. It will grow up and slowly perish, retreating back into the black soil of consciousness. It will lie there dormant until, inevitably, it will sprout another love. That is what Melissa thinks in any case. That is the faith by which she lives; no, not the faith, but the truth.

But I am the man who wants to freeze something in high summer, using the man made institution of marriage. I cannot accept nature and I look to God to overcome nature's mutability and give eternal happiness. But there is no "eternal" in the world, as Melissa knows, and God is not inclined to interfere. That is why everything slips so terribly from my grasp when I try to touch it. Even Melissa's touch is not entirely real.

Yet I still hope that everything with Melissa will go on forever. After all the cycle of man is not one season, but many seasons. Perhaps man has but one love which grows and perishes as he grows and perishes and human life is one season over nature's many seasons.

Jim Wilson could hear Father Swift splashing in the bath now. He was trying to sing snatches of Verdi's requiem and his bellowing, though hardly lyrical, was recognisable. Jim Wilson looked at his watch and went and took one of his cigars out of his cigar box. Mrs Carmichael would be arriving to cook tea in half an hour and Jim Wilson hoped that Father Swift would be out of the bath by then. He feared that Father Swift was perfectly capable of doing the dance of the seven face flannels in front of Mrs Carmichael, destroying her faith forever. The man was an impossible eccentric. He should, reflected Jim Wilson, be called "Bananas" because he speaks and acts as though he is slithering hither and thither on a banana skin.

Jim Wilson wondered why Father Swift had come. Perhaps the hierarchy really hoped to change his mind. Jim Wilson lit his cigar and looked down at the road where a drover was rising to the trot of his horse; his dogs in a panting muddle behind the flash of the horse's iron shod hooves. Jim Wilson threw open his French windows to hear the clip/clop of the horse's hooves. The drover rose and fell in the stirrups against the orange-yellow of the felled maize and the blue jellied light through which weak strands of golden sunlight ran. The sun looked like a bucket of cold milk. A puff of smoke wafted into the cold air above the rhythmically bobbing drover. Then he passed out of sight behind the hill leaving only the sound of his horse's hooves on the road and a dog that had been left behind, moving like a black rocket, its belly almost on the ground, skittering around the corner in pursuit of its master. All that was left was the distant blue hills and the faintly acrid taste of Jim Wilson's cigar.

Jim Wilson pushed his French windows shut, sat down, closed his eyes and continued smoking his cigar.

Twenty minutes later Jim Wilson was contemplating the imminent demise of his cigar when Father Swift came through to the lounge wearing carpet slippers, green corduroy trousers, a checked brushed cotton shirt and a fawn cardigan.

"Well, Wilson," he said, "how about that whisky?"

"Certainly."

"Cigars too, eh? I'll have one of those. Where are they?" Jim Wilson pointed out his cigar box and got the whisky out of the cupboard. He poured the whiskeys and got a jug of water from the kitchen.

"You'd better add your own water."

"Right you are." There was a knock on the door. "Who on earth is that? Not your lady friend, I hope."

"It'll be Mrs Carmichael to cook the tea," said Jim Wilson, a touch of irritation in his voice.

"I hope she minds her own business."

"She wouldn't do this job if she wanted to do that."

"Quite! Oh well, not to worry."

Once Mrs Carmichael was settled in the kitchen cooking the tea Jim Wilson went back into the lounge and sat in his chair facing the silent Father Swift. Father Swift puffed his cigar and looked at the smoke he blew towards the roof. Then he swirled his whisky and water.

"You want to leave us for this woman, then?" he asked without looking up.

"Yes," said Jim Wilson. He lit a cigarette. The cigarette tasted horribly sweet after the cigar.

"You're a talented man. No one wanted you to come and minister to these rustics in the first place.

"I don't desire worldly success, even in the church."

"All the more reason why you should have a position of authority. That's what's wrong with democracy. People who desire power only desire it for their own vainglorious motives, not to serve humanity."

"Perhaps, but I'd still rather strive to understand myself and God."

"There's nothing wrong with understanding yourself. It makes you a calmer person. Why do you think I'm such a nut? It's because I must exorcise my eccentricities by indulging them, so that I can think clearly when I have to think."

"You seem to imply that there's something wrong with trying to understand God."

"It's useless. God is not to be understood, but to be obeyed. Understanding is the sin of the Protestants and has led to the godless situation we now have in the west. Men have understood nature and made themselves comfortable and so they no longer worship God but their own intellect. But a few short years of comfort will not be much recompense for an eternity of hell. When men in less fortunate areas are starving, they send food and not priests, because they are so carried away by their own humanism. Sadly, God is not a humanist and when those men who have been saved by food eventually die, they are lost into hell because they were given food and not God."

"You mean that God has no pity, no indulgence."

"He has both, provided that you believe. To believe will gain you heaven, provided that you struggle against your sins, even though, on occasions, they overpower you. Man is fallen and cannot help but sin. But if you do not believe, even if you avoid sin, you are condemned. Sinless men are monsters of coldness and inhumanity."

Father Wilson shrugged and poured himself another whisky. He couldn't see what difference this was supposed to make to him. He was not going to betray either God or Melissa by continuing in his present hypocritical position. God's brutality didn't really surprise or shock him. After all, when someone is omnipotent, they can obviously do as they please.

Father Swift got up from his chair and walked over to the table and poured himself another whisky. The room seemed very silent suddenly.

"So, why not stick it out for a while? Love is only a toy, a shadow compared to the unseen reality of God." Father Swift tucked his extinguished and half smoked cigar behind his ear.

"You talk with some authority."

"I know that love was created by the devil to lure man away from God, if that's what you mean. It is a beautiful creation, a superb creation. One might be tempted to speculate that even God couldn't have done it so well. God, of course, has given us marriage, which is much less beautiful in every way. It is unavoidable, from a biological point of view, that man must expel his sperm, so God gave man a wife, someone who would not occupy his thoughts too much."

"I doubt that even you believe that, Father Swift."

"You can doubt what you like, but brute lust does not set a woman up as an object of worship, as love does."

"Yes, I see that."

"Anyway love, as the devil's work, does have one flaw. It is not eternal. It is the perfect trap; something that is so beautiful that it ought to be eternal, but is not. No man could have invented something so fiendish, eh Wilson?" He tossed back his whisky, leaped across the room, seized the whisky decanter by the neck as though he was about to strangle it and poured himself another drink. He might have been the devil himself, delighted by his own treachery and viciousness.

"So, by remaining a priest I scorn the devil's ultimate blandishment?"

"Exactly. You are brilliant, Wilson, brilliant. You must apply for a transfer to Wellington, when this woman's lost her sensual halo, of course."

"If you'll forgive me saying so, this doesn't sound an awful lot like conventional dogma."

"Of course not, but you can't tell people the truth. People are dim witted. That's why they all have to surrender their judgement and do what the church tells them to. The world is too complicated, too seemingly unjust and too grisly for all but a few of us to understand. Frankly, I think that this Pope is too meek, but he will go to hell for errors committed in his name and the faithful will go to heaven for doing as he told them."

Father Swift sank back into his chair and the cigar behind his ear fell onto the floor beside his chair. As he bent over to pick it up, he noticed that the door leading to the dining room and the kitchen was partly open and moving a little, as though someone was holding it."

"Scullion!" screamed father Swift. He rose from his chair and leaped into the air his voice going to falsetto as he screamed: "Scullion!"

"Mrs Carmichael, some out from behind the door," said Jim Wilson calmly. Mrs Carmichael came timidly out from behind the door.

"I knew there was someone behind the door," said Father Swift gleefully. "Your ears were flapping like a line of sheets on a windy day and I could hear them, Mrs Carmichael, I could hear them."

"I'm sorry Father."

"It's too late now. Go out and finish the meal. I expect you to give this woman notice, Father Wilson. There is no place for an idle eavesdropper like her in a place of trust." He looked savagely at Mrs Carmichael. "That's all. Get out."

Father Wilson blinked and sat back in his chair. Initially he had liked Father Swift whose eccentricity had been gratifying. But he didn't know if he liked what Father Swift had said and he certainly didn't like the way Father Swift had handled Mrs Carmichael. She was a painfully nosey old creature, but her life was full of petty trials and tribulations. Father Wilson did not believe in healing peoples vices by exposing people to fire. His instinct was to shield those prone to weakness and error from the flames.

Now Milton Harper was one for allowing people to sink or swim. He and Father Swift would have got on just fine. Both suffered from the same disgust with the world. They thought of the world as being full of petty baubles that had no significance. One clung to the viciousness of God to make sense of it and the other to violence. But there was a certain amount of peacock blue in the dark and soundless flame of Milton's being. Perhaps he was redeemed in part by his divine, if self created, physique; but Father Swift, in his heart, was pure black. Jim Wilson shivered, almost imperceptibly.

Father Swift relit his partly smoked cigar. The blue smoke hung in the dark shadow of the room. The cold, heavy air was rising out of the ground, blinking its eyes in every shadow, like a cat unwinding itself, to take possession of the trees and streams. The light was lower and more glaring now, a golden path to God, away from the steam snorting cows and the homely scent of wood smoke. Everywhere women and men were working towards the freedom of the evening, an evening once filled with silence and the weak light of one-hundred-watt bulbs and now profaned by the engrossing cold blue light of the television set. Once men had lived their own lives. Now they could lead any life except their own.

"Well, what about it Wilson?" Father Swift's voice exploded into the cooking moistened air.

"I'm resigning."

"Oh, I thought I'd convinced you."

"You did, but only to resign."

"Why? Why?"

"The God of my parishioners is a real God. He is like the flowering thorn or the twisted willow or the beam of sunlight in the mystery laden silence of a dusty country church. They demand of me a certain standard of honour which you do not understand, because your God is complex and enigmatic, an idea. But God breathes and moves, even if it is not as we breathe and move. He is not the cunning and heartless dictator of a populous state as you see him or an ineffectual idiot as Mrs. Carmichael sees him, but he does mean a greater level of fulfilment than we would be able to achieve without him."

"This is hysterical pagan rubbish, Wilson."

"No. Up until now I have been an atheist, because God has only been an idea. It is unfortunate that I have to try to know both a woman and God at the same time, though I'll try."

"Father Wilson, your evangelical language appals me! The church has never believed that God could rest on so flimsy a ground as reality, just as it has never believed that marriage could rest on so flimsy a ground as love. No Matter. I think you have made the right decision. This is very decent whisky. Remind me to tell Mrs Carmichael she won't be sacked."

"All right."

"This is a nice posi here. You'll be sorry to leave."

"Yes."

"Leaving the church will be worse for you than it would be for me. After all, I'm just a thinker; though don't quote me on that."

"I'll miss the respect. Normal people don't get much of that."

Chapter 25

The other pedestrians on the street were whirled and partly carried by the wind, but Milton moved stolidly along the street, faltering occasionally, but ultimately impervious to the blast. Lillie and Liz had taken him to the edge of the abyss of himself and he stood there looking in. Wherever he moved on the street he was always on the edge of that hole.

Milton looked along the wind silvered street, then stepped across the moving water in the gutter and out onto the wide and empty street. In the middle of the wide road he stopped and blinked, noticing a huge space of light between the dark cliffs of the two storied shops. He pushed up his shoulders, pulled down his eyebrows, snorted and then walked with a sinister tread to the other side of the road.

Reaching the pavement, he stopped and stared at the large, shiny leaved rubber plants growing out of a square of black earth littered with shingle chips. Then he looked up, through his own reflection in the window, at the rows of steel shelves filled with books. From where he stood Milton could sense the close, windless warmth of the library. Women with rain blackened coats were standing inside, their weight concentrated on one leg or another, browsing through books.

Milton moved along the street and went up the ramp into the library. The glass doors burst open with indecorous violence. Milton was standing there in the silence of the library looking around. A librarian behind the issues desk was looking at him, waiting for a request for assistance. Milton stood there savouring the papery, silver fish smell of the library. He didn't ask for assistance but instead walked across the thick carpet, treading carefully in deference to the scholastic silence. He collapsed into a black, vinyl chair in front of a table of foreign language magazines. A librarian with thick soled shoes went stomping past, her backside flicking with cultivated eroticism. Milton looked after her, caressing his nose with his fingertips. He shut his eyes and wriggled deeper into the chair. There was a hiss as more air escaped from inside the chair.

Milton heard the scuff of shoes on the library floor and caught a whiff of perfume. He opened his eyes. The hip swinging librarian was straightening up the magazines on the table in front of him. She smiled warmly at him. She had short, black hair, olive skin, white teeth and a very pretty little moustache.

"You read French?" she asked.

"No. I find English hard enough."

"Oh, you're just here to sit then?" she said, disregarding his rudeness. Milton felt a warm wave flow through his body and he felt his cheeks go hot. He realised that he was probably blushing,

"Yeah," he said, smiling broadly at the librarian. She blushed and walked off, her backside swinging.

Milton sat there, stiff, but blinking his eyes. A thick, choking lust wrapped itself around his body like a shroud. He stood up and turned his chair side on to the window and sat there waiting for the librarian to go past again. Rain, as white as flour, flew in sheets down the street, but made no sound on the roof. Milton leaned forward in his seat and waited for the librarian to come past again.

Five minutes later she came back carrying a pile of books in one hand. When she looked towards Milton, he beckoned her. He felt brazen and overt, though in the back of his mind he felt astonished at what he was doing. The librarian came up to the table, put her free hand on top of the pile of books and leant forward towards Milton.

"How would you like to help me with my reading?" he said quietly, a grin on his face. The librarian blushed, stood up and marched haughtily over to "Detective Fiction." She began to put the books in her pile in the correct places on the shelf. Milton relaxed back in his chair and put one leg on the table of magazines. Having shelved her pile of books the librarian marched back across the room refusing to look in Milton's direction. Milton's grin broadened. He half closed his eyes like a cat in the sun.

An elderly man smoking a pipe came and sat opposite Milton and began to read a "Paris Match" with great attention, occasionally plucking at the end of his long, drooping, white moustache. Another librarian came to shelve more books in "Detective Fiction." Milton wondered whether or not he had miscalculated. The second librarian, who was not at all unattractive, looked coldly at Milton as she walked past.

Finally, however, Milton's librarian came flouncing back. Milton caught her free hand as she passed him. She turned towards him, half in anger and half in surprise.

"I'll see you outside at five," he said softly. The anger in her face slowly dissolved and she stood there considering. Then she said,

"I finish at four thirty."

"Four thirty then." The librarian shrugged and walked off, but the shrug was one of acquiescence.

Milton was back in the street again. For the next few hours at least, his life was sorted out. In one hour, he would be picking up the succulent little librarian. His throat felt tight with expectation. Liz and Lillie were both expelled from his thoughts. He stopped under the gloomy awning of a saddler's shop and looked across the deserted intersection, its traffic light, painted with black and yellow hoops like a bumble bee, remorselessly changing from green to orange to red and then back to green again.

After he had stood there for several minutes Milton noticed a couple on the far side of the intersection waiting for the lights to change. The man had on a gabardine raincoat and the woman had on a fawn, goat's hair duffel coat like the one Liz had. Milton couldn't see the woman as she was hidden by the man's body. Milton heard the crossing indicator buzz. It came faintly to him through the roar of the wind. The couple hurried across the glaring intersection. Once across they stopped and the man pointed out something further up the street. The woman stepped out from behind the man and, for a moment was obscured by a passing shopper towing a trundle. Once the shopper had passed, Milton straightened up. The woman was his wife Liz. The man was lighting her cigarette for her now. Milton knew nothing of this man and he decided to follow.

He waited until they had disappeared from view and then ran into the open beside the harsh, high facade of a bank. He reached the main street and grabbed hold of a telephone box to stop being blown further down the street. He could see his wife and the man walking about half way up the block on the other side of the street. He could see them above the shiny, wet roofs of the parked cars. Then the man stopped and let Liz go in a door. He followed her in. Milton knew they had gone into a coffee bar. Milton stopped in the middle of the pavement and shrugged. So what? He had his generous arsed librarian. He had no worries.

The man in the gabardine raincoat pulled out a chair for Liz and she sat down. The coffee bar was dark, full of pot plants and had a lot of lights on stands. The lights had orange shades. The owner, who was sitting at a table talking to a girl in a post office smock, got up smoke seeping from her nostrils and walked behind the counter saying as she went:

"Wha'd a you want?"

"Two coffees, thanks," said the man, rummaging in his pocket for some cash. The woman put two saucers on the counter, put two cups on the saucers and slopped some dark coffee into both of the cups from the conical, glass coffee container.

"That'll be fifty cents, thanks." The man put a fifty-cent piece in the woman's palm. She hit the keys on the till, the till rang and there was a clack as she threw the coin in and another "ting", followed immediately by a bang, as she threw the drawer shut and started back for the table to renew her conversation. "Now, where was I?" she asked as she resumed her place at the table.

"She hasn't got much finesse," whispered the man as he handed Liz her coffee. Liz took the coffee without any response. She tore open a sugar sachet and shook the contents into the coffee. She dropped the empty sachet into the ashtray on top of her cigarette butt. Then she stirred her coffee.

"I'm still cold," she said and sipped her coffee.

"I love you Liz," said the man. Liz just shrugged. "What's the matter? You've told me your husband mistreats you."

"I wouldn't quite use that word. You're so inexperienced Peter. You think it matters."

"But it must."

"Milton could eat you, Peter."

"What does brutality matter?" Liz smiled gently to herself and shook her head. "I would never treat you like he does."

"That's your tragedy." Liz flicked open the top of her cigarette box, took out a cigarette and lit it. As she drew on the cigarette the match flared and hid Peter.

Peter was so nice it was terrible. He didn't seem to grasp that women wanted to admire men as much as they wanted kindness from them. Whatever Milton might do he had a certain inextinguishable splendour about him. No matter how controlled he was, he possessed something untameable. Poor Peter could never laugh with the abandon and strength of Milton. Liz thought of Milton, eyes glinting, mouth open, yellow dog teeth bared, bent backwards from the waist, laughing. She thought of the careless physical dominance he exerted when they made love. Milton's mind might have stopped questing, but his spirit was inextinguishable. He would never do anything, he was too poetic to achieve. The most he was able to do was celebrate being alive. It was a pity that Milton was unable to accept his own status as an artist.

"You still love him then?" asked Peter, rudely interrupting her reverie.

"He says I never loved him."

"Well, did you?"

"He wouldn't have said it without a reason."

"For God's sake!" said Peter pressing some tobacco into the bowl of his pipe with his forefinger.

"Up you too," said Liz angrily.

Milton walked up the main street as far as the town clock and then back down the other side of the main street. It was amazing how little time it took to walk up and down the main street. As he came opposite the coffee bar he increased speed. Out of the corner of his eye he could just see Liz, shaking a spoon at the man in the dark interior of the shop. The next time he went by they were still there, though this time Liz had her head thrown back and she was looking at the roof. The next time he went past the coffee bar it was almost 4.30 pm and Liz and her "friend" were gone.

Milton walked up and down on the pavement outside the library entrance. His dark, little, generous arsed librarian came out with another librarian and sauntered slowly down the ramp towards the street. Then she and the other librarian stopped and talked for a couple of minutes. Milton figured that his little librarian might want to conceal her rendezvous from the other girl, so he pretended to take no notice of them. Finally, the other librarian strode off up the street and the dark, little librarian came across to Milton. He looked at her over his shoulder.

"Where do you live?"

"Makaraka."

"How do we get there?"

"By bus."

"Well, we'd better catch a bus then."

"But I live with my mother."

"Well?"

"I don't understand."

"Let's catch the bus." Milton put his arm around the girl and pulled her in against him. He couldn't wait to run his hand over her smooth, heavy, bottom.

They reached the bus shelter on the corner. The wind banged straight into the mouth of the green, wooden bus shelter. Milton and the girl sat down. The wind played with the girl's hair as she sat there under Milton's arm, looking straight ahead and dignified. Milton held her a little tighter and felt her wiggle into his side. He looked at the brown, leather gloves that concealed her hands. Very elegant, he thought.

"Do you really have trouble reading?" she asked, looking up at him.

"Who cares?" he said looking away from her glance of enquiry at something across the road. She looked down into her lap, obviously afraid of this surly, ultra-confident man. He was so irresistibly forceful.

She squeezed her thighs together and wondered where Milton would have her.

The old lady in the bus shelter with them, unrolled a crumpled, brown-paper bag, put her hand in, extracted a sweet and popped it in her mouth. Pursing her lips she sucked the sweet, furtively glancing around to see if anyone had noticed what she was doing. Then she rolled up the bag again and held it in front of her, her hands in the same position as a kangaroo's paws.

The light was blotted out by the dark body of the arriving bus. There was a hiss as the brakes were applied. The door of the bus flopped suddenly open and the girl climbed the steps with Milton behind her. The driver lounged in his seat with his ticket punch in his hand, staring insolently at Milton.

"Two to Makaraka," said Milton. The man sat there looking unblinkingly at Milton. Milton looked at the driver. There was a long silence. Milton felt his cheeks go hot. "Well, how much?"

"Fifty cents," said the driver in a flat tone. Milton put a fifty cent piece on the wooden plate and began to walk down the aisle, grasping the seats on either side as he went. "Hey, you! You'd better take your tickets," the bus driver called out. Milton turned around, looked scornfully at the bus driver and said:

"I don't want them." The driver looked at Milton summing him up and then, as he turned away, he said:

"Have it your own way then." The door of the bus swung shut.

Milton sat down by his "dark lady". He didn't really know what he was doing. The girl was pushed up against the window and looking out at the passing cars. All he wanted to do was fuck her and get away. He didn't go around picking up girls for casual sex, but here he was doing it. He had always been able to measure desire before against love or some form of physical or moral beauty. It was as though he had come up against the brutality of human appetite, his own human appetite, for the first time.

It must be her, he thought. He looked at her closely. There was something soft and yielding about this girl, some capacity for blind abandonment that most women did not possess. Milton turned to her and pushing her coat aside slid his hand up her leg. She turned towards him, put both her arms around his neck and kissed him violently.

They stayed kissing until the bus stopped and they looked out the window and saw the old corrugated iron fence of the sawmill and realised they were in Makaraka.

The girl jumped off the step, landing on the far side of a puddle of creamy, yellow water. Milton stepped down beside her and trapped her under his arm again. They stepped back as the bus went bumping away over the pot holed surface of clay and shingle.

"Come on," said the girl hitting Milton in the small of the back as the bus, already on the tar seal, accelerated smoothly away.

They weaved their way between the puddles which looked like small craters full of water. The blustery wind almost knocked them into several of the puddles. They crossed the road, looking at the racecourse, which was behind a single line of houses. The grass on the actual track was long and the grandstand, standing alone in all those empty acres, looked forlorn in the darkening air. They passed the butcher's shop. The meat in the window was a dull red and sat on stainless steel trays between metal bars, whitened by ice. Pieces of red and green, plastic fern were scattered between the trays.

Just past the butchers they went through an old, wooden, picket gate. The gate was painted cream and the paint was peeling. They walked down a yellow, concrete path with moss growing in the cracks in the concrete. A privet hedge, which grew over the path, brushed their faces and sprinkled their hair with water.

Then they were in a dark alley between the hedge and the gleaming white, weatherboard walls of the house. At the back of the house, they climbed some steps of orange brick and the girl, who had already taken her key out of her bag, slid it into the lock, and twisted her hand and the door opened.

The door shut behind them and they were in the semi darkness of a high roofed hall. The walls were covered in white pattered wallpaper and the door frames of varnished wood had a dull, golden sheen. The tinkles of a candelabrum died slowly away. Halfway along the hall, on a big wrought iron table, was a brass vase full of proteas.

The girl dropped her black, leather handbag onto the floor and, standing on her toes, kissed Milton. She rubbed herself against him half groaning. He reached under her coat and skirt and pulled off her panties and her pantyhose. Her arse was every bit as smooth and heavy as he had imagined. Then they were on the floor in the semi darkness and she was clinging to him, half strangling him and all he could think of was her flesh and he was moving and she was grunting and he wanted to shoot into her.

Finally, he succeeded and they lay there, hot and breathless, her ankles sticking lightly to the back of his thighs. Then she started to kiss him again, warm, frantic, salivarous kisses. She joggled his softening penis inside her and finally it began to harden and she was throwing herself at him, pushing at his rump with her heels, all the time seeming to talk to herself, though Milton could not understand what she was saying, until she suddenly went completely still and just laid there. Finally, she opened her eyes, looked at him for a second and then pushed him off. She stood up and began to work her feet into her shoes.

"You'd better go now. Mummy will be home soon." She smiled at him with melting tenderness. "You will come and see me tomorrow, won't you?"

It was dark now and raining again. Milton stood outside the butcher's shop with its dark window and watched the streams of water pouring from the awning onto the ground. The water was like a fly curtain made of transparent beads and it clattered as it fell into the puddles. The orange street lights were distorted by the falling rain.

Milton walked to one end of the butcher's shop and looked out of the side of the awning. You could see the streaks of rain in the cones of the cars' headlights. Big, dark trucks wailed by: white spray rolling out from their wheels. You could see their red tail lights long after they had become shadows in the rain.

For several minutes Milton watched the red light of a plane, roving apparently aimlessly in the sky. His feet were cold because he had somehow got water in his boots.

Finally, he stepped out from underneath the awning and began to walk towards town in the rain. After a few hundred yards his hair was sticking to his scalp and his trousers were sticking to his legs. Each time he walked under a streetlight he could see the rain drops swirling in the air like a swarm of bees. The cars came towards him cutting a furrow through the water, slopping it on his boots. The power wires maintained a rhythmic oscillation.

Then the rain stopped, though the wind kept up.

Milton reached the golf course. As he walked by, he could hear the flags flapping in the wind, even above the roar of the swirling trees.

Then he was in the city, his heels clacking on the pavement, the occasional dog barking at him from the warmth of a lighted front step. Milton was completely soaked, though he felt pleasantly warm.

He turned into a succession of side streets that were dark and tree lined; corridors of darkness, broken by tubes of light from the lampposts, which receded into the distance. Above the dark land, shadows swirled around the moon's fluorescent pool. Milton was startled by the scratching sound of a piece of paper, which the wind was tumbling down the street. Eventually his joints began to ache, but he didn't worry. He was almost at Lillie's door.

As he stepped into the hall of the old house it felt amazingly dry and warm, though he could hear the "splock, splock" of the water leaking into the pot in the middle of the hall. The old house creaked in the wind. Milton looked behind him and noticed his wet footprints on the floor. He pushed open the door into the kitchen. Lillie looked up from her book. She was sitting in a chair, her feet on the table.

"Hi!" she said getting up and coming towards him. Then she stopped. "You're soaked."

"Yeah."

"Come on through. I'll dry you off." Milton walked towards Lillie's bedroom, removing his water-logged coat as he went. "Put your clothes there," said Lillie, spreading out several sheets of newspaper on the floor. Milton took off his clothes, slowly peeling the wet material away from his skin. Lillie rubbed his wet flesh with a towel until it was pink. "Sit down and I'll dry your hair." Milton sat silently. "Where have you been?"

"Whoring."

"With Liz?"

"No, with the Dark Lady of the Sonnets."

"How could you have got so wet between your place and here?" asked Lillie, misunderstanding the situation.

"I wasn't with Liz," shouted Milton. Lillie went on drying his hair, though less vigorously than before. "I was...." he paused, unable to make the admission, "disgusting."

"Because you had another woman?" asked Lillie' with a trace of incredulity.

"She was nothing. But she had a lovely arse."

"So? I've gone to bed with men for similar reasons."

"No, you like sex and when I'm with you I like sex. I didn't like this. I just had to get my end in."

"Don't be vulgar."

"Well, it's the only way of putting it."

Lillie didn't understand. She didn't understand the black, insane compulsion of the copulation. Neither beauty nor love had been the reason. He hadn't wanted to talk to his "Dark Lady." This thought drew him up short. He looked up slyly at Lillie and burst out laughing. He realised that he was a puritan a uniquely twentieth century puritan. For the old-fashioned puritan sex was exonerated by marriage. For the new puritan it was exonerated by love or beauty. Neither puritan could accept the bestial anarchy of desire.

Milton felt Lillie drape her heavy dressing gown over his shoulders. He looked up at her. She seemed like a stranger, a woman of no importance.

Chapter 26

I t was late on Sunday morning. The river flat was still glistening with dew, though the grass had lost its whiteness except in some of the smaller valleys where the frost would lie most, if not all, of the day. The sun was white and hot, though the hills and big trees still cast long, dark, arctic shadows. The snow, miles away on the ranges, made the air seem thin and brittle.

Dave Gibson sat on a deck chair on his patio, the sunlight seeming to flicker as birds flew across the face of the sun. He could smell the lamb his wife was cooking for lunch and, occasionally, he heard the fat pop and hiss. He looked at the etched black web of silver birch branches and shivered.

"Bloody Russian things," he muttered under his breath. At the far end of the garden the whippy, knotty chaos of a japonica was just starting to bleed crimson flowers. Dave Gibson frowned at the thought of the camellia, just around the corner, whose white flowers always went a rusty colour.

Dave Gibson re-lit his yellowed cigarette in the cavern of his hands, his jaw thrust out. The baby started to yowl somewhere deep in the cold house. The sound continued on and on, a backdrop to the chirp of the starling on the TV aerial, the cooking mutton and a passing flock of goldfinches. Dave Gibson gritted his teeth and shut his eyes. Why can't the useless bitch shut the thing up? he thought. I don't want to sit here, but it's Sunday and I can't do anything else.

"Shut the kid up!" he bawled suddenly. A blackbird flew away from under the silver birches with a cackle of alarm.

"Go to hell!" shouted Melissa, from somewhere in the house.

Gibbo's face froze and he stared across the flat. He reached down, picked up his glass and sipped his beer. The baby's monotonous wails became intermittent. Dave Gibson closed his eyes and watched the screen of orange swimming between his eyelids and eyeballs. He felt the sun, warm on his face. Through his clothes he could feel the heat of the sun on his skin.

He had given up trying to get any respect out of his daughter, Melissa. He was saving his efforts in case she thought she was going to avoid marrying the ex priest.

Jim Wilson had been an ex-priest for two days now. He was coming out for dinner today and Dave figured that today would do the trick. After all the man couldn't be totally without honour, even if Melissa was. Sometimes Dave thought that Melissa wasn't a woman, but a whore; a women with no heart and no weakness. Unless people were vulnerable, they ended up being scandalous. That's why handsome men and beautiful women ended up being no good for anything; they weren't vulnerable, they weren't human. Fortunately, all those types went to Hollywood or Avalon or places like that and left the ordinary, unattractive people alone. Melissa wasn't beautiful though, so she must be an aberration, an ordinary woman with no vulnerability.

There was silence again now, at least from the child. Dave Gibson stubbed out his cigarette on the yellow cardboard tobacco packet beside the chair and let his weight sag fully into the canvas. Jim Wilson didn't really seem a bad sort. He was obviously honourable or he would not have left the church and he was obviously intelligent or they wouldn't have let him become a priest in the first place. Perhaps he was an intellectual, though and not interested in real work at all? Still, the man had to make a living somehow and there wasn't an awful lot you could do around Gisborne. He must see how practical it was to marry Melissa. He was built like a horse too. Besides, if he marries Melissa and comes into the business I can die then. I will have lived for some reason. What I have created will go to my offspring and all this work will not have been wasted, which is what would happen if I died and the farm was sold to someone I've never seen. The kingdom that you pass on is the only thing of importance in life. Happiness, grief, love, none of them matter beside the land you pass on. A man can commit crimes for his land which could never be justified if they were committed for happiness or wealth. Land is more important than even women. You only have women to help you civilise the land and give you heirs. If they give you nothing except heirs they have served their purpose. If your work lives after you in the hands of your children and grandchildren, death is nothing. Melissa's worthlessness can be redeemed by Jim Wilson and their children.

There was a cracking, tearing sound behind him and Gibbo jerked in his chair and quickly looked around. Melissa was just applying a lighted match to a cigarette.

"Nice morning, Dad."

"Yeah." Melissa stared at the black worm casts sprinkled on the lawn. "When's this bloke arriving?"

"Eh?"

"When's Jim arriving?"

"I don't know. He shouldn't be long." Melissa sat down on the edge of the cold concrete. The feeling reminded her of childhood. She bent down, knocked off her shoes and walked out onto the lawn feeling the moisture, cold and gritty, between her toes. A kingfisher flashed a vivid blue as he flew away from his perch on a fence post in the shade of the house. Melissa smeared the tops of her toes on the lawn, dragging one foot and then the other behind her. The cold of the lawn was exhilarating.

"You'll get the flu," said Dave.

"I doubt it."

Melissa was worrying about Jim. She felt strangely cold and empty inside, as though her soul had become a winter shadow. Even so, she still believed she loved him. It couldn't have been going to last as short a time as this. They were entirely free now and could love as they pleased for the first time. What a funny compulsion love was! How odd that it should try to express itself through something as drab as human flesh. It had nothing to do with flesh or even, it sometimes seemed to her, with self. Perhaps love was something altogether alien to humans, something which merely possessed them to express its self and which people mistakenly took as being part of them? Perhaps love simply used and discarded human bodies and human personalities in some quest of its own, not really understood by men and women? That would explain its power and it would explain its inability to leave human beings completely satisfied.

A shadow seemed to pass in one side of her body and out the other. She felt grief beneath her eyes and in her back. She gulped in some cigarette smoke.

No. Love was human and comforting and warm and these suspicions she had about the ugliness of flesh were only signs of some psychological corruption. Yet there really was no reason why she loved Jim. She could describe a hundred loveable characteristics he possessed, but they were hardly characteristics that he alone possessed. Besides, she hadn't done a computation of characteristics to decide that she loved him. She just loved him. That was all: the beginning and the end.

Then everything suddenly seemed all right. She wanted to walk hand in hand up the creek with Jim and kiss him beneath the willows. She felt again that love righted the world and made her feel at home in it. But the world would eventually become boring again and she would no longer love Jim. She shrugged. Perhaps it wouldn't happen for a long time.

She climbed back up on the patio beside her father.

"Why aren't you helping you mother to cook the dinner?" asked Dave, lighting another cigarette.

"She's cooked the same dinner for the last quarter of a century. It would only throw her off her rhythm."

Dave looked up at his daughter and realised that he was afraid of her. She had the power to deny him something of ultimate importance. He realised, for the first time, the impotence of his own rage. For a man of his age, it was a terrible realisation. His own passion had always seemed to change everything that mattered, but he knew it could not sway his daughter. Her calm would defy his worst rages. The ex-priest won't be influenced by me either, thought Dave.

"Do you love your father?" asked Dave suddenly. Melissa frowned and then shrugged.

"Women exist to love men, not their parents."

"But you're part of my flesh."

Melissa looked at this little, sinewy creature who looked incapable of emotion or poetry. He looked more like a rock, or a tree, or any part of the landscape rather than a man with sensitivity and feelings.

She was his flesh though. She shivered with loathing. She felt repelled by his flesh and for that matter, by her mothers. I am the bloody bi-product of my parent's desire. I am flesh and blood and slime. My child is flesh and blood and slime. It's funny, I had never thought of it that way. I had always somehow thought of it as being pink and jolly and clean, because it was the product of love. But one day it will look at my flesh and think of our bond and be repelled as I am now. How funny, that on one level man is just like a frog.

"What's that got to do with anything?" said Melissa.

"I want you to marry him, Melissa. So, there's someone to carry the farm on."

"Shut up, Dad!"

"I want you to promise me you'll make him marry you."

""Dad, do you believe that I would do anything to deliberately hurt you?

"Don't change the subject. I want you to promise."

"No. You and I live in different places. Love only means love, not marriage.

There was silence again apart from the melodic peel of a roosting magpie. The sun was very hot and bright. Melissa could hear her father trying to draw in his breath. She didn't look at him. She was disgusted that he could have been so tasteless, so sloppily emotional in front of her. She realised that he must be getting old. She had been able to respect his animosity and savagery, but this grovelling was distasteful, doubly so because there was no choice to make anyway. She knew that Jim understood. She knew he realised that their love existed in defiance of the world and that there was no place in the ordered ways of the world for their love. The highest expression of their love was two bodies groping together in the dark. There was not any more to it than that. Their love had nothing to do with families or society. She wanted to have a child by Jim well enough, but she didn't want to spend her life washing rugby gear, bottling fruit and all the other horseshit that went with marriage. But she couldn't have the beauty without the drudgery. She was going to be frustrated by having children and she was going to be frustrated by not having them, but she figured that the latter was the lesser of the two evils and the less time consuming of the two frustrations.

Melissa picked up her shoes and walked out of the warm sun on the patio into the cold lounge. In the middle of the floor, she turned suddenly and walked through to the kitchen. The kitchen was warmer than the lounge, but still cold. Mrs Gibson was just cutting a cauliflower into floweret's and dropping them into cold, salted water.

"Hi," said Melissa, stopping in the kitchen doorway.

"Hello dear. You ought to go outside. It's cold in here."

"Why don't you go out mum and let me finish the meal?"

"No!" said Mrs Gibson, her body tightening with fear.

"Hell!"

"What's the matter now, dear?"

"Being in the arms of this family is like being festooned in wet kelp." Mrs Gibson looked up from her cauliflower, gave her daughter a puzzled look and went back to working on the cauliflower. "How come Dad wants an heir so badly?" Mrs Gibson's hand paused in mid air. She looked up again at her daughter and put down the vegetable knife.

"He just wants a bit of masculine fellowship." Melissa couldn't prevent herself from chuckling. "You may find it funny, but a woman can't supply everything you know." Melissa laughed again, no less cruelly. "He wants someone to help make the decisions, someone with a young body to take the strain off his old body, someone to go to the football with."

"You go out and talk to him Mum. I'll finish up in here."

"Alright," said Mrs Gibson reluctantly. "Thanks dear. I wouldn't mind a bit of sun."

When Mrs Gibson walked out onto the patio she noticed the light, but not the heat. She had carried the cold of the house outside. Dave was standing on the edge of the patio wriggling his toes and looking into the distance. His hands were in his pockets.

"Will you bring me over the other chair?" asked Mrs Gibson. Dave Gibson cleared his throat, went and got the other chair from the wall of the house and unfolded it.

"It's a beautiful day," he said.

"It's too cold. I even feel cold here in the sun."

"You shouldn't spend so much time inside. Make Melissa do more."

"You can't realistically have such expectations of your children now. There's too much choice. Once a man would have given his right arm to own land. Money's too easy now."

Dave Gibson coughed some more phlegm out of his throat. This time he spat it onto the lawn and then stood on the edge of the patio and pulled his greying eyebrows down over his eyes. Then he slowly walked back and sat again in his deckchair. The knotty, savage, little man and his clean, healthy austere wife sat on the patio of this expensive home which had as little to do with them as cubism had to do with Michelangelo. They were the products of an age of labour but they had survived into an age of leisure. They did not understand that Melissa was their spirit untainted by tireless labour and unreasonable standards of utility.

Meanwhile, Melissa stood in the kitchen looking out over the dog kennels thinking of the terrible suspense she would endure if she married Jim and they lived on the land and waiting each night for him to come home to see if their love had died during the day. Then there would be the happiness of the night, then the nervousness of another day and surely they would not survive.

Mrs Gibson put her feet on the deckchair and carefully arranged her dress over her knees.

"He's got to marry Melissa," said Dave in his raspy voice.

"He doesn't," said his wife calmly.

"The next twenty years won't be worth it for me if he doesn't."

"That'll be too bad."

"So he's got to marry her."

"No."

"Yes."

"No. You'll have to put up with twenty years of bitterness."

"I've worked hard."

"Who says hard work is rewarded?"

"It ought to be."

"Perhaps."

Dave Gibson looked up at the benevolent blue sky. It was the sort of day that would tempt a man to fly. The shadow of a hawk came sliding over the sun yellowed face of the first ridge until the dark bird itself reared into the air and flew away into the throat of the blue.

Dave Gibson wondered if there was always a time when fate caught up with you and rendered every future event, even pleasure, distasteful. Still, if it always happened to everyone he had been lucky to have delayed it for so long. What if it had come when he was eighteen? He realised that if it had come at eighteen he probably would have had the virility to dispose of himself.

Perhaps it was fate that compelled Melissa to act as she was acting. If there was such a thing as fate and God controlled fate, then obviously God was a shithouse. He could have let me have a son and I wouldn't have had to be so tough on Melissa. It wouldn't have cost him anything to let me have a son. It wouldn't cost him anything to stop kids dying of cancer or being killed in car accidents and if he can't stop those things he's not what he's cracked up to be. And if he could stop those things and chose not to he was simply a prick. I've never done anything to anybody half as bad as what's being done to me right now; so why do I deserve it? Perhaps every time you sin you get paid back with interest, which hardly seems fair.

I've never thought of this sort of thing before, but now that I do it is obvious that God is a bastard. Funny, I feel a bit better now. I feel that I'm not going to quite lose everything after all. If Wilson marries Melissa after all it is a bonus, a stream of piss in the eye of God. I'm not going to go down. I've always bloody fought and I've always loved fighting and I've always thrived on animosity and, for the next twenty years, or however long it is, I'll live on my hatred of God. The only thing that could get me now is the absence of God and, for a place to be as shitty as the world, there's got to be some prick behind it.

Dave Gibson filled his foam curtained beer glass, grinned all over his face and drank down the whole glass. He looked at the rugged hills, at the moment smoothed and softened by the new winter growth. The manukas looked like moles on the cheeks of the hills. Here and there was the yellow scar of a slip. Dave Gibson's grin broadened and his eyes began to glitter with tears. He realised that he was as hardened, as rough as the hills themselves and that he could beat any damned bastard there was, God included. As long as he was alive his spirit was indomitable. The land was his family, his children and his brothers and no matter who deserted him he still had that, provided of course he could remain financially solvent. As long as there was that there was something to live for and if he couldn't pass the land on, he would at least take it into his heart when he died and keep it there forever.

Gibbo held his beer bottle upside down and watched the foam dribble into the bottom of the glass.

"Melissa!" he screamed.

"Yes."

"Bring me another beer out of the fridge."

"Just a minute, you lazy old bastard!" Dave Gibson leaned back in his chair, pushed open his tobacco packet with his thumb, pulled loose a chunk of matted tobacco strands and began to go about rolling another cigarette. Melissa came walking through with an already open bottle of beer.

"Thanks dear. Put it beside me. You don't really have to get married if you don't want to." Melissa, who was already walking away stopped, turned around, frowned and said:

"Really Dad, I wasn't intending to." She passed through the square of bright light where the sun fell through the door of the lounge and disappeared into the dark lounge. Mrs Gibson opened her eyes.

"I feel like a beer, dear."

"Oh, Hell! Why didn't you say so before?" said Dave, rolling off his deck chair. "I can't ask Melissa to come back again."

"It hadn't occurred to me that I wanted a beer then."

Chapter 27

An hour later Jim Wilson arrived. When Melissa saw him getting out of the rental car, she knew she still loved him. She walked down the concrete path between the roses, half embarrassed at her joy, and when he came through the shrieking gate, she pressed herself against his bulk. The day seemed to explode into a greater brightness and she seemed to breathe it in through the pores of her skin. She wanted to say that she loved him but she didn't because the utterance seemed so trite and ridiculous. Words were a barrier between her emotion and his and to kiss was a way of overcoming that barrier, which was why kissing made so much more sense than conversation. Melissa gave Jim Wilson one last squeeze and, letting him go, took his hand.

"How does it feel to be free?"

"Confusing."

"How confusing?"

"Frightening I suppose. I feel new, pristine and unknown to myself."

They stopped on the doorstep by the gumboots and raincoats. Jim Wilson felt dizzy. He felt weak and afraid and he drew Melissa to him to try to draw on her strength and vitality. I've left it too late for this sort of turmoil. I'm too old for this sort of uncertainty. Perhaps Father Swift had been right. The world was an open sore and the only protection was Melissa's arms. Yet the world was more beautiful because of Melissa. It was as though the two parts were torn apart by love and man fell down the chasm in between.

"You'll come back to town with me this afternoon?"

"All right."

Dave Gibson carved the lamb at lunch time. By then he had changed into a jersey, an open necked shirt and sports trousers. Dinner was very quiet apart from the clacking of cutlery on plates. Periodically two people would catch one another's eyes, smile and then go on eating. Half way through the lunch Jim Wilson poured some more mint sauce onto his lamb, ran his finger under the spout of the jug and licked his finger. Flecks of gristle showed in the grey brown meat with its cooked, yellowish skin.

"Nothing like farm killed lamb, eh boy?" said Gibbo to Jim Wilson.

"No. You wonder how butcher's shops do it."

"Oh well, if you want to live in town you've got to eat like a townie."

"Do you think country beer is better than town beer?"

"I wouldn't know," said Dave Gibson grinning, "It's all fire water to me."

"Many a true word spoken in jest," said his wife. Mrs Gibson put her knife and fork side by side on her empty plate.

"Well, what are you going to do now that you're no longer a man of the cloth?" asked Dave Gibson.

"I'll have to become a tycoon." Jim Wilson laughed aloud at the thought.

"I'd offer you a job with me, except that Melissa wouldn't approve."

"I couldn't do that Dave."

"Oh well, think about it."

"Peaches and cream, anyone?" asked Mrs Gibson.

"We're still eating dear," said Dave.

Melissa lit a cigarette and looked out the window across to where the dogs were lying in the sun on their cage floors.

"You and Jim ought to go for a ride after lunch," suggested Mrs Gibson.

"I couldn't fit on one of those bikes by myself, let alone with Melissa."

"You mean we're going to walk?" asked Melissa.

"I'm a modern man. I wouldn't know how to walk," said Jim Wilson popping half a roast potato into his mouth.

After lunch they all went out onto the patio and sat in the glare of the already west falling sun.

"There'll be a frost tonight," said Dave. That's the worst of these fine days."

"I'll be going into town this afternoon with Jim," said Melissa. "I'll be home tomorrow morning." There was complete silence. Mrs Gibson closed her eyes. "You can take care of Mark can't you Mum?"

"I suppose so?"

Under the silver birches a thrush stood with a worm dangling from its beak.

"I could take him with me. What do you think, Jim?"

"You can't do that," said Mrs Gibson quietly.

"I don't mind," said Jim.

"Think the child might become a delinquent, Mum?"

"He'll be upset in a strange place."

"Yes, bring him with you," said Jim.

"What will your landlord say?" asked Dave.

"He lives miles away."

Jim and Melissa drove back into town flashing in and out of

shadows as though they were passing in and out of road tunnels. Melissa sat with the child on her knee. They passed a cow on a distant ridge, looking like a dinosaur against the violent sun. The yellowing weeping willows sat in the green flats like sagging tents. The poplars stood grey and pulpy; as though they had been abandoned by the breath of life. All the leafless trees seemed to have lost their rigid power and were waiting for the leaves to emerge and harden their almost fluid trunks. The uncovered, black earth glowed like coal in the sun. You could sense the water lying just beneath the cover of green pasture. There were no cars on the road and no men in the paddocks. Sunday gripped the land like a frost.

Once they were out of the hills and on to the main road there were cars full of people who were looking out of the windows and pointing. Some had elderly female passengers who were being whisked, half conscious, between the fences; fences that were half concealed by last summer's dead grass. A few leaves, either yellow or red, still hung on the knotty grape vines in the vineyards. The houses, scattered apparently at random in the fields, looked like old bones in a meadow. Smoke seeped faintly from some of the chimneys. The oranges glowed like fancy lights in the dark foliage of the orange trees. Rings of paler oranges lay on the ground beneath the orange trees. In some fields there was still standing maize, grey with mildew and withering slowly earthwards. A wall of cloud seemed to have boiled on to the horizon from out of the sea.

They passed one man sitting on the bonnet of his car, drinking tea out of a plastic cup and gazing across the flats. His wife, who was sitting in the passenger seat of the car, was leaning out of the window and gazing in the same direction. She turned to him, said something and then looked back again.

"It's a beautiful afternoon," said Melissa, smiling at Jim. The child, his face looking like a pink, plastic potato, burped in his sleep. Melissa smiled and blew it a kiss. "I'm glad we brought Mark. Perhaps I ought to move in with you?"

"I'd better get a job first."

They drove in through the town itself, the streets wide and almost completely empty under the blue sky. Here and there were groups of kids on bikes, in some cases cigarettes hanging from their barely adolescent lips. A few families, father, mother and children, strolled along in front of the shops under the cold awnings. Then there was only the empty street, the dark display windows occasionally flashing deluges of silver light on to the grey pavement.

The only set of traffic lights in the shopping precinct turned red as they approached and stayed that way for at least two minutes while the green light shone into a wide, deserted side street which led to a bridge over the river. Two boys on bicycles flashed past them and crossed the intersection against the red light.

The lights changed and Melissa nudged Jim who shook his head, grunted and started off across the intersection. They drove past the port, a tangle of rusting spars against old coarsely built wooden sheds. They watched the shadow of their car bobbling before them over misshapen tar seal. Above the roofs of the houses, they could see Kaiti Hill. It stood between them and the sea and its inland side was already in shadow.

They turned inland towards the treeless, grassy hills and, as the paddocks between the houses began to get bigger, they stopped outside a little, square, flat roofed, roughcast house with a long, rank lawn. In the very middle of the lawn was a rusting forty-four-gallon drum which served as an incinerator. A very large, lichen bearded plum tree grew against the house on one side of the front door. Melissa turned, looked at Jim and said:

"Very salubrious."

"Quaint, I think."

"It looks more like a water tank than a house."

"It feels like a water tank once you're inside."

"Is the power on?"

"Yes," said Jim angrily getting out of the car.

He got the carrycot out of the back while Melissa got out of the car holding the baby. She walked through the long, wet grass with Jim following her, feeling in his pocket for the house keys. She climbed the glossy, dark green, front steps. The house also had dark green window sills. Jim charged past her with the keys, unlocked the front door, opened it and managed to squeeze both him and the carrycot through the short, narrow door frame. He lumbered, rather like a gorilla, down the hall and disappeared through a door somewhere near the end of the hall. Melissa walked after him staring at the yellow, pinex walls. She passed two darkly varnished doors immediately opposite one another on either side of the hall. Cobwebs hung from the plastic lightshade which was yellow with age.

"Jim!" she called out.

"Yep," he replied from somewhere quite close.

She came to another doorway, the door open. She went through, blinking, in to the brighter light. Jim was filling a shiny, new, electric kettle in the sink. The sink had a wooden bench. In one corner of the room was an old, cream stove with old fashioned, solid, slow-heating elements. Through the window above the sink Melissa could see a weeping willow lying on its side just across the fence in a neighbouring paddock. The tree was still very much alive, even though it had fallen over. In the sunny paddock beyond the tree were clumps of arum lilies. There was an oblong horse trough in one corner of the paddock. On the far side of the paddock there was a row of modern houses.

Melissa noticed a couple of clumps of snowdrops growing in the shadow of the fallen weeping willow. There seemed to be some sort of ditch between the house and the willow.

"This place reminds me of Doctor Blood's Coffin."

"What about the view?"

"What happens when the stream floods?"

"It washes out the old tenants and allows you to put in a new lot of tenants at a higher rent. You can't go wrong with a piece of real estate like this." Melissa laughed.

"It's a challenge, I suppose."

"So 's torture."

Melissa put the baby in its carrycot. It promptly began to cry. Jim Wilson went on making tea.

"You don't own a pot, do you? I want to warm some milk."

"Under the sink."

"Why are you in such a foul mood? You've never been this shitty before."

"Well, it's not a very exotic place to bring you."

"Its exotic compared to some of the places I lived in Wellington. I quite like it actually. I hope we have a heater."

"We've got a fireplace actually."

"That's even better."

"I haven't got any wood yet."

"Never mind, we'll go to bed."

Later, when it was dark, Jim Wilson got out of bed and walked over to the window with a lighted cigarette. He felt frustrated by the barrier of his body. No matter how you twisted and turned the wished for liberation from the body, the wished for total contact with the beloved never occurred. It was like being a little man at the controls of a huge robot trying to touch someone who was at the controls of another robot. The two robots rolled and crashed and bumped together but the little man and the little woman were still trapped in the control rooms. The odd thing was that if the robots did not roll and crash, they were even worse off.

Besides, it is her body that is beautiful and, in striving to attain her, I find a happiness of sorts.

Perhaps ideal love, where the lady sat in the tower and the knight walked around plucking his lute underneath was so popular because it was a certain part of love. A woman's body was an unconquerable tower that imprisoned and protected her forever and the wise knight never tried to ascend to the top of the tower. He simply serenaded her from below.

Outside the road shone like a ribbon of steel in the moonlight. Across the paddocks, in the town itself, the dark roofs glistened from the already descending frost. In the house across the road Jim could see the back of three heads sitting in a line on the top of the window sill of the lounge. He could see, beyond the heads, three faces and three bodies reflected in the mirror that hung above the fireplace. The three pairs of eyes were staring intently at the same spot. Jim presumed that they were all watching television. He wished they would pull down their blinds. He didn't want to be a secret spectator of their domestic activities.

He shivered and walked back across the room and got back into the double bed beside Melissa who put out her hand and touched him.

"You poor thing! You're cold." She took his hand; eyes still shut, and tried to wiggle her way deeper into the bed. Jim Wilson leaned over Melissa, the smoke from his still lighted cigarette rising into his eyes.

He shut his watering eyes tightly while he stroked her hair. "I love you, but what does it matter?" He supposed that this feeling of shiny emptiness, like a scoured milk can, was something, but it didn't touch him somehow. He knew that Melissa loved him, but it seemed there ought to be more to love. It ought to be some sort of unending revelation, although exactly what sort of revelation he had no idea.

Jim Wilson leant out of bed and stubbed out his cigarette in the ash tray on the floor. He felt he ought to pray, but God had no place in his life with Melissa lying there beside him. He would have to walk unbelieving through life like a man walking across a lake on thin ice on a brilliantly sunny day who knows the walk can't go on forever but who is newly astonished each second that he has not fallen through into the icy water below.

He slipped down under the blankets and began to kiss Melissa's body. As he kissed that warm body, smelling slightly of decay, he realised that this was really all there was to his life and he felt rebellious.

Melissa, who had just been dreaming about a pig falling on a bed of daffodils, hugged Jim Wilson's head against her. She could be happy with him because she had already accepted the loss of love that would inevitably come. The pain came from expecting things to last, of rebelling against time. Just as a certain scene is only beautiful from a certain perspective and at a certain time, so it is with a man. Just as in a certain state of knowledge we may find a particular poem profound and beautiful we also find that tomorrow the same poem can seem banal and drab. So at a certain time we find a man beautiful until our fluctuating emotional desires demand another man to meet our changed needs and desires.

Melissa drew Jim Wilson to her without clearly formulating any of this. This understanding was so much a part of her that she didn't need to think. She held Jim against her to comfort him, to comfort this gigantic child who blundered around in the world like a seal on a rock. He had not the least comprehension of the world. He was struggling in the darkness of God. He understood with his heart but misunderstood with his mind. His insatiable desire for the eternal made him a maniac. Every man she had ever known was a similar maniac. Every man she had ever known wanted to live forever. Her father wanted his eternal monument of dirt, peopled by his grandsons and Jim wanted his unchangeable morality supported by God.

Neither of them could accept this dark, cold, quite sad little planet where men loved and lost and died, deserted by higher guidance and with only one another to cling to. If men did not embrace their sad destiny they became homicides and maniacs, saints, soldiers and politicians all dedicated to vicious rebellion against the world, the world of God. Men needed to get off their thrones and make love.

Jim lay there beside Melissa with only a few tufts of his hair sticking above the blanket. Melissa puffed her breath into the dense air. There was a creak from somewhere in the house. Melissa half sat and leaned on her elbows. There was another creak, though it seemed to come from a completely different place.

"Jim," hissed Melissa, "we've got an intruder." Jim emerged from the blankets and looked around in a startled fashion.

"Where is he?"

"I heard him."

"You heard him make the floor creak you mean?"

"Yes."

"This house is full of creaks. We've got them in place of cockroaches by special agreement with the landlord."

"Go and bring Mark in anyway."

"It's cold out there."

"Stop being silly Jim. You've just been up." Jim lay there preparing himself as you do before you jump into a cold river. Then, suddenly, he tore back the sheets and landed heavily on the wood floor. He ran on tip toe around the foot of the bed trying to protect his soft feet. He pulled open the door of the room. His silhouette bent at the knees as it passed through the doorway into the faintly milky light of the hall. Then there was silence, apart from a little scuffling and then the carrycot came through the door, dangling from Jim's fist. Jim's dark body followed his fist and forearm through the door.

"It's still asleep." whispered Jim.

"Mark's not an "it". Bring him over here."

"I'm freezing." Jim Wilson turned on the light and felt momentarily dizzy as the room became a lot of sharp edges and solid planes.

"Well. Give me the child and get into bed," Melissa took the child out of the carrycot and put it on the bed beside her. The bed groaned loudly as Jim got back into bed on his side. He lit another cigarette. A cloud of smoke hung almost motionless in front of his head. Seeing Melissa sitting there with the child made him desire her again. He desired not to love her so much as subjugate her, trap her beneath his body and force her into pleasure. Melissa let the child lie with its face on her breast. That was oddly arousing for her. It made her feel impersonally randy. She was faintly shocked. There was always something faintly shocking about those sorts of feelings. But the child was purely physical. It was warm and it crapped and it ate. It was purely physical, purely sensual. Its life was uncomplicated by high desires. Jim Wilson looked over at Melissa in her reverie. There was a flush at the bottom of his spine and a tingling in the back teeth of his mouth. He was jealous and the jealousy, if unchecked, could paralyse the strongest physical response.

"I don't like you being away from me. I don't like you thinking private thoughts."

"I'm sorry Jim."

"Your life is my life. It's not your own."

"I'm sorry, but I've got this legacy that reminds me of a time when I didn't know you."

"You love Mark more than you love me."

"Don't be stupid. It's not a competition."

"I'm sorry." Jim Wilson hit the bed with frustration. The baby woke up and started to cry. "Shut up!" hissed Jim Wilson. The baby began to cry louder and Melissa realised that her hand was warm and wet.

"You've made him piss all over me." Jim Wilson swung his feet out of bed and sat in sullen silence his back to Melissa. Unfortunately, the two, bulky, pink folds that sat on his hips were something less than eloquent. A giggle passed over Melissa's face as she noticed them. She felt like leaning over and pulling one of the hairs that were so abundant in the cleft at the top of his buttocks. Jim Wilson's body twisted hideously, as though it had been shaken by some invisible hand. "Get back into bed or you'll get the flu. With your smoking you'll probably end up in hospital if you do."

"Shut up and change that screaming shit machine!" The words forced their way between his teeth.

Jim Wilson sat there locked in his little emotional cupboard shivering from the cold. He was trapped by his own emotions and, at the same time, disgusted by his own pettiness. How could he be jealous of a mere infant? Something inside his body was wrenching this way and that. He wished he could reach inside his body and tear out this torment. He heard Melissa get out of bed. What was happening to him? His jealousy shut out his love. He hated Melissa. She was everything, all he had, but she insisted on going away from him.

He knew he couldn't stay trapped in this mire of hatred. He had to be tender in the hope that his display of tenderness would overcome his hatred. He shivered again convulsively and stood up. Mellissa was just pulling the wet nappy from underneath the baby. The baby was still crying. Jim Wilson walked around the bed and put his hand on Melissa. She shrugged him off.

"Wait until I've got him changed!" said Melissa shortly. Jim Wilson's teeth clenched with anger again. All she had to do was be nice for a second. Jim Wilson tried to swallow his grief.

"I'm sorry," he murmured, hanging his head like a tragic dog. Melissa pinned on the fresh nappy and put the child back in the bed which her body had warmed.

"I think I'll feed him now that I'm up. Melissa reached for her underclothes that were on a battered old armchair.

"Please kiss me," blurted out Jim Wilson. Melissa looked at him with surprise. Then she smiled warmly.

"I always get involved in what I'm doing." She went over and hugged him. "How's that?" Jim Wilson pulled her tightly against him and then shivered violently. They stood that way for quite a time. Then Melissa tried to wriggle free. "Let go, Jim. You're hurting." Jim held on to her for a little while longer and then, as Melissa tried to look up at his face, let her go. She went back to putting on her clothes. "Go back to bed, Jim," she said without turning round. Jim Wilson walked round the other side of the bed and got back in. The sheets felt cold again and he lay there as still as possible waiting for his body to warm the sheets.

"I'll ring up Milton." he said as Melissa was pulling on her jeans over her pantyhose. She was delighted to be able to wear tight pants again.

"Yes, I'd quite like to see someone from outside the family. Maybe, if we can lick this place into shape, he could come for a meal. He can bring his wife this time."

He'll probably still be fighting with her."

"Ask them both, anyway," said Melissa lighting a cigarette.

Chapter 28

iz Harper walked across the playground of dry mud. Here and there a few tufts of grass still grew. The low, winter sun sat just above the brick wall that separated one side of the school from the surrounding houses. The white sunlight shimmered and swam. The ground breathed warmly on the structures of man. A boy with a schoolbag on his back swung across the grey, unpainted jungle gym and dropped to the ground. He lay on his stomach on the ground, playing dead.

At the other end of the playground two boys, one with a torn shirt, were kicking at goal, bare footed. The silence of the late afternoon was broken by the "punk" of the ball as they kicked it. Liz looked across at the jumbled collection of prefabs which made up the school. The buildings had the look of a lot of vacant, slack jawed idiots. A tall, blond woman came striding between two of the buildings and walked in Liz's direction. There was something vaguely familiar about her, but Liz looked away and walked down to the end of the paddock to send the goal kicking boys off home.

"Mrs Harper." The voice sounded thin and musical. Liz looked back at the woman who was just breaking into a run, her long hair ballooning in the air behind her. Behind the woman, on the edge of the concrete playground, two male teachers were squatting, talking to one another. A blue haze of cigarette smoke lingered around their heads. "Mrs Harper." The woman slowed to a walk and came up to Liz, panting slightly.

"Yes, can I help you?" The blond woman laughed with strange familiarity. "Do I know you?"

"Sort of. I'm Lillie Foster."

"Really?" Liz started to walk on and Lillie fell in step beside her. "Why come and see me?"

"Milton has been unfaithful to both of us."

By then they had reached the goal kicking boys.

"Come on you boys. That's enough. Time to go home."

"Aw, Mrs Harper!"

"Don't 'aw' me Henry. I don't want to stay here all night watching you two kick goals."

"Hell!" said the boy putting the rugby ball under his arm.

"Watch your language or you'll go to Mr Holmes." The boy went off, his head hung in frustration. The other boy picked up his jersey by one sleeve and followed, dragging his jersey on the ground. Liz looked back at Lillie who was grinning.

"You're very strict." Liz shrugged and then laughed.

"You've got to give the parents what they expect."

Liz turned around, took her packet of cigarettes out of her pocket and put one in her mouth. She waved the packet at Lillie who leant forward and took one. Liz lit her own cigarette and held the match towards Lillie who poked the tip of her cigarette into the flame. Liz shook out the match and tossed it away.

"What do you want, anyway?" asked Liz who started to walk with a measured tread back towards the buildings.

"Milton's been screwing some librarian. She's drawing him away from us."

"Ah! So that's who you are. I knew I should know you. Even so, why use the word "us" all the time?"

"We did alright, sharing him."

"I didn't like my evenings alone."

"Neither did I."

They walked on in silence for a time. When they reached the edge of the grass the two male teachers nodded to Liz who nodded back to them without breaking her stride. The heel plates of Liz's boots clinked on the concrete.

"You're good looking, anyway," said Liz once they were out of earshot of the male teachers. They went around a corner and a group of sparrows, which had been squabbling over a crust of bread, burst apart like an exploding shell and flew away into the air. Then, one by one, the sparrows reformed in line on the spouting of an adjacent classroom. "I'll just get my coat. Come in if you like."

It was eerie in the deserted classroom. Coloured paper silhouettes hung from the roof, trembling slightly. The desks looked like a group of animals about to stampede for the door at any minute. Lillie looked at the symmetrical, white printing on the blackboard. The ledge underneath the board was scattered with pieces of coloured chalk and powdered with chalk dust. A glinting, golden fish swam in the emerald water of a fishbowl. In one corner was a table covered with shells and stones. On the wall above the table was a large piece of paper with autumn leaves stuck on it. In another corner there were some tall pieces of toitoi and bamboo.

Liz sat on her desk and looked at Lillie.

You love Milton?"

"I want him."

"So do I. If your existence allows me to keep him, that's alright."

"But he's got this librarian."

"I know."

"Why do you want him?"

"Let's go home and have a drink? I know you drink."

Back at Harper's Lillie and Liz prepared for their evening with a sort of sober gloom. Lillie fetched in kindling and firewood from the little room at the back of Harper's ramshackle garage and knelt at the hearth. As the kindling began to take, she dropped bigger and bigger pieces of wood on the structurally fragile blaze. Finally, Lillie tossed two white pieces of split pine on the blaze and stood up from the cold hearth. She sat down in an armchair. Liz came through with a flagon of sherry cradled in one arm like a baby. She had two sherry glasses in her other hand. She set the glasses on the carpet and carefully poured two sherries holding the flagon in both hands. She screwed the top back onto the sherry flagon.

"I like to put the top back on because I believe, quite erroneously, that it makes me drink less." Lillie laughed.

"Cheers!" she said, holding up her glass. They touched glasses. Lillie took a sip of her sherry, put it down, offered Liz a cigarette, took one herself and lit both cigarettes. They sat there in the dull light of the electric bulb, the fire crackling and a pot lid tinkling on the stove. Occasionally there was a hiss as some water fell from the pot lid onto the element.

Liz bent over, unzipped her boots, pulled them off and flexed her sinuous feet in front of the fire.

"I suppose," said Liz, starting off slowly, "it's a bit like this. When you're a girl and you have a special toy, you're somehow made special by that toy. Some men believe that because they own a special car that they are somehow special. Well, my special car, my special toy, is Milton. I feel special because I own him."

"Isn't that a bit of a vote of no confidence in you?'

"Not really. I'm not thick and I'm quite learned really, more so than Milton. But he picks up nuggets off the ground while I spend years mining them. That is something irreplaceable. At the moment though, he just won't talk."

Liz sunk once more into silence. She wanted talk out of Milton all right, but more importantly, she just wanted Milton. She wanted to walk along the beach with him when it was nearly dark, but when you could still feel the heat in the air and the cool hand of the flat, deep, blue sea. She wanted to walk through cities in the rain with the neon lights standing out, even in the middle of the day, with people flowing noisily and hotly onto the streets after having lunch in bars. She wanted to drag him from shop to shop, his face crinkled with distress, as she feasted her eyes on the unattainable extravagances of the world. She simply wanted him.

Lillie looked across at Liz and she too began to feel for words, for ideas.

"He knows something about me that I cannot quite grasp. I have always been very physical and Milton is the essence of the physical. It is as though, in looking at him, I see what I am who I am. If all men were mirrors Milton would be the only mirror in which I could see my reflection. Yeah, that's exactly it." Lillie tossed her cigarette but into the fire.

"We're not very alike," said Liz.

"No."

"What do you think he sees in this librarian?"

"She's an aberration. I don't believe she matters."

After that they slipped down the slide of drunkenness together, without ever ascending to any sort of gaiety. They sipped their sherries more and more infrequently, while their matches exploded more and more often. Their cheeks became hot and their eyes sore.

Lillie's throat became sore, as it always did when she smoked too much. Once Liz got up and opened the door, but the cold was so sharp she shut it again immediately and stood for a while leaning against the shut door.

Eventually they went out to the kitchen, moving with absurd deliberateness, and ate their tea. The potatoes were too salty and the lamb chops were shrunk into pieces of hard, brown wood.

"I could carve Pinocchio out of this chop," said Liz with apparent seriousness.

"The grain would be no good," said Lillie. Liz laughed without enthusiasm. First one and then the other tossed their cutlery onto their plates of mangled chops, broken potatoes and mashed silver beet. They both lit cigarettes.

"Sorry about that," said Liz. "I'm not usually this appalling."

"Who cares?"

"Perhaps we ought to have desert?"

"Good idea."

Lillie watched the apricots slip over the lip of the can like orange boats going over a waterfall. The peaches sat like water lilies in the white plate as the juice coiled around them. Lillie pushed Liz's hand up when she thought she had had enough. The rest of the apricots avalanched into Liz's plate.

"These look better cooked anyway," said Liz sitting down."

"You reckon you could do without him?" asked Lillie as she sucked an apricot off her spoon.

"Yes."

"No man has ever got me down like this."

"We'll get over him if he leaves, but I'd rather not have to."

"Yeah."

They retreated back to the lounge. Lillie threw some more pieces of split pine onto the dying fire and Liz refilled the sherry glasses.

"We might as well turn the light out."

"Might as well," said Lillie. Liz plunged the room into blackness. They sat there, two silhouettes, the fire light whirling and flickering on their legs. Their breathing sounded unusually heavy and loud. The red tips of their cigarettes bobbed erratically as they talked. Liz went and pulled up the venetian blinds and wiped a hole in the fog on the window pane and looked out at the navy blue, star pierced sky. Then she returned to her chair at the fire. The light came through the window like light from an open refrigerator door. Lillie began to feel as though her eyelids were very puffy.

"I'm tired Liz."

"Go through and lie down. Straight through the kitchen on the left."

Liz watched Lillie navigate her way through the darkness and out the door. Liz pushed her feet towards the fire again. She felt like a fuck. If Milton came home now, they could do it on the floor. Then he could go and have Lillie if he wanted to. She was not such a bad sort, Lillie. Liz figured she could get on all right with her. Perhaps living, all three of them in the same house, would solve the problem. Watching Milton have Lillie might be exciting. She shut her eyes.

Then, suddenly, there was a click and Liz looked towards the door. A blast of air, cold, wet and bestial wrapped itself around her. Milton came through the door silhouetted against the street light. Then everything went dark. Liz blinked.

"Hi," said Milton softly. For a second Liz felt as though the room was still empty.

"You've been with somebody?"

"No." Milton walked into the light of the fire. Liz stood up, took two unsteady steps towards him and clung on to him.

"I'm a little drunk." He kissed the top of her head. She reached down, unzipped his fly and began to fondle him. Milton sighed with relief and kissed her all over her face. Liz pulled him over to the couch and collapsed on her back. Milton pulled off her panties and touched her rump. There was a hiss as she drew in her breath and tried to wriggle away from his touch.

"Your hands are bloody frigid. Don't touch me!" She drew him to her with her heels. Milton felt himself slip into her smooth, moist, almost synthetic warmth. He joggled her gently and heard her sigh. "Come on," she whispered. Milton, who was gripping the back of the divan pushed hard against her. He felt Liz lurch hard against him and he heard her start to come.

When she had finished, he bent over and kissed her stomach. His prick felt cold, sticking out of his trousers like that. He stood up and put Liz's hand on his penis.

"No," she said quietly.

"Why the hell not?" asked Milton with shocking loudness.

"Shh," said Liz. "Lillie's asleep in the bedroom. You'd better go through and see her. Warm your hands first though. I'll make a cup of tea."

Liz turned on the light. Milton rubbed his eyes and then pulled his penis back into his pants. He walked slowly over to the fire taking off his coat. He threw two more pieces of wood onto the coals and extended his hands to the fire. He sat there watching the logs blacken and then, finally, burst into flame. He stood up and went over and let down the venetian blinds. They fell with a bang. He went and sat down by the fire again. Liz came through with a pot of tea and he reached up her skirt and squeezed her naked backside.

"You feel delicious."

"And what about Lillie? Will she feel delicious when you go through to her?"

"Of course." Liz pulled away from Milton.

"I'll get the cups."

Liz poured the tea and handed a cup to Milton. She stood with her back to the fire and sipped her tea.

"This is not supposed to work, Milton."

"It will, because now I understand. You, Lillie, weight lifting and running are all part of the same world, the purely physical. I live in a world of surfaces and sensations. Nothing is more beautiful than that world. The other world of self and analysis is a phony world. It is my world that leads towards perfection."

"I only partly see that, Milton."

"You've got too much cigarette smoke in your eyes," said Milton reaching out and squeezing her hand. Milton picked the teapot up off the hearth and poured himself another cup of tea. Milton looked at Liz's feet and her slender toes. Her feet were indescribably beautiful. The walls of the room suddenly looked like slabs of stone and a long way away. He was suddenly very tired. Milton took a long sip of tea and stood up, looming over Liz.

"Are you going in to Lillie?"

"Well, I'm sure as shit not going to sleep on the couch for the night."

Lillie was lying in the darkness half asleep. She could feel the soft wool rubbing her legs. Her back and rump were stiff and she was constantly changing position, winding and unwinding on the cover of the bed. Her mouth was beginning to feel dry. She pulled the woolly bedspread off the pillows and hugged one pillow tight against her stomach. A thick, heavy scent mixed with the smell of old carpet in the cold air. Lillie rolled herself up in the bedspread, completely trapping herself and the pillow. Being trapped so tightly was not at all unpleasant. Such a big bed too was a luxury. She had never owned a double bed of her own, though she had slept in other people's double beds. She rolled from one side of the big bed to the other. Then she lay still. Her body became hot, without moisture. Her stomach felt a little empty. The air in the room became soft and choking, like candy floss. Lillie felt her face twisting out of shape. She opened her mouth and started to pant.

Suddenly there was flash and the room was white and everything looked like a film negative. Lillie fought her way out of the tight blanket. The colours returned to the room but the light still blazed with unnatural intensity. She could see Milton at the foot of the bed, his hair a delicious gold and his flesh as white and smooth as marble. Further back, against the wall, Lillie could see Liz, standing with her arms folded her face framed by a blur of black hair. Milton was close to her now and Lillie felt her rump go cool and she shivered as an electric shock seemed to flicker in her cunt. She shut her eyes to try to perpetuate the illusion that she wasn't human.

Liz leaned back against the wall. She watched Milton peel Lillie, exposing the thick, soft fruit beneath the clothes. Then she watched Milton naked, writhing like the original serpent himself, on flesh that seemed as though it must burst in a gush of liquid. Reptile and woman, they struggled like two creatures in the desert until they lay there still. Finally, Milton crawled off Lillie's body with mechanical smoothness and slid under the sheet. Lillie stirred. She looked so young; like a big, blond walnut skinned child. She pulled her knees up to her chin and then straightened her legs out under the sheet. She wriggled her way across to Milton and put her head on his shoulder. She closed her eyes, a smile on her face. Milton looked up at Liz.

"Come on, come to bed."

"I'll just have a last cigarette."

She went out the door and the room suddenly seemed very empty to Milton. He lay there looking at the orange water stain on the white, pinex ceiling. Lillie was warm and heavy and burrowing further into his side. Liz came back with a chair, sat beside the bed and lit a cigarette. It suddenly struck Milton that the whole situation was rather like hospital visiting. Liz sat there looking at him and smoking her cigarette. Sitting there looking at Milton she felt as though she had somehow been abandoned. Finally, she stood up and undressed.

Milton lay there looking at her angular frame, her wide hips and her small breasts. Liz bent over and pulled the sheets back. Milton grinned at her.

"You'll have to put the lights out tonight."

"So I will."

Everything went dark. Milton felt the bed wriggle and heard a mattress spring ping. He reached out. Liz had her back to him. He reached over and grasped her stomach.

"I want you."

"Do you?" He felt her turn over. She gave his penis a painful squeeze. "So, you do." He felt Liz turn away from him again. Then he felt her rubbing on his hip. He turned towards her and Liz thrust her rump against his stomach. Lillie put her arms around him and pressed herself against his back.

Chapter 29

The sunlight shone, white but feeble, through the cold air. Jim Wilson looked across the oily, surging water of the harbour at the palm trees, their branches writhing above the river's edge. The railway lines were rusty on the sideless, curving bridge that spanned the river. Two seagulls hovered like kites, screeching above the masts of a fishing boat. Jim Wilson could hear the slop of the water around the piers. Behind him cars bumped their way over the tar seal and onto the heavy, grey, concrete road bridge. The berth for the big ships, towards the harbour entrance, was deserted, dwarfed by the empty sky and the open sea.

Jim Wilson turned from the harbour and looked across the concrete, past the cream weighbridge building, to the palm flapping on the piece of green lawn before the mouth of the bridge. Milton Harper was coming towards him from underneath the palm. Jim Wilson raised his hand in the air and Milton leaned forward and began to run, his black coat flapping around his thighs.

Jim Wilson stepped forward beaming and took Milton by the hand.

"How are you?" he said taking Milton's cold hand in his own fleshy grip.

"Fine," said Milton, "fine." Jim Wilson hugged Milton. "Shall we walk?"

"Yes, good idea. Let's walk.

So they walked round past the waterfront fish shops, past the lunching men in white pants, aprons and hats. Sometimes the men were just in groups sitting and smoking, talking and laughing noisily in doorways, in the sun but out of the wind. Jim and Milton walked side by side in silence; Milton Harper's slim explosive muscle beside the slow striding giant; Milton's hair curling and flying at Jim Wilson's shoulder. They walked in a cocoon of friendship which blotted out the people they passed. One of a group of girls in green smocks and hats wolf-whistled at them from a yard, but neither Jim nor Milton noticed.

They walked past the iron mooring pommels and the big, slightly frayed, loops of rope. The grey wall between the harbour and the river was streaked, in places, with vertical, black lines. A chugging fishing boat was coming in, its prow slapping irritably at the choppy water.

"How's love?" asked Milton Harper, finally breaking their silence.

"I don't really know," said Jim Wilson. Milton laughed warmly. Kaiti Hill was high above them now, glittering green in the watery sun and misty blue of the sky."

"How come you don't know?"

"I'm sunk in it, I'm drowning."

"I'm saved James, I'm saved," said Milton slapping him on the back. "I'm finally removed from all those things you seek."

"How?"

"Through physical pain and physical pleasure; through embracing the purely physical." Jim Wilson shrugged.

"There seems no point in suffering to me."

"Christ was purified on the cross."

"Yes, but he died to redeem mankind."

"I don't believe he died. I think he lived and realised that love, compassion, the things he lived for, were all fraud and that, if you shrugged them off, all you were left with was the flesh and your own, glorious Adam like aloneness."

"Well what happened to him?"

"He went and hid in a brothel." They both laughed.

Then they were out of the sheds and warehouses looking across at the blue sea, waves running alongside the sea wall, like blunt nosed whales slowly rising out of the water as it became shallower until there was no longer any water beneath them and, being out of their element, they shattered to pieces on the beach. Out on the sea, which was all undulation and bursting light they could see a gleaming, white boat angling across the bay like a hooked trout making a sudden rush across a pool. Before them and to their right, were the reefs, water gleaming on their dull, grey tables. The sea was frothing and splashing in clefts. Here and there the reef was stained with brown algae and seaweed.

Jim and Milton walked alongside the thin strip of tar seal that had been stained by whitish clay. As they went they were obliged to pick their way between the puddles on the sandy, brown dirt beside the chipped edge of the tar seal. The grass between the road and the beach was long, coarse and dank. Way out across the reef, at the seas edge where the blue water reared and retreated, a Maori woman and her son, with jute sacks in their hands, were jumping from rock to rock. The sacks hung stiff and flared from their hands.

"I wonder what they're after."

"Sea eggs maybe."

"Come on, let's go and sit on the beach."

They sat down amidst the stones and the broken shells. There were bits of leathery, brown-black kelp decaying between the stones and bits of brittle, black seaweed festooned with nuts, hardening between the shattered driftwood. Jim Wilson turned his back to the wind and lit a cigarette. Milton picked up a yellow piece of driftwood which had been smoothed like a bone by the churning waves and the rocks. He ran his hand over the surface.

"As sculpted as a woman's arse."

"Don't be revolting, Milton," said Jim quietly. "You don't treat women as having humanity."

"No," said Milton. He lay down and wiggled his back until the stones were arranged in a comfortable position. "What good would that do?"

Jim Wilson closed his eyes and felt the cool wind rubbing his sun hot face like a hanging willow frond. He put his hand to his mouth and felt for the cigarette with his lips. Milton watched the smoke come out Jim's nose and then slide over the surface of his cheeks and race away towards the steep, foliage green cliff face behind them.

"I've been thinking about love, Milton," said Jim, rather unexpectedly. Milton began to laugh, but instead of stopping after a reasonable interval his laughter continued and grew in intensity. Jim Wilson opened his eyes and saw Milton sitting on the stones, his elbows tight against his ribs, rocking from side to side, his mouth wide open and his eyes glinting with tears. Finally he wasn't laughing anymore, he was just panting, lying on his side now, hitting the stones with the bottom of his clenched fists. At last he managed to say:

"I wish you wouldn't state the obvious like that."

"Well, are you ready to listen?" asked Jim Wilson with a grin.

"Let me get my breath back, will you?"

"Be my guest." Finally, Milton blew the last laugh from his mouth, like a trumpeter blowing into a trumpet and settled back on his elbows.

"Let's have these thoughts then, shall we?"

"Are you sure you wouldn't like to laugh about something else first?"

" Nope," said Milton. "I don't see any more intellectually lumbering clerics in the neighbourhood."

"The commonest notion about love is that the woman you love is your other half and that you need her to achieve perfection."

"Yes. Don't you think it's true?"

"I don't think so. What happens if the woman is the earth and you are striving to be part of the earth?"

"Beats me. What happens?"

"What's the only way a man can get into the earth?"

"He could become a potholer," said Milton grinning. Jim Wilson scowled. "Or he could get himself buried," added Milton.

"Exactly."

Milton stood up, picked up a stone and hurled it into the air. It held up in the air before curling away to the left and skittering over the rocks. Then he stood there kicking a hole in the earth beneath the stones. An old car drove slowly along the road behind them. There was sudden burst of music as it drove past and the music died away very suddenly. The sea clashed over and over like cymbals playing in a distant orchestra. Milton put his hands in his pockets and looked at Jim.

"I don't know anything about love except that it doesn't work. It was just a force that I could never understand. Love isn't me. That's all."

"You don't know if I'm right then?" asked Jim walking down the beach and putting his hand on Milton's shoulder.

"It just seems to me a dangerous thought," said Milton, his eyelids being tugged by the wind coming out of the misty, blue sky.

Jim Wilson pulled Milton against him almost brutally, and then released him. Jim Wilson felt betrayed by Milton. Milton knew much more than he was prepared to let on.

As he made love to Melissa Jim Wilson knew that he was transformed and that she likewise was transformed; so that when they came back to themselves after having been away, they were both disappointed to return to the clear, cool light of everyday reality. It was as though, during the labour of love, Jim was drawn again and again into some fecund darkness of windless, dry decay where the air was choked with the fine dust of rotten wood. Time and again he reached out for the woman he loved only to find a place which seemed to have nothing to do with any woman or anything human. It was this place that was the final destiny of love, its final triumph. Nature was finally, through its ultimate weapon, love, calling man back to itself. In defiance of God it was calling man to rot, body and soul, in the suffocating dirt. So that he might feed the trees and the flowers and the creatures of the earth. As he caressed the woman he loved man stared at the spaded sides of the grave. It was love calling man to itself, to death.

By then Milton was standing up on the road looking back over his shoulder at Jim Wilson, below him on the beach. Jim had a stick in his hands and was breaking it into smaller and smaller pieces. Milton turned away from Jim and looked away up the hill at a small, dark brown, creosoted bach with white window sills and a white door frame. In the freshly cultivated space between the fence, also daubed with creosote, and the dwelling, a man with a pipe in his mouth was sitting on his heels planting onions along a string line. His was the last bach. After that there were only thin, tangled native trees on the increasingly steep hill face.

Milton looked back again at Jim Wilson, lost in thought and fumbling with his cigarettes. Milton silently cursed women. As long as they were beautiful, tender, frail, compassionate, needy of love, they were lethal. As long as they reached towards a man to reach out and possess them, they were murder, even if they did not know what they were doing.

Fortunately, Lillie and Liz were not of that sort. They did not want to be taken or possessed. They only wanted pleasure, to be transported out of themselves. They did not demand this terrible, obscene and frightening intimacy. Long live them and all whores like them.

"Come on, Jim. We're going back."

"Uh? What's that?

"We're going back," said Milton, walking to the road's edge and putting out his hand. Jim grasped Milton's hand and Milton pulled him up onto the road. Milton put his arm behind Jim's back and pressed him into movement. They walked, slow and meandering, in the middle of the road like a couple of lovers out to idle away the afternoon. "I think you ought to leave this woman," said Milton looking up at the side of Jim Wilson's face. Jim walked on; his face immobile. Milton grinned momentarily, feeling like a little boy staring up at an adult. "You know I'm not much of a guy really. I can be pretty shitty and pretty cold; but you're the only man friend I've got in this place." Milton took his hand away from behind Jim's back, put it in his coat pocket and shrugged. They walked on a little way. "I don't suppose it all matters." Milton suddenly breathed out, as though he was breathing on a hand mirror before he intended to wipe it. Jim Wilson looked down at Milton and smiled and winked.

"I know what you're saying. But right now, I can't bring myself to do what is necessary."

They sauntered past a fifty kilometre per hour sign. As they passed Milton deposited a neat, globule of spit in the middle of 0.

"I never could play darts," said Milton, "but boy could I hoick."

They walked on moving in among the warehouses and the small factories and back into the orbit of the petrol fumes. Like all dock areas, everything seemed to be coated with a varnish of grime. They walked over the horror grey pavement until they reached the wooden docks again. The fishing boats moored over against the wall that kept the river out of the harbour were still sidling in their moorings. A bike with a monotonously shrieking peddle was ridden past by an unshaven man in a crumpled sports jacket and khaki trousers. He had a yellow cigarette butt, which he seemed to have forgotten, hanging from the corner of his mouth.

Jim and Milton looked over the edge of the wharf into the water. *His reflection is broken by the water* thought Milton. Milton had been too weak to cope with the rebuffs of love and he had fled it. That had been the easy thing to do, like not dying. Not dying was easy and comfortable. *Jim,* he thought, *will ride it to the end, even if he's not there yet.*

Jim turned away from the water's edge. He had not been looking at his own reflection, but at the silver light that had been behind him. He felt sick. He did not want to die, but reason seemed to suggest that was the only option. It was not extinction he feared, but a transformation of consciousness, the apprehension a man feels before he takes a new drug. Of course, the difference was that death was the one trip you could never get off.

And, of course, there was his responsibility to Melissa. He felt that he had somehow used her, though it was not his fault. In his love for her was his betrayal of her. Whatever the situation, Jim Wilson knew that he was compelled to die; just as he had been compelled to love Melissa.

Jim Wilson and Milton walked back to the road to Kaiti where the traffic went by with the same monotonous rhythm. They stood there, looking at the traffic and then the sky and not knowing what to say. They both believed that this was a parting but the parting somehow made no sense because neither of them could believe in it, grasp its finality. So, they simply stood there. Periodically they would look at one another and grin. The tension became so great that both felt like laughing.

In the end Milton simply looked quickly at Jim and walked off.

Jim watched Milton walking quickly but deliberately towards the bridge. Soon he would be absorbed into the carnival atmosphere of the town's centre. Milton reached the horizon of the bridge and slowly disappeared down the other side. Jim Wilson turned away and began to walk towards home.

Chapter 30

Once he was in the city and out of Jim's sight Milton went into a phone box and dialled Jim's number. Milton stood in the phone box looking at the collection of soaps in a chemist shop window. In his right ear the phone went "drrrt, drrrt!" There was the desired click at the other end.

"Hello, Melissa. This is Milton Harper here."

"I thought you were supposed to be with Jim."

"I've just left him. He's on his way home. Can you get away now?"

"I can bring the baby in the car, I suppose."

"I want to see you."

"Where then?"

"I'll be on one of those seats near the Peel Street Bridge. Okay?"

"All right. I won't be long."

There was a clack and Milton found himself listening into a dead phone. He put the receiver back into the cradle and shivered. It was cold in the shade of the city awnings. He stepped out of the phone box and walked through the women with heavy shopping bags, strolling farmers with their hands in their pockets and girls in jeans, patrolling the streets, looking for God knows what. Periodically two plump, shiny faced businessmen would hail one another and stop and talk in the middle of the pavement, radiating well-being. If they smoked, they smoked as though they had never smoked before.

Milton turned down the wide street that led to the bridge, making sure he kept on the other side from the library. He reached the bridge, concrete and solid like the one over at the port. He ran across the road which edged the river, sidled between the parked cars, walked under the shade of the wind hissing Pohutukawa's and down the sloping lawn to the river's edge. Further along the grassy bank an elderly man was sitting at a brown table feeding birds.

Milton looked into the grey water of the river at a half-submerged brown paper bag. Wave after wave was flowing back up the river driven by the incoming tide. They were only small waves at the moment with long spaces between them. Between the boarded river bank where Milton stood and the grey circling water was an area of grey mud and brown matted grass. The lawn, sloping to the water's edge, was yellow in the sun.

Milton began to pace. He hated waiting. Ever since he had given up smoking, he had hated waiting.

Finally, he looked up to the heavy, green trees swaying above the cars that looked like billiard balls and saw Melissa, leaning slightly backwards and slipping as she came down the grassy slope. She looked pretty and plump in her flared, blue jeans.

"Hello Milton," she said smiling warmly. "I haven't seen you for a while, not since I got thin."

"You look nice," said Milton smiling. Then he wished he hadn't said that.

"Thank you," said Melissa looking pleased. Melissa came to a stop beside him, put a cigarette in her mouth and looked across the river. She adjusted the cigarette in her mouth and lit it.

"You look more sophisticated now that you're a slim smoker." Melissa laughed in a way that indicated she thought that Milton was being silly.

"You're much less suspicious than you were."

"I know you're not on the hunt." Melissa laughed again.

"What do you want, anyway?" She turned and began to walk downstream, forcing Milton to follow her.

"I think Jim's planning to leave you." She stopped suddenly and turned, her face pale.

"What?"

"Not like that. I think he's going to kill himself."

"Oh," said Melissa, sounding relieved.

"You don't sound exactly mortified."

"I can't stop him, Milton. I don't want him to die, but I can't stop him. You don't try to force someone you love. It would destroy that love."

"But if he dies there will be no one to love."

"At least our love will have been honoured and we can still respect one another."

"God damn it! He'll be dead."

"You don't understand, do you?"

"Whadda, you mean I don't understand? You think I've never loved?"

"If he dies, I might have to die too."

"Bullshit! Women are not like that."

"We aren't all empty vessels, Milton."

"You won't do anything then?"

"Not won't. Can't"

"Sorry for wasting your time then." Milton turned and walked away up the bank. Melissa could read defeat in his back. He's rather magnificent, she thought, fighting his lonely struggle against the world. There is nothing that guy would not fight. He was conceived rebellious and when he perishes, he will perish rebellious.

Milton topped the bank, moving with muscular power. You could almost see the wings under his coat, as though he was about to leap into the sky with a cry of triumph and laugh and mock the world in full knowledge that he would eventually fall exhausted to the earth and be torn to pieces by the waiting multitudes.

Melissa slowly climbed the bank. Men, she thought, are crazy for destruction. When I take Jim and enclose him and hold him there, there is always the knowledge that I am trying to protect him from his inevitable doom and I am flooded with the sweet tragedy of human mortality. Yet I cannot rebel, I cannot do. I can only be. But men, men can only become and it is that that destroys them. When Jim loves me, he seeks, while I merely live. Yet it is him I love and if he goes, I will be deserted again and I will have to wait in terrible immobility until I am allowed to love someone new. Men can only pass through my hands, no more. But perhaps there is a loyalty beyond time that needs to be honoured in spite of its absurdity.

The thick, wooden soles of Melissa's shoes clunked on the pavement and she threw her cigarette butt under the wheels of a parked car. The cigarette butt rolled back down the slope of the road and lay smouldering in the wet leaves in the gutter.

Chapter 32

Spring that year was not a season in itself but rather an interval between the hushed dead of winter and the sudden, dry, smoky heat of summer. The weeping willows finally shed the last of their leaves and within a month, like some quick-change artists, they were already shooting new, green tips. Some days it was warm and breezy, but there was no slow accumulation of warmth that spring often brings. The daffodils and jonquils were out and the flowering plums were pasted with pink blossoms as though some mad kid had been rushing round with crepe paper flowers gluing them to the trees. But rather than a perceptible change spring simply progressed and the flowers simply came out, one by one in their pre-established order. Then, at some point, people suddenly said: "Oh, it's spring."

Spring certainly had little effect on Jim and Melissa. They waited in a stillness of expectation, waiting for some unarticulated disaster to strike. Even when Jim was charming there was horror lurking beneath the gaiety. Melissa saw it all and suffered it all. Sometimes Jim would prowl the house with pent up grief until Melissa simply left, whereupon he would sit and cry. He wept for his own misfortune and the woman he was about to betray.

Each time Jim and Melissa made love he was seized by a cold dread because he knew where his love would take him but he also knew he had to go there because he loved the woman. He was wracked by the terrible duality of her flesh.

Once he had been to see Milton Harper and his harem, but the sheer trivial effervescence of their existence had sent him away sickened. They seemed to skate over the surface of life without ever seeing it.

That particular day Jim and Melissa had been to lunch at her parents. Gibbo had chomped his meal at the head of the table with unusual dourness, even for him. There had been a savage southerly storm several days before and he had lost a lot of his early lambs. When Dave uncharacteristically grumbled about having to go round the ewes Jim and Melissa offered to do it for him.

They climbed the ridge with their pants tucked inside heavy, grey, woollen socks. Jim's hobnail boots creaked as he laboured up the hill. The long yellow-green, spring grass fluttered in the slight breeze. The dead, woolly corpses of last year's thistles bobbed. They heard the faint sound of a spring and looked down at the fan of shining, water-wet grass on the hill below. Way down on the flat the house sat in its own shadow, looking almost as though it was sitting in a hole in the ground. The sun glared on the roof. Mrs Gibson, in a wide-brimmed, straw hat was crouching on the sunny side of the house digging in the garden with her trowel.

"Makes you feel funny to see something you know from so far away," said Melissa. Jim Wilson smiled and pulled her against his hip. They went on climbing into the blue sky which was swimming with spring light. At least the light had yellowed a bit since mid winter. Jim felt dizzy and his exertion distracted him, for a time, from his doom. He could see the white of Melissa's flesh between her blouse and her trousers. Her flesh was glowing with perspiration. Her blue, jeaned backside was thrust towards him as she climbed the hill in front of him.

Jim felt suddenly happy, meaninglessly happy. There was only the surface of this glittering world. Jim thought of Milton Harper and his physical exertions. Perhaps it was this that Milton was infatuated with. Jim let the thought drift away like a thistledown in the wind. He wasn't going to ruin this occasion when Melissa was pink, loveable flesh by an excess of speculation.

Eventually they were lost in the hills with no sign of a house anywhere. There was only the innocent, confident curiosity of the larks, the honk of a circling pair of paradise ducks who periodically disappeared only to return corrupting the lark tinkling, sheep-bleating air with their nasal honks. The hills, green and spring smooth, stretched away in waves like a woman's hair. In the valleys the thick, dark manuka was bent and shaken by the wind. The slopes of some of the steeper hills flashed like mirrors where port holes of bare papa had been exposed.

They walked through some fresh, green, new, spring thistles on the hard, yellow track. A pheasant planed down a ridgelet like a fast-moving cloud. Then they stopped and Jim put both hands on the top of a fence post and visibly sagged as he stood there panting while Melissa raised her binoculars to her eyes and swung slowly on her hips as she scanned the neighbouring hills. Then she let the binoculars hang below her breasts and turned and looked at Jim, whose eyes were round with exhaustion and said:

"You want a cigarette?" Jim looked at her as though he barely comprehended and then he nodded savagely because he felt it such an effort to nod at all. He slid down the post and sat with his back against it and slowly lit a cigarette with trembling hands. He sat there feeling the sun burn his face and the wind cool his sweat and soon his whole body was tormented by an itch that was a fusion of heat and cold that would not mix. Melissa still on her feet, said: "Come on! We've got to go and have a look at the Māori Paddock yet. Any way, we mustn't get cold."

They walked on towards the back of the farm on ridges that were like arrow heads of flint, tumbling in shiny terraces onto the boulder choked valleys below. In the bottoms of two of the valleys were still surviving stands of native bush. You could see silvery threads of water on the faces of the grey boulders that had blocked the gullies and forced the streams to flow over the tops of them. They disturbed a black cow under a couple of manukas and the cow charged off down the hill in panic, her huge udder swaying. Eventually she disappeared into another stand of manukas. Sheep lay in the shadows of the cabbage trees and others plodded the steep terraces nibbling grass. Jim and Melissa passed a staggering, still yellow, young lamb, apparently disorientated, jabbing his mothers udder. Coming over one hillock a savage eyed hawk heaved itself into the air; the lambs carcass he had been feeding on rising an inch or two off the ground before he could untangle his claws from it and drop the weight. The hawk flew off mechanically, leaving the white and red carcass lying on the ridge.

Eventually Melissa stopped and turned around, hands on hips, and watched Jim, who had fallen further and further behind her, coming up the ridge; looking at the ground, his body forward and rolling with each step. She felt happy. She was at home here and knew what she was doing. Maybe she had hated it all once, but it was undeniable that she got a great deal of pleasure from walking the hills of the farm. It was what she had been brought up to do, whether she approved of it or not.

Jim looked up the ridge at Melissa, a blurred, black silhouette in the blue sky. He had never been so tired, but he was free, not of reality because everywhere he turned there was a reality that was alarming, but free from the dark prison cell of his musings. It was like bobbing on the top of a gushing fountain of water, really living, and purely enjoying life. He fell in front of Melissa on his knees and kissed her stomach, which was wet and hot and had a red mark on it where the elastic of her panties had been before they had slipped down her hips. He could smell her hot skin and he licked her stomach. When his tongue disappeared off her skin Melissa felt a numbing coldness. She stepped back from Jim leaving him there on his knees. She looked at him kneeling amidst the sheep shit and the biddy biddy, staring at something far away in the sky. She laughed.

"You want to go for a swim?"

"I don't have any togs," said Jim.

"You don't need any togs here. There are only sheep around and they walk with their naked backsides in the air all the time."

"My flesh is scalding and I'm itchy as well."

"We'll go home along the big creek and have a dip then. I'll just have a look round first."

Jim stood up stiffly, lit himself a cigarette and walked backwards and forwards on the knoll to stop getting cold. Far off, in the blue sky above the endless succession of hills, three magpies were attacking a hawk. The magpies would climb above the hawk and shoot suddenly down slashing at the cumbersome hawk with their beaks. Vainly the hawk would turn on its side hoping to catch one of the passing shadows with its talons. All across the spotty hills the trees were moving and the fence posts looked like dark matches driven into plasticene.

Melissa walked back towards Jim.

"We've got to go down here. There's a sheep cast or dead over the other side." They started downhill and Jim found, to his surprise, that this was harder than walking up hill. That particular paddock was thick with manuka and the manuka tore at Jim's face and made it itch. He got manuka leaves down his shirt and that itched as well. At the same time gravity pulled him remorselessly down the slope forcing his legs to move faster and faster. Finally, he attempted to sit down on a patch of grass and moss, but he simply slid on his backside so he stood up and went on, half walking and half running. On one occasion he and Melissa burst into a clearing where there were several sheep. The sheep's eyeballs shattered with horror and they ran in panic towards the oncoming humans, only to veer away at the last minute, their bodies swaying like loosely stuffed pillows.

Jim and Melissa emerged out on the rush strewn flat. Melissa lay down on the wet ground laughing, feeling the moisture begin to seep into her clothes almost immediately. Jim Wilson sat on top of a rush looking like a giant sitting on a dwarf's stool. Melissa stood up. The back of her jeans and her blouse were wet and muddy.

"I haven't had so much fun since I was a kid," she said, panting and grinning. Jim Wilson sat in glum, body aching silence. The muscles of his calves were jumping like frogs trying to escape from a pit. He could hear his heart banging, apparently in his ears. He felt sad, but it least it was a worldly sadness. He looked at Melissa and smiled a rumpled smile. She looked at him and wished she hadn't tried to walk him off his feet. Still, at least they were both happy at that moment. She walked over to him and put her arms around his head. "Come on, you poor, old giant. Let's go and find this sheep." She stepped back and waited for him to get up.

The creek was in a gorge there and they walked upstream until they came to a dry slide of shingle and dirt which ended at the bottom where dark water ran between brown stones, all shaded by native trees. Down there it was a different world, like a dragon's throat, green and cold and soft coloured. Behind Jim and Melissa the land was man dry, but down there among the native trees, the moss, the ferns and the smooth, silent pools man went as a guest, a part of the landscape, not the owner of it.

"Ready?" asked Melissa.

"I suppose so. You go first."

Melissa jumped off the top of the bank onto the slide. Her feet started to move and she jumped again. The dust rose about her until she was just a shadow in the dust and all the time she was jumping and sliding, getting closer to the bottom.

She passed out of the sun and into the shadow of the gorge. On she went, jumping like a nimble goat into the dark below. Jim jumped onto the slide, felt the uncertainty of his foothold and jumped again. The dust trail left by Melissa meant that he got dust in his throat, but that was nothing compared to the dizzying haste of his descent. Jim had never known anything like it. It was like being a God yourself. He was descending as fast as a water fall, unable to place his feet, something beyond him controlling his movements. He became aware that he was cold as he passed into the shadow of the bush, but his descent still continued.

Suddenly, there he was standing in the middle of running water. The crackle of water was rich and thick. It seemed to Jim that he was still moving. He staggered around in circles a couple of times. Melissa was standing there in the green darkness on the other side of the creek.

"You're pretty agile for a heavyweight." Jim beamed with triumph. He splashed through the water. A cold thread of water ran inside the greasy oven of his socks. It ran in one, long, delicious dribble down the back of his ankle and on to his instep.

Melissa had climbed out of the creek bed now and Jim followed her into the trees, climbing over tracks made slippery by fallen leaves. The track zigzagged up the steep side of the gorge. Three quarters of the way up they passed through the green-yellow, flickering of sunlight and leaves, like walking through a mobile made of the lenses of sun glasses. The wind hissed in the perfect, soothing solitude of the native bush.

Finally they came out on the dry bank top looking at the sunlight lying over the hills like golden syrup and the slowly moving manuka and the brown and green rushes. A kingfisher flew like a blue arrow across their path.

"I think it's to the left," said Melissa. She led off, Jim following, listening to the thud of their boots on the hard ground.

A couple of hundred yards further up the creek they came across the sheep lying in some water cress in a shallow stream. They looked down at the sheep lying on her side. She stared at them, too exhausted for fear. She kicked a couple of times and then let her head fall back on the slushy ground and lay there still.

"Well, let's see what sort of a gynaecologist you are," said Melissa slipping into the side creek over the bank. Jim Wilson, feeling a sudden rush of idiocy, jumped into the air and, after hanging there momentarily, fell, embedding his feet in the muddy ground and splattering mud all over him and Melissa. "You big goat!" said Melissa grinning. They walked up to the sheep. She simply lay there, apparently indifferent to her fate. "Let's get her out, shall we?" Jim Wilson shrugged, leant over, took two handfuls of wool, lifted the sheep out of the quagmire and deposited it on the dry ground above. The side it had been lying on was so wet and muddy it looked as though it had no wool at all on that side. "Hold on to it!" shouted Melissa scrambling out of the stream bed on her knees and rushing over to grab the sheep.

"Well, what now?" asked Jim Wilson.

"You hold it!" said Melissa, rolling up her right sleeve. Jim Wilson could just see two black hooves protruding from the sheep. Melissa slipped her hand inside the sheep and, in a couple of minutes, had delivered the dead lamb. The lamb lay still in its afterbirth, looking as though it was wrapped in a plastic bag. Melissa stood there panting, her bloody arm dangling. It all seemed strange to Jim Wilson, very simple and superficial, yet profound. "Hold onto it for a couple of minutes," said Melissa, "then give it a kick in the arse." She slipped back into the little gully again, slopped some muddy water on her arm, clambered out of the stream bed again and stood there wiping her arm on the leg of her pants. She lit a cigarette in the cup of her hands like a man. "Okay, put it on its feet and kick its arse." Jim took two handfuls of wool on the sheep's back and stood it on its feet. The sheep immediately collapsed again onto its muddy side. "Kick its arse this time before it sits down," advised Melissa. Jim stood the sheep up and kicked it. The sheep staggered a couple of steps and then collapsed. "Garn," snarled Melissa leaping at the sheep and giving it a hefty kick in the rump. The sheep heaved itself to its feet, hobbled a couple of slow steps, then just stood there and shook its head. "Have a smoke and then we'll chase it along a bit," said Melissa.

Jim Wilson lit a cigarette and gulped the bitter smoke into his lungs. He felt a little dizzy. He had never had much to do with animals before, except of course pets. He hadn't understood that anyone could be so matter of fact about life. Suddenly life seemed to have been enormously simplified for him. Melissa in this situation was a changed person too, much more drab and utilitarian. Yet it occurred to Jim that it was always that solidity that made her so attractive to him. She had been born here in the centre of things, the true heart of the world, so she was completely reliable.

Actually she had a lot in common with her father, though she lacked his streak of savagery. She also lacked the moral vulnerability of her mother. Mrs Gibson had probably come from a normal home and suddenly, coming face to face with matter-of-fact brutality, the trauma had been too much and she was left emotionally weakened. But Melissa had avoided becoming emotionally lopsided. Culture had allowed her to avoid vulgarity and the practical brutality of farm life had given her certainty.

Jim looked up and saw Melissa walk over to the sheep and nudge it with her toe. The sheep moved off a few steps and stopped again. Melissa folded her arms and went on smoking.

When they started back towards the house Jim realised that he had lost all sense of direction. There were only hills and gullies and manuka and fences and the blue sky and the yellow sun beginning to fall out of the sky.

He and Melissa strolled down the river flat. The shadows of a few isolated pines on the green flat stretched long and black towards them. The air had taken on a secret heaviness. Groups of sand flies pulsated in the shade. The air was full of seams of heat and cold.

"Why didn't we come up this way?" asked Jim Wilson.

"We couldn't see anything from here," replied Melissa hugging him. Jim Wilson kissed her moist, hot hairline.

"I wish we could stay here forever."

"So do I," said Melissa, giving his stomach a squeeze.

"Suddenly the world seems altogether changed."

"You mean you no longer look for death?"

"No, I don't; but I suppose it will only last as long as we're here."

"Shall we stay the night?"

"I wouldn't mind."

"Shall we have that swim?"

"I wouldn't mind."

They came down to the water's edge across the moist, grey silt that had choked the grass during the last flood. The downward rush of the creek was impeded there by a ridge which turned the flow of water and created a large, deep hole. They walked in under the orange branches of the basket willow and went to the water's edge. The sun came through the bare branches of the tree in a series of vivid explosions. They stood still under the branches of the tree and looked at the tree's reflection in the slowly swirling water. The sunlight had turned the grey mud on the bottom of the pool an ochre colour.

Melissa retreated from the water's edge, sat down on a big piece of poplar that had been washed down by some earlier flood and began to unlace her boots. Then she removed her socks. Her feet looked very white. She tip-toed across the soft, grey mud under the tree. The warm mud slithered up between her toes. She stood right on the water's edge, stretched out a leg and dipped her toe in the water. She gently stirred the water with the tip of her toe. She withdrew her toe and turned around.

"It's cold."

"Chicken," said Jim.

"Oh, yes?" said Melissa, striding purposefully back to the log. She took off the binocular case and dropped it on the ground. She pulled down her pants and stepped out of them. She quickly unbuttoned her blouse, pulled one arm out of the blouse and then pulled the blouse off the other arm. She reached behind her back, unhooked her bra and, lowering her arms and rounding her shoulders, took it off. Jim Wilson sat there languorously smoking a cigarette. Melissa had a matter-of-fact way of getting undressed which he found very arousing. Melissa padded back to the water's edge and stood there for a moment. Suddenly she just dived out into the sunlight; her back arched her flesh looking as white and thick as cream, her form momentarily like a butterfly. There was a quiet plop as she entered the water and the waves raced out in rings rocking on the edge of the mud. Melissa popped up out of the water like a cork, rising up until her breasts cleared the water and then settling back down again. Her hair had gone a glistening grey and clung close to her head and neck. Jim Wilson looked at the white shadow of her body in the dark, gold water. "Come on!" shouted Melissa and she swam towards the shore.

She lay there on the grey mud at the edge of the pool, her body bobbing in the wavelets of her own making, looking at Jim. Then she retreated back into the pool and, stiffening her arm, slapped the water sending a stream of curling silver through the air towards Jim. The water fell well short of him.

"All right, all right." Jim slowly stood up and reluctantly undressed, putting his clothes in a pile on the log beside Melissa's. Eventually, he stood there beside the log: pink, huge and barrel like, the blond hairs coating his chest and his penis dangling.

"You look like a mountain!" shouted Melissa from out in the water. Suddenly Jim leaned forward and began to run, taking short strides and his feet slipping in the mud, until he stretched out into the air above the water, like a log and fell belly down in the water with a report like a cracking stock whip. Melissa bobbed in the waves and watched Jim's pink body sliding across under the water, his hair streaming out away from his head. He surfaced right on the other side of the pool and stayed there, his chin just above the surface of the water.

"It's not hot," he shouted loudly.

"How would you know?" Melissa shouted back. "You're fatter than a polar bear."

"Cheeky little harlot," laughed Jim. He struck out across the pool with huge, water slapping strokes. Melissa swam away from him up the pool with short, neat little strokes. Once it was too shallow to swim anymore, she stood up, drops of water shining on her goose pimpled flesh. She took a stride towards the crackling silver water above the hole, but she was too late and Jim Wilson's back rose out of the water like the back of a pink, breaching whale and he shot out a hand and grasped Melissa's trailing ankle. She shrieked and tried to pull clear but the big hand was firmly around her ankle. Melissa's hands flew in the air as she fell backwards towards the pool. She felt herself land on Jim Wilson's chest and she felt him wrap his tree trunk legs around her waist.

"What's that thing sticking into my back?" she said, trying to find Jim Wilson's chest with the back of her head.

"Must be an eel," said Jim, paddling with one hand to keep them steady.

Finally, they got out and stood, knees slightly bent, in front of their clothes. Melissa's teeth were chattering and she had a headache. Jim picked up his shirt and began to dry Melissa's back with it. Then he pulled her against him and dried her stomach and her breasts. His clammy flesh sticking to her back made her feel secure and she lost the sad feeling that the cold and headache had brought on. Jim bent over and kissed her just behind the ear.

"I love you," he whispered. She turned around and looked up at him.

"Come on!" she said turning away from him and running out of the other side of the trees into the sun. Once she was above the grey silt she lay on her back on the grass. Jim came stumbling over carrying their clothes clutched against his stomach. Melissa lay there with the blue sky in her eyes. The sun was beautiful and warm and the clover under her back, was soft, though a little itchy. She could smell the grass and hear the magpies. She looked at Jim.

"No one will see." He lay down on top of her.

Never had love seemed more innocent and unspectacular. There was only Melissa's small, feminine body huddled beneath and around him and the world seemed to enlarge and the sky flatten until they seemed to be squashed between the two planes, one green and one blue. The birds sang as though they had microphones and the sun was on Jim's back and Melissa laid beneath him small and warm and needing protection. Then he was lying there on the grass beside her, feeling a little dizzy and weak in the infinite sunlight of the world.

They got up, put on their clothes and walked home, blowing

cigarette smoke into the evening air, seeing who could blow smoke higher into the air.

Twenty minutes later they came, panting and dishevelled through Gibson's fly door and heard it bang shut behind them. They sat down at the kitchen table. Mrs Gibson, who was standing by the sink, stood there staring at them.

"Will tea be long, Mum? We're starving." Mrs Gibson turned away. She wanted to ask what they had been doing, but since they were adults, she didn't dare.

"Oh, it won't be long," she said vaguely. Melissa stood up, walked behind her mother and lifted her off the ground.

"Eeeeee! Mrs Gibson screamed. "Put me down!" Melissa put her mother's feet back on the floor.

"We went for a swim, Mum," said Melissa, sitting down at the table again and lighting another cigarette.

"You shouldn't be swimming without togs now. You're not a child you know."

"You think Jim saw something he hadn't seen before?"

"No, but you shouldn't do it. Your father's shepherd might have come across you."

"He was probably doing what we were doing in his own four walls."

"How could he be swimming in his own four walls, dear?" Jim and Melissa looked at one another. Melissa grinned and Jim blushed.

Jim and Melissa finished cigarettes, sitting at the kitchen table. Finally Melissa stubbed out her cigarette and announced;

"I'm going to have a bath. Are you going to come and scrub my back, Jim?" Jim blinked and looked at Mrs Gibson.

"You go and scrub her back," she said quietly, with a little smile.

"I think we'll stay the night too, Mum."

"That'll be fine. Your father and I get a bit lonely here on our own."

After they had finished tea and Melissa had fed and quelled the baby, they all sat in the lounge looking at the television set. Gibbo sat, surly, withdrawn and toothless in his chair, mouthing his cigarette. They watched a local talent quest programme. Gibbo sat through the whole of the programme muttering:

"Couldn't sing a note if I was pulling his balls out."

When that was over, he looked at his watch.

"Christ! Now we've got this historical Pommy shit. A waste of overseas exchange and about as interesting as a parson's sex life. Will you have a beer with me Jim and help me drown my sorrows at this lousy Sunday night viewing?" It was the first time Gibbo had said anything to Jim all night. "In fact, we'll have a whisky. That way I'll drown them faster. I suppose you want one too, daughter dear? You ought to be like your mother and have tea."

"I thought I might have a whisky tonight too, dear," said Mrs Gibson.

"Hell!" said Gibbo going out to the kitchen for the glasses. "Hell's bloody teeth!"

Gibbo poured whisky and water for everyone and they all sat there listening to the still house and the ongoing hiss of the wind, which had risen a little. Mrs Gibson would sip her whisky and then her knitting needles would stab and flicker in the semi darkness. Jim Wilson felt very alone.

"Melissa and I were talking, Dave," he said. There was a terrible silence. The shadowy figure of Dave Gibson was looking straight ahead at the extinguished television screen. Dave took a sip of his whisky and a drag on his cigarette; but he said nothing. "We were thinking you might want to employ me as a farm labourer for a year or two until I know something. Then, maybe, we could consider that partnership." There was another long silence. Mrs Gibson's knitting arms moved like pistons on a train. Melissa looked into her glass and swirled the whisky as though there was ice in it.

"Why should I give you a second chance?"

"There's no reason why you should," said Jim.

"It's what you want Dave," said Mrs Gibson, without daring to look up.

"I've got used to being without. Why should I change now?" said Dave Gibson with ominous quietness. "Why should I change?"

"Okay, Dave. It was just an idea," said Jim, collapsing defeated back into his chair.

"You two have got a bloody nerve, a bloody nerve," said Dave Gibson. He jumped out of his chair and shook his fist at them.

"Dry up, Dad. Can't you behave like a normal human being for once?"

"This is my life, my life!" said Dave Gibson his voice rising to a shriek. "This is what I've always wanted. First you take it away and now you give it back. I don't trust you; in my heart I don't trust you."

"We are being serious, Dad."

"But will you marry him? After you're married you can do what you like, but you get nothing from me if you don't get married."

"We wouldn't have suggested this dad, if we hadn't decided to get married." Gibbo collapsed back into his chair, dropped his cigarette butt on the white carpet and ground it out with his heel. Then he stopped and looked down at what he had done.

"Fuck!" he shrieked in full falsetto. "Now I'll have to buy a bloody new carpet!"

""Don't get so excitable, dear. I'll put a rug over it," said Mrs Gibson. Nothing could shatter her serenity in this moment of triumph.

"Give me a tailor made will you, dear," said Dave Gibson to Melissa. She threw him across a cigarette. He lit it and puffed without taking the cigarette out of his mouth. The cigarette pointed straight at the ceiling. "Boy, those guys at the pub will have to take notice of me now, said Dave dreamily to himself, "otherwise I'll set Jim on them." He sent up clouds of smoke towards the ceiling.

Later that evening when Jim and Melissa were getting undressed for bed Jim said, without turning around:

"Will you fix up the house for me?" I don't want to go back to that place." Melissa walked up behind him and put her arms around him.

"Mum and I can fix all that."

"Please,"

"Are you happy?"

"Yes."

"Are you safe?"

"I hope so."

At that moment Jim Wilson believed that he had escaped the real end of love.

Chapter 33

t was summer again and the air was as itchy as dry twigs, though the hills were still a livid green and the poplars were still spring pale. However, the scars on the hills had already changed from yellow to white and the dust clung to the shrubs and nettles that grew by the roadside. The sheep were panting under the willows that looked more welcoming than pools of water

Lillie Foster had collapsed back in the front seat of the Mini. Her blue and white bikini top barely controlled her brown breasts. Sweat glistened in her cleavage. Her bikini bottom was merely two, small triangles of cloth linked by narrow tapes of the same material. She leaned forward to peel her sweating flesh off the vinyl seat cover and then sank back into the seat again. She put a foot across into Milton's lap and he squeezed her toes. Milton was looking at the road and the passing landscape through the dusty windscreen. His eyes were narrowed against the glare of the sun on the red bonnet of the car and the glistening white of the dusty, summer road. Lillie watched a globule of sweat wiggle down his temple and the flickering of his muscles on his sweat-shiny, brown arms as he swung the wheel. There was a dark sweat stain under both armpits of his singlet. Milton could feel the runnels of sweat wriggling down the side of his ribcage. He wound down the window and shuddered at the cool of the breeze on his hot flesh. It was almost as bad as a breeze blowing on you when you were running stripped to the waist.

Milton wound his window up and Lillie languidly lit a cigarette and breathed smoke out of her nose.

"Open your window. That Thing'll choke me," said Milton. He slewed around a sharp corner, the car wiggling in the dusty shingle.

"Faster!" said Lillie, laughing with exhilaration.

"It's too hot to go fast," grouched Milton.

"You're running out of steam," teased Lillie. "Must be too much weightlifting."

"Too much fucking, you mean." Lillie laughed an open-mouthed, liquid laugh.

"You'll have to tell Liz to leave you alone."

Milton grinned and wriggled in his seat. He was looking forward to seeing Jim. He wanted to know how Jim had exorcised his suicidal demons.

Milton stopped at Gibson's front gate and Lillie slipped her feet into her Roman sandals, got out of the car, walked to the gate, unhooked it and, lifting it a little, walked it open. Milton drove through the gate. There was a crunch as he slid to a halt on the soft, grey shingle. Lillie shut the gate and walked towards the car. Suddenly Milton rammed the car into gear, let out the clutch and raced away showering Lillie with stones. She quickly stepped out of her unbuckled sandals, picked them up and pursued him, running on the grass beside the drive. Milton slowed and admired her powerful stride in the rear vision mirror. Lillie's breasts swung with each stride. He stopped the car.

He realised that he shouldn't have done that when she was so scantily clad. Lillie pulled the door open and climbed, panting, into the car. She hit Milton playfully on his head with one of her sandals.

"You fink!" She reached over and gave his hair a sharp pull. Milton sucked in his breath. Lillie laughed and stroked his hair. They started off again.

There was rumble of planks as they drove over the swing bridge. They finally came to a halt behind Dave Gibson's Jaguar. Milton got out of the car and into the grass cooled sunlight. Before he shut the door he leaned in and said:

"You'd better throw on your dress. That thing's likely to excite a certain amount of comment."

"Aw, Milton!"

"Come on, put it on. If Dave Gibson sees you like that his false teeth will probably fall in the dust and he'll go rushing off into the hills jumping in the air and banging his heels together." Lillie slipped a brown patterned, loose dress over her head, swung her feet out of the door and bent over and did up her sandals. Mrs Gibson came out the door looking pale and rather strained.

"Hello Mr Harper," she said, "Jim's over in the yards."

"Yeah, I saw. Thanks Mrs Gibson."

"Hello," said Lillie looking up and beaming.

"Hello," said Mrs Gibson, smiling shyly. "You must be Mrs Harper."

"No. I'm Lillie Foster."

"Oh!" The sound trailed away into the balmy, claustrophobic, green day. The air was full of the smell of willows, at this time of the year managing to compete with the smell of sheep dung. Lillie, having buckled on her sandals, stood up.

"Well, I suppose I'll see you later, Mrs Gibson?"

"Probably," said Mrs Gibson turning and going back into the house.

Lillie walked after Milton and took his arm. She closed her eyes as she walked. She felt the grass brushing the tips of her toes and her feet felt deliciously cool. The scent of Milton's straw smelling armpits seemed to engulf her. Her arms and shoulders burned and the material of the loose dress plucked at her flesh.

They were leaving the eye soothing dark shadows of the garden now and walking across to the sheep yards. Above a maze of grey boards Milton could see Jim Wilson in a wide brimmed straw hat and a black woollen singlet, drafting sheep. His arms, chest and throat were the colour of brick. His face was hidden by the shadow of the straw hat. Melissa was there too, sitting on her hands, on the top rail of one of the grey board fences. The sheep in the holding yard were shuffling nervously around in a slow circle. Milton climbed over the gate into the holding yard and turned back just in time to see Lillie vault the gate. Milton felt a tinge of envy and then looked across the yards at Gibbo who was leaping in the air waving his arms and going, "Ya, ya!"

A couple of dogs, tied up in the adjacent yard, were peering between the boards in the direction of the race and barking in the intervals between their pink tongued panting. Dust hung in a thin, swirling cloud above the race. Milton looked at Lillie who was trying to pick her way through the liquorice-coloured sheep dung.

"I'll carry you," said Milton and he walked over, swept her off the ground and carried her across the yard like a bride across a threshold.

He put her down on the other side of the holding yard and wiped his forehead with the back of his wrist.

"Hello, Milton!" shouted Jim, looking back immediately at his drafting. Gibbo looked around once momentarily, turned back, kicked a couple of sheep and then turned back again his eye lingering on Lillie. Then he hurled himself in among the sheep in the race again. Melissa slipped off the top rail and waded through the sheep in the yard.

"Hello Milton," she said smiling. Milton smiled at her warmly, but said nothing. Then, suddenly remembering, he said:

"Melissa, this is Lillie Foster. Lillie - Melissa." Milton looked away at Jim Wilson who was completely focussed on working the doors of the race.

"Hello," said Melissa to Lillie with smiling warmth. Lillie looked at her, laughed and said:

"Hello." Melissa took a packet of cigarettes out of her blouse pocket and offered one to Lillie saying;

"Smoke?"

"Thanks," said Lillie, taking a smoke and leaning forward for Melissa to light it. Then they both stepped away from one another on the opposite sides of the fence and began smoking.

Gibbo was standing in the grey dust of the empty race looking lonely and lost. Jim Wilson, his face relaxed and open for the first time walked towards Milton and the two women.

"We'll have smoko, eh Dave?" he said as he walked.

"Okay, boy," said Dave collapsing against the wall of the race and pulling his packet of tobacco out of his pocket. Jim Wilson vaulted a low rail and came across to Milton through the sheep, a smile on his face.

"How's things?" he said.

"Fine," said Milton grinning. "What's all this vaulting stuff?"

"I'm fit," said Jim, feeling in his pocket for his cigarettes. "Good for the four-minute mile."

"What shit you talk!" said Milton, looking away at the hills, which seemed to have been made denser by the heat.

While the others went inside Milton and Jim walked down to a stretch of creek where there were no willows, just a long, deep, mud bottomed pool flowing slowly between banks of buttercups. They sat on the bank and dangled their feet in a couple of big clumps of cutty grass, which were growing down near the water's edge. Red and black dragon flies buzzed like helicopters across the surface of the water. Under the water cock-a-bullies darted on the warm mud.

A twig of willow floated slowly down the pool, dragging its shadow across the pool bottom. At the bottom of the pool the water crackled and disappeared into a scented cave of willows. Milton lay back on his elbows in the grass and looked at an ineffectual puff of white cloud that hung almost motionless in the sky.

"Well," said Milton, "what are you doing?" Jim Wilson shrugged as he lit another cigarette. "You don't know what you are doing then?"

"I think I'm probably living for the first time in my life."

"Yeah," said Milton.

"Probably."

Milton stood up and walked around, kicking the tops off buttercups. He felt disorientated. It was like all of a sudden talking to a stranger.

"Why the change?"

"Suddenly I realised that it was possible to be happy living on the surface of the world. Suddenly I knew I could just experience. Suddenly Melissa was just pink, friendly flesh."

"Yeah," said Milton, turning his back on Jim Wilson.

"I have a right to be happy, don't I?"

"I wouldn't know."

"Besides, don't you live for the surface of things?"

Yeah, but I get little peace out of my surfaces, because I know they only cover endless darkness. You believe in yours."

"Yes I do."

"What about God? You must be an atheist now?" Jim Wilson kicked the river bank with his heel.

"Yes," he said in a whisper, as though he didn't dare to say it any louder.

A fantail came whirling and fluttering across the clearing, going from one group of willows to another. Milton felt the ache of grief in his back and behind his eyes. Jim had driven him just that bit further into isolation. As long as there is someone treading the path that you have trod, who is learning the things that you know, there is some consolation for your loneliness. But Jim had cut him off by rejecting all his knowledge, simply refusing to admit that the darkness was there. He was joining the rest of humanity and condemning Milton Harper to oblivion.

Milton looked at Jim and shrugged.

"We'd better go up. We have nothing more to talk about."

"There's no reason why our friendship can't continue is there?"

Milton shrugged and turned away. He walked up the bank past an old apple tree that had split down the middle. The fallen half was in flower, even though it was lying on the ground. Jim Wilson looked at Milton wearily climbing the bank. He stood himself and threw his cigarette butt into the water. There was a faint hiss as it landed and Jim Wilson followed Milton into the house.

Throughout afternoon tea Milton was very stiff and formal. Lillie and Melissa both watched him uncomfortably out of the corners of their eyes. Jim ignored Milton, but exchanged pleasantries with Lillie. Mrs Gibson was too busy being the gracious hostess to notice anything and Dave was too busy dipping biscuits in his tea and surreptitiously eyeing Lillie to notice much either.

The air was beautifully mild in the house and the curtains barely moved in the faint breeze. Apart from the noise of conversation and the rustling sounds, the air was very still, resonant with silence. The sounds of the birds and dogs outside seemed very far away. Milton briefly shut his eyes in the hope that the silence would heal him, but he was distracted by a story of Dave's about how he had won one hundred dollars one day at the races and then, in a fit of madness, had put it all on an outsider in the last race and lost the lot. Milton could not see the point of this story and neither could Lillie, though she smiled encouragingly at Dave.

Jim broke up the afternoon tea by getting up noisily and saying:

"Well, I suppose I'd better get back to work." Dave grunted, stood up and lit a half-smoked cigarette. He and Jim went out the door. Milton sat there glumly looking at the three women who all looked at each other. Then, Mrs Gibson stood up in the quiet room and began to gather up the cups and the plates.

"I might go down to the creek for a swim. Are you coming Milt?" asked Lillie

"You go on down. I'll come down in a minute." Lillie got up and strolled out humming. Melissa and Milton sat there looking at each other as Mrs Gibson went in and out. They sat there staring into each other's eyes. Finally, Melissa stood up and walked towards the door. Milton followed. Melissa sat on the back doorstep lacing up her hobnails, pulling each cross tight in turn and finally tying a double bow at the top. She stood up and they walked down between the roses, Milton just behind her right shoulder. They passed out the gate.

"How do you like it all?" asked Milton suddenly. Melissa shut her eyes. The sudden yellow sunlight and the bright green of the grass made her head ache. She opened her eyes, blinked and then lit a cigarette.

"It's a solution of sorts," she said after inhaling.

"Do you like it?"

"Yes and no."

"How yes and no?"

"I keep him, but our love loses its seriousness. It has become a source of joy, but it's not really serious anymore." They walked on. "I don't know," said Melissa flapping her arms. "I don't know. I can't really do anything, you see."

"Yeah, I know."

"Our happiness, living like this, really destroys our love."

"Yeah."

"Are we wrong?"

"No. But he's betrayed me."

"I wouldn't like to have to make his decision. I don't though."

They walked towards the sheep yards where Dave Gibson was flapping his arms behind the sheep in the holding paddock while his dog ran back and forth behind the mob with soft mechanical movements, occasionally pausing to bark. The sheep all crushed into the dusty gateway leaving the grass in the holding paddock flattened behind them.

"Once Lillie's had her swim we'll go," said Milton to Melissa.

"All right. Will you come to our wedding?" Milton looked at her for a long time. Melissa hung her head in embarrassment. Milton simply shook his head and walked off.

Milton walked across the wide river terrace towards the willows and the creek. He passed a piece of rotten wood, left there by a previous flood and largely obscured by the grass that surrounded it. He was very aware of the lowering sun, shining into his eyes just above the tops of the willows. His skin began to tighten in the heat. He walked in under the green fronds of the willows and stood on the debris of old twigs and leaves. Lillie was moving slowly on her back in the shaded water. The water looked as thick as oil. She kept floating, her limbs slowly spreading apart until she looked almost like a star.

She looked dreamily at Milton. He was sitting there cross legged against a rough willow trunk looking like the Buddha. Outside the shade of the willows, she could see the blue of the sky. The water splashed softly as she moved gently down the pool until she stopped in a shaft of sunlight which had penetrated the canopy of willows.

There was a swirl on the water and Lillie disappeared only to re-emerge back up the pool, rising into the air like a brown column, shedding gouts of silver onto the trembling water that surrounded her. Then she just bobbed there in a thin slit of sunlight.

"Come in," she said softly to Milton.

"Na!"

Lillie kicked her way to the bank, the water behind her bubbling like a spring. She reached up, put her hands on the bank, bobbed a couple of times and then rose out of the water straightening her arms. She got up from her kneeling position and walked towards Milton, drops of water tumbling off her. Milton stood up and pulled her towel off the branch of the tree and Lillie stood there while he dried her. He touched her shoulder and her flesh was cold and clinging. She turned to face him and pulled up his singlet and dug her finger tips into his knotted muscles. Milton's face hardened and his eyes took on that cold, far-away look. Lillie put her arms around him and tried to pull him to her. She couldn't shift him.

"What's the matter?"

"Let's go home."

"I want a fuck."

"We'll stop on the way. Under a roadside bush," said Milton smiling and tousling her hair.

"All right," said Lillie, laughing.

Chapter 34

When Lillie and Milton returned home it was nearly dusk. The sky was a pale, spray-whitened blue and the air was cool. Milton leaned on the letter box with his shirt off feeling the air slide damply over his aching body, aching today from accumulated sweat and heat rather than exertion. He could hear the sea washing back and forth and the growl of a small plane echoed in the empty sky. The smell of freshly cut grass flooded his nostrils. Milton took off his shoes and walked around on the cool lawn. The freshly cut grass clippings clung to his feet.

Another summer and soon all the green world would be burnt off by the sun and the whole world would be Milton Harper brown, Milton Harper bone dry. Milton disliked this flush of opulence, this emerald world of early summer when the foliage had not yet been dominated by the sun. He felt that it was that that had corrupted Jim Wilson. This moment of paradise in the human cycle turned men's heads. Beauty such as this, the beauty of the cultivator, had to be rejected. To be a real animal you needed to embrace the pain of the body, the self-absorbing brutality of the chase and the migration. To be real you had to live without pleasure, to lack it until you cried and wondered why you were alive.

Liz came treading across the lawn in a bra and skirt in the hazy treacle light of the dusk.

"What are you doing Milt?"

"Just thinking."

"About what?"

"How the fuck should I know?" Liz hugged him.

"You crabby old bastard!" Her arm was warm against his now cool flesh. He felt her hip bone pressing against him and could smell her scent and cigarette smoke. He leaned over and kissed her forehead.

"You go back in. I'll be in, in a minute." Milton watched Liz walk back across the lawn with that soft walk of hers. The white of her bra stood out in the darkness. She mounted the steps like a silently flying bird and disappeared through the door. The fly door clacked behind her and the wooden door shut. Milton stood there staring at the empty porch. It was as though, for a moment, Liz had left part of herself behind.

He turned back towards the road. Perhaps Jim Wilson's betrayal had been all for the best. Milton felt as though he had been softened by the affection of Lillie and Liz and Jim Wilson's friendship. He still could not understand why simple humanity made him feel so awful. It was like a snake that wound itself around him and crushed him. Trying to shake off emotions was a sort of physical struggle.

He had always despised human beings and their simple absorptions. Perhaps he should never have been on earth in the first place. He felt he belonged in some harsh, far away part of the universe. He knew he should go back there, but like Jim Wilson, he was afraid.

Lillie lay on the divan in the lounge, completely naked under her loose-fitting dress. She sipped her gin and lemonade and looked across at Liz, who was also drinking gin and lemonade. Lillie missed the frantic nature of her old life and the loneliness of it. But she could not go back because she was held by the physical impersonality of Milton Harper. She had lost her freedom, but she could not have done otherwise. She looked out the window at the blue-gold sky, the dim land, and Milton walking slowly on the lawn, his hands in his pockets. She swallowed the remains of her gin in a gulp and lit a cigarette. Liz looked up from her book, noticed Lillie's empty glass and got out of her chair, draining the remaining liquid out of her own glass as she did so. She walked across the room and picked up Lillie's glass.

"Thanks," said Lillie, absently. Lillie lay there, her body slowly tightening. She drew on her cigarette, but instead of soothing her, the effect of the nicotine only lay over the top of her tension. Lillie lay there, still and tense. Liz brought her another gin. Lillie took it without a word and drank it down. Then she lay still again. She badly wanted to wrestle with something. She stood up, suddenly and decisively.

"I'm just going out to do a bit of modelling."

"Tea' ll be ready in quarter of an hour," said Liz, but Lillie was already disappearing out the door her dress swirling and billowing. Liz heard the back door bang. She stood up to turn on the light. Before she did, she leaned on the divan and watched Milton wandering forlornly on the lawn. She smiled, turned on the light and sat down.

Milton looked once towards the house as the light came on. The room, through the window; seemed Spartan and misshapen. The sensation pleased him. He looked away.

Lillie pulled open the old door at the back of the garage and walked across the smooth, dusty, dirt floor. The air in the room was close and hot but she could feel the evening breeze curling around her ankles. Everything in the room appeared a faint, fawn colour. She walked over to the old, unpainted wooden table and, bending over, she pulled a large plastic bag of clay out from under the table and, leaning backwards at her hips, lifted it into the air and then fell forward with it onto the table top.

"Whew!" She undid the wire that kept the heavy, semi-transparent bag closed. Then, pulling apart the mouth of the bag she plunged both hands inside it and drew out a slippery, hard block of clay, one of several in the bag. She threw it on the table, where it made a "plunk". She squeezed it and felt the cool, wet clay mould itself to her hands. She put it to her nose. It had the smell of earth. She lifted up her dress and put its cold, slipperiness to her belly and rubbed the wet clay all over stomach, leaving yellow smears. She threw the clay on the table and pounded it with her hands. The clay on her stomach began to dry and pinch her skin. She stood there looking at the clay. It was beautiful, but there was nothing she could do with it. She had no vision, only a body. She picked the clay up with both hands and threw it against the wall. It hit the wall, stuck momentarily and fell like a big shadow onto the floor making a beautiful, soothing thump.

"It's tea time," said Milton quietly. He was standing there, in silhouette, leaning against the door frame as though he had been there for some time. Lillie squealed with anger, pulled her dress off over her head and ran at him, putting her legs around his waist, crushing his hips and grinding her elbows into his ribs.

"You feel so nice, so nice," she said maniacally and prodded and grasped his flesh and crushed his hips tighter. Milton gritted his teeth, closed his eyes and began to stroke her arse. Lillie sat there, legs around his waist, her head sideways on his chest. He kissed the top of her head. "I've only got my body, Milton," she said in a small voice. "I've only got my body and sometimes it drives me mad." Milton carried her over to the table and laid her on it. He pushed the bag of clay onto the floor. He bent between her legs. Lillie lay sobbing with relief.

Chapter 35

The wedding breakfast had been consumed and everyone who was not staggering was dancing. The band had well-rehearsed expressions of enthusiasm, especially the saxophonist, who stood there blowing and grinning at the same time. Men with suits that smelled of mothballs were gliding around the dance floor looking like a mixture of Fred Astaire and Groucho Marx. Their faces, red from alcohol, seemed to have swollen to draw attention to their facial defects. Cigarette smoke whirled under the yellow lights. The doors of the hall were open, an escape route to the soothing oblivion of the night.

In one corner there was a huddle of suited males and, caged in the middle of them, Dave Gibson rocked and hawed. This was his celebration, the greatest celebration of his life. Coarse ribaldry gushed from his mouth into the ears of relatives he hadn't seen for years.

Jim and Melissa sat quietly in a corner. Jim reached out and lit her cigarette. She looked at him gratefully. Their wedding was a celebration in which they were alien. Melissa's brown, Victorian style curls shone richly on the white satin of her wedding dress. Jim Wilson looked as huge and immobile as a Minotaur in his brown suit and matching waistcoat. He gazed at the revellers rather like a managing director watching his managers making idiots of themselves.

Mrs Gibson came shuffling timidly up to them and leaned forward saying:

"How are you dear?"

"Utterly exhausted," said Melissa, smiling at her mother.

"And how are you Jim" asked Mrs Gibson squeezing his hand.

"Fine thanks," said Jim, smiling in response to Mrs Gibson's genuine concern.

"You're not drinking very much."

"I don't feel in the mood. Too drained."

"Well, you won't ever have to do it again."

"If I do," said Melissa, "it'll be deep in the forest where only the birds can see."

"Don't say that, Melissa. You shouldn't be having doubts now."

"Mum!" said Melissa sternly.

"I'm sorry dear," said Mrs Gibson turning and scuttling away, her long, emerald dress swishing over the dusty floor.

Melissa and Jim shrank back into the corner, crushed by the noise of the band, the shouts from around the hall and the scratch of sliding shoes on the dance floor. All around the walls there were bunches of flowers, but they failed to completely disguise the drab utilitarianism of the hall. A youthful couple, who had been dancing among some sedate elderly couples at breakneck speed, fell over and lay there laughing. Eventually the girl scrambled up, pulled the boy to his feet and they went careering on.

Jim looked up, through seams of cigarette smoke, at the dark windows all along the top of the hall. A couple of long cobwebs swung from the roof. Melissa put her hand inside Jim's.

"This is God awful music. If I could dance properly and had the nerve, I'd get up there and do a strip. It's a pity Milton and Lillie didn't come. I bet she would have done one." Jim leaned back against the wall and watched the couples, pressed formally close together, sliding around the floor. It was a wedding from another era.

All Jim Wilson had ever been was a priest and this seemed absurd to him. If I had played in a rock band, he thought, I would have been driven out of my mind. I was lucky that I made it a rule as a priest to avoid the after-wedding bun fights.

"I'm going out for a breath of fresh air," said Jim standing up.

"Good idea," said Melissa, dropping her cigarette butt on the floor and grinding it out with the ball of her foot. They sidled around the edge of the hall, smiling at this one and that one. Jim's body ached from the heat and the food and the excessive amount of smoking he had done that day. Since he had been working with Dave he had been smoking 15 fewer cigarettes a day, but today he had relapsed back to his old number.

"Hey, Jim!" Gibbo bawled as Jim and Melissa passed his group. Jim turned towards Dave. "I was just telling these blokes about you carrying that strainer up the ridge the other day." Jim shrugged, smiled amiably and then walked on. "I reckon he could kill a bull with his bare hands," he heard Gibbo saying as he walked after Melissa, who had not stopped in case her father said or did something embarrassing. As Jim walked, he raised his eyes to heaven momentarily.

In the last stride before the door the cold hit them. It was as though it had managed to get one foot into the hot hall, but no more. Their feet crunched on the shingle and they stood in the square of hot, yellow light feeling their sweat turn cold. Jim walked on into the darkness and suddenly the music seemed very far away and he was embalmed in the stillness of the night. He struck a match and lit his cigar. He

313

stepped off the fine shingle onto the dewy grass. The hot day had turned into a dewy night and the night would doubtless turn back into a hot day again. He walked under the still, tent like oak tree and kicked the grassless dirt with his toe. Once he had disturbed the wet surface puffs of dust, barely discernible, rose beneath the tree. The white street lights were reflected off the roofs of the cars parked beside the drive. The other houses in the street stretched away beneath the dark, milky sky like tombstones. Melissa came up behind Jim holding her long frock in one hand.

"We can go if you want to. We're allowed to sneak away for our first night of wedded bliss. It's the done-thing, or at least it was twenty years ago." Jim looked at Melissa with her white dress, her dark hair and the lunar landscape of her face. He pulled her against him and held her there. He smoked his cigar over the top of her head.

After a minute they walked hand in hand out from under the tree. They passed a couple of Melissa's male relatives grinning in the doorway, cigarettes smouldering between labour -thickened fingers. Very few of Jim's relatives had come to the wedding and Jim's parents, who wouldn't forgive him for leaving the church, had both stayed away.

Melissa and Jim went into the back room of the hall while Melissa got changed. As Jim unzipped her wedding dress Melissa said:

Just think. I won't have to minister to Mark for two whole weeks."

"Yes, that'll be a relief."

"You're not jealous of him anymore?"

"I just don't think about it," Jim said and he drew on his cigar with sinister softness. He closed his eyes and collapsed back against the wall. He didn't know where he was or what he thought. There was only one way to describe the day and that was "extraordinary". Even his resolve to live on the surface of things had been absolutely shattered by the tension of the day. He seemed to be doing one thing after another without having any idea why he was doing them. He had given up trying to understand and judge and had just acted.

"I don't want to go out through the hall much," said Melissa.

"Let's go out the window."

Out in the hall the band stopped playing.

"Ladies and gentlemen, the bride and groom will be leaving soon," said the MC over the loud speaker. People began to crowd around the doorway of the back room. Jim and Melissa could hear the sinister silence in the hall and the shuffling feet outside the door. Jim tip-toed over to the window and gingerly raised it, while Melissa quietly snapped her suitcase shut. Melissa, in a blue trouser suit now, though she still had on her white wedding shoes, tip-toed over to the window and put one leg through. Then, bending at the waist, she put her trunk through. After several seconds her other leg disappeared into the darkness. Jim dropped her soft, white suitcase out the window and climbed through himself. Just as he disappeared into the darkness someone outside the room began thumping on the door.

"Come on! Ya not s'pposed to be doing that until you get to yer hotel." There was great laughter as Jim and Melissa jogged across the lawn behind the oak tree. A suited youngster bent down and peered through the keyhole.

"Hey, they're not there." Someone else pushed the door open and they all saw the open window.

"They've escaped!" someone shouted. Three or four young men raced across the hall whooping like Indians and were absorbed into the night. Some of their girlfriends stumbled after them, getting tangled in their long frocks.

Jim Wilson was just putting the car into gear when he saw three young men come out of the darkness under the oak, straightening up and slowing down as they looked around for the car. Jim Wilson let out the clutch of the Humber Hawk and it lumbered away, the youths renewing their speed and giving chase until the car's red tail lights were far away in the night.

Then they walked back laughing to the hall to go on drinking and perhaps dancing.

Gibbo sat, momentarily deserted by his cronies, but feeling smug about Jim Wilson's cunning escape. No grass grew under the feet of that boy.

Chapter 36

Jim and Melissa drove between the summer-still houses of the city. The street lights glared in the moonlit sky and the houses seemed deserted. The stars seemed weak and out of place in the navy-blue sky. Jim didn't like it. Whereas before he felt confused by the rush of events, now he felt threatened by this civilisation. He had stepped outside his ritual of action and he was already sinking again, sinking into the tropical darkness of his doom, remembering his adoration of Melissa that had replaced his adoration of God, or at least a sort of a God. He blinked and looked around at the moon pale roofs. It was like driving through a dinosaur cemetery, with huge white bones protruding from the earth.

That was what he had forgotten. He had worshipped Melissa and hoped to find salvation in her, but had ended up fleeing her for a little safety. Melissa was sitting stiffly in her seat, her head turned away from him, looking out the passenger window. Then she turned towards him and, inside her hair, instead of her face was a skull. Jim threw himself against the closed driver's door. The car veered towards the centre line. Melissa wrestled with him as he tried to get away.

"Jim!" she screamed. He recognised her voice and stopped struggling. He looked at her, eyes wide. Melissa drew away from him and screamed. Then she broke into sobs. "What's the matter?" she sobbed. "What's the matter?"

"I don't know," said Jim driving on. "You gave me a fright."

"Don't do that again, Jim," she said clutching his arm.

"I won't," he said patting her hand.

They stopped on the roadside outside the motel they were staying in. Jim took the key out of his waistcoat pocket. There was a restaurant attached to the front of the motel and they could see couples sitting at the tables in the dimly lit room. The couples were leaning forward as they ate. A slight breeze lifted the front of Jim Wilson's hair. He looked at the orange lights of the bar, bottles hanging upside down. A barman wearing a white shirt and a black tie was cleaning a glass, his elbow high in the air. The air seemed milder here beside the sea.

Melissa and Jim walked down the side of the restaurant towards their motel. The yard was full of natty, new cars their colours just discernible in the dull light. Jim unlocked the motel door, opened the door and turned on the light. The room seemed more than real, as rooms often do when you encounter them for the first time. They walked into the brightly lit kitchen-dining room and Melissa pushed the door shut.

"I wouldn't say no to a cup of tea," said Melissa flopping on one of the kitchen chairs.

"Okay," said Jim, taking out the jug from under the bench and filling it with water. "I suppose I've got to go out to the car and get the tea?'

"I'm afraid so."

Melissa lit a cigarette and opened the door that Jim had shut behind him. Then she took off the jacket of her trouser suit and stood looking down the drive until she saw Jim trudging back towards her. His head was lowered, as if in thought. She felt confused and suddenly panicky. She never should have married him. She thought of the span of their lives stretching in front of them and, like anyone who looks across the future rather than into it, she was afraid of the dreadful predictability of her life. She would watch her son grow up and then, in the short time it took him to grow up, she would be a woman in her late middle age. Life seemed very short and death, very near; the only thing between her and death, years of tedium. She tried to think of tomorrow and their holiday, but the thought couldn't attach to her imagination. She looked at Jim's solid, material form looming as he walked across the grey shingle. He was still a consolation for this sudden agony. What she couldn't understand was why she had been thrown back so completely into the agony of love.

Jim came through the door and pushed it shut again. Melissa put her arms around him. He stood there not responding.

"I love you," said Melissa, a little desperately.

"Yes," said Jim standing there, his flesh rigid as he stared at the wall.

"What's the matter?"

"I love you too," he said pulling roughly free of Melissa. "That's what the matter is." He banged the tin of tea on the bench and turned around and looked at her. His eyes were glassy with suffering. They stood there, both in pain, both magnetically drawn to one another in their pain. The jug began to boil and Jim Wilson turned around and wrenched the plug out of the wall. He looked at Melissa again. Slowly, almost imperceptibly, they moved towards one another. Then, at the same moment, they lunged towards one another and fell sobbing and kissing, on the floor; groping for one another's flesh, trying to pull off the clothes that kept them apart from one another. Then Jim Wilson was back in the dark place of his destruction again and he knew there was no escape now. He kissed Melissa's warm, moist flesh and listened to her small, bird-like noises under him and suddenly there was only Melissa and Melissa was nothing except blackness and death, the death that she promised, the death that she embodied. His "normal" life had gone.

They lay there half panting, half sobbing in a confusion of clothes. Then, saying nothing, tears glistening in their eyes they stood up and got dressed again. When Jim finished tucking his singlet and shirt back into his pants he sat at the table and lit a cigarette. Melissa stood there wiping her groin with a towel, her pants still hanging on her right ankle. She threw the towel on the floor and put her left foot back in her stocking again and worked the pants and the pantyhose back up her hips. Then she zipped up the slacks, sat down at the table and lit a cigarette as well.

"We almost destroyed ourselves," said Jim.

"Yes."

"I've got to do it this time. I owe it to you."

"It's vile that we love one another so much that we have to die."

"It's not our fault. That's the way the deck is stacked; for everyone in the end." There was a long pause. Then he said: "Anyway, you don't have to die."

"What will I do without you?"

"I don't know. Anyway, it's not my business."

They finished their cigarettes in silence. They heard some laughter outside on the drive. A car started and there was a crunch of shingle under its tires as it drove away. The world was going on living.

They both sat there hating the world that could not see their pain and, if it did, would pronounce it madness. The final insult, the final horror was that they would be accorded no recognition for what they had done, except by one person.

"Do you think Milton knows?" asked Melissa.

"Yes, Milton knows." said Jim flatly.

People were such little things, wrapped up in their own pleasure, not realising that their lives were not their own. They did not see the glory of darkness, the velvety, purple flowers of death. Jim Wilson felt his face flush. He was suddenly exhilarated by the thought of his own death, even though he had no idea of what it might be like. Death seemed draped in a halo of splendour.

He stubbed out his cigarette and stood up.

"Let's go down to the beach." He took off his coat and waistcoat, unknotted his tie and pulled it out from his collar. "I'll get a jersey and a knife from the car."

Melissa stood up, stubbing out her cigarette. She looked at Jim vaguely. She felt, suddenly, as if she was in a white cell no bigger than a box and that nothing existed except herself and the white walls of the box. She felt herself go out the motel door and she felt the change of temperature on her skin, but she knew no more than that. She was moving behind Jim onto the drive, walking like a stiff legged puppet. She could see Jim striding purposefully ahead. She was vaguely aware of the eyes of the passing cars and she could hear the swish of their passing. There was the dark shadow of the land and the lightness of the sky over the sea.

They stopped while Jim unlocked the car and rummaged around in his suitcase for a jersey and a hunting knife. The hunting knife had been a wedding present from Dave.

A bus came up the road at great speed, its noise building, until Melissa dropped her head and put her hands over her ears. The sound receded. Then Jim was very close to her, pulling his black jersey over his head like a man putting on a mask before a robbery. She could feel the heat of his body and his breath blowing on her forehead. He put his arm around her shoulders.

They hurried, leaning slightly forward, across the dark road. They could see the lights of expensive houses glittering against the hills on the landward side. The white line of the road seemed to stretch away into eternity.

Even in the moonlight the grass between the road and the beech looked faintly brown and the air all around the coast looked like a meandering milky river as the moon shone on the spray. There was a rustling noise as they stepped off the sand onto the grass. Melissa could feel the grass plucking at her trousers and her feet began to feel uncomfortable as sand spilled into her shoes. Once or twice she stumbled, but Jim Wilson had her firmly under his wing and he dragged her until she found her feet again.

Suddenly they were at the edge of the grass looking down onto a smooth stretch of sand. The sea slipped over the white sand like a black mantilla. The offshore breeze ran its fingers through Melissa's hair. The sea stretched away and away, like a ploughed field. Down here the moonlight was so strong you could have seen a cork bobbing on the tide. To their left and right the sea water sucked and slithered around the reefs and the rocks. The sea water became silver in that moment before it slid off a rock back into the sea, leaving the rock like a shiny, furred seal in the darkness.

They slipped down the sandbank and walked out onto the hard beach. The silence was overwhelming apart from the faint hiss of the running film of sea water and the faint background sound of the traffic. Melissa bent down, took off her shoes and walked along the sand in her stockinged feet. The sand felt cold and firm, while Jim's hand was warm and firm. They walked along the sand until they came to where some rocks stuck out of the sand like pieces of coal. They turned around and walked back the way they had come. Up above the hairy back of the sand dunes they could just see the shining, orange street lights. The street lights made the inland hills, which rose up quite steeply, no more than a faint shadow. They stopped and stared out across the ruffled plane of the sea towards the horizon. Melissa stepped close to Jim and smelled his acidic sweat.

Suddenly Jim sat down, cross legged, on the beach and sat there very still looking across at the waves. He drew the knife out of its sheath and tossed the sheath on the sand. He tested the knife with his thumb. It was very sharp and its edge clung to his skin at the slightest movement. Jim sat there and the cool of the earth invaded his rump and his thighs. He did not look at Melissa because there was part of her that could weaken his resolve to do this.

As he sat there, he became filled with an almost childish delight. It was as though he had suddenly been absorbed back into the moment of his life and had lost all sense of the past and the future. There was only the present, the dizzy joy of the present. He was free; he was wallowing in his freedom. He had no fear now because his death was now and not in the future.

This was what it meant to be eternal, this abandonment of three-tiered time. Man lived surrounded by fear because he had a future. But when the lamb ran from the wolf it did not know it was running to preserve itself and so was free of the knowledge that tormented man. The more man knew the less he was able to live in the present and so the more intelligent the man the more imperfect he was. Milton was right in the end. Knowledge was the original sin.

Death was on Jim Wilson now. It had mounted his back and was caressing his face. There was something smooth yet loathsome about its touch, it was tender and hideous. I have got to go, thought Jim, because that is where all men must go. He pulled his jersey up over his head and there was a moment of dark confusion like being cast into a well, and then there was the milky sky and the stars half extinguished by the brightness of the moon. He put the upper part of the knife blade to the far side of his throat. He drew his hand across. There was a momentary stab of pain which vanished leaving his mouth full of a hot, sickly, thick substance. He felt his eyes roll in his head. They sky spun over and over, like when you are a child and spin round and round and then stand still and fall to the ground with dizziness.

There was sand, slightly white and pitted by feet. It was coming towards him and then, somehow, he had passed into it. He was in some forest clearing of creepers and cool leaves. It was pleasantly hot and the water dripped from the leaves to cool him. Underneath his back there was cool moisture. He looked up and suddenly there was a great wall of pink larva squeezing between the tree trunks and coming on at a terrible speed. Then it was there, over the top of him, looking the same colour as the blocks of salt you leave cows to lick. Then Jim Wilson was dead.

Melissa looked down at Jim crumpled up on the sand like a cardboard box that had been stood on or a kerosene can that had all the air driven out of it and was squashed by atmospheric pressure. The stench of his blood glistening on the sand like a clot of oil was sickening. Melissa looked at the grass on the top of the bank moving slowly in the breeze. She didn't know what to do. It was so stupid, so silly, but so unavoidable. Jim was permeated with doom and his highest aspiration was doom. The world was sick and life was sick and if anyone was responsible for this, they were sick. Suddenly Melissa rushed blindly to the edge of the sea. She bent forward and dropped vine after vine of vomit into the slopping sea. The sea tossed the vomit back and forth as it dissolved and dispersed. Melissa stood up. She felt somehow purified.

She looked down at Jim, lying in the sand. I do not love him now, she thought. Like Milton Harper there is only room for one emotion in my heart and that is hatred. The world is detestable. The world, which through love I loved, is vicious and doom ridden. Its beauty is nothing but a mockery.

Melissa turned from the sea, scrambled up the sandbank on her hands and knees and stumbled through the grass. When she reached the edge of the road she bent over and put on her shoes. A car came towards her out of the night like a huge bumble bee. Then it was gone.

Melissa ran across the road, along the drive and burst into her motel room. She picked up the phone and dialled Milton Harper's number. She stood there panting. The phone rang for a long time. Finally the phone clicked and she heard Milton say:

"Hello."

"Milton?"

"Yeah?"

"This is Melissa."

"How are you?"

"Jim's dead. I will be too in five minutes. Will you do something with our bodies? We'll be on the beach in front of the 'Chalet.' You were right. Real love is impossible."

Milton stood there looking into the mouthpiece of the dead phone. Then he slowly placed the mouthpiece back into the cradle. He walked back to the lounge. Lillie was lying snoring on the divan with her mouth open. Liz had her feet curled up underneath her on the chair with volume two of Toynbee's History of the World open on her lap.

"Who was that?"

"Melissa. I have to go and see them."

"What for?"

"It doesn't matter." He walked over and kissed Liz. "I mightn't be back for awhile." He walked across and looked down at Lillie lying asleep. He picked up her long, loose dress, looked underneath it and smiled. Lillie tossed a little and he let the material go. He looked back at Liz who was reading her book and wriggling a little in the chair. Then he picked up his jersey from off the floor and went out the door. Lillie woke up and looked around as the door shut. Then she collapsed back into sleep.

Milton drew up behind Jim Wilson's Humber Hawk and turned off his engine. He got out and tied his jersey around his waist. Two girls in thick, cork soled sandals walked past and looked at Milton's heavy arms dangling from the sleeves of his tight, stretched singlet. One blew a stream of cigarette smoke out of the side of her mouth and, when she was past Milton she said:

"What a bloody animal! Nice though."

Milton smiled and then laughed. They turned and looked back at him, but Milton was already crossing the road towards the beach. He walked through the long grass He could hear the sound of the sea and watched shivers run across the tops of the grasses on the dunes. He could see a dark indentation in the surface of the grass to his right. He figured that that was where Jim and Melissa had walked down to the beach. Milton reached the edge of the bank. The sea was boiling like black tar now and there were leaves of silver on its muscular back. Milton looked down at the black lump on the white sand. It looked like a collection of stones. Holding his arms out to his sides like a bird he ran down the sandy bank and then trotted along the beach. He could smell the sea and then, as he approached the pile of matter on the sand, he smelt something that he remembered was blood.

Melissa was lying there across Jim. He could hear a faint trickle. He reached down, took Melissa by the arm and turned her over. There was a little blood still running from the gaping red mouth under her chin. She was very warm. Milton felt her wrist, but there was no pulse. He bent over and picked her up and holding her small, generous body in his arms rocked her back and forth and looked up at the sky. He kissed the top of her head and looked up at the sky again. Then he began to walk back and forth in front of Jim Wilson's body holding the still warm corpse of Melissa.

"If I could love I would have loved you," said Milton softly. "I would have loved you because you loved him and there are not many who can love anymore." Milton sniffed loudly, trying to draw the tears out of his nostrils. There was nothing for him to do now. They were dead, just as they had been dead from the first time they had seen one another. Nothing changed, nothing could be influenced. They were just matter now, just as all people were matter. They had become their strongest element.

He laid them out, side by side, on the sand, on the dark, water-smooth sand near the creeping rush of the water. Then he sat on the sand behind them. I am alive, he thought, still alive. All I am doing is waiting for what they have found; the end of love.